Deadwood Destiny

by

Nancy Kovats

Deadwood Destiny

by

Nancy Kovats

Copyright © 1986 as "Passion's Gold"
by Nancy Kovats
ISBN 0-8217-1781-2
Reprinted 2009
ISBN 978-0-615-29462-9

First printing: February 1986 by Zebra Books
Second printing: June 2009 by Last Gold Mine Press

Cover design by The Image Engineer, Fort Collins, Colorado

Printed in the United States of America

To order additional books of Deadwood Destiny,
visit www.DeadwoodDestiny.com

This book is dedicated to the memory of my great grandmothers, Francisca Niethammer of Austria and Suzanna Kukura of Czechoslovakia.

In the early 1900's, they followed difficult husbands from their home countries to America and to the mining camps of Montana.

They, too, were pioneers.

The Mysterious Black Hills

or

Shall Pa-ha-sa-pa Be Invaded?

As spring approaches, there is but one question on the lips of the thousands of adventurers who have gathered throughout the winter in Nebraska and surrounding territories: Should we try for the Black Hills?

Ever since the first hardy trappers explored this island of pine-clad mountains in the midst of our Great Plains territory, rumors that gold sparkles in its clear mountain streams have filtered back to civilization.

But a full-scale exploration of this region, so enticingly close, has been prevented by the cession of the Black Hills to the Sioux as part of the Laramie Treaty of 1868. It has been government policy to remove by force any white man found trespassing.

Yet this same government, two years ago, sent General George Armstrong Custer and over a thousand men of the Seventh Cavalry on a scientific expedition to map the region with the stated purpose of establishing a military outpost in the Black Hills. The news that the Custer expedition found gold on French Creek electrified the nation and brought suspicion to many who questioned the true purpose of the government in sending such an expedition into the Hills.

These suspicions seemed confirmed by the outfitting of a second expedition a year ago. Ordinary citizens have not fared so well. Last spring a party from Sioux Falls was tracked down by the military and forcibly removed from the Hills, but not before they confirmed the finding of gold on French Creek.

Last summer General Crook continued to uphold official government policy when he escorted some 600 miners from the area. It is reported, however, that many wily miners eluded the military and wintered in the Hills, no doubt staking their claims in the choicest spots.

It should be pointed out that it has by no means been proved that a bonanza on our doorstep does exist. The geologist with Custer's expedition claims he saw no gold, though Custer himself supports the claim of his men that they did pan gold from the creek. Custer is also reported to have said the region is almost unsurpassed in its pristine beauty.

And so to those waiting for the snow to clear the prairies so they might risk their scalps seeking fortunes in the Black Hills, we say there are three questions to be answered: First, does gold exist in paying quantities? Second, will the government relent and offer its protection, or will the U.S. Military continue to remove trespassers by force? And third, but perhaps most important, is it right for the white man to invade Sioux lands?

To the last question, we point out the Sioux hold the Black Hills in great regard. They call it Pa-ha-sa-pa, which means "Hills That are Black," and consider these hills their sacred hunting ground. Others argue that since the red man neither plants nor tills these lands, it is the white man's destiny to tame this new territory.

One thing is certain: with the whole country still in the grip of a depression and many out of work, a beckoning bonanza of gold nuggets provides an almost irresistible lure. Those of the pioneer persuasion say there is no more fitting endeavor in this year of our nation's Centennial than for the hearty sons and daughters of Liberty to extend civilization by exploring and settling the Black Hills.

Whatever the right or wrong of the matter, this writer predicts the summer of 1876 will see the question of the Black Hills resolved at last.

Hugh Everett's first and last editorial for The Carpenter Sentinel, Nebraska Territory's Leading Bi-Weekly Newspaper.
—April 13, 1876

CHAPTER ONE

Spring was near and promise should have been in the air. Instead, a cold wind swept soil from prairie and fields and shifted it to the crusted drifts of dirty snow banked along the road down which Jake Lewis drove his mules while the boy, Edwin, nestled close to him on the wagon seat. The road went west and led to the railroad which could take Jake to Sidney, Nebraska, the gateway to the Black Hills, but although half of Iowa's discouraged homesteaders in that spring of 1876 were dreaming of joining what was to be the last great American gold rush, it never occurred to Jake Lewis to do so.

He was not a man who dreamed of escape. He knew his homestead was a sorry place, but he figured if he kept at it, his luck was bound to change. He'd been lucky once and gotten Molly to wed when she was the prettiest girl in the county, and he only her father's hired man. He'd never regretted paying the price on that luck, and he figured that sooner or later he'd be lucky again. So he kept his eyes on the road and his goal in mind. He was depositing Edwin at the Tuttle homestead and fetching Lizzie Tuttle to sit with Molly through her ordeal. He was a man with responsibilities.

He was also a man who lacked imagination and seldom wasted his energy in idle thought, but after arriving at the Tuttle homestead he had to wait for Lizzie to settle Edwin with her oldest daughter and gather her things, so he lit a pipe and found a moment to envy Sam Tuttle. Tuttle had a large and healthy family, a prospering homestead, and even a frame house with four glass windows — just the sort of house he'd promised Molly when he brought her West.

Tuttle came out with his wife and attempted to strike

up a conversation while Lizzie settled herself on the wagon seat. Jake puffed his pipe, scratched his beard, and nodded often enough to be polite. He had never found conversation easy with the Sam Tuttles of the world, and he didn't like finding himself, once again, in the position of being beholden to his neighbor. Just once, he'd like Tuttle to owe him a favor.

He finally judged he'd endured enough talk and made to turn his mules. Tuttle, still talking, took hold of the lead mule's bridle and turned the team for him. The gesture annoyed Jake.

If there was one thing he understood, it was mules.

"Make sure it's a boy!" Tuttle fired a parting shot at him.

"Don't mind Sam," Lizzie said, "I guess it's in a man's nature to want sons, but I expect you and Molly would be satisfied with a girl this time."

Jake just nodded, and she went on filling in both sides of the conversation. "Just so it's healthy. I know how you feel. That was real sad last time, but those things can't be helped. You didn't need to go to the expense of having Dr. Morgan. I've birthed ten of my own and Lord knows how many for other people. But I expect after last time you'd feel better having a doctor. Though I don't know what a doctor could do that I couldn't with a baby that never lived." While Jake tried to think of a decent way to shut her up, she patted his arm and talked on, "How's Molly been feeling lately?"

Jake tried to picture Molly. Pretty, he saw her, but he couldn't say that. Big. Couldn't say that. He finally settled on "tired."

"Land sakes, I imagine she's tired. That sod house would wear anybody out. You can't keep one clean."

"I thought I'd have her out of it before now," Jake grunted and clipped the mules with his reins to hurry them. "I can't seem to get the cash ahead."

"I know. I know. It's terrible, ain't it? Between the drought and the grasshoppers, why nobody's had a good year since you two moved out here."

Something in the way she said it made Jake know she was thinking, *Still, you've had worse luck than anybody. Some people just never get ahead.*

"And now with the whole country in a depression," she rattled on, "it almost makes a body wish the war was still on. I don't know where it's going to end. Something's got to get this country moving again. Why, I think a man like you, a man with nothing to lose, would want to join the gold rush and head for the Black Hills!"

Jake felt like turning the wagon around and taking Lizzie home. What kind of lout did she think him? He might not be a great provider like Sam Tuttle, but he didn't abandon his family to follow crazy dreams. He prided himself on having his feet solidly rooted in the earth. He didn't answer, and finally Lizzie grew tired of butting against his taciturnity, and they finished the trip in silence.

Lizzie Tuttle was right. The Lewis homestead had the look of a place haunted by failure, a failure made worse by the evidence someone had tried. There were curtains hung at a window which admitted no more than a memory of light, a foundation laid for a frame house never more than a promise, and the skeleton of a cottonwood tree which had survived long enough to make its loss loom larger. The dead tree and a broken fence stood guard over a patch of ground that looked to be the beginning of a cemetery, but even this seemed unfinished. And the wind endlessly shifted the soil against the sod house.

The doctor opened the door and came outside. Jake didn't have to see his face to know something was wrong. Doctors don't meet you outside in their shirt sleeves in a March cold snap with good news. Dr. Morgan was a skinny man with thin, gray hair. He had a bad eye and wore a little eyeglass on a ribbon pinned to his vest. When he was being professional, he put the glass to his eye, holding it in place with a lopsided squint. He wore it now.

Skirting the mules, Dr. Morgan came around to Jake's side of the wagon. His face was grave and careful, as composed as it could be and still keep the monocle in place. "It's over, Mr. Lewis. Your wife is fine, but the baby was born dead."

"Again?" Jake heard Lizzie gasp the word and wanted to put his hand over her mouth. "Again?" she exclaimed. "Just like last time! Isn't it awful! I delivered the poor little girl for her, Doctor, and I knowed there wasn't nothing I could do, and now here it is, the same thing again. It's like a curse."

Jake sat silent on the wagon seat. He closed his eyes for a moment, heard the doctor moving around the back of the wagon saying, "Come on, Mrs. Tuttle. Let me help you down. I know Mrs. Lewis will be glad to have you here. Come in and sit with her, and I'll get my coat and help Mr. Lewis with the mules."

So there's more, Jake thought. *He's got more to tell me. Doctors don't help you with the mules unless they want to talk to you away from the women.*

He had only a moment to hold his grief to himself before the doctor was beside him in the wagon, putting on his coat as he talked. "Let's get the mules out of the wind and I'll talk to you."

Outside the lean-to, the monocle disappeared, and the doctor worked with him unhitching the mules from the wagon, but leaving them in harness so Jake could drive him back to town later. The doctor followed Jake's lead in slipping the bridle from his mule so as to replace it with a feed bag. Jake thought, *He's a good man if he can handle women and understand mules too.*

"I did everything I could, but the baby was already dead." The doctor put more grain in his feed bag than Jake would have allowed. "It was a boy this time." He said the last hurriedly as if he wanted to get the information out while they had the mules between them.

Jake put his head down against the warmth of the mule's neck. For a while the only sound was that of the animals' crunching their grain. It would have been a boy this time. His son.

"I know how you feel, Mr. Lewis. It's unfortunate, but we don't know why these things happen. Some would say it's the sins of the fathers, but I'm inclined to take a more scientific view. Something in the blood, perhaps." He'd put the monocle back in place, and, as he looked at Jake, one eye was big and accusing.

The doctor went on discussing his theories, but Jake had caught his meaning when he said *sins of the fathers*. He thinks it's something I've done, Jake thought. He tried to think of something terrible he'd done. Getting drunk was all he could think of, but it didn't seem that should count. A man was entitled once in a while when his luck ran sour. He wondered if it had to be sins of the *fathers*. He figured it did. Women's sins wouldn't count for much. Molly had sinned once, but that had been long ago and she had paid the price. Molly was good, so it had to be his fault, but he couldn't reason it out. He'd put it out of his mind.

"At least you have a fine boy there in Arnold," the doctor said, his monocle gone now.

"Edwin."

"Yes, of course, Edwin. How old is he now?"

Jake had to stop and think. "Almost six."

"A fine boy."

Jake accepted the compliment. He had so long thought of Edwin as his son that only in the loss of the male child did he remember. He did not dwell on it. At least he had one boy to help around the place.

"And your wife. A fine woman, your wife."

Jake thought he caught something in the doctor's tone. Where was all this talk leading? "You sure Molly's all right?"

The doctor walked around the mules, but instead of heading for the house, he stayed in the shelter of the lean-to. "So far as I can tell. Of course we'll keep her in bed. Mrs. Tuttle can stay a few days?"

Jake sighed and nodded, feeling there was more to come.

"There is one thing," the doctor busied himself with wiping his monocle with a none-too-clean handkerchief while he spoke.

"What's that?" Jake felt himself go hard inside.

"Well..." the doctor hesitated. "This isn't easy to say to a man, but if she was my wife . . . well . . ."

Jake had never seen an educated man look so uncomfortable.

"I wouldn't try again," the doctor finally said.

"Try again?"

"Try to have children. What I mean is you shouldn't try to have more children, for a while anyway." He raised the monocle.

"No more children?"

"Yes," the big eye peered at him. "I think you should be content with the boy, Arnold — er — Edwin, for now. What I'm saying is you shouldn't *try* any more."

"You mean we can't —"

"That is correct." Morgan's face was red. "You, Mr. Lewis, will just have to control yourself. That's what I'd do if it were my wife. I've already explained the situation to Mrs. Lewis. She seemed to think you'd be reasonable. You will, won't you?" The big eye in the monocle stared.

"What?"

"Be reasonable!

"Oh ... yes ... sure," Jake nodded. He had always been a reasonable man.

Lizzie Tuttle had entered the sod house almost eagerly for she felt that by sharing this latest tragedy with Molly Lewis she would gain another opportunity to penetrate the mystery of the woman and her husband. They did not seem a couple made to each other, and Lizzie had speculated on how they came to be wed. She had pried openly, but, although Molly accepted her friendship, she did not confide her innermost thoughts in the usual way of women who are too much alone. There was something secret and sad about Molly. That she came from a good family was revealed by her speech and manners and the china proudly displayed on a rough plank shelf. The dirt floor of her sod house was well swept and the walls were covered with layers of newspaper and whitewash and pictures — all wifely attempts to make pretty with what she had.

Her only son was kept so neat and had so diligently been taught his manners, his letters, and his prayers, that sometimes Edwin seemed more like a young prince than the son of a bearded old farmer like Jake Lewis.

Lizzie had often thought that Molly herself was more like a queen than a homesteader's wife. She had been beautiful and young when Jake first brought her to Iowa some six years before, and somehow, despite the plagues of grasshoppers and drought and the general misery of the times and climate, she had managed to retain her looks — not just her prettiness, her womanly and graceful figure, her corn silk hair and cool blue eyes and well-shaped mouth, but her vitality, her quick laugh and blush and way of reaching out to life. Now Lizzie wondered if Molly could survive this latest tragedy with her spirit intact.

Lizzie strode through the main room and pulled aside the curtain that separated it from the bedroom. Molly lay on the bed, covered by a faded quilt. Lizzie, seeing the way her arms still protectively cradled her belly, burst into tears.

When Molly saw her friend crying, her own tears began, and that was good, for since it had happened, she had been beyond tears. Lizzie's hug released more tears. Molly thought, *I want my mother,* and Lizzie hugged harder as if she understood. And then Molly's face was being washed and her hair smoothed, and Lizzie was talking about making soup while Molly lay back, comforted by the touch of the other woman's hands and the way she brought something of home to the dark little house.

Then Molly heard the outside door opening and closing and thought, *Jake's home. The doctor will have told him by now.* There were footsteps, and the doctor pulled aside the curtain. "Feeling better?" he asked, his monocle gleaming in the lamplight. Without waiting for her answer, he added brightly, "Here's your husband!"

Jake stood in the doorway, silent and awkward, his hat in his hands. He was only thirty-six, fifteen years older than she, but he had looked middle aged ever since she had known him. He had never been handsome, and he had been clean shaved only on their wedding day, but sometimes there was a look of gentleness about his eyes that moved her, and today his whole face was so filled with suffering that she could hardly bear her guilt. She tried so hard to love him, and it always ended in failure. She closed her eyes and tried to control herself, but she could feel more tears coming.

"You got pain, Molly?" Jake stepped to the bed.

She shook her head.

"Sure?"

She nodded. He patted her hand silently for a long time. Then he asked, "Will you be wanting some wood?"

She opened her eyes, trying to fathom his meaning.

"Wood. For a box." Jake shifted his weight awkwardly. "I thought I could get it when I take the doctor back to town."

"Box?" Then she understood. She nodded to stop him from saying the word, *coffin*. Was that all he could think to say, to talk about a *coffin*? Couldn't he say something to ease her pain?

"I'll get something real nice, Molly. I'll make it strong!"

He's trying, she thought. There are some that wouldn't think of making a coffin for a baby that never lived. It was the only gift he'd ever give his son. She forced herself to whisper her thanks and he kissed her on the forehead, gently, awkwardly, his beard scratching.

"I'll get the wood when I take the doctor home. Lizzie will stay with you." She nodded but he didn't leave. "The doctor wants to examine you again," he finished lamely.

She must have winced at the word *examine*, for he added, "We got to get you well. That's all that's important now. Don't worry. I'm not going to ... bother you anymore!"

His words stuck in her mind throughout the doctor's brief and silent examination of her body. *I'm not going to bother you anymore.* When the men were gone, Molly lay listening to Lizzie puttering in the kitchen and was glad to be alone. So the doctor had told Jake. She could no longer try to be a wife to him. She had not minded doing her duty to Jake. She had tried to find joy in giving to him and, having only once tasted of passion, did not know there could be joy in taking. She had no expectations from Jake's embrace other than it should give him release and give her children to love. Now she had no son for Jake, and no baby to hold to her breast. She touched her breasts. It seemed they were already fuller, and knowing she must have Lizzie bind them against the milk that would come unbidden and be wasted, she thought she could not endure the pain. She wished for Edwin, needing to hold him. But she knew her son was already growing up and taking on Jake's ways. She saw her future, even more lonely than her past, and pictured herself shut away in the sod house, safe from the heat of the summer and the cold of the winter, but always alone.

She was afraid and thought the fear must be another punishment, a punishment for once again thinking of Hugh. For even in labor with Jake's son, she had thought of Hugh. Needing so desperately to escape the pain, she had let her mind return to home and family, and that led to remembering a walk in a spring meadow. And after all the years passed since he had gone away and she had married Jake, she had escaped to the world that was sweet and secret and beautiful in the memory of their love. Then as the next pain mounted her, she had tried to push away the memory, and when it would not go but only turned dark, she was afraid that in the anguish of childbirth she might forget and call his name.

Hugh. She had pushed the memory away then, terrified for the child within her, the child that like the last one, had grown still in her womb. She had told herself it could not happen again, that this child would live, and she had promised God that if he would deliver her of a live and healthy child for Jake, she would never think again of Hugh. She would ask for no more, dream no more, but be content.

But the baby had been born dead, and she could not fathom what that meant. Why had she born a healthy son to another man while the babies of her lawful husband stilled within her?

She wanted so badly to be a good wife to Jake, for though plagued by bad luck and not given to saying and doing the tender things a woman foolishly yearns for, he was a good man. He had saved her from disgrace, treated Edwin as his own, and been as good as a father to her. He had never thrown it up to her either, never even spoken of it, though sometimes she almost wished he would, for when so much welled up inside her that needed sharing, Jake's silence was oppressive.

She had tried to love him, and in a way she did, but she had never succeeded in quelling the longing in her heart, the feeling that something was missing and needed to be searched for. She had never been able to forget her first love and moments made intimate not just by touch but by a sharing of the spirit she could not hope for with Jake.

She thought that it was for cherishing that memory that she was punished, not for the act itself. That had been sweet and good, and she too young to realize the consequences of giving herself to a boy who knew no more than she the price of love. It was the remembering that must be wrong, the way she took out the memory and held it to her as if it were a real thing like her mother's cameo necklace or like a locket concealing a faded tintype of the beloved and kept in a secret place to be taken out for the pleasure and pain of it. It was her refusal to let go of the memory that she thought kept her from being a truer wife to Jake. She believed that if she could but will it she would stop thinking of Hugh forever, except, of course, in those moments when Edwin smiled a certain way, and she knew it was his father's look about him.

Molly did not know it was the memory of love that sustained her through the cold and lonely winters on the homestead, and it was the never-quite-lost hope of recapturing it that enabled her to feel the promise of spring. She did not know, and would not have admitted it if she had, that life with a man like Jake can never be more than comfort and duty, can never be a love that sparkles and gleams even when lost, and that once having known this kind of love, a woman can never be satisfied with less.

She thought she would be happier without her longings and be a better wife. And she might have been. There are women who do not remember, or who have nothing to remember, and if they marry men who are good and steady, all is well. If they do not know the heights of passion, neither do they know the depths. But Molly Lewis was a woman with that nameless yearning for something more. She belonged with a man who had a restless need of his own to strive and fight and build and love in a way beyond the ordinary.

But she was married to Jake and she didn't know, nor was ready to know, any of this. She thought only of going home, returning to Pennsylvania and being her father's daughter again. She looked at her work-worn hands on her faded bride's quilt and remembered the reason she had left and why she could not go home. Many a day she had kept herself going with the dream the homestead would flourish and they would go home with new clothes and a family so large and beautiful no one would remember why she had married Jake Lewis. But now she could dream that dream no more. She was barely past twenty, but it seemed her life was over. Her pain spilled over into more tears.

Lizzie, bustling in with steaming cups of tea in the china teacups, saw her tears and commanded her not to start up again.

"We had ourselves a good cry and that's enough for now."

Molly accepted a cup of tea and held it carefully while

she regained control. She did not want to break another cup, one of her last links with home.

"He don't have much to say, does he, that husband of yours?" Lizzie pulled her chair close to the bed to drink her tea.

"No. But he's a good man."

"Oh, I know that," Lizzie rocked and sighed. "Anyone could see how hard he took it, but he sure don't have much to say."

"No, he's quiet." Realizing Lizzie had seen his awkwardness in comforting her, Molly felt protective of Jake.

"I guess men are all like that," Lizzie sighed, "I can't hardly get a word out of my Sam unless it's about crops and such. Nothing tender, and he's a real talker compared to Jake. I guess it's just not in a man's nature to want to talk with women."

"I knew one once who was different. He made me want to share my secrets, and he told me his and —"

"And?"

Molly blushed and studied her teacup, knowing she had said too much. "Oh, he was just a schoolboy I once knew. It was a long time ago. I expect they all change, get to worrying about life and all and get too busy to ... you know."

"Oh, I know. It's a man's way, but you'd think once in a while, like with your loss and all, Jake could say something more, show he cares."

"He shows by doing. He works so hard here. He really tries."

"I expect he'll feel better driving into town and doing his chores. He'll take real good care of you now. "Course he'll probably stop off at the saloon."

So Lizzie knew. "You can't blame him, can you? I mean a man has to have some release, losing his son!"

"I know. Don't blame him a bit. Even Sam would

today. It's just that you'd think he'd want to talk about it. But not Jake. He won't ever say how he feels. If he sees men he knows today, he'll talk about something else, politics or crops or going to the Black Hills. But he'd never confide in anyone. He'll leave it to Sam and me to spread the word about your loss. Why I tried to talk to him on the way over. I asked him about going to the Black Hills, but he shut me off. He wouldn't even answer me."

"You and Jake talked about going to the Black Hills?"

"I talked. Not him. No imagination, that man. You'd think he'd want to make a try for it. They say there's a fortune in gold there for those that have the gumption to face the Sioux!"

"You think Jake should go?"

"I didn't say that. Just said I'd think a man *like* Jake would want to go. It's not like he's got anything to lose. Sam said he'd go, but he's got to get crops in this spring!"

"So does Jake."

"Of course."

So Molly said what she knew Lizzie was thinking, "It doesn't do much good to plant if it doesn't rain or if the grasshoppers come. Lizzie, if our luck doesn't change, if it hits us worse than anyone again this year, I don't think I can go on."

"Now don't you worry. Jake will make a go of this place yet," Lizzie said without much conviction in her voice. "The last few years have been bad for everyone!"

"But not like it was for Jake and me," Molly picked at the edge of the quilt she'd made as a girl for her hope chest, "We just get farther and farther behind. Jake tries so hard and everything he does goes sour." She stared at the curtain which shielded her from the other room where the doctor had laid the little bundle containing the baby. She felt the tears coming again. "And this failure is mine."

"Don't talk that way, Molly. It's going to get better. Jake's going to make a fine farm here."

A fine farm, Molly thought and remembered that morning. Just before she started labor she'd felt restless and asked Jake to walk with her. They stopped to examine the cottonwood tree and saw that despite all the water they'd hauled for it, the tree had finally winter-killed. It might come back from the roots, but there would be no shade again that summer. The tree was to shelter the grave of the child she had lost two years before. Jake had run a few strands of wire to protect the grave and the tree from livestock, but the fence was sagging. He'd marked the grave with a homemade wooden cross. You don't put up headstones for babies that never lived, but the grave looked like something made by children to bury a dead bird. Jake must have seen it through her eyes because he said, "I thought I'd make a real fence this summer. We could plant flowers again."

"They won't grow," she said, already afraid for the new baby which seemed to have stilled within her. She saw her remark had hurt, but her fear spilled into anger. "We can't even have a real graveyard on the place."

"Christ, Molly, what do you expect?"

"I'm sorry. I shouldn't have said it." But looking at the homestead, the flat, endless loneliness of it all, she closed her eyes and thought, *this isn't home and never will be.* Home is white houses and streets lined with trees and folks visiting back and forth and sitting on their porches after supper. She'd wanted to do something desperate, to send Jake out into the gold fields, to risk his life even, anything to get them beyond that place, but it was then she had felt the first pain of labor and realized she could not care for a new baby and the homestead without Jake. Now, realizing there would be no baby, but only another pitiful little marker in the cemetery to symbolize their failure, she felt again a desperate urge to find a way out. She sensed that if she did not act now, she would simply dry up and turn inward within the walls of the sod house, never again touched by anything. She clutched her friend's hand.

"We've got to get out, Lizzie. I can't take this place any longer. I'll go crazy. I want to go home."

"Hush," Lizzie pushed her down in the bed and tried to cover her up. "You're talking crazy. This is your home now, and you got to accept it."

"I can't. I just can't. I'll die!"

"You won't die. No woman dies of it. You'll just grow up. Get practical and forget all the fairy tales and dreams."

"And just die *inside*. I'll go crazy if I stay here, Lizzie. I've got to get home."

"If you could go back to your people for a visit, that would be what you need. But Jake can't afford to send you. What about your family? You told me they're well-off. Why not write and ask them for the train fare?"

"I'd never do that. That would be admitting . . . no, I can never go home unless . . . unless it's all right with Jake and me. We have to have the money to go on our own. So they see . . . so they see I've . . . we have made a go of things."

"There ain't no way Jake Lewis is going to come up with that kind of money. No way anybody could come up with that kind of money short of striking it rich in the gold fields!"

"Then you think he should go! You really think I should send Jake to the Black Hills?"

"My God, woman, where did you get such a notion? I only brought it up to him because I was only trying to find something he'd talk about. Nobody but a fool would try for the gold fields."

"Why not? You said that was the only way to make enough money. Go where there's gold nuggets just waiting to be picked up."

"If the Sioux don't get you first. And if you've got rail fare to Sidney and cash to buy supplies and horses to get you to the Black Hills. Just suppose for a minute Jake was brave enough or fool enough to face the Sioux. How would he find the cash to get there? And how are you going to get a crop in here *alone*?"

"We could sell the homestead."

"Sell the homestead? Your only security?"

Lizzie saw Molly's reaction to her blunder and began to talk faster. "And what would you do while he was gone? Where would you live? And how would you feel all alone with Edwin, not knowing what was happening with Jake? And maybe never coming back, and you not knowing if the Sioux got him or what?"

Molly was silent, and Lizzie gave a grunt of satisfaction and began to gather up the tea things. She had her back to her friend and was about to leave when Molly spoke again, her voice calm and controlled, "I could go with him. Now that there's no baby, I could go with him. Edwin and I could go too!"

Lizzie dropped the tea things with a crash and, turning back to the bed, felt of Molly's forehead.

"You must be getting the fever. That's crazy talk. The whole country is crawling with Indians. It's bad enough a bunch of fool men think they can go in there, but to take a woman and boy! Why, the only women going to a place like that would be camp followers! It's not the place for a lady from good stock, like you."

"But I've heard women are going in, and, even if they're not, even if I were the first one —"

"Not even Jake Lewis would be fool enough to take you!"

The remark momentarily stunned Molly. She slumped

back against the pillows and Lizzie, thinking she had done her duty, bustled off. But Molly was not defeated; she was angry. She was tired of people telling her Jake was foolish, that he didn't have luck or gumption. He was a brave and good man, and if it was right for them to go to the Black Hills, then he would find a way to take her and he would protect her.

But was it right? She tried to reason it out, but she was tired and confused. Her vision began to blur and as the kerosene lamp flickered, the sod walls of the house seemed to be closing in on her. She willed herself to think. There had to be a way out of this place.

She had heard the Black Hills were beautiful. In the summer they would be cool and green, like the hills of home. It would be good for Jake to have an adventure. All men need adventure. It would make up to him for the fact she could no longer be his wife. Maybe his luck would change. If she could only get him to go, it would give him new hope.

She made up her mind. She would ask him in the morning. She would make him see the right of it.

She truly believed she was doing it for Jake and not to still the longing in her own heart.

CHAPTER TWO

The whole country was talking of the Black Hills that spring. The possibility of following the gold rush, should it develop in earnest, aroused particular interest among the men who plied their trade in the gaming rooms of the great riverboats of the Mississippi. On the river the talk was relaxed, idle, speculative, without the desperate yearning for opportunity and adventure that marked the yearnings of the men of the western territories. Among the frock-coated men who worked the river there was no need to prove one's manhood by conquering new territory, fighting the red men, or staking a claim. There was no need to be among the first. It was better, in fact, to watch and wait, to let others risk their scalps with the Sioux, bend their backs hacking out the wagon trails, and break their hearts proving the worth of the new strike.

There was time in that spring of 1876 for a frock-coated gentleman to stroll idly along the streets of a Mississippi port town. There was time to pick and choose from the enticements offered such gentlemen by the shops, saloons and bawdy houses which serviced the river traffic.

Such a gentleman could play gamblers' games with himself. He could glance idly into a shop window; and if he saw something he liked, he could take it or leave it. He could set up a challenge for himself, and call it *destiny*.

Sally O'Brien's Ready to Wear and Fine Dressmaking occupied a side street. It was not an impressive shop, except that, due to Mrs. O'Brien's persistent nagging, the window was sparkling clean and, among other things, displayed a fine assortment of men's handkerchiefs.

A man who stopped to admire the handkerchiefs and looked beyond them into the shop would have seen two women unpacking a shipping crate. One was old and fat and gray. The other was startlingly beautiful, even in the brown serge skirt and high-necked white shirt of a shop girl. Her profile was fine, not with the classic lines of a cameo, but with the upturned nose and saucy pouting lips of a dance hall girl. Her skin was fair, and her raven black hair escaped from its knot in enticing tendrils. One could not tell about her eyes from the shop window, but her body, as she bent over the shipping crate, was graceful, yet excitingly round.

Such a man could have admired and walked on. He could have carried the image of the woman and the need it invoked to a bawdyhouse. Or, he could have stared, admiring his own reflection in the window as much as the woman within.

He could have taken out a coin, flipped it and caught it on his sleeve, making a wager with himself. And then strolled across the street to watch and wait.

"Oh, Ma, isn't this lovely?" Emma O'Brien exclaimed as she unpacked the bolt of green velvet. "Isn't this the loveliest piece of goods you ever saw?" She unfastened the bolt and pulled out a length of the fabric to touch to her cheek. "It's so soft and rich feeling and look — " she held the fabric so the light caught its sheen, "the color! It's the color of emeralds!"

"And how would you be knowing the color of emeralds?"

As she reproved her daughter, Sally O'Brien's speech lilted in the Old Country way, though it was her husband who had been Irish.

"I saw some in the shop down the street. Emerald earbobs. They were the most beautiful things I ever saw. They would match my eyes."

"Emma! I've told you a hundred times not to be loitering around shop windows. A girl can get in trouble that way." Her mother dipped into the box Emma had been unpacking and began to lift out the heavy bolts of fabric. "They were probably fake, anyway."

"Yes, Mama, I'm sorry." Emma sighed and lowered her thick lashes, trying to look demure and succeeding, for she was a natural actress. Longingly she fingered the green velvet until she could no longer resist asking, "Ma, couldn't I have a piece of this? I could make me the most elegant gown. Please, Ma? I won't ever ask for anything else."

"Why, I never heard of such a thing! Did you look at the price of that stuff? That's the most expensive goods we've ever had, imported and all. I only hope we can get our price for it with times so hard."

"Maybe if we don't sell it, if there's a piece left over ... maybe it will get a little faded and —"

"And, nothing, Missy. Even if you needed a new dress, which you don't — your blue serge is still plenty good if you turn the cuffs. Velvet is not for shop girls. You know that."

"But, Ma, it's so lovely. Couldn't I, just this once?"

"I don't want to hear another word about it. You're a hard, selfish girl to be thinking of taking money from my pocket. Money I need to feed your brother and sisters. Besides, I told you. Velvet is not for the likes of us." Sally O'Brien let her stubby fingers touch the material for just a moment. "This will go to some fine lady, or to some whore. Though whores are partial to red, and I don't cater to such anyway. Now forget it, girl, and give me a hand with this unpacking. "

Emma sighed, rolled up the bolt of green velvet and put it on the shelf, a little apart from the rest. It was no use arguing. And she certainly didn't want to get her mother off on the subject of whores. Sally O'Brien was daft on the subject, talking as if it were the camp followers instead of his duty to help save the union of his adopted country that had impelled Cornelius O'Brien to march off to war a decade before. He had left her with five children, Emma, the oldest, barely nine and the only one who could help in the store. He had never been heard from again. Sally O'Brien had run the little dry-goods store herself after that, setting up her sewing machine in the back and featuring fine dressmaking as well as high quality ready-to-wear as it became available after the war.

At the same time, she had left Emma to manage her large brood of children in the rooms above the store, Now the younger children were in school, and Sally was feeling her age, so she had turned most of the shop work over to Emma, having taught her to sew a perfect seam by pinching her every time she daydreamed and stitched crookedly.

Emma hated the shop. Their customers were all women and all dull. But at least by working in the shop she could make beautiful clothes and dream they were hers, for she loved fashion and read the pages of *Godey's Lady's Book* like some girls read the Bible. Her fantasies of a world beyond the shop were fed by Godey's, the beckoning whistles of the riverboats, and her memories of the theatre.

Although she'd not yet dared dream of anything so wicked as being an actress, drama was central to her life. This was thanks to her lovable rogue of a father who had secretly taken Emma to the vaudeville shows. He saw no reason why his favorite daughter should not have a taste of something he loved, despite the fact his wife regarded theatres as no better than bawdy houses.

Sally O'Brien was not a mean woman; she was a realist who had learned that dreams and dreamers only bring troubles, but she knew she had been harsh about the velvet. It would have matched her daughter's eyes.

"Don't be pouting, girl. If we end up with a piece of

that gabardine left, I'll let you make up a new collar and cuffs for the serge. I let you make that waist there last spring, didn't I?" She studied the white top Emma wore with her brown skirt. "Now that's suitable for a shop girl and right pretty the way you did it with the eyelet edging. We don't want you to look too poor to catch a husband."

"If you want me to find a husband, why don't you let me have something really pretty to wear?"

"Because you tend to be a bit flashy-looking, as it is, with all that black hair and green eyes. You got your father's good looks, curse that it was. If I don't watch you, you'll attract another man who's no good. A nice, steady business man, that's what you need. Not someone who's here today and gone tomorrow."

"Father was a nice, steady business man, wasn't he?" Emma bit her lip as soon as she said it. She should have known better than to bring him up. She remembered her father as a handsome, laughing man whose black hair fell over his forehead and green eyes danced. She hated to hear her mother speak bitterly of him.

"That was different. He had the grand and glorious cause to run off to. Though if you ask me, he only joined to get away from the responsibility of a family. The war was no cause for an Irishman, and with half Missouri on the other side, he could as easy have stayed home. But some men got to have their adventures. Got to go and find trouble as if enough doesn't come to your door."

"Don't women need adventure? Don't women need to have excitement and to dream and ... to wonder?"

"Wonder! Oh, yes, think that way, girl, and you'll wonder. You'll find one that will leave you wondering night after night 'till he's finally gone for good. You listen to me, Emma. Life is hard enough. Don't look for trouble. And don't think about love and such foolishness. It's all a trap. You go to meeting and dress proper, and learn to keep your mouth shut, and we'll find you a man who will make you a respectable living and never, ever leave you wondering. That's what you need, girl. Not green velvet."

Emma nodded as if she believed it all, biding her time, and the moment her mother left the shop for the afternoon, made for the green velvet.

"Cranky old bag," she said to herself, listening to her mother's footsteps on the outside stairway and then moving across the rooms upstairs. Soon she'd be sprawled on the bed, sleeping the afternoon away while Emma slaved in the shop. As if she would ever meet an interesting man at church. It was full of women, plus a few doddering old widowers who'd killed their first wife or two with child bearing. Oh, and beardless boys who blushed just to look at her! Besides, her mother rushed her away afterwards so fast that even if she should see someone interesting, she'd never have a chance to make an impression. Emma doubted if her mother intended to ever let her be courted. Her first born daughter had learned the trade too well. Besides, her younger sister, Colleen, pretended to be a simpering idiot who couldn't add a column of figures or sew a simple French seam, so she could stay in school and avoid Emma's fate of being trapped in the shop.

Emma picked up the bolt of green velvet and carried it to the mirror at the dressmaking end of the shop. If she could only make a dress from its lush folds, she told herself, she could find a way to escape spending the rest of her life under her mother's thumb.

Lighting a kerosene lamp, she arranged it on the bracket beside the mirror. She could at least see how she would look. Holding one end of the fabric, she let the bolt drop to the floor. Holding the velvet up before her and studying herself in the mirror, she saw the color was perfect. It brought out the green of her eyes.

Smiling, she unbuttoned the top of her waist and pulled it open. She would just tuck this velvet into the top of her chemise to see how it would look against her skin. How she would love to have a low-necked gown like this! What was the use of having skin that was white and smooth as silk and breasts that swelled over the top of your chemise if no one was ever to see them?

She pulled the pins from her hair, releasing it from its knot so that it tumbled around her shoulders in lush waves. The lamplight sparked her eyes and danced around her naked throat. She caressed the velvet. It was almost as pleasing to the touch as her own skin.

The bell jingled as the shop door opened. They never had customers at that time of day. She turned, still holding the green velvet tucked into her bodice. She was aware of the nakedness of her neck and breast and her hair tumbling down around her shoulders. It was a man. The kind of man she'd seen strolling along the riverfront where the steamboats docked. The kind of man who made her mother walk faster and jerk at Emma's arm.

For a moment they stared at each other.

He spoke first. "That shade of green is perfect for you. It matches your eyes. All you need to set it off is a pair of emerald eardrops. I just saw some in a shop down the street."

She felt herself blushing. Pulses deep within her began pounding. She turned back to the mirror as if embarrassed, and in the moment before she pulled the velvet from her chemise and began buttoning her waist, she saw herself as he had seen her. Beautiful and desirable. She also saw his face reflected in the mirror and knew he was enchanted.

He turned his back as she arranged her clothes. Obviously he was a gentleman.

"Pardon me. I didn't realize you were indisposed."

"We don't usually have customers after dinner, but

you are welcome to look around."

"Then you are the proprietress?"

"I just work here. The velvet is not for me. I wanted to see how it would look made up."

"But you should have it. It's made for you."

"It's really not suitable for a shop girl. Now what can I help you with, Mister —?

She drew out the *Mister,* surprised at her own boldness. But she had to know his name. And whatever he had come for, she intended to keep him there as long as possible. She had not seen a man this handsome since her father had gone to war.

He studied her a long time before he answered, then he removed his broad-brimmed white hat and swept it before him in a courtly gesture.

"My name is Austin Avery."

"Austin Avery. What an elegant name."

"It is a name well respected down the river. Or it was until *the war,* although it is a comfort to think that even we who lost so much in that dreadful holocaust kept our good names."

"You're a Southerner?" She hoped she could avoid revealing her father had fought on the other side. In Missouri, the war was still a touchy issue.

"Yes, from Louisiana. But now you know more about me than I of you. May I be so bold as to ask your name?"

It was bold, of course. She was surprised that a gentleman should act so and prayed her mother would not take a sudden urge to come downstairs. Emma knew she should turn the subject to business, but he was so handsome. God knows when she'd get another chance to flirt with such a man. She knew she had hesitated too long, but she hated to say her name. Here he was a Southern gentleman, and Emma O'Brien sounded as common as wash water.

"My name is Em —" she began and then her eye caught the green velvet, "Emerald. My name is Emerald O'Brien."

"Emerald O'Brien! How perfectly it suits you! I could not have thought of a better name myself! "

Now, what does he mean by that? She wondered, but his face was impassive. She'd not let him disconcert her. Making her voice cool, she said, "And what are you *looking for,* Mr. Avery?"

He looked straight into her eyes and what she saw there made her blush and look at her feet. Then, just when she emboldened herself to meet his gaze again, he turned the conversation to talk of fine handkerchiefs and ruffled dress shirts. They did not carry the shirts, she told him regretfully, but they had a large stock of handkerchiefs. She praised the merits of each, until at long last he selected the most expensive, those of India silk at a dollar each. She had known he would choose the best. Wanting to keep him in the shop as long as possible, she suggested that shirts could be made for him, but he said he was just passing through on his way up river.

She wondered frantically what she might do to detain him. Then, after he paid for the handkerchiefs and she was wrapping them, he peeled off a wad of greenbacks and tossed them on the counter. "Would this be enough for a gown of that green material? Made up and ready to wear, I mean."

She stared at the bills, dumbfounded. "Why, yes," she stammered. "It's more than enough." *Of course, you fool,* she thought. A man like that would have a wife or mistress. She made her voice cool again. "Will you bring the lady in to choose a style? We have the latest copy of Godey's Lady's Book, and I can copy whatever she —"

"That won't be necessary," he said. "Make it up to suit yourself. I'm sure you know the latest style."

"But," she replied, almost trembling from both fear

and hope. "How will I know what size to make it?"

"Make it to fit yourself. I'll be back at the end of the week. Can you finish it by then?"

She hesitated only a moment before saying she could, knowing she'd have to sew day and night. Without further comment, he left. She stood there with her head spinning and her heart pounding. What did he mean? Did he have some other woman who was just her size, *or did he mean what she thought he meant?* She had not dared to ask. If she were wrong, she'd have made a fool of herself. She stared for a moment at the green velvet while she tried to sort it out.

Then she picked up the bills and shoved them into the cash drawer. She reached under the counter and got out the latest copy of Godey's. She knew just the dress she would copy. It had a fashionable bustle back and a low neck to show off her breasts and a cunning little jacket for daytime. She would have to think of an excuse for her mother. A new customer with lots of cash. Maybe even an actress. A rush job.

She turned the pages rapidly, her heart hammering, knowing something momentous had begun.

An adventure. A drama in which she, Emerald O'Brien, would star.

CHAPTER THREE

In Carpenter, Nebraska, in that spring of 1876 there were two main topics of speculation among the men who hunkered around the stove at Hornbringle's Hardware or the brass rail of the City Saloon. The first was the endless possibilities in and the ramifications of joining the gold rush to the Black Hills. The second was whether or not there would be a fight between Phineas P. Crandall, editor of The Carpenter Sentinel, and the Everett boy. The men followed Crandall's lead in calling his new employee *boy* despite the fact Hugh Everett was obviously a man — one who looked like he could hold his own in a fight. But that was the fun of it! Old man Crandall persisting in calling Hugh *boy* and expected him to act humble and do all the dirty work around the Sentinel office when Crandall barely reached five feet in height even in his high-heeled, patent-leather, spat-covered shoes, and Hugh Everett was as tall and strong as a young oak and had the steely gaze and powerful grip of a frontiersman.

Most of the men figured it had to come to blows, though some argued that Everett seemed to be the idealistic type who felt he owed Crandall his loyalty for the editor's letting him take over his father's position while old John Everett coughed his lungs out and his poor wife worried herself into the grave beside him. Hugh Everett, they argued, was an educated and civilized man, having been away from Carpenter reading law until his father's illness brought him home. He would control himself and never pick Crandall up by his embroidered silk lapels and give the pompous old goat the shaking he so richly deserved.

Further complicating the speculation was the question of Luther Everett. Everyone knew Mrs. Everett's last words to Hugh had been *take care of your brother*, and everyone knew sixteen-year-old Luther was going to need a firm hand. So by the time Luther's name came up, it was generally agreed that Hugh was stuck. Such a responsible young man would not dare give up an office job in a first-class establishment like the Sentinel, not with times so hard and so many out of work.

There were even those who argued that a young man who wanted to get ahead could do worse than to follow in the steps of Phineas P. Crandall. True, he was arrogant, an unscrupulous businessman, and personally obnoxious; but he was also, one had to admit, a businessman who was amassing both capital and power. And, moreover, he was loyal to his advertisers. He had successfully promoted the Nebraska route to the Black Hills as being safer than the Wyoming route by playing up every skirmish with the Sioux in Wyoming territory and downplaying any on the route from Sidney, thus profiting the local economy. It was difficult to find fault with a man with such a keen editorial policy.

The men hunkering around the hardware store and saloon were not the only ones in Carpenter to speculate about Hugh Everett. The thoughts of most of the unmarried women and even some of the good wives of the city turned frequently to the need to comfort the young man in his bereavement with gifts of homemade bread and jam and even washing and ironing. The women said they would do the same for anyone who had suffered such a loss, but each knew in her secret heart she offered more than sympathy. And each knew her cause was hopeless. For although Hugh responded with smiles and a squeeze to the hand or even the waist, and he might have taken a woman who dared to offer herself without marriage, it was obvious he would not be won easily. He acknowledged a woman, but he seemed always to be looking beyond her, as if what was promised was not enough, but he dreamed of another woman in his past, or in his future, who would offer something beyond even the dreams of the women of Carpenter, Nebraska.

Some women thought the distant look in Hugh's eyes was only the haunted gaze of a man who has suffered tragedy and that in time he would be ready to settle down. Others, older and wiser women, said young Everett had that look about him when he first came to Carpenter; that he had the wanderlust and was best left alone, being the kind of man who must roam and will bring grief to any woman who dares love him.

The truth was no one in Carpenter, Nebraska, understood Hugh Everett, least of all Hugh Everett

Phineas P. Crandall had studied the young man ever since Hugh gave up his law studies to help his father by taking over his duties at the Sentinel. The editor had decided, almost immediately, that he wanted Hugh working for him. He did not have the delicate hands of a natural typesetter as did Crandall, but he was intelligent and skillful and had been quick to master the layout of the print drawers and the mechanics of the lever-operated printing press. Most important, he was an articulate man who could write polished copy. With such a man running the office, Crandall would be able to devote his full attention to the various schemes he fancied would establish him as one of Nebraska's leading entrepreneurs.

First, however, Crandall decided, Hugh must be taught who was in charge. Though Hugh was always polite, there was something about him that Crandall found disturbing, even threatening. He sensed there was a fire inside Hugh that Crandall needed under his own control. He told himself that Hugh, like all men, had within him a beast, a beast that must be leashed for the boy's own good.

He did not admit his true motive, which was that if he could take down someone as tall, strong, and handsome, as Hugh Everett; then he, Phineas P. Crandall, would be a bigger man.

Crandall fancied that because of his respect for Hugh's grief over the illnesses and deaths of his parents, he had been easy on him. But on the day he read Hugh's Pa-ha-sa-pa editorial he decided the time had come for a showdown. He had not seen the editorial until it was in print, having trusted Hugh to fill in a gap on the front page while he took a long lunch at Meyer's Saloon. Although he was pleased by parts of the editorial, other parts infuriated him. Clearly Hugh needed some strong leadership!

Hugh was setting type for the next edition, wearing his black apron and matching sleeve protectors and standing before the California job case, a waist-high rack containing drawers of various sizes and styles of type. Crandall folded the newspaper so as to display the Black Hills article and slapped it down on the case.

"What is the meaning of this Pa-ha-sa-pa garbage?"

"Sir?" Hugh responded politely, but Crandall saw something flaring in his dark eyes.

"I said, what is this Pa-ha-sa-pa garbage?"

When he set out to intimidate someone, Crandall had a way of peering over the top of his wire-rimmed spectacles so his piercing blue eyes seemed to look right through his victim. He was doing it now, but Hugh did not intend to be intimidated. He set down the frame with the line of type he was setting before he spoke.

"I believe you asked me to fill out the front page by writing an article promoting the Black Hills."

"That's just it," Crandall sputtered, "An article promoting the Black Hills, not a theological discussion! Not 'Sacred Hunting Ground of the Sioux' and," he snatched up the newspaper and scanned the article as he talked, "and questions of right and wrong. *Never questions of right or wrong!*" He threw the paper down.

Hugh picked it up and studied his article. He remembered how much he had enjoyed writing it. He had savored the word, "Pahasapa," saying it over and over to himself. The word seemed to evoke images of mysterious, beckoning mountains wreathed in fog, deer grazing at the edge of meadows, valleys with clear, sparkling creeks where the sunlight caught the gleam of golden nuggets. The longing that came to him when he thought of the forbidden lands was sharp. It was as if, although the area was off-limits to whites by treaty, something was calling him there. He felt something great would happen there and he longed to explore this last frontier.

"What are you doing, boy, *dreaming?*" Crandall broke his reverie. "You see! That's what I wanted to get on you about! Dreaming all the time. You think too much. 'Sacred Hunting Ground Horse Shit!' Whose side are you on, anyway?"

"Naturally I'm for opening new lands to civilization," Hugh measured his words carefully, so his anger wouldn't keep him from making his point, "but until the government succeeds in negotiating for the Black Hills, the Treaty of '68 clearly —"

"The Treaty of '68? You're talking like a bleeding heart, pap-sucking Quaker. Trust me, there are enough bleeding hearts in this world without a responsible paper like The Sentinel admitting the Black Hills belong to the Sioux."

"But the point is, they do —"

"The point is the goddamn treaty commissioners in Washington have to be made to get off their fat asses and write a new treaty and take that land away from those heathen redskins!"

"You talk like a —!"

"I talk like a *realist*. That's what I am, and that's what you're going to have to be if you want to get along in this world. Your father got you over-educated; that's your trouble. I warned him about it, but he didn't listen, and now he's dead and you're writing about 'The Sacred Hunting Ground', for God's sake!"

"Listen, Crandall, if you didn't like it, then why — "

"Then why did I let it go to print? Is that what you're asking? Not because I didn't see it." His expression told Hugh he hadn't, but the old man had his steam up. "No, it's because. . . because I *like* you and want to see you get ahead. Figure I owe it to your father. That's what I told Hornbringle when he joshed me about your little essay. 'He'll learn,' I said. 'He'll learn running a paper is a business.'"

"Yes," Hugh replied. "I'm aware the gold rush is important to a hardware man like Hornbringle, and we have to be loyal to our advertisers, but you make it sound as if the whole gold rush is nothing but a business opportunity!"

"And what do you think it is, boy, *a goddamn crusade*? You've got to learn there's nothing wrong with business. It's the free enterprise system. Why, if enough people invade the Black Hills, and the goddamn government can be brought into line to protect the rights of its law-abiding citizens by wiping out the Indians, then a whole new land will open up right on our doorstep. Can you see what that will mean for us? For the railroad and for Nebraska?"

"Crandall, I think —"

"Civilization! That's what it will mean! Miners digging down and breaking rock and getting all that gold, and timber men cutting trees, and farmers clearing the land, and people building houses and barns and chicken coops!"

Warming to his subject, Crandall struck a pose with

one hand on the type case as if it were a podium and the other hand hooked in the front of his vest. He looked senatorial with his natty suit and his snow-white mutton-chop sideburns setting off his bald dome. "What would be a more fitting way for this nation to celebrate its Centennial than by opening a whole new territory to the free enterprise system? Think of it, 1776 to 1876, and hundreds of new businesses thriving, livery stables, hardware stores, hotels, boarding houses, and brothels, and even newspapers! Why there might be an opportunity for some enterprising entrepreneur to own a whole chain of newspapers! Progress, that's what it is!"

"But what about truth?" Hugh demanded as Crandall paused for breath." Don't we have some obligation to inform people of the truth? Don't people have the right to know about the moral issues and the risks involved in such an endeavor?"

"Truth? Now where did you get a fool idea like that? No one cares about truth, boy. Not even the ministers. Why there wouldn't be a church in operation today if people cared about truth. No sir! What people care about is *economics*. Business, getting on!"

Suddenly Hugh could stand no more. He wanted to slug Crandall, get out of the office and keep going. He wanted to bust loose and follow the crazy idea that had been in his mind all week.

He was sick of grief and responsibility and Carpenter, Nebraska, and especially, moral decisions.

He ripped off the sleeve protectors and the black type-setters apron and threw them on the floor. No man should have to wear an apron.

"What are you doing?" Crandall demanded. Hugh hesitated. He had no plan, and from somewhere inside him a voice said, *Remember Luther. Take care of your brother.*

Crandall was staring at him accusingly. Hugh fought for control. He told himself he was a civilized man and must behave logically. He needed time to think. He spied the empty coal scuttle. "I need some fresh air," he said. "The bucket's empty. I'll fetch some coal." Without waiting for Crandall to reply, he grabbed the scuttle and took his exit.

Outside, Hugh took deep breaths of the cold afternoon air. The air held just the promise of spring in it. It was the second time in as many weeks that he had come to the point of telling Crandall off. The first was shortly after the funeral when he asked Crandall to set a value on his father's share of the partnership.

"Did he mean in dollars and cents?" Crandall had asked. "What else is there?" Hugh demanded. "Well, there's good-will," Crandall said pleasantly, "and loyalty and reputation. Intangibles built up over the years of a partnership." Hugh persisted, "In dollars and cents." And then Crandall had told him.

Nothing.

His father's share of the partnership, which he had assumed would be sufficient to keep Luther in school while he returned to the law, was worthless. "It has not had a cash value for some time," Crandall went on explaining while Hugh, through a red mist of controlled rage, saw his dreams slipping away.

Hugh could not believe it and said so. According to the banner on the masthead, The Carpenter Sentinel was "Nebraska Territory's Leading Bi-Weekly." How could his father's share be worthless? With a great show of affronted dignity, Crandall produced evidence in ledger books that the sizeable investment his father made in the partnership six years before had dwindled away. In Crandall's precise script was the record of dozens of withdrawals of capital made when his father's illness had prevented him from earning his salary, and he still insisted on providing his sons with the luxury of education. Hugh's certainty that Crandall had cheated his father was shaken by the old man's implication that the family's financial ruin was somehow not his fault but Hugh's.

"I told him it was your responsibility to take over. I told him to call you home months before he did."

"If only I'd realized how sick he was. His lungs had been bad for years, but we somehow never expected —"

"To know the will of God? No, Son, few understand that."

Hugh shut out the words as best he could while Crandall launched his sermon about what a blessing it was that his mother had followed her husband in death to be his helpmate in the beyond. Crandall wasn't the first to voice this platitude; it was one Hugh especially hated. Hugh thought he should have discovered some answers to the meaning of life and death himself, but he had not. He avoided thinking of the deaths of his parents; deaths which had thrust upon him the responsibility of his brother, Luther.

As if Crandall could read Hugh's mind, he finished his speech with, "How old is Luther now?"

"Sixteen."

"Ah, yes, sixteen. Well, some are men at that age and some are not. It is my impression your brother has not yet *settled?*"

Hugh frowned. He supposed a certain amount of rivalry between brothers was natural, but Luther was always out to prove there was something he could do better than Hugh; then getting hurt and angry when he again came up against the fact that Hugh was the smarter and the taller and even the better-liked of the brothers. Hugh did not regret his promise to take care of his brother; he loved him. He only wished he could *like* him a little more. None of this was Crandall's business, however, so he replied only that Luther was still in school.

"Then you will need to provide for him as well as for yourself? Had you planned to go on reading for the law?"

"I don't see how I can afford to right now."

"I don't either," Crandall said cheerfully, "and that is why I am prepared to make you an offer."

The offer was for Hugh to take over his father's duties at a figure so low Hugh could not trust himself to answer, but Crandall seemed to assume it was settled; Hugh would spend the rest of his life as the all-around work horse of the Sentinel. It was a job which should have been easy to quit, but Hugh was only too aware the whole country was still feeling the effects of the post Civil War depression. Thousands of families like his had followed the new railroad lines west, but the lands they took up had often proved barren and worthless.

Throughout the western territories men were looking for work or waiting for the spring thaw to clear the land so they could make a try for the Black Hills. The hills seemed to be hope's last frontier. Hugh wanted to go himself. Sometimes it even seemed it was his destiny to go. But he told himself such feelings were irrational and he, an educated and rational man who knew better than most the risks of such a venture, could not go chasing a will-o'-the-wisp. Especially not when any decision he made would effect Luther's future as much as his own.

There has to be a reasonable solution to this, Hugh thought, standing with his filled coal scuttle in the alley behind the office he never wanted to enter again. *I can't be as trapped as I feel.* There had to be some compromise between duty and desire. Some way he could provide for Luther and still have his adventure.

An idea had occurred to him as he wrote the

Pahasapa editorial but he had dismissed it; suddenly his notion seemed reasonable. He would talk Crandall into sending him into the Hills as a special Black Hills correspondent. He'd send back objective reports on the gold rush. Luther could board with someone in town. Hopefully, he'd come home rich or could afford to send for Luther.

And if the gold rush was a bust, he'd have kept his link with the newspaper and at least have a job to come home to.

He decided he'd thought enough. It was time for action. Resolutely he strode back to the office. Crandall was sitting at his own desk. He had taken the drawer of type with him and was finishing the galley on which Hugh had been working. He looked up as Hugh came in. "Well, it's about time you came back to work. Get to setting this type. My eyes aren't as young as they used to be."

Hugh knew Crandall expected him to pick up the drawer of type and take it meekly back to the job case to finish. He wanted to keep the old man happy, but he didn't want to make another submissive gesture. He busied himself with picking up his apron and sleeve protectors.

"Crandall, there's something I'd like to talk over with you."

"Of course, Son." Crandall was obviously expecting to be asked advice.

"I'd like to go to the Black Hills. I've been thinking it over and I know you'll agree the Sentinel owes it to its subscribers to discover the truth of this gold rush thing, so I was thinking if you could outfit me, I'd —"

"Go to The Black Hills? You can't be serious. Only a fool would do that."

"What's so foolish about it? The paper's been urging people to go for months."

"People with nothing to lose. People who don't matter. People who can be used to open up the lands. Not people like you."

"Why not? Why not me?"

Seeing he was serious, Crandall stood up and walked toward him. "Because you have something; you have prospects!"

"Prospects? What prospects have I?"

"Why I told you, boy. You can work for me. I'll train you up in the business. Just like you were my son."

"Son? I'm not your son! And don't ever call me *boy* again. I'm twenty-two and I'm a man!"

"Not while you've got such fool schemes in your head. What do you think you'll accomplish by going? What do you think you'd find there?"

"I don't know — *something!*"

"Wealth? Power? Land? Adventure?"

"Yes! All of those! Gold! I'll find gold!" Even as he said it, Hugh felt foolish. It was something more than gold he sought, but he couldn't put a name to it.

"You really think you'll find gold? That it's just lying there waiting for you to strike it rich?"

"Is that so crazy? That I could stake a claim? That I might be lucky? Why not? At least there I'd have a chance for something!"

"You're a fool dreamer like your father!"

"I'd rather die a dreamer than spend my life as your slave!"

"You'd hardly be a slave," Crandall said, backing away from Hugh's anger. "I was thinking that I'd make you a partner one day.

I wasn't going to tell you yet. Was going to see how it worked out, but seeing as how you've been bit by the gold bug, I'll tell you now."

"A partner?" Hugh almost choked over the word.

"There now, Son," Crandall moved closer to him. "I

figured that would make a difference. Can't turn down an opportunity like that, can you?"

"*A partner?*" Hugh sputtered. "You'd make me a *partner!*"

"Just like your father," Crandall beamed and picked up the drawer of type from his desk and offered it to Hugh as if it were a gift. "Now you take this type back over to your case and finish up. We'll discuss the details later."

"Shove it." Hugh said evenly.

"What?" Crandall blinked from behind his glasses. He clutched the drawer, suddenly wary.

"I said you can take that drawer of type and shove it. And you can take the whole damn Sentinel office and your goddamn lousy job and do the same!"

"You've gone crazy." Crandall backed away.

Hugh saw his fear and took a step forward, enjoying it. And then it happened. As he retreated from Hugh's anger, Crandall clutched the drawer to his chest, and the type rained down like hailstones.

"Look what you've done!" Crandall shouted. "Now look what you've done!"

Hugh had to laugh as he watched the little editor drop to his knees and begin frantically to gather the type. Some had fallen between the cracks in the floor. He'd never get it all.

"Don't just stand there, boy, help me!"

"I'm sorry, Crandall, *Sir*," Hugh had turned the word into an insult. "I'm sorry, but I've got better things to do. I'm going to the Black Hills."

"But what about Luther? Have you forgotten your brother?"

Hugh hesitated. He had. Just for a moment.

"Will you take him with you to face the Sioux?"

"Yes! Why not? It'll make a man of him."

"You're crazy and you're a fool," Crandall muttered,

still down on his knees gathering the type. "You're a fool, but you'll have to find out the hard way. Remember I said that! You're a fool!"

"Maybe I am," Hugh said evenly. "Maybe I am. But there are some things a man has to discover for himself."

CHAPTER FOUR

Afterwards, whenever Hugh or Molly thought of that meeting in the camp on Lodge Pole Creek, and they would think of it often, they would wonder if it had been their destiny to meet again. In her dark moments, and there would be many, Molly would think of the meeting as something arranged by God to test her strength and honor. While Hugh, although he too wondered about God's will, was more likely to think of their meeting as a joke planned by malevolent gods who found pleasure in watching humans struggling in the tangled skein of emotions set in their paths to torture, confuse, and tempt.

Both, in those moments when each sensed a purpose to their being together, the thought that *it was meant to be* would triumph; but that notion was always followed by the fear that such thoughts were only a way for their troubled consciences to justify what they allowed to happen.

In truth, it was neither the hand of God, nor the malice of evil spirits that brought them together; it was simply that Jake Lewis was feeling so good about himself and his team and wagon that late April day, as he joined with the other members of Hobart's party who were camped just outside Sidney, Nebraska, to plan the expedition to begin on the morrow. Molly and Edwin were to wait back in the town while the men did their work.

In the few miles between the town and the camp, Jake had forgotten that going to the Black Hills had begun as his wife's idea. He had forgotten that he was a man cursed by bad luck and failure and that he had been beholden to Sam Tuttle for buying the homestead and their farm equipment, and that beyond his wife and child, a team of mules and a wagon and supplies, he had not a thing in the world to call his own.

For he had a fine team and a fine wagon. Not, of course, the heavy wagon of the freighters, but as good as could be had in Sidney, the jumping-off point for the Black Hills. He had plenty of flour and beans and bacon stowed away in the wagon. Molly's trunk and a few sticks of furniture were well concealed. A pickaxe and gold pan were prominently displayed, though he would not need them until the party reached Custer, the gold camp on French Creek named for the leader of the expedition which had proved the existence of gold in the Hills and thus inspired the gold rush.

In the days it took to sell their possessions and arrange for train transport to Sidney, he had become as consumed by the promise of good fortune in the Hills as any other down-and-out farmer in the territories. His optimism did not weaken when they reached Sidney and saw how many were already mounting expeditions. Nor was he discouraged by reports that not just the Sioux would oppose them, but the U.S. Cavalry was under government orders to stop and turn back anyone suspected of entering reservation lands in violation of the treaty already breached by that same government.

Jake felt his luck had changed. That good fortune was finally coming his way. His optimism was reinforced when he succeeded in being accepted by the Hobart Expedition, the group he'd heard would be the strongest and best-armed Black Hills expedition.

Jake was not a man easily impressed by other men, but Emmet Hobart had the aura of a true frontiersman. Jake saw plenty of men on the Sidney streets who wore new buckskins and loaded cartridge belts across their chests, but who revealed in their manner, or their grandiose speeches about supposed deeds on the frontier, that they were mostly acting. But Hobart's buckskins were as worn as his face. Moreover, he was almost as taciturn as

Jake himself. It was from others that Jake learned Hobart had served the North bravely with the 43rd Wisconsin Volunteers and, after the war, had done it all — fought Indians, killed buffalo, and worked on the railroad.

And not only was their leader a real frontiersman, but his expedition would have the benefit of an experienced guide. Donnelly was a fat Irishman who told bad jokes and looked like he'd be more comfortable tending bar than riding a horse, but he had wintered in the Black Hills and knew the way to Custer City. It would be a grand expedition of at least a dozen wagons and some thirty-five men armed with single-shot rifles, or even with repeaters. The party was small enough to travel fast, but big enough to impress the Sioux who, it was generally agreed, didn't organize their opposition, but only formed small war parties and watched for stragglers who promised easy scalps.

Jake's reticence had helped him win acceptance. His team and wagons were scrutinized by Hobart himself, as well as by Donnelly and Pearson, whose position was not clear but who made himself part of the group around Jake's rig. Pearson remarked on the size of Jake's wagon and wondered if he planned to haul gear for men walking or on horseback. Jake said that was what he planned to do. No one had thought to ask him if he had a family along, and he had not volunteered the information.

This secret was the source of some uneasiness as he hung around the camp that day, listening to tales of adventure and plans for breaking camp at dawn. Molly and Edwin were waiting in the hotel in town; he figured he'd just show up with them in the morning, maybe even keep them down in the wagon until the party was underway. Once Hobart's Party was on the road, he didn't think they would make him turn back. He hoped not. He was determined to be part of this expedition. For once, he had as much chance for success as anyone else. It made him feel bold and generous and a little bit testy. And that was why he acted as he did when the Everett brothers showed up. That — and perhaps — *destiny*. It might seem strange that the men so easily accepted Jake into their group, yet questioned the addition of the Everett brothers. But Jake, though he was a farmer and not a frontiersman, was clearly one of them. He, by the leather look of his skin and the hardness of his palms when he shook hands, had labored outdoors. His clothes were work-stained and old. He spoke like the other men, simple, direct, uneducated. The Everett boys were different. Anyone could see that, even as they approached the camp late that afternoon. Their clothes were rugged, but so new the creases showed, and the young one was wearing Napoleon boots, kneehigh in front, made for riding, not walking and so new they must hurt.

The Hobart Party, almost to a man, labeled the newcomers as *boys*. Had they looked like wilderness scouts, they might still have been denied admittance to the expedition solely for *coming late*. Hobart had camped on Lodge Pole Creek while he recruited the best of the men who gathered in Sidney. The others, even Jake Lewis, the last to join, had since early morning smoked, planned and forged their group. They named the expedition officially, decided on a line of march, and agreed to set out at dawn the next day. They were a unit, *The Hobart Expedition to the Black Hills*. And there is no way better to solidify a group than by excluding some Johnny-Come-Lately-Greenhorns, which was how they saw the Everett brothers.

"Well, look what's coming down the road," Jake heard Pearson sneer. Jake saw two young men approaching the camp. One looked strong enough, but the other was short and limped a little, carrying a rifle over his shoulder. It was a man-sized weapon, but Jake was reminded of Edwin with a wooden gun, playing solider.

"Faith," Donnelly drank from his pocket flask, "It must be the schoolmaster and his star pupil come to see us off."

Hobart rose as the two entered the camp, and the tall young man stepped up and offered his hand to Hobart. "Emmet Hobart? We've been looking for you. I understand you have an expedition leaving for the Hills tomorrow."

Hobart merely nodded. Jake felt a subtle shift in the attitudes of the men lazing around the fire. Donnelly and Pearson stood and moved close to Hobart. The rest of the party grew quiet, so as not to miss anything. Jake stood himself, but took a position well behind Hobart while the young man continued speaking.

"I'm Hugh Everett, and this is my brother, Luther." He shook hands with those standing and gave friendly nods to the others. Hobart and his crew responded coolly. Hugh stood straighter, but Luther blinked nervously, managing to look like a kid hoping to go to a circus.

"We hear you've got the strongest party ready to go," Hugh concluded, "and we want to join up." Jake thought he sounded manly, but the young one had to pipe in, "We'd sure like to ride along with you!"

"This ain't no wagon ride," Pearson intruded, taking a position a little apart from the rest. "Ain't no riding, and we mean to make time."

"You might find someone to freight your gear," Donnelly said, "but you'd be walking. Unless you got the price of horses, but them's dear in Sidney. Course, you can always wait a few years until there's stage service to the Black Hills."

"Walk all the way?" Luther blinked.

"That's right," Hobart spoke at last. "Some three hundred miles, and the last of it all uphill."

"We can walk," Hugh said. "We're fit enough."

"Sure you are," Pearson snorted. "You and your little brother."

Hugh Everett looked angry, but Hobart let it be known by his manner, that it was his job to vet the newcomers. "There are other expeditions," he said not unkindly."Parties are still forming on down the creek. You can probably find a place in a day or two. We're ready to pull out in the morning."

"As are we!" Hugh declared. "Our gear is ready in town. We'll haul it out tonight. We want to go with this expedition. We want to be among the first."

"You're already late for that," Donnelly interjected. "Miners been sneaking to the Black Hills all winter. The choicest diggings go fast. I've already staked my claim, but you folks can't waste time."

During this talk, Pearson had settled back against a wagon wheel and begun to whittle as though no longer concerned, but now he spoke again, "How old is your brother?"

It was more a taunt than a question. Pearson kept whittling as if he wanted them to notice his knife. Jake saw it was not the pocket knife most men used for whittling, nor even a hunting knife, but a weapon known as an Arkansas Toothpick. Its long, thin blade was useful only for sticking pigs or other men. *Or*, Jake thought, *making men think you're a killer*. Pearson was not a big man; he might be the kind who conceals his weakness by acting sinister.

Hugh stood his ground and answered straight out, "seventeen," but his brother's expression made Jake think Hugh had exaggerated. Well, every man's entitled to lie a little.

"Sev-en-teen," Pearson drawled, twisting his knife so a long sliver of wood curled around the blade.

"Pearson is trying to point out," Hobart interjected

"that this is a dangerous expedition. Or at least it will be if we don't stick together. We can't have anyone turning back. The Sioux won't bother a party of any size, but they'll pick off stragglers. I don't like to turn anyone away, but your brother seems kind of young, and you don't either of you look like you've spent much time outdoors!"

"Luther's been doing farm work. He's stronger than he looks. We're neither of us greenhorns. We've grown up hunting, and we're good marksmen, and we're well supplied."

"And well-armed!" the kid raised his rifle above his head.

"Hurrah for you!" Donnelly and Pearson snickered.

"We both have new Springfield rifles. Single shot, but accurate," Hugh tried to address only Hobart. "I can't see where having two more armed men can hurt your party. We'll find another party if we have to, but we want to go with you."

"We'll go by ourselves if we have to," the young one popped off, and Jake couldn't help but grin. He figured he'd catch hell from his brother later.

"I don't like to turn anyone down," Hobart began, "But —"

Donnelly finished for him, "It's no Sunday School picnic."

"We ain't got time for coddling no kids," Pearson wiped the blade of his knife on his pants leg, as if he was done. Jake felt the urge to speak up. He was debating what to say when Hobart turned to the men around the fire.

"I say this should be a group decision. It's up to you men. Anyone here willing to freight their goods?"

There was an awkward silence as the men looked at each other and shrugged. Hugh faced the group squarely. He looked to Jake like a good man to have along on a fight. And a decent sort who would not be a trial to Molly.

"They can freight with me," Jake said.

"Well, then I've no real cause to object," Hobart said. "Just so you boys know the danger."

"We do," Hugh shook Jake's hand.

"We've already divided into messes," Hobart said. "You'll have to find someone to share cooking chores with."

"They can mess with us," Jake said.

Hobart nodded, turned as if to walk away, then stopped. "You said *us*. You got someone else along?"

Here it comes, Jake braced himself to speak. "My wife and son. They're waiting in town."

Hobart frowned. Hugh looked at Jake in surprise. Tension rippled through the group. It was Pearson who spoke. "You got a woman and kid along?"

Jake nodded.

"How old is the lad?" Donnelly asked.

"Edwin is seven."

"Lord have mercy."

"Why didn't you tell us this before?" Hobart demanded, his voice angry.

"Didn't know it was important. Nobody asked. I got room in the wagon for them to ride. There's been women in there already, ain't there? They had to go in with someone."

"Not decent women." It was Pearson again.

"Decent women don't take up any more room in a wagon than the other kind" Jake replied.

"If there's one thing the Sioux hate to see," Pearson snarled, "it's women and children. To them, that means settlers. They'll maybe tolerate men passing through, but if it looks like a party's come to settle, they'll fight for sure."

"We'll be ready for them!" Luther hefted his rifle.

Hobart was still frowning. "I don't like it."

"Myself, I'd welcome women decent or not," Donnelly said, "but there's no sense in tempting the heathen red devils —"

Jake didn't like the way it was going. He would fight, if need be, for the right to take Molly and Edwin along, but he didn't know how to argue the matter reasonably. And then Hugh spoke.

"It's smart to take them. Women and children must be included if Americans are ever to occupy these lands. As long as no one but prospectors go into the Black Hills, we will always be portrayed as trespassers." Hugh had not studied law for nothing; he knew how to make a case. "Families going in makes us settlers; thus, the government will have to offer military protection."

Jake was impressed. The young man had a good mind on him. The others were quiet until Hobart spoke. "It makes sense, but I wouldn't risk my wife that way."

"It was her decision," Jake said. "She knows the risk, and she's willing to take it."

"Women got no business making decisions," Pearson said.

"I don't like it," Hobart declared. "I didn't plan on being responsible for a family when I let you join!"

"We already shook on it," Jake said, "and the responsibility is all mine."

"All right," Hobart sighed. "I won't go back on my word." They shook hands all around. All except Pearson, who threw down his whittling and slipped his knife in his boot. As he stood, Jake got a good look at his face. There was something narrow and twisted about it, but it was to Hugh that Pearson seemed to direct his parting shot.

"Women always make trouble!"

Hugh acted as if he hadn't heard, but Jake knew by his expression he had, so he offered to give the boys a ride to town to load their gear from the hardware store. They decided to spend their last night in town, but Jake figured he'd best move his family to the camp that evening after they'd eaten and just as darkness fell. Molly needn't know about the ruckus, and it would be easier for her to spend her first night of camping close to civilization. The boys helped Jake hitch the mules to his wagon, and they were driving away, when Donnelly, took his own parting shot.

"Be here at dawn with the women and children, or we'll leave without you!"

Hugh kept silent, but Luther muttered, "Children. Donnelly called us *women and children*. I'll show him. I'll show everyone."

Luther's immaturity and attitude worried Jake, but he figured a day or two of hiking the trail was bound to settle the kid, so his optimism returned. He'd done right. Luther would be a companion for Edwin. And he would have two more guns to protect his wagon and family. Molly would appreciate that. And she would like Hugh. Of that he was certain.

Molly was horrified. Not at the thought that Jake was talking about *her* Hugh, but at the thought that she would *even imagine* such a thing; that she was so foolish that after all the years and all the miles that lay between them, the very mention of a name that sounded like his, of a description that could have been Hugh, the boy she had loved, turned man, she would grow faint.

She had always thought they might meet again. Someday when she was back home, much older, and perhaps even a widow. Hugh might return to Pennsylvania and call at her parents' farm, and finding her there, it could be just a reunion of classmates. They could reminisce of childhood, without acknowledging what had transpired. If she were to show him a tintype of Edwin, he might sense the truth, feel a moment of recognition, perhaps even pride, but she would speak of Edwin only as *her son* before sending Hugh away. This time, *he would be the one wondering and remembering.*

But to imagine that they would meet now in Nebraska, with she in faded gingham, married to a man like Jake, and already fighting fear and guilt because they were about to risk everything because she could not face another winter on the homestead? It was crazy of her to even think such a thing, *just because the name sounded like his.* Jake never got names straight; he would find it odd if she questioned him too closely, and then what? How could she speak now of what was never spoken of between them?

She never seriously thought it might be true. She pushed the thought aside. She would think only of the journey. Then, the next morning, the hope denied, the prayer of her heart, never spoken, the glimmer of so many dreams denied, at last come true.

She stepped down from the wagon and there before her was Hugh. For a moment, she thought he was a vision, haloed, as he was, by the rising sun. She felt faint, the world misting around her, the wagon train a blur, and then he spoke.

"How do you do, Mrs. Lewis?" Odd to hear his familiar voice, the formal tone, "Allow me to introduce myself." Then his voice broke, and she knew he recognized her. What was she to do? How could she have prepared herself? There was another figure behind him. The brother perhaps, but she had never known his brother. He would not give them away. Unless Hugh did first. Then she knew what she must do. She thrust out her hand and shook his, very quickly, very formally.

"I'm pleased to meet you, Mr. Everett."

She saw his confusion and tried to think how to signal his silence. She was aware of Jake to the side, looking pleased and cordial, showing off his wife.

And then Edwin clamored down from the wagon, wailing about lost suspenders. She pulled him close, letting him bury his face in her skirts for a moment and then turned him and held his fair face up for Hugh to see.

"This is Edwin," she said. "Our son."

She hoped he understood.

CHAPTER FIVE

There was no time to think or to react. Even as they stood staring at each other dumbly, Emmet Hobart galloped up on a big roan horse shouting commands. "Day's wasting. Line 'em up and move 'em out."

Jake hustled her and Edwin up on the wagon seat. There was a flurry of activity around them as men shouted and swore, kicked out their campfires, and stowed their gear in the wagons. In the confusion she did not know if Hugh understood about Edwin, did not even know if she *wanted* him to know; but at least he understood she intended to pretend this was their first meeting.

Sitting on the wagon seat trying to hold Edwin close and quiet despite his excitement as they took their place in the line of wagons, she wondered if she had done the right thing. Should she have admitted knowing Hugh? Tried to pretend that they had been only friends; should she now turn to Jake and tell him the truth?

She studied her husband and knew she could never tell him. In all the years of their marriage, he had never once alluded to the fact he was not the sire of the son he loved. He had assumed that she had been taken advantage of and was not responsible in any way for the predicament that had caused her to leave school and hide at home. When Jake, who worked for her father had asked him for her hand and then come to her, saying he wanted to go West and needed a wife, she knew Jake and her father both thought of her as a woman wronged. Only she knew it had been as much her doing as the boy's, that one sad, sweet afternoon of their last goodbye before the Everett family went West.

She had lain awake and cried for her lost love all that night and again the night she accepted Jake's offer and his promise never to "hold it up to her." Jake did not know how to speak of love, but he had shown his devotion to her in his deeds. How could she tell him the true identity of the man he had so good-naturedly befriended?

They journeyed in silence.

As for Hugh, he wanted desperately to talk to Molly, to know if what she had implied about Edwin could possibly be true, and if she intended never to acknowledge even knowing him, but he had no opportunity to speak to her alone. When they paused for dinner, they saw another party of men coming downhill toward them. To the surprise of the Hobart party, these men were headed back toward Sidney. It was obvious by their appearances they had not struck it rich. Needless to say, this backwash of discouraged Black Hillers put a damper on the high spirits of the Hobart party. And the men themselves, seemed bent on tormenting the new pioneers, telling horrendous tales of death and scalping by the Sioux. Yet, when pressed, not one man could say he personally had seen an Indian fight. It was as if this sorry group of men had gotten together on their stories to justify their quitting; few had even reached Custer.

Hobart hustled his own party through their meal and got them moving again so fast that the only contact Hugh had with Molly was the exchange of another dreadful, confused look as she handed him his tin dinner plate.

There was a critical moment as the two parties separated, with some of Hobart's Expedition looking uncertainly at the road leading back to Sidney, but Hobart spurred his horse like the commander of a battalion, delivering a battle cry. He dismissed the party trailing back toward Sidney with one contemptuous word. *"Greenhorns!"* The Hobart Party was different, he told them, stronger, smarter, well-informed, well-armed and properly outfitted. Hobart made it seem as if only cowards would have doubts. Because they had to, they believed him. They had all cut themselves from home in some way; there was no easy retreat.

And then, after they were again underway, they heard a vaguely familiar sound, mournful, and faint on the morning air, yet reaching them all the way from Sidney. It seemed impossible but there it was. *A train whistle.* Hugh looked up from his place walking beside the Lewis wagon and saw Molly tilt her head to listen. And then from the other party, the one returning to Sidney, he heard the sound of cheering. Hugh looked back. The men were throwing their hats in the air and shouting.

All for the sound of a train whistle.

It was the first sign of civilization for the celebrating men, Hugh realized. *And our last.* He looked again at Molly. She had turned pale.

Molly was so disconcerted by Hugh's presence that she'd even thought of begging Jake to take them home, but then she realized, *they had no home.* And Jake, who never looked down on anyone, had faced these men with disgust. She realized there was no way to go but forward. She was unnerved by it all, but still more afraid of the confusion in her heart than of the danger of the journey. By evening, when her family and the Everett brothers gathered together around the campfire for their meal, she was almost in control of herself again, when Luther, making small talk over dinner, asked Jake conversationally, "So, where you folks from originally?"

"Back East," Jake said. "Pennsylvania."

"No kidding," Luther said cheerfully and turned to his brother. "Didn't we live there for a time?"

"Very briefly," Hugh said quickly. "We were moving

west. The doctors said the drier air might help our
father's lungs. It did for a while."

Molly realized that he was giving her a pointed
look. She knew he was asking if he should mention the
months they'd lived near her parents' property, so that
they might pretend to suddenly "recognize" each other.

No! she signaled him with the slightest shake of her
head, and he swiftly launched into a lengthy description
of his father's health and the death of both parents,
obviously to distract his brother from further questions.
But when he paused for breath, Luther interrupted.

"So, Jake, how'd you come to move to Iowa?"

"Always wanted to homestead."

"And you, Mrs. Lewis?" Hugh was speaking to her.
"What did you want?"

"Me?" What a foolish question to ask a woman.
She could not remember anyone ever asking what she
wanted.

"I wanted what my husband wanted."

Hugh seemed satisfied by that, but something perverse
made her add, "I wanted to be married."

It was not the sort of thing a woman said. But he
had asked her a foolish question and left her no choice.
As he had once left her with no choice, but to marry
the hired man. Of course, he couldn't have known the
consequence of their last afternoon. He hadn't wanted to
leave; he'd made that clear, but his family needed him.
Then he started to leave but turned and swept her into
his arms desperately. Their lovemaking had begun and
ended with farewell. Still, what gave him the right to ask
her now what she'd wanted after he was gone.

After Molly spoke, Hugh was quiet, letting Jake and
Luther, mostly Luther, carry on a conversation with
dreams of what they would do when they struck it rich
in the gold fields. Luther was rattling on about buying
himself pearl-handled revolvers and several pairs of fine

boots, when Hugh turned to her again.

"And what will you do, Mrs. Lewis, when Jake strikes it rich? What do you want now?"

It was a question she could answer. "To go home."

"To Iowa?"

"No!" She almost laughed. She stood up and stared into the dying embers of the campfire. "To go home to Pennsylvania. Then I —" she seemed to catch herself, "or rather, We will buy a house on a street with trees, near my family, and I'll have a piano and put Edwin in good schools and — I don't know — What do rich people do? Go to dances and parties, I suppose."

Dances and parties, even as she spoke she realized she was beyond the foolish entertainments of girls. She had lost all that becoming a woman. Because of him. And he was free. Or was he?

"And you?" she asked. "What will you do when you get your gold? Have you a sweetheart waiting?"

"No. No sweetheart. No one waiting."

She felt a moment of joy. She could not meet Hugh's eyes, but stared into the dying campfire and finding a shred of girlhood vanity left inside her, wondered if the firelight flattered her face. She wondered at the picture she made before the fire with the barrenness of Nebraska behind her and the hope of the Black Hills before her. She wondered what Hugh felt for her. He had written her three letters she'd had no way to answer. He'd promised to come back. Had he, too, endlessly remembered what they'd done?

And then Jake stood and shattered the moment with one word, "Bedtime."

He'd said it as he did every night. It signified nothing, but that it was the end of the day and a woman's place to be beside her husband, but when Molly took Jake's arm and turned away from Hugh, she felt as if she somehow betrayed Hugh. They had made promises. They had said words never spoken between her and Jake. But Jake was her husband. She climbed into the wagon, feeling infinitely weary.

They made a long drive the next day. The men seemed to recapture their enthusiasm for the journey, but Hugh saw in the well-worn trail evidence of how many had gone before them. They were coming very late to a race that would go to the swiftest. And Molly's presence had changed everything: Molly beside her husband on the wagon seat and with him at night, neither confirming nor denying what she had implied about the boy Edwin who always grinned as he scampered along the trail or peeped out from the wagon. The boy he hardly dared to look at, not dark like Jake, but blond like himself. He had to talk to Molly alone.

Molly knew she couldn't keep avoiding Hugh. When they made camp the evening of the second day and Luther and Edwin followed Jake to find grazing for the mules, Hugh brought her a bucket of water from the creek, and she knew the time had come.

"I have to talk to you, Molly."

She said nothing, but took a seat on a fallen log. He sat down on the other end of the log, not facing her at first. They observed the men in camp. No one watched them, but if anyone did, they would appear to be two people resting and chatting after a long day.

"You didn't answer my letters," he said.

She was surprised. It was almost an accusation. He was angry at her. It had been hard not to answer that last letter and tell him of her predicament and Jake's solution.

"There were only three letters, and no address on the first two. I had no way to answer you at first, your family wasn't settled, and then, later, there seemed no point. You were gone. Far away."

"I didn't want to go. I had to stay with my family. Dad was sick. My mother needed me. "

"I know that."

"I thought of seeing you again. I dreamed of it."

"Did you?" She felt a rush of pleasure.

"Molly, we may not have much time. We must talk." She nodded. She knew it was coming. The moment she had both prayed for and dreaded.

"I have to know. The boy, Edwin. You called him our son. Surely you didn't mean?"

"Please don't make me say it again."

"My God!"

It was a moment before he spoke again. Then, he seemed angry. "Why didn't you let me know?" He looked as if he really cared. Yet it seemed such a foolish question. He sounded like the boy she remembered; not the man he'd become.

"It was too late," she said at last. "It was months before you were settled in Nebraska and had an address for me to write to. By that time —"

She paused studying her hands. She had never discussed such things with a man before. "By then, it was too late. It would have taken weeks to hear back from you, and what could you have done, anyway?"

"I would have married you. I would have come back!"

"How? How could you have gotten back and how could you have married me? I was sixteen and you weren't much older. You were a school boy. You had no way to take care of a wife and baby."

"I'd have found a way."

"You say that now, but you have to remember how young we were. You've had two days to think about this. I've had years. You were young and free. Free as you should have been. You were a boy, and I had become a woman. I remember your letters, all three of them. They were sweet, but they were a schoolboy's letters, full of longing and promises and pretty words, but I needed a husband."

"So you took Jake."

He made it sound as if she had betrayed him. Again, she felt a strange mixture of anger and guilt and another emotion she could not name, but which was making her heart and her speech too fast.

"He worked for my father, and he had known me since I was a child. He was a good man, and he'd always liked me, and when he knew about my trouble, he offered to marry me."

"The hired man. You had to marry the hired man!"

"Don't you ever say anything against Jake Lewis! And don't you accuse me. I never lied to Jake; I did what I had to do!"

"I didn't mean it that way. I just meant, my God, I did that to you and — Molly, did you love him at all? Do you?"

"Oh, Hugh," She gave him the same smile she gave Edwin when he was being foolish. "It didn't matter how I felt. I was four months gone and the neighbors knew. He said he was going west to homestead and told my father he'd marry me and take the child as his own and never hold it up to me. And he was true to his word."

"He's been good to you then?"

"Yes."

"You've been happy?"

"Happy? The questions you ask! What is happiness? I've been safe, protected, loved, in a way. I've been happy enough. As much as I deserved. It's not easy homesteading. And we haven't been lucky."

"You don't —" he started to say something and then couldn't get it out. She knew what was coming and she faced him as he finished, "You don't have other children."

It was a question. She looked at the sky for a moment and took a deep breath before answering. "If you're asking me if I've been a true wife to him, I have. I've tried. I lost two babies. I probably can't have more."

"I'm sorry, Molly. I'm sorry. For everything."

"It was God's will. I sinned and I was punished."

"Don't say that. You never sinned."

"What would you call that day in the barn?"

"Beautiful. I thought it was beautiful, the way it happened. It was the first time for us both. It was the best thing that ever happened to me. It was beautiful. It was wonderful!"

She felt such a rush of emotion she could not look at him. Yes, it had seemed wonderful. She felt even more guilt, for it was not that way for her with her lawful husband. Not the way it had ever been again. She could never say that that one perfect hour of making love with Hugh had been beautiful, but he had said it and she was joyful that he remembered her that way. A sudden thought came to her and she had to ask.

"Have I changed much?"

Hugh was touched. It was such a feminine question. She was, of course, the most feminine of women. He was glad he was not sitting too close to her. He might not resist the temptation to reach out and touch the strand of golden hair that had escaped its knot and lay along the curve of her neck. She *had* changed. She'd lost her youthful prettiness; now she was beautiful. He didn't know what it was exactly that made her so, the hair maybe, or her eyes. She had pale blue Scandinavian eyes, cool and far-away looking, but there was about her mouth with its full lips, a hint of sensuality. Did she want him to tell her she was beautiful? Did she want him to make love to her again even though she was another man's wife? Or did she only want a reassurance that she had not been robbed of everything in her that had been fresh and lovely? It would be a small lie. "You're just the same."

"That's not true," she said to keep in check the thrilling surge of emotions his words brought, "but thank you for saying it. Life's hard. I'm not the pretty girl I was then. I'm not that girl."

She looked down at her work-worn hands, ashamed she had been foolish enough to speak of such things. "I'm a mother. I've had to work hard, but I have a fine son and that's what matters."

"He is fine. He's a beautiful boy. And smart too. You've done a fine job with him."

"I always hoped you'd see him. I always thought that someday you'd come back and know the truth." *Know that I never stopped thinking of you*, she longed to say.

"If only you'd let me know."

"Would you have been happier, knowing?"

"It would have driven me crazy."

"So I was right. It was better to not to know, to forget."

"And did you forget?"

"Don't ask such questions. We have no right to talk this way. I don't know why we've met again, why God let this happen. Maybe it was meant that you should see your son, but there is nothing between us. It's over."

"How can it be, Molly? How can it be over when you have my son, when you're — When I feel so —"

"Stop!" She almost shouted, suddenly terrified, not just by his words or the fear that someone was watching them, but by her own feelings. "Don't talk that way. He's *not* your son!"

"What?"

"Forget I told you. Forget all of it. He's Jake's son. Jake was the one that helped me birth him and raise him. Jake woke up nights and walked the floor with him when he fussed or was sick, and it was Jake who taught him to — to ride a mule and to pee like a man. All that counts for something! He's more Jake's son than yours! And I'm Jake's wife. What happened before doesn't matter. Don't think you can just walk up and change things!"

"Don't think I want to — to change things." He stood up as if to walk away. "Don't get the idea because I had to know about you and the boy that I still — that I want anything from you. I came to the Black Hills to look for gold, not to look for you."

"I know that. Don't you think I know that? You could have come east looking for me, but you didn't, you went on west first chance you got, so don't think I want anything from you. Go off on your adventure and leave me behind *again!* Our meeting doesn't change anything."

"Of course it does. It matters. I feel different knowing I'm responsible for what's happened to you, and for Edwin. But what can I do now? You're right. You and the boy, you're Jake's now."

"Yes, Jake's. Not your problem."

"Don't say it like that. I couldn't take responsibility then, but I would now." He paused and took a step forward, "Would you ever consider leaving Jake?"

"My, God, how can you suggest such a thing?"

"No, of course, you wouldn't. I shouldn't have asked." He stared off into the distance before saying very quietly, "I think it's better if I leave the party."

"You can't do that," she was afraid. "You can't just walk to Sidney by yourself. The Indians would get you for sure!"

"I didn't say I was going to Sidney. I'm going to the Black Hills, but I'll stay away from you, if it's going to hurt you and Jake and the boy, if you want me to leave —"

"I don't want you to leave," she stood up and held her

hands out to him, palms up. "I want you to stay with the party."

"Make up your mind, woman."

"Don't leave the party on account of me. You have the right to think of yourself and of your brother. How could you explain leaving after all your trouble to join Hobart? We can handle this. Jake won't be hurt. He'll never know there was anything between us, and they'll be nothing more, except —"

"Except?" He stared at her, his eyes intense and searching. "What would you have of me now?"

Molly was stunned by his question. What *did* she want from him? What did she want that she could have? There were so many barren spaces in her life, but she could not put a name to any of them. She had learned to live only for her son. She would think of him now.

"I want you to spend time with Edwin."

"Edwin?" he pulled back a little, his expression changing, losing its intensity.

"You could help with him," her words tumbled out. You could help protect him. And you could pay attention to him. Get him to talk more. Jake's so silent. You could help teach him his letters. You're an educated man. You could do things for him Jake can't."

Hugh hesitated, as if he sensed some fallacy in what she asked. But it was true, she told herself. She was not being disloyal to Jake to admit he was not an educated man. And then, as if on cue, Edwin came running up, complaining that Jake and Luther had sent him back while they stayed to play cards and talk with the men.

Hugh looked from the boy to her as if he were pondering something. Probably worrying about his freedom, she thought. His adventure. He'd avoided Edwin so far. Not wanted to be involved, she suspected, or to acknowledge what she'd implied when they met. She held her breath, sensing the importance of the moment, and then Hugh squatted down and spoke to the boy.

"Edwin, would you like a piggy-back ride? When my brother was little, he used to like to climb on my back. Would you like that?"

Edwin nodded solemnly and Hugh indicated he should use the log as a mounting block. With the boy on his back, he turned back to Molly.

"It's only until Custer City," he said. "When the wagon train reaches Custer, we'll disband. It's only for this little while. Till you're in a safe place again."

"Yes," she whispered. "Just for a little while." She was moved to see Edwin clinging happily to Hugh.

Oh, look at them together! Of course, Edwin can love him as well as Jake, she told herself, not just when she first saw them together, but later when she was forced to face the consequences of that evening. She would tell herself that her mistake was not in persuading Hugh to stay, nor in letting the boy mount his back. It was in not turning away soon enough, in taking just a moment to stand there beside Hugh and Edwin and allow herself the tiniest fantasy that they were *a family.* For in that moment, the three of them standing together with the setting sun lighting their fair hair, that was how they looked.

And that was when Frank Pearson rode up.

He had a brace of jack rabbits slung over his saddle horn. He halted his horse and stared at the three of them. Then he sat back, and his scarred face broke into a grin that revealed yellow jagged teeth. He acknowledged Molly with a fingertip touch to his sombrero.

"Evening, Mrs., I brought you a rabbit. Don't know if your man," he looked at Hugh, "had any luck hunting."

"Mr. Lewis has been occupied with his mules," Molly said coolly. "Mr. Everett was about to give Edwin a piggy-back ride."

"I see that," Pearson said, then turned to the boy. "How'd you like to ride a real horse, son? You can climb right up here behind me."

Edwin had been riding astride with one man or another for much of the day, but he hesitated, even as Hugh took a tighter grip on his legs.

"Thank you,'" Molly said, "but it's his bedtime. Mr. Everett was taking him to the wagon."

Edwin whined, but Molly cut him off, "Do as I say, Edwin. It's past your bedtime." Hugh didn't give Edwin another chance to argue but took him to the wagon, feeling both foolish to be seen toting the boy and angry at the man's efforts to be friendly with Molly. He hoped Pearson had not been observing them long.

When Hugh returned, he found Pearson staring at Molly.

"Say, that boy's the spitting image of you!"

Hugh was stunned; then realized Pearson was talking to Molly, but she made the same mistake.

"What a terrible thing to say!"

"Huh?" Pearson cocked his head and stared at Molly. Hugh started to step forward to try to shush her, but it was too late.

"What a terrible thing to imply. How dare you!"

Pearson's eyes flickered between them. He grinned suddenly. "Why, I meant he looked like *you*, *Mrs. Lewis*. I wasn't even thinking of *Mr. Everett*, but now that you point it out to me, there is a sort of resemblance. You folks neighbors back in Iowa?"

"Of course not," Hugh said, trying to keep his voice even. "That's a poor sort of joke." He wanted to drag Pearson off the horse and clobber him, but reason told him he could know nothing, and overreacting would only make matters worse.

"Sorry," Pearson grinned. "I was just thinking out loud. Didn't mean to offend. Never like to offend *a lady*."

He started to ride away, then swung back, "Forgot to give you your rabbit."

He produced his knife and separated the brace by slashing through the haunches of one rabbit. He let it drop to the ground, grinned, spurred his horse, and rode away.

Hugh was livid. "I'll get that bastard!"

"Stop it, Hugh," Molly grabbed his arm. "Stop it. You'll only cause trouble. You'll draw attention to us."

"You heard what he said! Saw how he treated you!"

"He didn't mean anything. I took it wrong. I thought he meant Edwin looked like you, and —"

"He's got to be made to shut up."

"Leave it alone, Hugh. I don't think he'll say anything to anyone. He's got no proof. We just have to act like nothing happened, and Pearson will forget it."

Finally, he agreed. She persuaded him, just as she had persuaded him to stay with the wagon train. He cleaned the rabbit, though she insisted she could do it herself. He told himself she was a lady who needed to be cared for. He told himself he was doing it for Edwin. And that it was all a temporary interlude. And he was still off on an adventure to the gold fields and could leave her behind at any time.

He told himself that nothing had changed.

CHAPTER SIX

When Austin Avery came back on Friday, the green velvet dress was finished and hanging on the rear wall of the shop, Emerald having just pulled out the last of the basting threads. He came into the shop as boldly as he had the first time. Her mother had just left; it was almost as if he had been watching, though Emerald did not then think him to be so calculating.

He was as handsome as she remembered, tall and elegantly dressed, a neat moustache, his hair as black and his skin as fair as hers. His eyes were more brown than green; his skin looked to be the kind that would tan if he was the sort of man who worked outdoors, but obviously, he was not that kind of man.

It was not just his appearance that excited her. It was the scene they made together, he darkly handsome, elegantly dressed and she, still dressed as a shop girl, but confidently beautiful. Thinking he might surprise her, she'd primped all week, arranging her hair on top of her head with extra ringlets, and whenever her mother was absent, daring a touch of rouge and face powder. When she'd heard the shop bell and caught sight of him, she had raised one hand to her throat without thought; now she held the pose to symbolize an uncertainty she did not feel.

For a long time they simply looked at each other. Aware of the scene they created, the play that was about to begin, she felt it was hers to begin the action, so still touching her throat, she pointed dramatically to the dress.

In turn, he stole the scene by holding out a jewel box. Thrilled beyond measure, she nevertheless reached for the box slowly; but when she opened it to find the emerald ear bobs she had admired in the shop window, she had to choke back a sob. The sparkling green stones and delicate gold filigree were so beautiful, and the gift so magnificent, she was stunned. How had he known she coveted them? It seemed a sign. Something wondrous had begun. Something meant to be.

"For you," he said at last, only the hint of a smile playing about his eyes and never reaching his lips. "The dress, too, of course."

She recovered her poise, for she'd expected the gift of the dress and rehearsed her response. She lowered her chin and raised her eyebrows, meeting his gaze, "And what, sir, do you expect from me in return?"

"Everything"

Everything! It was just the response she had dreamed of; her heart leapt towards him, even as she stepped back, as if frightened. It was unfolding just as she envisioned. He would be visiting the shop often when her mother was gone, bringing her more gifts and begging her to become his mistress. Then he stunned her again.

"I want you to come with me tonight."

"What?" This she had not expected.

"I want you to come away with me tonight. I'm taking the Mississippi Belle up river on my way West. I plan to be gone some time securing mining interests in the Black Hills. I want you to come with me tonight."

"Tonight?" Emerald's jaw fell open. She knew it was an unattractive expression and quickly bit her lip, then realized that was no better. She had expected him to ask her to be his mistress, and had expected a long and thrilling courtship before she gave herself to him. To expect her to go that very night away on a riverboat was an astonishing request. In her limited experience with men, she had found them easy to manipulate, but if she went with Austin Avery that night, she would be giving herself up to a will stronger than her own. It was both threatening and exciting. Yet it was possible he too was playacting. If she had met her match, perhaps he had also met his.

"I don't know what to say, Sir. Your suggestion is very bold." She did not especially like the line, but she was playing for time, trying to sort out her emotions. It was the moment a good girl would hand back his gift.

And then, as if reading her mind, he said, "The dress and the ear bobs are yours whether you choose to come with me or not. They were meant for you."

She had, of course, never considered giving them up, except as a pretty gesture, but instead she made up her mind. There had never been any real doubt about it from the moment Austin Avery first walked into her shop the week before. Still, she intended to play out her scene.

"You have overwhelmed me, Sir, to walk in here and make such a suggestion. To ask me to leave my poor widowed mother and my dear sisters, to —"

"You don't have to decide now," he'd interrupted a bit too brusquely, especially when she'd brought the back of her hand to her forehead and was about to set off her eyes with a few tears.

"I realize you need time to think," he said evenly. "I'm sorry I cannot make my offer in a more traditional way, but my business interests in the Black Hills will not allow me the time to court you in the more leisurely manner of the old South."

It was on the tip of her tongue to ask what he meant by the word *court*, when he tipped his wide planter's hat to her.

"So, Madam, the choice is yours. If you wish to throw your hand in with me, be at the dock at 8 o'clock tonight. When the Mississippi Belle leaves, I will be on it. With you or without you."

He turned and, before she could speak, was gone.

It did not take her long to decide. She knew this was her one best chance to get away from her mother and all that was dull and dreary about the Mississippi waterfront town. More than that, this was her chance for something she could not quite name, something that was wondrous and exciting and *destined*. She had always known she was beautiful, but never until seeing herself in the mirror through Austin Avery's eyes did she have any sense of the woman she could become. She knew he wanted her, and he had known the green velvet and emeralds were meant to be hers!

As young as she was, she sensed a great truth: *There are few men who sense what a woman wants, and fewer still who will give it to her.* True, he hadn't mentioned marriage directly, nor even love, but surely these would come later. She was not without wiles.

Emerald wove for herself a fantasy of a life with Austin Avery. She made of it a tapestry even richer than the green velvet. It was a tapestry threaded through with stately houses, beautiful clothes, elegant dinners, and all sorts of theatrical evenings. In her fantasy admiring eyes were always on her. Her dream included Austin Avery regaining his fortune in the mines and returning to the South in triumph to buy back the old plantation. She would reign there in splendor, as his bride, wearing the emerald earbobs and, at her throat, a matching choker. How people would stare at her then!

Her fantasy was not of love. She had known little of that in her life, only the feeling she had lost when her father went away; then she had lost the satisfaction of knowing she came first in his affections, for she could always win his smiles and hugs away from her plainer sisters with her little songs and dances and pretty ways. She did not, of course, articulate these thoughts. She knew only that she had been waiting all her life for Austin Avery. He was unlike any other man who had noticed her. Other men she could make foolish with the merest frown or tilt of her chin, but Avery had known instinctively what it took to win her; he would know how to continue the drama. Yes, he would make love to her. She did not know the ways, but she knew he did and she knew they would all be done well. And so, it did not take her long at all to decide to run away with Austin Avery.

That night for a few hours, the fantasy came true. The Mississippi Belle was like a floating wedding cake or a fairy castle and she the princess. She had often dreamed of escaping on one of the steamboats churning up and down the river. She was not disappointed, for inside it was a palace of carved wood, gilt and scarlet paint and red plush. There were servants to wait on her, gentlemen to admire her, and women to peer at her with envy. And the food! Each day she was served things she had not known existed: seven kinds of meat and three soups and fishes and dozens of desserts all cunningly displayed with raisins and bananas and oranges and figs. And the drinks! Champagne in goblets so thin and clear and delicate she was almost afraid to pick them up. She tasted everything and thought she would never get enough.

And through it all, Avery's eyes were on her, saying such things to her across the table.

And then late that night, in their cabin, Avery slowly unbuttoned the green velvet and removed everything but her chemise, before carrying her to the bed. Avery kissed her lips, her neck, her breasts. She was trembling and a little afraid; her mother had warned her men did terrible things. He'd not turned off the lamp, but shame disappeared as he not just touched, but looked at *everything*. At last, just before entering her, he paused and studied her face. She looked into his eyes and saw how beautiful she looked reflected there. He'd told her over and over that he wanted her to feel pleasure, and she gave herself willingly.

It was that moment with his eyes she would remember later. It would take her some time to appreciate what happened next, though appreciate it she would. But that moment of having his complete attention she would seek again and again.

The feeling of mattering most to Avery did not last long, although she was able to recapture it in other moments when he made love to her. He took her again and again that first night as the riverboat chugged up the Mississippi and her body cried out in pain that was mixed with the beginnings of a pleasure she had only dreamed might exist. That he slept close to her all the first night did not seem important.

But it seemed very important that the next night was different. He insisted she wear the emerald green dress and watch him gamble. She enjoyed the furtive stares she received from the other men at the gaming table. Even the game was exciting at first. He won over a thousand dollars that night, and when they finally returned to their cabin at two in the morning, he made love to her, calling her his lucky charm.

Then, to her amazement, he got up, dressed and went back to the game.

That night set the pattern of their life together, but it took many nights of his leaving their bed to play cards until dawn, that she finally admitted to herself that he was exactly the worst sort of man of her mother's warnings — a professional gambler

That was bad enough.

Worse was the knowledge that she had given him her whole life and he had something that was his alone.

CHAPTER SEVEN

Hugh stood on the shore and stared at the river. The North Platte was a challenge at any time, but Hobart's party had arrived to find it flooding, sweeping debris downstream and muddy water overflowing its banks. It seemed an impossible barrier. Donnelly said they must camp and wait; eventually the river would recede. The others used the time to secure the wagon loads, rest the stock, and practice shooting, but Hugh returned to stare at the river and brood. They were now only four days away from Sidney, counting the day wasted at the river, but it seemed to Hugh that not only the country but he himself had changed. His body seemed stronger; he'd stopped shaving and his growing beard was coarse, for Molly's innocent plea that he stay with the party for Edwin's sake made him feel as if something in his gut was being slowly twisted and tightened.

Another party waited to ford the river, a freight caravan of a dozen bull whackers, their heavy freight wagons and herds of oxen. The presence of these men and beasts seemed to intensify Hugh's conflict. The bull whackers were crude men, who smoked, drank and swore with enthusiasm. They welcomed Hobart's party to their campfires and regaled them with tall tales. Most had begun their frontier experience as buffalo hunters; they were proud of their deeds, but Hugh was disturbed to hear confirmed that killing off the buffalo had been a sanctioned, if not official, government policy to destroy the Indians' way of life. Whether of man or beast, these men seemed to regard the killing as sport. And the Hobart party was fascinated.

Just the night before when the Lewis family had joined the men around their campfire and listened to yet

another tale of hunting buffalo, Edwin had remarked,
"I wish I could have killed me a buffalo," and Luther
chimed in with, "me too!"

And then one of the bull drivers had said, "Don't
worry. You'll get you an Indian."

Luther had grinned, but Molly jerked the protesting
Edwin toward their wagon while Hugh gave a little
speech, rebuking his brother as well as the stranger,
saying that although the Indians had certainly killed
many settlers, they were not beasts but human beings,
and white men, too, had committed atrocities.

Luther conceded no trace of humanity to the red man
but declared his intention to notch his gun for every
Indian he shot.

"A good Indian is a dead Indian."

"Damn it," Hugh replied, "You sound like Chivington!
In his own reports he admits he led his men to slaughter
innocent women and children! And him a former
minister!"

"Chivington was right," Luther grinned. "Wasn't he
the one that said, 'Nits make lice'?"

Jake laughed when he caught the meaning. "Oh, I get
it! "Papooses make Indians! That's a good one!"

Hugh walked away from the men then and found
Molly at the wagon where she had settled Edwin for the
night. She turned to him and almost shouted, "You see?
Do you see now, how it is with these Western men? And
now Jake talks like one of them! I've got to get Edwin
back to decent folk. I can't have him raised out here with
people who make a joke out of slaughter."

Hugh wanted to hold her, but of course, he could
not, so he gritted his teeth and said, "I'll try to guide
Edwin."

He had helped her into Jake's wagon and then
walked to the river. Though he could tell the river had
barely receded, the bull whackers were to attempt a

crossing the next day, and if the bull teams succeeded, Hobart had declared his party would attempt their own crossing. Thoughts of Molly and Edwin adrift in the wagon and careening downriver tormented Hugh, but other pictures arose in his mind which troubled him more. Molly as he remembered her, young and unafraid, laughing and running toward him when he would meet her after school. Her turning to him, her cool blue eyes suddenly merry that day they both ran through the rain to the barn. And in the shelter of the barn, Molly was warm and yielding in his arms.

Now, the next morning he faced the river again, knowing that whatever came next, whatever dangers Molly and Edwin and Luther would face from this final crossing into the forbidden land, the responsibility was his. He had by his own foolishness brought them all to this. And if Molly or Edwin was hurt, or Luther should actually kill an Indian, it would be on his conscience. *And what of yourself, Hugh?* He wondered, touching again the new stubble of his beard. *What of the beast within you? Are you sure you can cross that river yourself and still remain a civilized man?*

As Donnelly and the bull whackers predicted, the waters had continued to recede during the night; soon the freight teams began their crossing. It was an impressive sight. On the trail, three freight wagons were usually hooked together and pulled by a team of seven pairs of yoked oxen, but to test the river, the trailing wagon was unhitched, part of its cargo stacked upon the other two wagons, and three teams attached to the lead wagon. That made forty-two oxen to pull the two wagons. It seemed impossible that the bull whackers could handle such a large number of the great long-horned beasts, but they did.

The bull whackers mounted horses to cross the river. Each swung a long buckskin bullwhip over his horse's head. The popping of the whips was accompanied by stunning profanity. The line of oxen nearly spanned the stream before it dragged the first wagon down the muddy bank and into the swollen river. Hobart explained that if one ox or even a yoke should stumble or flounder in quick sand, the long team would keep the wagons moving. If the heavy wagons stopped for an instant, they would quickly sink to their hubs. The crossing took most of the day, as once having crossed, the great ox team was loosed from those wagons and driven back across the river to fetch the next ones. It was late afternoon, before it was their turn.

The flood waters had receded farther, and after all Hugh's foreboding, the crossing of the North Platte was anticlimactic. Hugh had no assigned task. The crossing was the responsibility of the mule drivers. He and Luther had only to sit beside Jake and let him do his job. The mules struck into the water surely, and even when the current lifted and swayed the wagon did not falter, but at Jake's urging leaned harder into the traces.

And yet something did happen at the crossing of the North Platte, something that marked a change in Hugh, as if he had, indeed, left behind the civilized man.

It was after Jake had driven their wagon across and gone to watch the remaining wagons cross. Hugh helped Edwin and then Molly out from their places inside the wagon so they could watch the other wagons cross. It was something he'd done a dozen times before. One hand taking hers and the other at her waist in the polite manner of a gentleman, never giving in to the urge to grasp her to him, yet always sensing something passed between them.

That day after the crossing of the North Platte, it happened that as Hugh helped Molly from the wagon, Pearson rode up behind them. He saw the smile Molly gave Hugh and the way their hands clasped for a moment longer than was necessary. He saw the way Hugh stared after her as she followed Edwin down the bank to watch the crossings. When Hugh turned back to latch the wagon tail, Pearson tipped back his sombrero to reveal his face.

"So, you did it, didn't you? You got some of that."

Hugh was startled. His premonition of danger at the crossing of the river had just minutes before seemed foolish. He didn't react at first, not believing that Pearson would dare to taunt him with such a remark.

"Can't say as I blame you," Pearson continued, "Even if Lewis is your friend. I wouldn't mind having some of that myself."

Hugh lunged toward him, but Pearson only laughed, spurred his horse, wheeled, and rode away, sending a spatter of mud into Hugh's face.

I'll kill him, Hugh thought. *I'll kill him. I swear it.*

And so after the crossing of the North Platte, it was not just the threat of the Sioux that caused Hugh to keep his rifle at the ready. One part of him burned to seek Pearson out and shut him up, but his more logical self argued that Pearson's accusation might be revealed in a fight. Hugh hated the lie he was living, but he knew he had no right to expose Molly and Edwin, and he wanted never to hurt Jake. Still, he resolved to take no more from Pearson. He wondered how long he could hold back his rage. As if sensing Hugh's mood, Pearson avoided the Lewis wagon.

The Indian danger was real now, and Hugh noticed the entire party seemed uneasy as they ventured farther into the forbidden territory. Hobart took to riding his big roan along the line of wagons several times a day, reminding them to keep together. The country was dreary, the trail, tedious. But only when they reached the first, and last outpost of civilization, on the trail to the

Black Hills, the Red Cloud Indian Agency, was anyone truly afraid.

Hobart's Party had looked forward to visiting the agency; they hoped for good news of the government's negotiations with the Sioux, even expecting to learn that the Black Hills were officially opened to white settlement, and they could expect military protection on the rest of their journey.

They were to be disappointed.

The Red Cloud Agency was situated pleasantly enough on a fine bit of bottom land near the White River, set against extensive buttes of sandstone rock. But the agency, and especially the agency store, was a dreary place. The store stocked only the most basic of necessities. Hugh bought Edwin some horehound candy, but there were so many Indians loitering about the place Molly kept the boy close to her. Jake tried to joke. Hadn't she expected there to be Indians at an Indian agency?

Donnelly told them there was nothing to fear from the agency Indians. They were *tame*. It was the wild bands of northern Sioux they had to fear. Hugh noticed the Indians seemed sullen. Even the squaw men, white men who lived with Indian wives, seemed hostile. He did not like the way they eyed Molly. They seemed fascinated by her fair hair. They had strange accents. French, Hugh guessed. They all said the same sort of thing, *"Go back. Trouble for you if you go on. No young mans here. Old mans yes, squaws, papooses, yes. What that mean? Trouble. All young men leave agency. They go north to Sitting Bull. I see fresh scalps two days ago. White scalps. You go back now."*

No one liked being threatened, especially by whites who drew government allotments for their wives and half-breed children, moved freely on agency lands, yet tried to intimidate other whites. Hugh realized they spoke the truth. There were no young men at the Red Cloud Agency. *Where were the warriors?*

There were soldiers at the agency. They came from nearby Fort Robinson and, like the Indians, loitered about the store. The fort had been built four years before to house the Indian agent and his family, but there had been times in those years that the agent had been a virtual prisoner of the Sioux. It made Hugh wonder. If the government couldn't control Indians who were supposedly at peace, what protection could it offer from the renegades?

What are your orders?" Hugh boldly asked a young officer.

"A few months ago our orders were to remove all whites except government employees from the Hills. That order has never been rescinded, but we have no current orders. So we stand by and watch parties enter. There's too many trespassers now to stop without declaring war on the civilian population."

"Then the army won't be trying to stop us?" Hugh asked.

"No, but — but we don't have orders to *protect* you either. *You're on your own.*"

The others seemed to think that was good enough. Hugh might have thought so too, if it weren't for Molly and Edwin. He felt they needed more information. He asked if anyone there had actually been to the Black Hills. The squaw men looked at each other and smiled, but none would talk.

There was, however, one young non-commissioned officer who dared to show excitement about the gold rush. He said he had been in the Hills with Custer in '74 and seen the gold discovered. Plus, he declared, it was the most beautiful country he had ever seen. Whenever the squaw men heard the name Custer, they sneered. "You know what the Sioux call Custer's trail to the Hills? The one you'll be following? 'The Thieves' Trail,' that's what they call it. They hate Custer the most, but all white men who come to the Hills are thieves and deserve to die."

Hugh stifled his anger and asked about the present location of troops. The soldiers hadn't much information to give. General Crook had been in the field since March to round up the Sioux and bring them back to the reservation. According to rumor, Terry and Custer and the Seventh Cavalry would be campaigning that summer. If so, they were certain to meet the Sioux in a battle that would once and for all settle the question of the Black Hills in favor of white occupation and civilization.

This news made everyone feel better.

They camped that night within sight of Fort Robinson. The fort conveyed little more security than the Indian agency, but when Hugh said as much to their leader, Hobart made a little speech about the fort and the Indian agency it stood to protect.

"Fort Robinson is as good as most army posts. It serves its purpose. The agency permits a lot of white men to profit off the government by cheating the Indians. It is an efficient agent for spreading disease, cholera, diphtheria, small pox and others, which serve to reduce the Indian population."

Hugh was shocked by that admission, but to argue with Hobart would be to argue with years living experiences Hugh knew only from books, but Hugh did not want to admit his government was engaged in a systematic program to wipe out the Indians. He had left Nebraska with the notion the Sioux would be peacefully persuaded to adopt an agrarian life and would soon allow civilization to proceed. Now he felt angry to see a solution to the Indian problem would not come easily. He did not know if his anger was at the government for ineptly trying to impose a new way of life upon the Indians, at the Indians for refusing to accept it, or at himself for becoming part of a movement that seemed destined to lead to war.

When they lined up the wagons to move out the next morning, they were five men short. Hobart got them moving before they had time to think about the desertions. It was the strong who remained, he assured them. They did not need cowards and weaklings on their venture. They were better off without them. It was only five men, after all.

But Hugh knew it was five fewer guns and that worried him. To turn back now would have made him feel a fool, the sort of man who deserved to grow old within the limits of Carpenter, Nebraska, but he was afraid for Molly and Edwin. Jake's confidence seemed unshaken and Hugh wondered if he should try to persuade him to take his family back to civilization, but he did not. Later he would admit to himself that it was Molly and not just his dreams of adventure and gold he was unwilling to give up. Hugh concentrated instead on talking others out of their discouragement. By the end of the day, he seemed to have convinced not just the others, but himself to keep going, but those on foot trailed behind the wagons.

Hobart galloped back to them to urge them to keep up. He had Edwin riding behind his saddle, hanging on and grinning. Hugh was both relieved and frustrated at the way Edwin had become the camp pet. Reason told him not to care too much for a son that would never belong to him.

Most of the walkers slowed their pace once Hobart and Edwin galloped back to the head of the column. Hugh paused to let Luther catch up with him, and was oddly pleased at the sight of his brother. The journey had toughed him; he was thinner and even seemed taller, and Hugh had the pleasant thought that the journey was making a man of him. He had not been wrong to bring

him, after all. He felt happy. They had not let Red Cloud
get them down.

Hugh was whistling when he saw them.

Horsemen topping the ridge to his left and boldly
riding down to the wagon train.

There was no mistaking them for another band of
discouraged Black Hillers or the ragged agency Indians.

These were the Sioux.

CHAPTER EIGHT

There was no comfortable way to ride in a wagon, Molly decided. She preferred walking, but walking could too easily make Hugh her companion, something best avoided. The moment of joy at finding him beside her was hardly worth the pain of having to pretend he was just Jake's partner on the journey. As she struggled to cook over the campfire, she told herself it was Jake and Edwin she was "doing for." Yet when she handed Hugh his dinner plate she could not help but blush. Her fair skin had always betrayed her emotions, but Jake and the others seemed oblivious.

Sometimes she stared at her reflection in the old mirror she kept in her trunk, trying to find a composed expression for her face, and could not help wondering if she was still pretty. She told herself she had asked Hugh to stay only because it was dangerous for him to go on alone, and for his protection and help with Edwin. Having denied her own feelings for so long, it was sometimes possible to convince herself she was doing right.

Such thoughts often kept her from sleeping, but on the day the party marched away from Fort Robinson, Hobart offered to let Edwin ride on the back of his horse, so she had the opportunity to doze in the wagon. When Jake halted the wagon suddenly she awoke surprised that it was time to camp. Then she heard Jake's shouts.

"Indians! Indians coming!"

She thought he must be joking, though he was not a joking man. She started to climb out onto the wagon seat, but he pushed her back inside. Jake's no longer stoic manner alarmed her.

"Edwin!" she cried. "Where's Edwin?"

Just then Hobart galloped up beside their wagon,

alone. "Don't get excited, Lewis," he said reining in his horse. "Soon as I spied them, I stuck Edwin in the lead wagon. It's a party of braves, but I doubt they'll want to fight. Looks like there's more of us then of them, but they must not see the woman or boy, so keep out of sight!"

"I have to get Edwin!" She struggled to get past her husband but he gently, but firmly held her back.

"Stay in the wagon, Woman, Hobart shouted, "and keep quiet! We'll try to keep them away from the wagons, but we don't want to provoke a fight. They'll probably just look us over, palaver awhile, and maybe do some trading. If they see they can't scare us, chances are they'll move on."

"But what about Edwin?"

"I can't bring him back now. Morris will keep him safe. Besides, Morris has a gun, and you don't." Then he commanded, "Lewis, you get her stowed in the wagon and come on with the men. The more guns they see, the sooner they'll stop trying to buffalo us."

Hobart had made Molly feel helpless and angry, but she told herself the men knew best. Jake jockeyed the mules into the circle the others were forming, then poked his head inside to announce he was joining the others.

"Stay with me, Jake!"

"I can't. All the men got to be there." He dropped the wagon flap and was gone. She had never felt so alone. She thought of Hugh, but realized he too would take his place with the men. She tried to control herself. She was a grown woman; she must be brave. She tried not to think of what Indians did to captured white women. She tried to peek out from under the canvas wagon cover, but she could see only prairie grass. Words were shouted, but she could make no sense of them. Then suddenly, it was quiet. She told herself the scare was over.

Then the shooting started.

She could not believe it. Hobart said the Sioux wouldn't attack. If they were already fighting, seeing her would make no difference. She must get to Edwin. He would be afraid. She reached the end of the wagon and was about to pull aside the flap when it opened. She jerked back, gasping. The Sioux were coming for her.

"Howdy, Mrs. Lewis, how you doing in there?" It was Frank Pearson. His scared face grinning.

"Oh! Pearson, It's you. I thought they were coming for me!"

"Who? The Indians?" He stepped up on the back of the wagon "Did you think a big naked buck would climb in the wagon and do it to you? Is that what you thought?"

He was climbing into the wagon. She backed up, clutching at the collar of her dress.

"Now ain't that something to be thinking? Imagine you thinking about some young buck putting it to you. Just goes to show, you're the kind that can't get enough. Just like I figured. Wanting it all the time, ain't you, Mrs. Lewis?"

"Go away! Get out of my wagon!"

He was crawling toward her. "And leave you all alone? With all those big, bad Indians coming? They'd take your scalp too. They'd love all that blond hair. How does it look down?" He reached for her hair, "I been wondering ever since I first seen you."

She had retreated as far as the wagon allowed. She told herself to keep calm and try to talk him out of it. "Please get out and leave me alone!" She didn't mean to cry, but she did.

"I won't take long, Mrs. Lewis. Unless you want more, I'll do you fast and I'll be real careful not to tear your clothes, you being such a lady."

"I'm going to scream!" But he was on her. One hand held her mouth and the other jerked the pins from hair.

"You can't scream, Mrs. Lewis. You'll bring the Sioux down on us. Unless, of course, you'd rather have all those bucks do it to you. I don't think you'd like that though. Even one like you that pretends to be a lady wouldn't like how the Sioux do a woman."

He used her loose hair to pull her around so her back was against his chest. He kept one hand over her mouth and she could hardly breathe. With the other he began unbuttoning her dress. She struggled frantically, digging her fingernails into his hands.

"So you think you ought to fight a little, just to make it look good? You don't have to put a show on for me. I know you're no lady. You done it with that Everett kid. And he ain't half the man I am. Wait till you see what I got!"

His other hand squeezed her breasts hard. She couldn't get enough air, and his hand covering her mouth smelled rancid. She was afraid she would gag and then choke on it.

"I can't wait," he whispered in her ear. "I can't wait any longer, Mrs. Lewis. I got to do it now." As he turned her and laid her on her back, she saw his eyes. Dark piercing eyes that looked right through her. She twisted her face away from him. His breath was foul when he tried to kiss her, slobbering on her and scratching her face with his whiskers, then his mouth on her breast, wetly biting and sucking at it. She kept trying to push him away, but he was so much stronger than she.

"I'll tell," she said, shoving at his greasy head, grabbing his hair and trying to pull his head away from her breasts, "I'll tell my husband, and he'll kill you!"

"No — you — won't," he said slowly. "I already figured it out. I've had lots of time to plan since I figured out about you and Everett. You won't tell your husband what I done to you, Mrs. Lewis, because if you do, I'll tell him you done it with Everett. He don't know that, does he? He don't even know the kid ain't his. That would be a shock, wouldn't it? For him to find out you got your lover boy along on this outing? How do you think he'll take that, Mrs. Lewis? Who do you think he'll try to kill first, me or the one that's been putting horns on him right in his own wagon?"

"He hasn't! You're lying. Jake wouldn't believe you!"

"Wouldn't he? You want to take a chance? Maybe you *want* to get Jake killed. Is that it? Do you think Everett could take him out in a fight, or do you think that tough old man of yours would win?"

"Jake wouldn't fight Hugh. "

"Really? You said he'd kill me, didn't you? And he'd have to *try*, wouldn't he? He'd be honor bound to defend his property. Has your husband ever killed anyone, Mrs. Lewis? I have. I've stuck a lot of men with my knife. I'm real good at it. So if you tell Jake, then the three of us can fight it out, and if I kill both of them, then you and me can —"

She moaned. All the time he had talked, his hands had been using her. She shut her eyes and held herself still, trying to sort it out. It would be another thing she could never tell anyone, especially not Jake. He wouldn't stand a chance against Pearson. Jake had never been in a knife fight. She was so tired of struggling.

"That's right. You just relax and enjoy it, and if we're lucky, we can figure out some way I can visit you regular all the way to the Black Hills."

He was pulling up her dress. She had to try to fight him again. She couldn't let him —

He raised up for a moment, and she opened her eyes. Maybe he was going to stop.

He was unbuttoning his pants.

Hugh had seen Indians before. He had seen the Poncas, Pawnees, and Omahas in their tribal dances, and he had seen the squaws and old men at the agency. But he had never seen Indians like these. These were the Sioux. And although they had ridden their ponies to the edge of the trail without raising their weapons or uttering the shouts that would signal an attack, it was evident this was a war party. There were twelve of them, eight men, four half-grown boys, as confident in their bearing as the men. Only twelve. There were twice as many white men, all well-armed; yet the Sioux seemed greater.

The war party had stopped about a dozen yards from the first wagons and sat their horses, stoic and calm, while the mule drivers sweated and cursed as they maneuvered the wagons into a cluster. Hugh and Luther and the other men ran to catch up to the wagons, where Hobart galloped up and down issuing orders.

Luther was out of breath. Hugh wondered if his brother was afraid, but didn't ask. Hugh spotted Jake leaving his wagon and cutting over to where the rest of the party formed a line confronting the Sioux.

Hugh caught up to Jake. "Where's Molly and Edwin?"

"Hiding in the wagons. Hobart told me to keep them out of sight. Edwin's in Hobart's wagon with Morris."

"Is there going to be a fight?" Luther asked.

"Hobart says not. We got them outnumbered. He claims they'll just want to palaver — whatever that is. Talk and trade, I guess."

"Well, I aim to have a fight!" Luther dropped to one knee and raised his needle gun.

Hugh stepped in front of him. "Damn it, Luther, Stop! If the Indians see you like that, they'll start shooting."

"There's twice as many of us as them!"

"Hugh's right!" Jake helped block Luther from the view of the Indians. Luther lowered his rifle reluctantly.

"You can tell by the way they're lining up they want to intimidate, not fight," Hugh gestured to the line of

Indians still sitting stoically on their ponies facing them.

"Hobart's talking to them," Jake said. "Let's get closer and find out what's going on."

As they walked deliberately toward the others, Hugh grabbed Luther's arm. "Keep hold of yourself! Think of Molly and Edwin back in the wagons."

"I won't start anything," Luther muttered, "but if the redskins do, you can bet I'll give 'em what for."

Keeping a tight grip on both Luther and his own rifle, Hugh followed Jake to the line confronting the Indians. Hobart stood ahead of his men, talking to an Indian Hugh figured was the chief.

"What's happening?" Hugh asked the nearest man.

"Hobart and the chief, Old Steals Many Horses, been talking it over. Or rather, the chief's threatening, and Hobart's listening."

"What did the chief say?"

"What you'd expect. We better keep out of the Black Hills. Says many whites will die. Said he dreamt it in a vision quest or something like that. Seemed real certain about it."

"We're not turning back!" Luther sputtered.

"Course not," the man spat. "The chief knows there aren't enough of them to stop us, but he's going to make it tough on us. Besides, it gives 'em credit, facing an enemy like this. They can go home and brag on it."

Hugh knew Indians considered it a mark of bravery to touch an enemy in battle, and as he studied the line of warriors, he could see the men all wore marks of honor to signify the times they had counted coup or killed an enemy. Several horses were painted with a red hand; the same mark appeared on the clothing of their riders. Hugh knew the mark meant they'd killed an enemy in battle, as did the crosses painted on their leggings. The number of eagle feathers they wore in their hair was important, he'd read, and the angle at which the feathers were worn also had significance.

In contrast to the marks of their bravery and their quill-decorated buckskin shirts, leggings and moccasins, the Indians wore government-issued blankets, signifying they had made at least a paper peace with the whites. The boys were armed with bows and arrows, but all the men had new rifles. They were Henry's and Winchesters, fine repeating rifles, better than the single shot guns Hugh and most of the others carried. Hugh wondered if the rifles, too, were government issue.

One look at the face and bearing of the chief and the others tore away all the theories Hugh had held about educating the Indian to the white man's way of life. These people could no more be tamed than could timber wolves.

Hobart seemed to have reached an impasse with the chief. The Indian still on his horse, seeming to look beyond Hobart, his face impassive, one hand resting on his rifle, the other holding up a lance. Hugh couldn't help but admire the warrior. He had the narrow eyes, reddish-brown skin, blue-black hair and hooked nose that marked his people; but he was nothing like the Indians at the agency. One of his braids was bound in red cloth; the other flowed free over his shoulder. He wore three upright eagle feathers in his scalp lock, one dyed red. There was a shell choker around his neck, and a bone breastplate covered his chest, while his buckskin shirt was decorated in quill embroidery over his shoulders and down his arms. His shirt, unlike that of the other men, was fringed with long hair, which Hugh suspected was human.

Hobart was talking to the chief, admiring his gun. It was a Sharps forty-five, as fine a rifle as was made. The chief refused to look at Hobart. He stared ahead as if he didn't hear what the wagon master was saying. Then suddenly, he handed his lance to the warrior next to him. As he did, Hugh realized with a shock the lance was decorated with scalps, and one of them was blond.

The Indians backed off a little as if to give the chief room. Something was about to happen. With a deliberate, broad sweeping gesture, the Indian pointed to a tree some distance away. A magpie sat on one of the branches. Slowly and with a great air of showmanship, the chief raised his rifle and sighted on the bird. Hugh was thinking it an impossible target when he heard the shot and saw the magpie fall. The Indians did not react visibly, but a little murmur of awe and confusion passed among the whites followed by a deadly silence as the old chief challenged them with his eyes.

Hobart stepped into the silence and, also with a flourish, pointed to a white spot on a boulder near the foot of the tree, raised his rifle and fired. The sound indicated the shot hit the boulder, but the white spot remained, so one of the Indians galloped over to check. Without waiting to see what he would report, Hobart picked a stick from the ground, took out his pocket knife and notched the top.

Hugh moved closer to see what he was doing. Hobart stuck something in the notch, and one of the men nearer him passed word back that it was a nickel. Hobart stuck the stick in the ground and walking up to one of the Indian boys, pointed at the stick and made a gesture as if he were shooting with a bow and arrow. The boy's face showed a trace of a smile and he looked to the chief for permission. The old man nodded imperceptibly, and the boy kicked his pony, galloped away, then wheeled and raced toward the stick, taking aim with his bow and arrow. While still some distance away, he shot, trailing the arrow and dislodging the nickel with its shaft. He gave a little cry of triumph and leapt from his pony to retrieve the coin.

Hobart quickly picked up the stick and affixed another nickel, gesturing to another boy. Hugh saw the wagon master was trying to defuse the warriors' hostility, yet allow the Indians to save face by showing their skill and bravery. Hugh had to hand it to Hobart; he knew how to handle a difficult situation.

At this point, the chief dismounted and pointing to the rock, sent another brave to set up a target.

"Okay, boys," Donnelly said, "the best marksmen among you get out there and show them what white men are good for. But don't start gambling because they'll take us for all we're worth. Just put out some nickels for the kids and act impressed when they do their stuff."

It was a strange shooting match; not sport, but a series of taunts. Yet, as the men took turns demonstrating their skill, the tension of the Black Hillers eased a little, and the Indians too became less silent as they acknowledged an especially good shot by one of their braves with a little whoop of praise.

Hugh and Luther took their places in line, and shot when their turns came, but it was evident to Hugh that even among the whites, they were far from the best shots. Hugh dropped out of the shooting and let Hobart, O'Connell and Luther continue the challenge. Finally Luther had to admit he was outclassed. Pearson quit at about the same time, which made Hugh wonder, for he had noted uneasily that Pearson was an excellent shot.

Hugh turned his attention to the young boys who were still shooting at the sticks with their bows and arrows. He marveled at the way they maneuvered their ponies as they rode about in circles, sometimes hanging off the side of their mounts as if to show how difficult a target they would present in a real battle. He wished Molly and Edwin could watch. He considered getting them from the wagons, but if Hobart was right, the sight of a woman and child might unleash the carefully controlled anger of the Sioux. No one doubted each time the Indians shot, they were pretending it was one of the trespassers they hit. Although on the surface, the shooting match was friendly, it was having the desired effect on their party, for Hugh saw reflected in more than one face his own awe at the skill of the warrior Sioux.

He decided against bringing Molly and Edwin out to watch. Besides, it was Jake's place to tend to his family, but Jake was completely involved in watching Hobart and the chief compete. Hugh wondered if he should slip away to reassure Molly and Edwin and perhaps reposition them so they could see what was going on but stay hidden. It was too risky, he decided, but thought he could go and relieve Morris from guarding Edwin. He looked around for Pearson but couldn't spot him in the crowd. It made him uneasy. Every since Pearson's threat at the crossing of the Platte, Hugh had kept an eye on him, making sure he never got the chance to bother Molly when she was alone. But now he had disappeared.

Surely not, he thought. Not in the middle of a confrontation with the Sioux. Even Pearson wasn't that crazy. Hugh started for the wagons, breaking into a run. It seemed to take forever to get to the Lewis wagon. He kept his right hand gripped around his gun and with the left jerked open the flap. Even as he did it, he could hear moaning and the sounds of struggle.

He saw Pearson on top of her. There wasn't room to shoot without hitting Molly. He threw down his rifle, and with an angry roar pulled himself into the wagon and charged Pearson, wrapping both arms around him and dragging him away from Molly. He threw him sideways across the end of the wagon and began to beat him. Hugh's blows were confined by the wagon, and the smaller man put up a mighty struggle. Hugh wanted to kill Pearson, so he got his arms around him again, and with a mighty heave let his anger carry them both over the end of the wagon and onto the ground.

It was a mistake. Outside the wagon, Hugh lost the advantage of his size and strength. Pearson landed cat-like on all fours while Hugh was on his knees, momentarily stunned from the fall. Hugh was too filled with rage to remember Pearson's agility. So when he threw himself toward Pearson again in a bull-like charge, the greasy little man simply backed himself against the wagon, grabbed the sides and launched a double kick that knocked the wind out of his attacker.

Hugh regained his balance as fast as he could, but Pearson was already crouching and reaching into his boot for the knife. He brought it up and snapped his wrist back and forth so that Hugh could hear the blade as it cut through the air. It gleamed wickedly. Pearson grinned, and with his other hand beckoned Hugh to him. There was something in his eyes that was almost hypnotic; like a king cobra in his death dance.

Hugh could hear Molly sobbing in the wagon as he pulled his hunting knife from its sheath. It seemed a clumsy weapon compared to Pearson's, but he was too angry to be afraid. He wanted to taste blood. Hugh knew he should play for time, holding his body sideways to protect his vital organs, but his anger was stronger than his reason, and he charged, holding his blade like a knight's lance.

At the last moment, Pearson simply stepped aside, and Hugh buried his knife in the soft wood at the end of the wagon. He started to pull his knife out, but Molly's scream warned that Pearson was striking. Hugh managed to evade the blow but couldn't get to his own knife. He came up swinging and managed a blow to Pearson's face.

They circled each other. Pearson seemed in no hurry to make his move but Hugh could see he, too, was in a killing mood. Hugh's eyes flashed between Pearson and the ground, seeking some sort of weapon. He felt Pearson was delaying his move, playing with him, enjoying himself.

Then Hugh saw his rifle lying where he had dropped it. He would have neither time nor space to raise the long barrel for a shot, but he could use it as a club. He dove for the rifle and had it by the barrel before Pearson realized what he was about. Pearson made a jab with the knife, but it went too high, and then Hugh got the rifle barrel in both hands, raised the gun over his shoulder and gave a mighty swing. He had telegraphed his intentions, and Pearson ducked smoothly with a sneer. Enraged, Hugh swung the gun back low with the vicious strength of a medieval battleaxe. Pearson was still crouched. The stock hit him squarely in the temple.

Pearson looked startled. Then his face seemed to collapse as he fell forward into the dirt.

The knife was flung far from Pearson's fingers and, still clutching his rifle, Hugh grabbed it and waited for Pearson to get up. Then, seeing the man was out cold, he turned his attention to Molly in the wagon.

"Are you all right?"

Her eyes were wild, her face flooded with color and her hair tumbling around her shoulders. She was cupping her exposed breasts with one hand and holding onto the wagon frame with the other. He wanted to touch her, to reassure her, to reassure *himself.*

"Did he —? He didn't *hurt* you did he?"

She seemed for a moment unable to speak. Then as she managed to pull her dress closed whispered, "You came in time."

"Are you sure? He didn't —"

He couldn't say it. As he stepped toward her, Molly seemed to shrink away from him. She glanced anxiously toward the clearing where Hugh realized from the sound of firing, the shooting match continued. Only minutes had passed. It seemed like hours.

"Where is Jake? Did anyone see?" she asked, now clutching the dress closed. Hugh stepped back a little so he could see the men and still keep an eye on Pearson

"No, they're still busy with their shooting match."

"Shooting match? It's a shooting match?"

"They've set up targets and are trying to outshoot the Sioux. It's a way to diffuse tension."

Molly seemed to fall apart. "The men are having a shooting match! All this time I thought they were fighting Indians, and Edwin was maybe being killed while I was —"

He saw she was on the verge of hysteria and putting Pearson's knife in his belt, he started toward her, but again she pulled away from him. "What are we going to tell people? Jake and the others. What are we going to tell them about Pearson?"

Hugh looked at Pearson still lying spread-eagled on the ground. "We'll tell what he was doing to you. They'll probably hang him for trying to —"

"You'd have everyone *know*. Know what he tried to do! What he thought he could do with me because — because of you and me." She was crying, "He said he'd tell!"

"You mean about us?"

"Yes! He said if I told Jake, he'd tell everyone about us."

"No one would take him seriously. Besides, if he starts to open his mouth, I'll kill him."

"Hugh?" Molly's voice was suddenly small like that of a little girl's. There was something in her eyes that alarmed him. "He isn't moving. Are you sure you didn't —"

"He's just out cold," Hugh gave Pearson a poke with the rifle barrel and then with his foot.

Pearson didn't move.

Hugh put the rifle down and pulling his knife from the wagon kept it handy as he knelt beside Pearson and turned him over. He seemed very still, like something had gone out of him. Hugh didn't believe it.

Molly said it. "I think he's dead."

"No! You're overwrought. He's just out cold. I didn't hit him that hard."

"You caught him in the temple."

Hugh picked up Pearson's wrist and felt for a pulse. "I couldn't have," he groaned. "I was mad enough to, but —"

Molly disappeared in the wagon. Hugh couldn't find a pulse. He told himself he didn't have the right place and kept trying. He looked to where the men were still gathered. Hobart would know what to do. Molly climbed out of the wagon.

Hugh stood, "I'll get help."

"No, wait." She knelt beside Pearson. She was holding something in her hand and Hugh almost laughed when he saw it was a mirror. She looked like a little girl kneeling there with her hair streaming around her shoulders, holding the mirror beneath Pearson's nose.

"Molly, what do you think you're —?" He began; then saw what she was doing and shut up. The minutes passed silently and slowly. Even before she held up the mirror to show him, he knew. It was unclouded.

"Oh, my God," he groaned. "I never meant to — I was so angry, but I never thought I could actually —"

"I'm glad. . . I'm glad he's dead! Hugh, he was going to give us away. Jake would never understand if he found out now. He'd think . . . he'd think there was still something between us. He'd think I still want you. I'm glad Pearson is dead. Besides, he . . . he hurt me."

Hugh stared at her. Her face was flushed and her eyes almost mad. She was both beautiful and terrible to behold. And what did she mean that Pearson had hurt her? He should get help.

"I'd better get the others. "

"You can't do that!"

"What else can I do? He's dead. I've killed him. It was self-defense. They'll understand that. Besides he was *hurting you.*"

"You can't tell them that. You can't tell them you killed him for what he was doing to me. They would — They would talk about me and you and they might banish you from the wagon train."

"They won't banish me. And if they find out what he was doing, why, they'll hang a medal on me!"

"Get rid of the body."

"What?" He couldn't believe she had said it.

She looked around frantically. "No one's seen anything yet. Do it now. Quick. Drag him out there to that rocky place. Out behind the camp."

"I can't do that!"

"You have to. It's the only way. Hurry before someone comes this way."

"But they'll notice he's missing. They'll look for him. I haven't time to bury him and the ground's too hard. They'll find the body."

"It's getting dark." She spoke purposefully, "No one will find him until morning. They'll think the Sioux got him. That he wandered off from camp and the Sioux got him."

Hugh looked between the men in the distance and the body at his feet. What she said made sense, but it was wrong. "No, I'm going to tell the truth. I'll take my medicine like a man. I think they'll let me stay with the party."

She climbed out of the wagon and grabbed his arm, "And what about me? Do you think I want the whole party knowing what he tried to do? Do you think I want them all looking at me and wondering if he succeeded?"

"They wouldn't think that," he said even as the thought came to him.

"They would. They'll all say he had me. Even Jake. My God, don't you think I know how people talk? How they stare? I went through that once. And it was because of you! Would you ask me to go through it again?"

He saw the buttons had been torn from her dress. He had brought shame on her once. This time he must protect her. He picked up Pearson's booted feet.

"Get in the wagon and mend your dress. I'll take care of him." Slowly he dragged the body away from the wagon, keeping his eye on the men in the clearing, sure he'd be discovered at any moment. Even as he did it, the shooting stopped. The Indians mounted, shouting and brandishing their lances. It was almost dark. If the men would just watch the Indians a bit longer, he thought he might make it.

He was out of sight of the camp now, but on rocky ground, so it was harder to drag the body. It kept catching on things. He figured he'd better go where he wouldn't leave tracks. He'd have to cut a piece of sage and try to brush out the track where he had dragged the body from the wagon. There was sure to be a search in the morning. Maybe they wouldn't look too hard; they wouldn't dare to spread out too far with the Sioux still watching them. But he couldn't take long hiding the body. His absence in the clearing might already have been noticed.

He saw a little gully, as good a place as any, and rolled the body down it. Pearson landed face up. Hugh remembered to put Pearson's knife back in his boot. The dead man's fly was still open, and Hugh had to close his eyes a minute, thinking what that meant, but then it gave him an idea. If someone found the body, maybe they would conclude he had stepped out to relieve himself and an Indian had picked him off silently with a war club. Pearson's eyes were open. He seemed to be staring at him. Hugh reached down to close his eyes and then stopped. The Sioux wouldn't do that.

It had to look like he had been killed by Indians.

Hugh realized there was one, perhaps two other things he should do. He hesitated for a long time. Then, suppressing a shudder of revulsion, he took out his knife.

CHAPTER NINE

No one missed Pearson until morning. When the Indians had finally galloped away, still brandishing their lances and muttering threats, they camped less than a mile from Hobart's party. The glow of the Sioux campfires was barely visible once they had their own fires lighted, but the sound of their drumming seemed to fill the air and go on all night. Although everyone agreed the Indians wouldn't attack, the drumming was almost more than nerves could bear. Hugh realized it was a lucky break for him that no one could think of anything else. No one wondered why Molly was pale and trembling or why he paced restlessly back and forth. And no one missed Pearson.

The next morning, as if by magic, the sun came out, and the Sioux were gone. Once again there was easy conversation and even laughter as they ate. But as Hugh was busying himself helping Jake to hitch up the mules, Morris came around looking worried and announced that Pearson was missing. No one remembered seeing him since the shooting match, but since Pearson had no friends, when he had disappeared no one knew. His horse and gear were still there, so something had happened to him. Morris asked Jake and Hugh to join in the search. With a glance at Molly, Hugh picked up his rifle and followed the men.

They formed small groups for the hunt, staying near the camp. Pearson would not have gone far, they reasoned. An hour passed and the men became restless. No one wanted to stay long in the place they had been threatened by the Sioux. They were about to give up the search when Morris yelled, "*Here!*"

Hugh followed the others to the edge of the gully and reluctantly joined in looking down at the corpse.

Morris had thrown his coat over Pearson's head. Hugh was glad he did not have to look again on the dead man's face. A few clamored down the gully to examine the body. Hugh remained behind. Hobart appeared and strode down the gully, sending little avalanches of gravel toward the men as they stepped back to acknowledge his leadership. Morris jerked the coat off Pearson dramatically and Hobart knelt over the body. Finally he stood and motioned for Morris to replace the coat. Hobart's expression as he climbed the gully was carefully composed.

"Indians?" the waiting crowd asked as if one man. "Did the Sioux get him?"

Hobart nodded. "It was Indians all right. He must have gone to piss, and some bloodthirsty redskin got him."

"You think so?"Donnelly probed. "Pearson was never shy about pissing in the middle of camp."

"It was Indians all right," Hobart seemed to be looking directly at Hugh as he said it. "The heathens got his scalp. *And worse.*"

No one was anxious to linger so they planted Pearson in the gully, covered the place with rocks, said a few words over the mound and marked it with a cross. They were on their way by noon.

When they had gone a little distance up the trail, Hobart rode to the end of the column and looked back. He remarked that it was the kind of place one could never find again. But Hugh, looking back at the same place then down at his hands, knew he would never forget the place or what he had become there.

In the days that followed, the country began to change, growing more rugged. They began to see antelope, small bands at first, then great herds which bounded away as their wagons approached. They all itched to hunt, but after Hobart expertly picked off two bucks and distributed the meat, he forbade the rest to hunt, warning them again to stick together. Subdued by Pearson's death, the men followed orders, although Luther was not the only one to complain. Most of them had once lived in some choked-off city place where they felt stifled by the rules and limitations of other men. They had come to the frontier not just to find gold, but to cut loose in some way, to explore and build and even destroy, and somehow be their own men. They had come too late for the buffalo, and now they were told they would miss the antelope too. The restriction chafed; yet they were afraid of meeting Pearson's fate.

Life is as unfair to men as to women. A man can yearn and fight and die and get buried without ever finding whatever it was he was looking for, or even knowing just what it was. Women don't often get what they want either, but they more often know what they seek.

Hugh longed to talk to Molly alone, thinking that she could somehow salve his guilt. She seemed to avoid him, sitting stiffly beside her husband on the wagon seat days, and nights around the campfire, keeping Edwin close by.

It was the first week of May, but cold drizzling rain mingled with spurts of snow made them miserable. Hugh and Luther had a tarp but no tent, so Jake insisted they spread their bedrolls under his wagon at night to stay dry. There was no way to decline without drawing questions, but it was agony for Hugh to sleep so close to Molly that he could hear her turn and moan. He lay awake, listening to the night sounds, trying not to imagine Jake taking his rights with her. He had been enraged to the point of murder by Pearson's lust; now he wondered if his own feelings were any more civilized; for, though he tried to deny the feeling, he wanted his partner's wife.

Molly was also tortured. She could not control her
endless remembering. It had been raining then too; they
had been walking in a hillside meadow when a sudden
spring thunderstorm sent them running for shelter.
Hugh knew of an abandoned barn. The roof was leaking
and broken, but had held in the remains of a box stall,
and here the two were as dry and safe as if they existed
only in their own special world.

She wore a blue dress, and her blond hair hung loose
about her shoulders. His shirt was a bit short in the
sleeves and she said she could sew him a new one. When
he rolled up his sleeves, she longed to touch his strong
arms and felt a new warmth within her. They were alike
in so many ways, but their bodies were so different. She
thought to ask him about that, realized she could not,
and wondered why such things were secret. He smiled,
and she knew he was thinking of the same things.

She laughed nervously, then busied herself arranging
the straw, talking of playing house. "Just last night I
dreamed we were building a house together."

And then he said the thing which broke her heart.

He was leaving. He had learned the news that
morning but kept it from her to allow her a few more
happy hours. Now, he could not keep from hurting
her. His father had made a decision. The Pennsylvania
climate had not helped his lungs and the doctor had
advised them to move west.

She began to cry, and saw tears glistening in his eyes,
tears he held back with the boy's need to be a man.

He declared he would stay with her. She reminded
him of what he knew: he could not leave his mother and
his little brother with his father so ill. Duty came first,
they agreed.

But they had only just found each other! Only yesterday
had first dared to kiss and to speak of love. Now they
clung together, frantically willing the moment to be a

lifetime. And then it began, the touching that was so new and so infinitely tender. They undressed and explored each other in innocence, wondering at the beauty they found in each other's bodies and unaware at first of the passion, not connecting something so sweet with the sin they had been warned against. They wanted only to touch and to give as a special, secret token of their love. They thought only of the wonder of it, discovering lovemaking together from the first touches to the last sweet shuddering sob.

Even afterwards, they felt no guilt but only a bonding, as if their bodies were still joined. For each, it was their first and only love. They swore it would bind them together for all time.

And now, so many years and miles later, it seemed they were indeed bound together, but in such a tangled knot Molly was certain she would never sort it out. The future uncertain, the present so enmeshed with emotions she could not admit feeling, Molly could find refuge only in the past. How she felt about the present Hugh, the man who had done an awful thing to save her from Pearson, and now walked beside her wagon days and slept under it nights, she could not say, even to herself.

The trail to the Black Hills steadily grew more difficult. The rain and sleet so dreary, the men found themselves praying for snow so the ground would freeze. Anything seemed better than the mud, a thick gumbo that gathered on the wagon wheels so they had to stop often to scrape it off. The men's boots were so heavy with it that sometimes they could hardly lift their feet to take another step. Molly and Edwin had to stay inside the wagon all day, and Hugh alternated between chafing that there was no opportunity to see Molly alone and relief that he was spared the opportunity to make a fool of himself by saying or doing something so rash he would offend her.

Someone suggested they camp a few days until conditions improved, but Hobart reminded them there was neither wood nor water so they might as well push on.

Then after nearly a week of gray skies, the weather began to clear almost magically. Hugh found himself walking faster in anticipation, and then, through swirling mists, he caught his first glimpse of the Black Hills, looking like an enchanted land. Like most of the party, who had lived their lives on farms and prairies, he was surprised to discover, the Black Hills were actually mountains. Nor were they black but shades of deep muted blue. For two days the Hills appeared and disappeared through the clouds, each time a little closer and more beautiful, but also foreboding.

Finally the party began to climb the first pine-dotted slopes, following the low places between the foothills so they were barely aware they were climbing except that as the trail wound higher, the air became colder, and the clouds became a light blanket of fog all around them. The weather now seemed to grow more miserable with each step they took; their spirits were so low no one bothered to comment that they had left behind the barren plains sometimes called, "the Dreary Black Hills," and could expect any moment, the sight of high mountain peaks and great beauty.

They camped at a place Donnelly identified as 'Buffalo Gap,' and the next morning awoke to sunshine and the sound of singing birds. The sun changed everything. For a week the men had been surly; now Hugh heard them whistling. He and Luther bickered good-naturedly as they had in the old days, and for the first time they were aware of the fragrance of the pine forest and the beauty of their surroundings. Molly was talkative as she cleared up the breakfast things, saying how the sunshine had changed the world and that she felt certain the worst of their journey was over. Hugh agreed, realizing that the burden he had carried since Pearson's death seemed lighter,

Molly was sick of riding in the wagon and weary of her husband's silence; she wanted to walk, but Jake told her the grass was too wet, she'd soak her shoes; so she stayed on the wagon seat, chafing at the restraint, talking about how the sun and the clear mountain air made her spirit light. She knew Jake considered her to be *prattling on.*

Then, late in the afternoon, when Edwin was napping in the wagon, Molly saw Luther was again limping and invited him to take her place. She climbed down and stood in the deep, lush grass for a moment, watching Jake drive away, feeling free and very aware that their wagon was the last in line, and behind her Hugh approached, also alone. She told herself she would not have planned it this way, but she so wanted to share her joy in this spring day. It felt right to wait for Hugh, especially when she saw the way his face gladdened at the sight of her.

They walked together, him quiet at first as she talked about the sudden flowering of the land, the beauty of everything, the scented air, how good it was to again walk together. Hugh was reluctant to break her mood, but in the past days thinking about what Pearson had done to her was driving him crazy. He wanted to know if he'd come in time to keep Pearson from violating her, but could not ask her, for whatever the truth, it would shame her to speak of it. He was burdened with his own shame, not just for killing Pearson — that had been an accident — but for what he had done to cast the blame on the Indians. He realized he couldn't even ask if Jake had told her that part.

Now, the sunlight breaking through the clouds seemed to wash away past wrongs. They would begin again.

"And how do you like the Black Hills now?"

"Beautiful," she said with a smile, "I want to sing, they are so beautiful."

Beautiful is what you are, he wanted to say, but did not; though she, looking at him, knew his thought, and longed to hear him say it aloud. The trail narrowed until they found themselves in a deep forest of pine. The trees seemed to form walls beside the trail, but the effect was not unpleasant. They could still hear the slow progress of the wagons so Molly did not feel entirely left behind, yet could savor the fragrance of the pine and the sunlight flickering through the trees in little patches of gold. She could hear water tumbling over rocks and knew they were near a brook.

Suddenly Hugh stopped and stared at something off the trail. He put his fingers to his lips and motioned her to follow. When she did, hesitantly, she saw a little clearing barely screened from the trail by a scattering of young aspen, and sheltered there a doe and her fawn. The others had driven past without seeing the deer who stood calmly watching Molly and Hugh, their heads alert, the black muzzle of the doe sniffing the air. Molly realized they must be innocent of humans to stand so calmly. Finally the breeze changed and brought their scent to the doe and she turned and bounded away, the fawn leaping after.

"I've never seen deer so close before," Molly whispered, as conscious of Hugh's nearness as of the beauty of the time and place. They stepped into the clearing; their shoulders were touching now, by accident surely, but touching, and they dared to prolong the moment. Neither moved nor spoke. It was as if the gods had turned them into two marble statues transfixed in the forest, caught in a spell; the very air teasing with all that was unsaid and forbidden between them.

She told herself the moment was innocent and could be savored and prolonged.

"How graceful the deer were. I've never seen anything so beautiful!" She said, aware as she said it of the reply the remark invited, and he did not disappoint her.

"I've never seen anything as beautiful as you. There is no other beauty when you are near me. You are more beauty than my eyes can hold!"

Even to himself his words sounded stilted, as if it was a speech rehearsed which in a way it was, for in his mind he'd said such things to her so often, the words were as familiar as a prayer.

His words brought Molly intense joy; she closed her eyes to hold to herself the overpowering pleasure of the golden sunlight, the lush awakening of the spring woods, and the glory of his speech. It was almost beyond anything she had dared dream.

Hugh, too, was flooded with emotions long held prisoner by distance, honor, and the dangers of the trail. Unlike Molly, he was not content with words. Touch, he must. His hand found her face almost without his willing it. He touched her skin ever so lightly but it was like a blessing. Ever since that day when she had stepped out of Jake's wagon and he had seen her again, he had longed to touch her, to soothe her fears, hold, protect and cherish her. With her eyes closed and her lips smiling, she looked like a woman in a painting; his caress was gentle.

Then Molly held his hand against her face with her own. She had so often longed that Hugh might touch her just so, knowing that only his touch could truly comfort her. Then, remembering what such a gentle touch had once begun, she pulled his hand away and grasped it between her own to hold them both fast against temptation. But then she found she could not release his hand but must take the other and press them to her and hold them locked against her heart.

Again they stood as statues, neither daring to move. Both sensed that in lingering together they risked more than discovery by the Sioux. For the Sioux would make a swift end of them; but another touch, another promise would bind them in something from which there was no escape. She looked at their joined hands, longing to see again the love in his eyes, as when they were young, but they were not young, and she must keep her eyes down, for if she met his gaze, then he might then capture her lips, and what could follow would damn them both.

Hugh pulled his hands away, and she felt both disappointment and relief until he touched her cheek again, "Please don't turn away from me, Molly," and he raised her chin so that their eyes met and then their lips.

Past and present, time and eternity joined, so they seemed to stand not just in a forest clearing, but in a place that hid them from this world and carried them to another, where nothing mattered except that destiny had promised them to one another; she returned his kiss.

All reason abandoned Hugh. He held her to him and caressed her. She seemed to offer an earthly paradise, richer than even the promise of gold-washed streams and unknown lands. Destiny had led him to find her again. He knew that now. He forgot Jake and the wagon train, and when he remembered that the Sioux might discover them, he thought that if a war lance found his back, he would die happy if only they could enter paradise together.

His urgency was too much for Molly. In that moment of his body against hers, she was as afraid of her own desire as of his.

"No, Hugh, stop!" She struggled against the power of his body, pushing at his strong shoulders, even as something in her joyously protested that it might already be too late.

Hugh hesitated just long enough to caress her face, again, and when he saw her confusion, his senses returned, and with an anguished groan he stepped away from her.

They stood facing each other, and she saw he was as stunned as she by what had happened. She felt herself on the edge of a precipice, as if she took one step forward they might fall together there in the grass like beasts in a field. She felt her breast heaving with emotion and knew her hair had tumbled down. She must stop this.

"We can't do this, Hugh. We have no right."

"You know we are meant to be together!"

"No. It can't be!"

"But you wanted to be alone with me. You wanted me to tell you I found you beautiful. I know you did!"

"Because of what we meant to each other a long time ago. That time I can't forget, but there can be no more."

"So, if neither of us can forget, what do you want now? To keep me just as a memory? Hidden away someplace? Like a mourning locket made out of the hair of a love who died? Something that you take out when you are sad and alone to remember your lost love?"

"Or like the cameo necklace that is too fine to wear but reminds me of my mother and home?"

She almost laughed. It was too close to the truth. An image, yes. A picture of Hugh always in her mind, like her mother's cameo. The cameo she kept hidden away, first in the sod house and now in her trunk. Looking at the delicately carved image of a woman's face carved from pink shell always evoked her childish longing for the treasure her mother had promised would one day be hers, but now held more pain than pleasure, for now it evoked not just her childish love of the thing, but the disappointment in her mother's face as she'd pinned the precious jewelry to the old dress Molly had worn for her travesty of a wedding with Jake.

Yes, she sometimes held it, the symbol of all she had once had and all she'd lost, her gracious home and family, a town and a school and the boy she had loved. Yes, she loved the Hugh of her memories, memories she could cherish or put aside when she must. Not this very real man before her. Not this man with his passion and needs. He moved toward her, still reading her mind.

"I'm here now, Molly. I'm real and I need you."

"No, Hugh, stay away."

"Just let me hold you again. Just for a moment. I know there can't be more now. Not until we work it out with Jake somehow."

His arms were open to her, gentle, beckoning, and she was terrified by what she felt.

"Don't touch me" she screamed. "Don't talk about Jake, and don't say those things to me. You're, you're acting like Pearson!"

"How can you say that to me when I —"

"Killed him! Yes, you killed him *and you wanted to.* You know you did."

"To save you. To protect you. His death was an accident, you know that!"

"And the other thing?"

Even as she said it, she hated herself, but she must keep him from her, drive him away. She spat out the words.

"What you did to Pearson's body! Did you do that to protect me? Was *that* an accident?"

It was as if she had struck him, and she was instantly sorry she had said it, but what Pearson had tried to do, and what she saw that even now Hugh wanted, was lust, not love. Not shy glances and tender words, but a wild rush of passion that must be denied. He turned away, but not before she saw the defeat and hurt in his eyes. She knew he felt guilty. He was a civilized man, almost as bound as she by right and wrong.

She was about to reach out to him and tell him she understood; but that they must somehow bridle their feelings and not tarnish the memory of what had passed between them, when she heard in the distance sounds that were familiar, yet in her present state, unrecognizable.

"Gun shots! Someone's shooting up ahead."

Again they were statues, too stunned to move, pondering what to do when Luther crashing through the brush towards them, shouting and brandishing his rifle.

"There you are! My God, come quick. There's shooting ahead. The bloody Sioux have ambushed some pioneers."

CHAPTER TEN

There were three of them. Two men and a woman. Dead, scalped, mutilated.

Lingering as they had been at the end of the wagon train, he and Molly had been the last to see. By the time they got back, the massacre had been pretty well discussed, and the men were standing there silent, just looking at the bodies. The Indians had killed the oxen too. Hugh had the irrational thought that after all their days of traveling on the narrow trail, it was convenient the bodies were found in a clearing, so they could all stand around and gawk. He was angry at the others for staring and at himself for not knowing what else to do.

Finally someone spoke. "They killed the oxen too. You'd think Indians would take a good team of oxen."

"Mother of God," Donnelly spat. "The heathens have no use for oxen unless they're hungry, and these weren't. They didn't even take the food, just scattered it around and fouled it so no one else could use it."

"They weren't hungry," Hobart broke in. "No matter what your bleeding heart Quakers would say. These Indians been eating off Uncle Sam all winter so they could go off in the spring and kill honest folk."

"They did it for meanness," Donnelly agreed. "Pure devilishness."

"They did it for a sign," Hobart said, "to warn us to stay out of the Black Hills."

"You mean they knew we were coming?"

"Sure," Hobart said. "This party was just far enough ahead of us that the Indians knew we could hear their shots. They probably been stalking us for days, but we're too big a party to take on, so they were just waiting for someone to wander off so they could pick up a couple of easy scalps."

"My God," Hugh said as he realized it could have been them, he and Molly, murdered, even while they embraced. It would not have been a pretty ending.

Molly, standing behind Hugh, thought how awful it would have been if Hugh had died thinking she hated him.

"We came upon them too soon," Donnelly said. "That's why they didn't take time to set the wagon on fire and mutilate the bodies."

"That's not mutilated?" Hugh stared at the bloody mess, thinking, *that woman raped and murdered could be Molly. And it would be my fault for trying to get her alone.*

"Hell, no." Donnelly laughed. "They're laid out real nice, Sioux style. Mutilation is cutting off hands, arms, fingers, what-have-you. Like was done with Pearson."

Hugh felt sick with rage at the brutality of it. He clenched his fists, holding back his anger. How could Hobart and Donnelly take it so coolly?

"Let's go after them," Luther shouted, brandishing his needle gun. "Let's get after them and make them pay for this!"

Hugh was ready to go.

"You think they're waiting for you to get a shot at them?" Donnelly laughed. "They're miles away by now."

"He's right," Hobart said. "Nothing we can do now but bury these folks. We can't be more than a day from Custer City, where they came from. We can see if they have any letters or anything on them to identify them, and we can leave word in Custer."

Hugh kept staring at the bodies. Hobart was right. Going after the Indians would be both futile and foolhardy, but he still wanted revenge. Hobart spoke at last.

"Well, let's get them planted."

"No need to cover them over too fancy," Donnelly added. "Let's just roll them into a gully somewhere and pile on rocks to keep the coyotes from making them dinner."

"If they matter to anyone," Hobart added, "someone will come out from Custer some time and bury them proper. They must have been heading home."

Several men nodded assent, and one grabbed the feet of the less bloody of the male corpses to drag it away. Another stepped up to the woman. Someone had already made an attempt to cover her exposed body with a coat.

"Faith" Donnelly said, crossing himself as he uncovered the dead woman. "Judging by the paint and clothes on this one, the Indians didn't get anything she hadn't already sold to half the miners in Custer."

Someone in the crowd dared to snicker at his implication.

"Here's a gully that should hold them all," another shouted. Donnelly began to drag the woman away.

"Stop this. Stop this right now! "

Hugh looked up, startled. It was Molly speaking. He hadn't realized she was still there. She should be in the wagon with Edwin. This was something a woman shouldn't have to see. But Molly was elbowing her way to the front of the crowd. She kept her head high like she didn't want to look at the bodies, but her voice was steady as she confronted the men.

"We're going to give these people a decent burial. Just because we are in this god-forsaken place doesn't mean we have to be as uncivilized as the Sioux."

The men shuffled uncomfortably, but a few nodded. All kept their eyes downcast. Hugh was ashamed. Molly was right. They were all barely civilized, thinking first of themselves, wanting to dispose of the bodies and be on their way. And he had been no better than the rest. He stepped forward to organize the burial, but Molly was in command.

"I want several of you to start digging. We will want three graves. Three *separate* graves. I think under that tree over there. And you will please make them deep enough so there will be no worry about animals."

She hesitated then, glancing quickly down at the half-naked bodies and then back at the circle of men.

"These people are not decently clothed. Will the rest of you look around the trail where the Indians scattered their belongings and see if you can find enough to cover them decently?"

"Everything is pretty well torn up," Hugh said.

"In that case, if you can't find enough clothing, perhaps some of you have something you can spare." She seemed transfixed by the scalped head of the woman.

"If you can't find her bonnet, I will give her mine."

The men began to move.

"And look for identification too, as Mr. Hobart said, so we can notify the families."

The men started picking up bits of clothing. Someone got a shovel out of a wagon.

"Wait," Molly added. "I will need some water. Would two of you bring some buckets of water?"

She paused, biting her lip, then holding her head high and speaking with the voice of authority said, "Jake and Mr. Hobart, will you please wash the bodies of the men and dress them for burial?" She paused and seemed to be steeling herself. "I will wash and dress this poor woman."

Jake touched her arm. "I'll tend to it, Molly. You never laid anyone out before."

She hesitated. Hugh thought she had never looked so fragile and he stepped forward, wanting to shelter and protect her from this, when she shook off Jake's hand.

"It's woman's work," she said. "I can do it. This poor woman is going to be laid out decent. I don't care what kind of a woman she was. That's not for us to judge."

Jake nodded and stepped toward the body. "Where do you want her?"

For the first time Molly faltered. "I can't take her in our wagon. Edwin could wake up any time."

Hobart stepped forward. "You can use my tent."

"Thank you." She gave him a thin smile and then looked around anxiously. "I don't want Edwin to see until they're all laid out. Luther?" She found Luther in the crowd, then hesitated, "No, it best be Hugh. Hugh, would you go sit in the wagon and keep Edwin in there in case he wakes up?"

Hugh hesitated. It seemed so little to do. He wanted to dig the graves. It would be good to feel the shovel bite into the earth. He needed man's work to vent his anger. But she was right. Someone should be with Edwin, and she wanted it to be him.

"I'll stay with him." He started to leave, but she was staring at him. "Is there something else I can do?"

"Yes, there is,'" she said. "Do you have a Bible?"

"No, I'm sorry, I don't."

"You'll find mine in the top of my trunk. Please get it out and choose something to read at the service."

"We didn't do no Bible reading for Pearson," Donnelly interrupted. "Hobart said a few words over him and that was good enough."

"I didn't think about it then," Molly kept her eyes on Hugh. "Besides, I'm not sure Pearson was a God-fearing man, but these innocent people have been cruelly murdered, so we must do the best we can for them. Hugh, will you do it for me? Will you conduct the service?"

His immediate impulse was to turn the job over to Hobart. He would feel like a hypocrite conducting a service, but then, searching her face, he thought perhaps she was trying to tell him something. Perhaps that she understood about Pearson and forgave him. Surely she would not ask him to read from the Bible if she thought he was a callous murderer. He nodded his acceptance and started for the Lewis wagon, feeling his guilt eased.

Hugh noticed Luther was still standing in the clearing, not joining the men who were digging, nor helping those who were moving the bodies and setting up the tent.

"What are you going to do, Luther?"

His brother shrugged. "I'm tired!"

"We all are," Hugh tried to keep his voice even, "but we have to keep a hold on ourselves. We'll need a marker for the graves. You can do that. And, Luther, try to make a decent cross, not just sticks tied together."

His brother just stood there. Finally he sniffed and wiped his nose with the back of his hand.

Without waiting for a reply, Hugh said, "I'll get you an ax out of the wagon."

"You're getting just like him!

"What do you mean? Getting like who?"

"Like Hobart. He's always telling people what to do. Now you're giving me orders. You're not the boss of me."

"Damn it, Luther," Hugh felt suppressed anger boiling to the surface. "I wasn't trying to shove you around. I just wanted a marker for the graves. I thought you'd want to help Molly."

For a moment the two brothers stood, face to face, their fists clenched. Hugh decided maybe it *was* time to show Luther some attention. He was about to jerk the boy up by his collar and lay into him when Luther backed down.

"Oh all right. I'll do it. But I'm warning you, Hugh. I'm sick of you treating me like a kid. You're no better than me. And if I hadn't found you and Molly in time, the Sioux would have got you too!"

Hugh had never before felt the calling to preach and he never would again. But that night at the burying, he the used all the skills he'd learned arguing the law and writing for the Sentinel. He practiced and found a cadence and tone in his voice, remembered from the preachers of his childhood. He was good with words and he'd found a message in the Bible.

Later, lying in his blankets and staring up at the stars with Luther snoring beside him, he wished he could have said more. He had wanted the burying to be done right. Not just for Molly, but for all of them. He knew they were disheartened by the massacre, and he wanted to give them hope, but his words were not as strong as his emotions. Besides he'd been a hypocrite, standing before them holding a Bible in hands stained in a man's blood.

He pondered what he'd said: Even though, they didn't know those they were burying, they knew they had come to the Hills with hopes and dreams like their own. These three, however, had allowed themselves to become discouraged and had turned back. This should not be a sign to them, for perhaps if these people had just stuck it out a little longer, they would have been rewarded.

Yes, turning back was always a temptation, and prudence was always advised. They had all learned going to the Black Hills wasn't just an adventure, but a test of their strength and courage. The important thing was to have faith in God and themselves, to keep on searching and working for the stuff of their dreams, and let no man call them fools for dreaming.

Then he'd read from Isaiah 2:4, the part about beating swords into plowshares, and prayed aloud that soon they would be turning from war to peace. For they were nation building. Perhaps they had come expecting an easy path and wanted only to find gold, but they must understand that anything of value was worth working for, and they were working to win a new land. Some of them were destined to live out their lives in the Hills, bringing civilization to the wilderness. And maybe they would be remembered as pioneers.

Even as he said those words, he had looked across the open graves at Molly standing with her husband and son, her hair pulled back and her face solemn and pale, and found her magnificent.

He'd had a thought then, one he could not speak aloud, for he had no right to speak of another man's wife, but that night, lying under the stars it came to him again. For looking at her over the open graves, he had seen growing in Molly a remarkable strength and spirit and had thought that if any of them was ever to be remembered or spoken of as pioneers, it would be Molly.

Molly Lewis, who said she wasn't the pioneer type, who dreamed of home and pianos, but who had taken charge of the men and given a proper burial to the gold-camp whore.

CHAPTER ELEVEN

In Custer City Hugh bought a small ledger book. He wanted to record his pioneering experiences, for he saw that the Hobart party was part of history in the making. He hoped also, that by filling the ledger pages with well chosen words, he would make sense of it for himself. Perhaps men did need the restriction of civilization to keep themselves in check; perhaps keeping accounts that balanced and recording words in rows of black ink served a purpose. He intended to record in careful penmanship his impressions of the land and the milestones of the journey, all while carefully censoring his feelings. Thus he might bring order to his troubled soul.

He had only so many pages in his book and had left some of the first ones blank to record the markers of the trip that began at Sidney and was supposed to end in Custer City. Even as he wrote his first entry, the story of their great disappointment, he was not pleased with his words, but he didn't have enough pages to allow for revision, and he sensed his journey had only begun.

We arrived at our destination, Custer City, after nearly three weeks of arduous travel, to discover no more than 100 residents remaining in a city we were told only days ago numbered thousands.

A large hotel stands half-completed and the city's most pretentious building, a theatre, has likewise been abandoned after one night of merriment. Even the sawmills, with one exception, have been carried along by a population bound for a new stampede.

The gold rush now proceeds to diggings in the north to a place they call Deadwood.

The demise of Custer seems tragic for it is most attractively located in a beautiful parkland and surrounded by mountains of considerable *magnitude. The city seems destined to become a center for farming and ranching once the Indian problem is settled.*

Massacres in this vicinity have occurred almost daily. Just before our party reached Custer, it was our unfortunate duty to bury three victims of an Indian attack. We were unable to ascertain their identity, but gave them Christian burial.

There are many such graves in these Hills, bearing only the fading legend, "Unknown Man, killed and scalped by Indians!"

Burley Bemis, the city's first mayor, and possibly the last, urged us to remain. He assured us the "Black Hillers," as we have begun to be called, would soon return, but most of those in the Hobart Party have deemed it more expedient to throw our lot in with those who have stampeded to the new Mecca of Deadwood.

Or is it to be labeled, 'Dead Wood'? Surely my guess is as good as anyone's.

Here Hugh found he could write no more. It seemed pointless to remain in Custer and foolhardy to venture on alone; but when the others decided to proceed, he held back, suggesting that he and Luther might linger a few days. He had promised Molly he'd stay with her until they reached Custer. He did not want to leave her now, but they had not spoken since his words and actions had revealed to both of them that he desired her. Now, it seemed the decent thing was to remove himself from temptation before he did more damage.

Custer City was a disappointment for Molly too, but a disappointment of a more personal, womanly nature. She had been so delighted by the sight of hundreds of log and frame cabins, that she hardly noticed the lack of population. When Jake remarked that there was something mighty strange in the mayor riding out to meet the wagon train and inviting them to take their pick of cabins to use until the owners returned from the northern diggings, she thought him unnecessarily suspicious.

She took satisfaction in choosing the best of the cabins, unpacking the wagon, doing a wash and even baking bread. By the time Jake returned from a day of what he called "reconnoitering the situation," she had fed Edwin and herself and was thoroughly settled. She took it badly when Jake told her they must move on. She put his dinner on the table and made Edwin go outside to gather kindling before taking her place across from him at the table and demanding, *Why? Why* when the spot was so pretty and they had a cabin for the taking?

Because the stampede had moved north, Jake said, and when she demanded to know why they could not look for gold in Custer as well as anywhere and accused him of having the wanderlust, he patiently tried to tell her what he had learned that day about what it took to mine gold.

Water, he said. There was not enough *water* in Custer City. And when she protested that French Creek was the loveliest little stream she'd ever seen, he tried to explain to her about the need for fast-moving water.

It takes water rushing downstream fast to wash the gold from the homemade rockers filled with gravel dug on the creek beds, he told her as if he'd reasoned it out for himself. There was little hope now to find actual gold nuggets, for those first to arrive, had taken them all. The task of those who had come later was to find *placer gold*. This, he explained as he ate, was sort of a gold dust hidden in the gravel and sand miners would shovel from the creeks and which, gold being heavier, would sort of fall out as they washed the gravel through the rockers. Eventually this would lead them to find *the mother lode*, the hillside vein into which they could sink a shaft to take the gold from the heart of the mountain.

He told her something else. Of a kind of gold she would hear of again and again in the weeks and months to follow until she would curse the name itself.

Poor Man's Gold. Gold to be found in a place they called *Poor Man's Diggings.* A place where the gold could be found on the surface, washed down in the stream beds, so that it could be mined with *placer methods.* These involved a sluice box and rockers or even a simple gold pan. Poor Man's Gold was gold that could be mined with hand labor and no investment of capital in the machinery necessary to going underground. Gold that could be won by a man with just his hard work, thus *a poor man* who would become *a rich man.*

This is what the thousands had abandoned Custer City to seek, he explained, pleased with his new knowledge. *Poor Man's Gold* in a place they called *Deadwood.* She thought both names sounded foolish, but she knew she would have to follow Jake and Hobart if the party decided that Deadwood was to be their new destination. She respected Hobart's judgment, and although she felt almost heartbroken, she would have soon started repacking, had not Jake concluded with words which shattered her calm.

"Everyone's going on in the morning but the Everett brothers!"

"Hugh and Luther aren't going with us?"

"Nope. Hugh said he figured it would be faster to cut across country since there's hardly a road for the wagons. Could be he's right, though it would be a risky business. Anyway, he said to tell you he hoped you'd understand that they had best go on alone!"

"You mean he's leaving? Just like that, without saying goodbye?"

Jake shrugged and held out his plate for more stew. "Oh, I expect he'll do that before we push out. I think he figured it was too much trouble for you cooking for them and putting up with Luther."

"Didn't you tell him it wasn't? Did you ask them to stay? Did you tell him we need them?"

"Course I did. Maybe not the needing part, but however you put it, Molly, there's no telling a grown man what to do."

Molly was stunned, but tried not to let Jake know how upset she was. Just that morning she had been almost happy, thinking that if she could make the cabin into some semblance of a home, she might make peace with herself, and return to the calm of their time in the sod house. In those years, only Edwin brought her feelings like joy, but having a home and chores had made her believe her life was in order. In the sod house, emotions could be stifled. She had given up her girlish notions and learned that spring and summer were for planting and not for dreaming. She had told herself the sad feelings of autumn and approaching winter were merely the loss of sunshine and not of her spirit; that she did not need pretty words and the sweet sharing of wild flowers in summer and hands held before a fire in winter. She could simply *endure*. Many women did. She believed it was enough to have a husband who was decent and hard working. To be living again in a city of sorts meant she would might in time not forget, but at least put away, those moments on the trail when lost love had miraculously returned to her.

She knew she should not risk being alone with Hugh again, but she had never considered that he might no longer be nearby. How was she to go on *enduring* if she must once again, let him go entirely? Need she spend her whole life doing her duty to Jake simply because he had once saved her from disgrace?

She looked at her husband, wanting desperately for him to sense her distress and reach across the table to hold her hands, or even get up and hold her close. She needed him to be, at the least, the comforting father figure she had made of him. But Jake was busy wiping up the last of the stew with his bread. Watching him and thinking all these things, she could not hold back her anguish.

"I don't want Hugh and Edwin to go on alone."

"Then go to him."

"What?"

"Go to Hugh. Tell him you *want* them to come on with us. He'll listen to you. He likes you."

She put her head down in her hands at the irony of what her husband had just said.

"Go on, Molly. Their cabin is practically next door. Take Edwin with you. He can finish gathering the kindling tomorrow."

Still she hesitated.

"It's going to be dark soon. If you don't go now, it could be too late. If they push out before us, you won't see them again."

Not see Hugh again! It was too much! She could not let him go without even saying goodbye. She could not let him go, thinking she hated him for what he had done to save her from Pearson and for kissing her and wanting her.

She rose from the table. She would persuade Hugh to stay with them, or if he insisted on going on with Luther alone, at least she would send him with the truth. She got her shawl and walked to the doorway, and then as she felt the sweet, cold mountain air, she knew she could be taking a step that might risk her marriage, her security and her sense of right and wrong. She turned back to her husband.

"Jake?"

"What?" He had picked up a piece of harness that needed mending.

"Come with me?"

"You can go that far alone. No need to be afraid."

"Please?"

"I got to fix this and then tend my mules."

Suddenly he seemed a stranger to her. It was difficult to believe she had really married this man. It was as if she was seeing him for the first time, or perhaps the last. She stepped out of the door, hesitated, and then called Edwin to come with her.

Hugh had known it was a coward's way to leave the party at Custer without even saying goodbye to Molly; but he had known he could not say to her face that he would never see her again. That was why he had decided to walk out of her life. He knew he could not forget her but he thought if he left her to Jake and got on with his adventure, threw himself into the search for gold, then at least he would be free.

Hugh was no coward but the depth of his feelings for Molly once he had dared to hold her again made him almost hate himself. For all his talk of civilization, he knew there was a beast within him who might make him lose control of his passions. He feared something else that was within him, a great well of love that ran so deep he might drown in it and never again be his own man.

Often when a man senses himself on the verge of such an all-encompassing love, he pulls back, runs away, or does something to push away the very love he yearns for. Hugh had resolved to leave Molly and, had she let him go, it might all have turned out quite differently. But she came to him.

He'd been amazed to look up from where he and Luther were organizing their gear before the cabin to see her approaching with Edwin beside her, and surprised at the way she had taken charge of the situation. She had let Edwin beg them to continue with the expedition, listened while Luther made a great show of protesting the high-handed treatment he fancied he'd received from Hobart, while all the time his nervous blinking betrayed his insecurity at striking out alone. And then, while Hugh was still trying to think of some excuse to talk to her alone, Molly had reached into her pocket, produced two pennies, and asked Luther to take Edwin into town for some candy.

"I had to talk to you alone," she said as they watched Edwin and Luther trotting down the path to town.

He nodded, wanting to make it easier for her, but being without words.

"You aren't really leaving us, are you?"

"I think it best."

"Why?"

"God, Molly. You know."

"Is it because of what I said about Pearson?"

"Partially —"

"I didn't mean it, what I said about what you did to his body. I understand why you did that. I know you did it to protect me."

"It's not just that, Molly. There's more. You know."

"Because of what happened when we were alone?"

"Because I kissed you, Molly, because I can't keep my hands off you. Neither of us can forget what happened. I made a fool of myself. I was an animal. I was like Pearson. You said it yourself."

"I shouldn't have. That's what I had to tell you. I acted like I hated you, and then later when I realized it could have been us the Sioux got, when I heard you preach at the funeral, when Jake told me you might be leaving, I couldn't let you go without telling you —"

"Without telling me what?"

She was confused, afraid. She pulled her shawl closer around her, bit at her lower lip, and could hardly get the words out. They came at last in a whisper, "Just that I don't hate you. I don't hate you at all. I never could. I forgive you for what happened to Pearson, and for what happened to me back home and, and I could never hate you."

It was not enough. It was just not enough. Something

inside Hugh sensed what Molly was driving at, even knew why she could not say more, but he wanted more. He sensed that he might win her. That she had come here to keep him, and that if he were cautious, if he played her gently — but he did not want to win her by subterfuge. He wanted her to come to him of her own volition. It made him reckless.

"You're trembling, Molly. It's cold. Come inside the cabin. I'll light a lantern."

She looked alarmed, and although the hand he reached out to her never touched her shoulder, she began to tremble.

"I can't come in. I have to get back. It's getting dark. I just wanted to ask you not to leave the party because of me. Jake wants you to stay partners and it's not safe for you to go on alone, so please, please just forget what I said because it wasn't true."

"You don't hate me!"

"No, of course not. It was just that I was upset because —"

"Because I kissed you. Because I love you."

"Don't say it, Hugh. Please don't say it. Don't you see? If you say it aloud, then we can't go on."

"And if I don't say it aloud, then we can go on as if nothing happened? Is that how you manage, Molly? Not saying things? Not admitting the truth? Do you think if you never say that we've been lovers, if you never admit it, even to yourself, that we can pretend to be just friends? Is that what you want? To be friends?"

"Yes, friends."

"Can't you see I can't go on like this? If you won't leave Jake and come away with me, then I've got to get away from you."

"Leave Jake?"

"Yes. You don't love him. You can't possibly love him, so come with me."

"How can you say such a thing? How can you even think it? How could we do that to Jake?"

"He's strong. He'll understand once he knows how it was with us before. We'll explain how we loved each other, and that will make it easier once he knows I'm Edwin's father."

"Take Edwin away from him? I couldn't do that to him. He loves Edwin. He raised him and he'll never have another son. Can't you see? Jake is my husband. We were married in a church."

"Because you had to. Because of what I did. I'm glad you had Jake to save you, but it doesn't mean you have to stay with him forever. I know it's hard, Molly. Jake's a good man; he's my friend. I don't want to hurt him, but —"

"I won't hurt him. I will never hurt Jake. He's my husband and, and —"

"And you love him? Tell me you love him."

She backed away from him, looking helpless. He pressed his advantage, grabbing her roughly by the shoulders

"Say it, Molly. If you won't say you love me, then tell me you love Jake!"

"I love ... Jake. Jake Lewis is my husband and I love him." She said the words with her eyes closed and her whole body trembling. He sensed she might break any moment, and he knew he could not love her and hurt her any more. He let go of her shoulders and she slumped against him weakly. He stood there holding her ever so gently while she sobbed.

"I'm sorry, Molly. I'm sorry, sweetheart. I don't know why I'm doing this to you."

She looked up at him. "I'm so confused. Oh, Hugh, I hurt so. I never hurt so badly before. I don't think I can stand it if you go away. I'm so afraid. I'm so afraid."

He held her in his arms, wiping away her tears,

comforting her like a child.

"What are you afraid of, Molly? The Indians?"

"Yes, no... I don't know. I don't know. I'm just so afraid."

He wondered then if she could fear the same things he feared. The beast within, the thing that might cut loose and wreak havoc. Or was it the great whirlpool of love that might suck one down? He thought a woman's fears must be different; it had to be the Indians or Jake's finding out or something terrible and unknown outside of her that made her tremble, and so he told himself he must protect her.

And she, sensing perhaps the one thing that would make him stay, looked up at him and said, "Please don't leave me, Hugh. Stay with me."

He said nothing more then but only held her close, knowing she would soon withdraw from even this chaste embrace. He knew if he followed her to Deadwood, he was as good as lost.

"I won't ever leave you again," he said.

CHAPTER TWELVE

"So if it's this Deadwood place we're going to, why don't we go?" Emerald asked. She was dressed only in a chemise and underskirt and had arranged herself artfully on the great mahogany bed, so the soft swell of her breast was revealed in a manner that was seductive without being bold. Austin Avery seemed to like it best when she was coy.

"I'm bored to death with hanging around Cheyenne," she added, but Avery seemed bent on ignoring her. He was dressing to go out and intent on studying his own reflection in the beveled oval mirror of the ornate mahogany dresser.

Emerald lowered her chin and stared at him with wide eyes. She felt the emerald earbobs jiggle against her neck and hoped the light was striking them so they brought out the green in her eyes. Sooner or later he would look at her: she would be ready. She had asked the question petulantly, more to attract Austin's attention than to gain information. He was dressing to go out. She was bored to death with watching him gamble, but she didn't fancy another night alone. She did not have any illusions that Dakota Territory would be any more pleasurable than Cheyenne, Wyoming, but she figured the sooner Austin Avery struck it rich in the mines, the sooner they could be on a riverboat steaming back to the luxuries of civilization. She decided to rephrase the question; this time taking a strand of her long black hair and twisting it around her finger as she spoke.

"I said when are we leaving for Deadwood?"

Now she kept her eyes downcast so Austin would notice the lushness of her eyelashes. Then, when she looked up at him, her wide green eyes would show their full effect. In the weeks since she had thrown in her lot with the gambler, she had often been alone, and had made use of her time looking into hotel room mirrors, practicing her lines and posing, seeing each time less of Emma O'Brien, shop girl and dreamer, and more of Emerald O'Brien, woman of the world.

"I told you, we'll go when I say the time is right." Austin finally acknowledged her presence, although he kept his eyes on his own reflection in the mirror. He'd stroked pomade on his hair to make it gleam. Now with a tiny scissors he trimmed a stray hair from his luxuriant mustache, and then tilted his head back to check for offensive hairs in his nostrils. There were none. He smiled at himself in the mirror, revealing a well-polished gold incisor. Sliding open one of the drawers which framed the mirror, he selected a set of diamond studs and began arranging them in the front of his ruffled shirt.

Emerald shifted on the bed in annoyance, then arranged herself, so her ruffled underskirt appeared to have fallen back by accident to reveal the inside of one leg, almost to the place where the black silk stocking met the garter. She had kept her shoes on.

They were new, after all.

"I just don't understand what we're waiting for! We came all the way to this god-forsaken town just to go to the Black Hills, and everyone in Cheyenne is packing out every day like there's some kind of a race on, and we're still here. All the gold mines will be found before we get there!"

"Precisely, my dear," Avery said, donning his brocade vest.

"But you told me you intended to acquire mining interests. That you owned mines in Montana before you sold out to go back down the Mississippi. You declared you were going to the Black Hills to acquire more mines. So why are we just sitting here in Cheyenne while everyone else finds all the gold?"

"That's just the point." He turned to her at last, actually smiling. "There are much easier ways to get gold than by digging for it. I thought I'd taught you that by now."

She should have known he was going to the Black Hills to gamble, yet somehow she'd pictured him in the mountains with a pick and shovel. Of course Austin would never get his hands dirty, and of course he could acquire a mine by gambling. She had seen him win over a thousand dollars in a night. It was just that it was still hard for her to admit that gambling wasn't a mere diversion with Austin Avery, it was a whole way of life.

"I still think we should get going. They're leaving Cheyenne by the hundreds every week."

"All in good time, my dear. We want to be sure this new Deadwood digging is truly the mother lode. We'd have risked our scalps going to Custer for nothing. I want all those eager hard-working souls to be successful and then bored enough to "invest" their winnings at my table. And, of course, we want to wait until a road's been built, a stagecoach operating and the Indians back on the reservation. We wouldn't want the Sioux to get that lovely hair of yours, would we? The Cheyenne route to the Black Hills is notorious for that sort of thing."

She smiled at the reference to her lovely hair and ignored the remark about Indians. She wasn't afraid. Danger only made things more exciting.

"It's just that I'm so bored with Cheyenne I could scream."

"Are you now?" He seemed to really study her this time. "Do you mean I'm not keeping you entertained?"

She cast her eyes down modestly, letting the tip of one finger caress her breast casually. "It's just that you come in so late when you gamble all night. You don't like me to watch you play because although I do a good job of distracting the other men, when I can see your hand you say my face is 'too expressive.' And you won't let me go anywhere in the evening without you, and you won't take an evening off to go to the theatre with me. And you sleep all day."

"And, my poor, little Emerald," he studied himself in the mirror, tying his flowing black silk neck scarf. "I thought you were having so much fun shopping. I see you have some new shoes."

At least he had noticed. They were genuine French kid. She smiled and made the most of the opportunity to reveal the inside of her thigh as she showed off the shoes. When she noticed a quickening of his interest, she closed her knees and pulled her underskirt down demurely.

"But, Austin, Cheyenne is such a dreadful place. A decent woman can't walk down the street even in broad daylight without some terrible man making a suggestive remark."

"A decent woman can probably manage quite nicely." A flicker of amusement crossed Avery's usually impassive face.

"Are you saying I'm not a decent woman?"

"Not at all, my dear, but you should know there is a an established custom on the frontier which makes it very easy to distinguish decent women from, the other kind."

"Nice women," he lectured, now watching her behind his own image in the mirror, "do not paint their faces. *The other kind do.* Surely you've noticed a certain sort of women in Cheyenne. They chalk their faces white and paint their lips scarlet and wear red feathers in their hats and walk little dogs on leashes. Therefore, my dear, if you wish to be distinguished from such, all you need do is wash your face and refrain from acquiring a little dog. Thus, you will be able to stroll the streets of Cheyenne or Deadwood, I'm sure when the time comes, without fear of molestation."

"Are you saying I don't look nice?" Emerald allowed her lower lip to tremble. She spent hours each day arranging her looks to please him and now this!

"My dear," Avery turned to study her. "You would not be here if I did not find you delicious. I did not mean to imply that your little artifices with powder and rouge were in the same class with the painted ladies. I'm merely telling you how you may walk the streets without fear of being mistaken for an indecent lady."

"I was a decent lady until you came along."

"Come now, Emerald. You were ripe for the plucking. If not been me, it would have been some fat Missouri merchant. Is that what you want? Do you wish you were married to some respectable merchant and safe behind the counter of his dry goods store?"

"I wouldn't mind being married!"

"Well, if that is the case, my dear, I'm sure you will have no trouble finding some upstanding young man here or in Deadwood who will be delighted to make an honest woman of you. I never promised you marriage, and I can tell you right now, you wouldn't like it!" He stopped talking to arrange a diamond stickpin in his ascot, then turned and looked her in the eyes.

"You're like me, bred for adventure and excitement. That's why I picked you out of that miserable little shop and brought you along. I'll tell you another thing, Emerald. I'm the right man for you. You might think you'd be happier with some man who would offer you marriage and respectability, but you wouldn't, because it's all a game with you just as it is with me. We play parts for each other, and I know all the parts you want me to play."

It was true. He did know somehow what she wanted and had known since the moment they met. But she had a power over him too. She sensed that.

"Doesn't it work both ways? Don't I know what you want?"

He seemed a bit taken aback. "Yes, you seem to. You've been most satisfactory."

"It's because I love you."

"No, you don't. People like us don't need love. Love is like the promise of a hereafter. It's pie-in-the-sky for those who can find no choice but to live their lives on earth in suffering. You and I take our pleasure where and when we find it. We make our own rewards. It's only those who believe in sin and eternal damnation who must talk about love to justify their lusts or the fact they get so damn little pleasure from their sanctified mating."

"But, Austin —"

"Now that you've finally said it, I know you'd like me to say it to you. Well, I won't do that. Love's an illusion, like one of my card tricks or what magicians do on the stage. And it's the worst kind of a trick because it's a trick you play on yourself."

She started to dispute what he'd said, although she hadn't quite sorted it out yet, but she was struck by something she saw in his usually impassive face. Even as he denied love, his manner had changed, so he looked for a moment as if, even as he denied that love was real, he wished it were so. Then he regained his composure, his dark eyebrows lifted and he gave her a look she understood.

"Will you be a good girl and help me with my cuffs?"

She nodded, demurely, knowing what he wanted. He sat on the bed beside her, offering her his open hand with the tiny diamond studs. She was hurt by what he'd said. Love could be real, couldn't it? And she did know about real life. Life could be dull, even painful. People could be ugly, even lonely.

With Austin Avery she was always beautiful, like an actress on a stage. What she could not understand was why he did not wish to play the scene as she'd have written it, complete with pledges and golden rings, as in a fairy tale.

Perhaps he sensed that she too feared the boredom of marriage. Austin did seem to have a sixth sense about her, knowing what she wanted just as, at this moment, she knew he desired her. She took the studs from him and put one through his cuff, holding his hand and drawing out the action, knowing his eyes followed the top of her chemise where the swell of her breast rose and fell as she breathed. Pretending to be unable to fasten the stud, she slumped a little to allow her breast to just touch the top of his hand.

He tore his hand from hers and put it to her breast. She looked into his eyes, still wanting to see adoration in his face, but again it was impassive. He pushed her across the bed, demanding. It was happening faster than she liked. She had lost control of him, but she felt her blood pounding in excitement. He kissed her neck and then began to tug at her chemise. His breath was hot and his moustache scratched as his lips moved down her body and found her breast. He smelled of Bay Rum and something else, hot and masculine.

Despite herself, she moaned. He leaned back and smiled into her face as if he had won something. She had determined never to let him know how much she enjoyed the things he did to her, so she held him away from her.

"Tell me you love me," she teased.

"Tell me you want me," he countered. "Tell me I pleasure you, Emma. Tell me I pleasure you."

"No," she said, still holding him back.

"Damn you," he said, and then his lips moved down her body and words no longer mattered, so that in the end it was she who pulled up her underskirt.

Afterwards, while she was arranging her clothes, her face and breast hot and scratched from his mustache, and her hair completely disarrayed, he rolled off the bed and began searching for his jewelry. It made her furious, especially when he straightened up after only a moment and held out the diamond, declaring, "Gambler's luck!"

"Don't tell me you're still going out!"

"Of course. It's the shank of the evening. And you just gave me my good luck charm, Emma."

"Don't call me Emma. Don't ever call me Emma."

"Why not? It's your name isn't it? Emma O'Brien?"

"It isn't! I don't know where you got such an idea." She burst into tears before remembering tears might smudge the smoky kohl around her eyelids. As she wiped her eyes on the bed sheet, Avery concentrated on a speck of dust on the lapel of his coat.

"Why are you so hateful to me?" she cried. "I do everything to please you, give up my family and everything and you treat me like I was common."

"You seemed to be enjoying my treatment well enough a moment ago. I called you Emma then and you didn't seem to mind."

"That was different!" She had been out of control, had almost let him know how much he affected her. She sensed there was danger in letting him have too much of her. That first night, she had given herself to him totally, but now she knew better. He had the gambling. She had nothing but him. That was why she must always be Emerald O'Brien. *Emma* O'Brien could be hurt.

"Call me Emerald," she said quietly but firmly.

"Emerald," he whispered, patting her breast.

She didn't particularly care for the gesture. It was meant, she supposed, to be conciliatory, but he acted as if he owned her.

"Be a good girl and perhaps I'll bring you a bauble,

though there aren't so many men traveling with their wives' jewels as we found on the Mississippi. Still, perhaps I can win enough greenbacks to buy you something you fancy."

He tipped his hat to her as he walked out the door.

Later, after a good cry, Emerald got out of bed and went to the massive walnut wardrobe. Opening it, she rummaged around behind her valise and took out the beaded purse in which she kept her jewels. She knelt on the floor, spilling the contents out on her lap. She had an emerald-and-diamond necklace to match the earbobs, her first gift from him and the only one she cherished, two ornate gold watches with chains, a half-dozen diamond stick pins of varying quality, and an assortment of gold chains and jeweled clips. The jewels gave her no satisfaction.

They were not given out of love. Only the earbobs had been selected for her; the rest were gambling winnings. If he lost, which he seldom did, he would borrow them back, replacing them when his luck changed, often the same night. She merely served as his bank. She sat on the floor before the wardrobe and looked at her clothes hanging above her. Seeing the emerald-green gown, she reached up and stroked it, then impulsively, pulled it off the hook and into her lap. Avery had bought her a trunk full of dresses but she would never have another gown she loved so much. She buried her face in the soft velvet folds and would have cried, but she did not want to water spot the material. Poor dress, it was already showing signs of wear.

It had all begun with the green velvet. It made her think of her poor mother. How she must have cried when she found Emerald's note. How she must wish she had her daughter back. For a moment, Emerald thought about going home. If she sold the jewelry she would have enough money to go, but she knew her mother would never take her back and if she did, would make Emerald's life a misery with wailing about sin and repentance.

As disappointed as Emerald was that everything was not going her way with Avery, she knew in her heart, the last thing she wanted was repentance. A life of sin was occasionally depressing but seldom boring. Sitting on the floor of the frontier hotel room, she asked herself, *What do I want?*

She had dreamed of going back to the South as the respectable wife of a plantation owner, but Avery seldom mentioned the plantation anymore, perhaps it was also a fantasy. In any case, she found it increasingly difficult to conjure those images which had only a few weeks ago seemed so attainable, images of herself on Avery's arm, beautifully gowned, gliding down an elaborate curved staircase and into the grand ballroom of the plantation, every eye upon her.

Now, thinking of how the men in her dreams stared at her, and how even in reality other men seemed to envy Avery and want her, she stood up and held the green dress before her. She looked at herself in the mirror and knew she could get what she wanted from any man, including Austin Avery.

But what was it she wanted? She remembered Avery's speech about love. He said they didn't need it. He never told her he loved her. He was determined to keep that emotion to himself, even as he teased her to say she wanted him.

Love will do for a starter, she decided. *I'll make Austin Avery say he loves me.*

Then I'll decide what I want next.

CHAPTER THIRTEEN

They were two days beyond Custer and camped within the luxuriant grasslands of the southern Hills when Hugh next had time to write in his journal. The Hobart party was making its last camp on level ground before beginning its climb into the rugged mountains in which Deadwood was supposed to lie. It was evening and Hugh had climbed a hill so he could be alone to write and watch over the camp, without making himself a target for Indians. Hobart warned that the Sioux, who were horsemen and plains fighters and avoided the narrow trails of the inner Hills, might take advantage of their last camp in the valley to make a raid. Heeding his warnings, many of the men cleaned their guns as they sat before their campfires. Jake was busy hobbling his mules and adding picket lines as a precaution. Luther and Caleb Dexter, the old prospector who had joined the party, were taking advantage of the last minutes of daylight to work their gold pans in the creek.

Hugh looked up from his journal, unable to concentrate. He had been keeping an eye on the Lewis wagon and saw Molly climb out, stretch, and walk about as if to enjoy the evening breeze before retiring. Her hair was loose and hanging in a pale mist about her shoulders that made Hugh's throat tighten. She saw him and waved but returned to her wagon. Once she would have joined him, but the days of casual conversation between them were over. They had become *friends*. Friends who did not trust themselves to be alone.

Hugh turned back to the map he was making of their journey, but he found himself wondering if it would have been different if they had met again in a civilized place. Would he be a better man if they were not two hundred miles from the nearest church? Or would he still promise

to be her friend and burn to be her lover? It had occurred
to Hugh that something might happen to Jake. Jake was
a middle-aged man and they were in a dangerous land.
He was angry at himself for the thought and angry at
Molly for driving him to it. His only consolation was
that, although he had already killed a man, he was not
capable of premeditated murder.

He was also concerned about their journey. Custer
had shaken him. The rows of abandoned buildings
were stark reminders of the riskiness of their venture.
His doubt was compounded the next day when they
came upon Hill City. Donnelly remembered it as a
thriving mining camp of over 100 cabins. Now it was
a ghost town, eerie, abandoned; with doors standing
open, dishes left on tables as if not a moment could be
wasted by those who joined the new stampede. They
were in a race, he realized; a race that would go to the
swiftest and strongest, and the Hobart party was already
very late. Increasingly he feared they were on one of
history's greatest wild goose chases, and somewhere up
that steep and precipitous trail to whatever waited in
the mountains above them, he must abandon his hopes
and dreams, or perhaps find his fate lay in yet another
unmarked grave.

Yet, despite these gloomy realizations, more often
Hugh was driven by a spark of hope, a feeling that he
was among the chosen few. Like Pip in the Dickens
novel he had enjoyed the winter before, he persisted in
having *Great Expectations*.

He wanted to write some of these thoughts in his
journal, but the light was almost gone, so he returned to
watching the camp. There was a movement by the creek
and he reached for his rifle, before seeing it was only
Luther and the old prospector, Caleb Dexter, returning
from their gold panning. Hugh wondered again what
Luther found so appealing about the foul-smelling, bad-

mouthed, perpetually drunk old reprobate. Luther caught
sight of Hugh and waved. The old man beckoned Hugh
to join them and pantomimed taking a drink. Hugh shook
his head *no* and the old man tottered off cheerfully, but
Luther came up the hill to press the invitation. Again
Hugh declined, but Luther persisted.

"Come on, Hugh. He's got enough for all of us. I
never got drunk before."

"There's no sense to be drinking when there's danger
of Indians!"

"You never want to have fun," Luther whined. "You
spend all your time *thinking*."

"We didn't join this expedition for fun."

"We don't have to get drunk. Just one drink. You can
have one lousy drink with us."

Hugh refused again, and this time Luther turned on
his heel and marched back down the hill purposefully. He
joined Dexter and they drifted out of sight. Hugh had the
uneasy feeling he should have gone along. It reminded
him of all the times in the past he'd rejected his younger
brother's efforts to be buddies. He wondered if he had
made Luther angry enough to go on a binge; started
to go after him, then thought better of it. The damage
was done and besides, he was not his brother's keeper.
It was a role he had tried to fill on the trip but with
every mile they traveled, he became more aware of the
futility of trying to control or even influence his brother,
for his efforts only increased Luther's resentment of
his authority. Had he realized how immature and bull-
headed Luther was, he would not have taken him along,
Hugh decided, but in the same breath told himself the
pioneering experience might yet make a man of Luther.

Of one thing Hugh was certain. Caleb Dexter was
not going to be a good influence on his brother. They
had picked up the old man in Hill City, and their first
sight of him, holed up in a buffalo robe in an abandoned

cabin, nursing a jug and as rank as a hibernating bear, should have convinced them he was not fit company for civilized people. But it seemed only decent to see if the old man needed any help, and before they knew it he had latched onto their party. It seemed he had been on a solitary prospecting trip when the Indians ran off his burro and almost got what little hair remained on his scalp. When he made it back to Hill City, he found the town abandoned, so he'd holed up with his cache of jugs to wait for the next party to come along and transport him to the new diggings.

He wheedled his way into their party with offers of chaws of tobacco, snorts of his jug, and stories of his adventures in the gold camps of the West. He had been to them all, Cherry Creek in '58, the Comstock in '59, and Alder Gulch since '63, from which infamous diggings he proudly displayed his good luck charm — a gold nugget as big as a tooth. He certainly looked like he'd been long on the trail. His mangy, graying beard almost covered his shirt, which appeared to be the top half of a set of once-red flannel underwear; his baggy pants were so patched with buckskin it was difficult to determine their original fabric; and his knee-high miner's boots had obviously seen years of wading in creeks and mud. Under their craggy brows, his eyes were bloodshot and crafty.

His odor was beyond description. Hugh doubted if the old man had bathed since leaving the California gold rush of '49.

It seemed the old man had been to every gold field there ever was, and knew everything there was to know about gold mining. He talked about flour gold, specimen gold, and conglomerate gold, the technical details of underground mining and hydraulic operations and capital investment, but he always returned to tell of the magic lure of *Poor Man's Gold*, that beautiful bonanza of nuggets just waiting to be picked up.

The men shook their heads in wonder as the old man talked. It was obvious there was a great deal more to mining gold than any of them had realized. Hugh saw that himself, but he didn't know if it justified what Jake did. He invited Caleb Dexter to travel with them; agreed, in fact, to haul his pack and remaining jugs for nothing. Luther was delighted, being somehow fascinated with him, but Hugh had great reservations. He wondered aloud why if the old man knew so much about finding gold, he had never struck it rich and was answered with tales of fortunes made and lost and hints of secret stores of wealth in eastern banks.

"Besides, it's the gold fever," the old man concluded. "Once the gold bug bites you, you got to keep searching; no matter how much you've got socked away. It's the thrill of the thing, searching for the big strike, always hoping to find the mother lode!"

The explanation didn't settle Hugh's doubts, but the decision was Jake's. Now as Hugh sat looking over the camp, he wondered again if Caleb Dexter's knowledge would be worth the trouble of having the old man along. His fears were confirmed an hour later when, as he spread his bedroll by the dying campfire, Luther came staggering up, obviously drunk. Hugh was annoyed, but he kept silent. The damage was done and in a way it was his fault for not going along to keep Luther in line.

Luther sat down on his pile of bedding and, grinning foolishly, attempted to remove his boots.

"Need some help, little brother?" Hugh felt a touch of tenderness at his brother's helpless condition.

"Don't 'little brother' me" Luther said in a thick voice, "I'm as much a man as you!"

The comment annoyed Hugh, but he decided it was not worth answering. Luther, apparently sensed he had overreacted and, not able to manage the boot alone, thrust his foot out in a conciliatory gesture.

"Okay, Hugh, if you want to give me a hand, I am jus' a little bit, let's say worn out from the trail!"

Hugh helped him out of his boots, and Luther studied them sadly before using them for a pillow under the head of his tarp.

"Poor boots, all ruined. Thas' the first thing I'm gonna do when we strike it rich. Buy me some new boots." He struggled to remove his belt and then gave up, curled up on the canvas and pulled his blankets over him. "You shud of come along. Me and my old pardner, Caleb Dexter, Jus' had ourselves the best old time.'

"I can see that."

"I knew you'd be mad," Luther said. "You an' Emmet Hobart are always telling people what to do. But I'm going to show you both a thing or two one of these days."

"Sure you are," Hugh took off his own boots. "Now get some sleep or you'll be sick in the morning!"

"Already feel a little funny."

Serves you right, Hugh stifled the urge to say it aloud.

Just as Hugh was arranging his own bedding, Hobart came by on his evening rounds. "You boys got guard duty tonight?"

"Not tonight," Hugh wished Hobart would not call them *boys*, and hoped Hobart would not notice Luther's condition.

"Well, keep your rifles close by anyway."

"Sure thing, Mr. Hobart. Whatever you say, Mr. Hobart" Luther muttered, rising long enough to pat the rifle at his side.

"I see you and Caleb killed another jug." Hobart said with a trace of humor in his voice.

"Wasn't a jug, it wuz a flask," Luther mumbled. "Flasks is easier when you're out prospecting."

"A flask then!

"You want to make something of it?" Luther whined.

"Not at all. It's a man's own business if he wants to get drunk. Just stopped by to remind you about the Indians!

"Don't you worry about us. We're alert as hell!"

Hobart grinned and walked away.

"It's a good thing he didn't want to make nothing of it," Luther told Hugh, "I'm too tired to take him tonight. Besides, I think I'm gonna be sick." He began to vomit.

Hugh moved away in disgust spreading his bedding about halfway between Luther's snoring form and the Lewis wagon. He usually avoided sleeping near the wagon Molly shared with Jake. It had been miserable on those rainy nights he and Luther had slept under the wagon, but somehow tonight he took a morose pleasure in being near her. He lay awake, almost savoring his loneliness, and then was startled to notice a figure coming through the darkness toward him. Instantly he was alert. He recognized the lean and slightly stooped figure. "Jake?"

"That you, Hugh?"Jake whispered. "Sorry if I woke you. I've got the dysentery. I'll probably be out in the bushes half the night. Where's Luther?"

"Over there," Hugh pointed.

"Snoring got to you, huh? He'll be sawing wood after what him and Caleb Dexter was up to." Jake climbed into the wagon.

Lord, Hugh thought, *please let me sleep.* He had a hard time getting to sleep and realized he actually missed the sound of Luther's snores, a sound he'd grown accustomed to in the years he'd shared a bedroom with his brother. Jake disturbed him coming and going on another trip to the bushes and finally Hugh picked up his blankets again and moved away from the Lewis wagon and back to his brother's side.

He was finally sleeping soundly when, as if from far away, he heard Luther's voice and felt a jerk at his shoulder. He was certain he must be dreaming, but he could hear Luther saying, "Wake up!" His eyelids flickered open. It was near dawn. There was just enough light to make shapes barely discernable.

"Hugh, wake up! There's somebody sneaking around in the bushes. Must be Indians."

"Indians!" Hugh raised up on one shoulder, trying to force sleep away. His heart began to hammer and his eyes searched the dim light appearing at the edge of camp as the sun rose. There was a figure there all right.

He was reaching for his own rifle when he realized who it was. He turned to Luther. Couldn't he see? Was he still drunk?

Luther stood erect, his rifle raised to his shoulder, taking careful aim.

He was about to shoot Jake Lewis.

CHAPTER FOURTEEN

Austin Avery had decided not to gamble at the Railroad House that evening. Though it was Cheyenne's largest hotel, it was never a good policy to work the hotel where you boarded. He tossed a coin to decide between the American House and the Inter-Ocean Hotel and was pleased when the Inter-Ocean won. The American House catered to the tenting crowd, and there would be more action and news of the Black Hills, but the Inter-Ocean featured fresh oysters and he needed to replenish his vital juices.

Emerald had been especially amusing that day. Of course, she could become a problem if her willfulness and pouting persisted, but so far her little shows of temper had merely served to whet his appetite. His impulse to take her along had certainly proven auspicious, he decided, but then things generally went in his favor when he trusted his instincts. Taking a chance on Emma O'Brien had been an excellent move. The girls available in gold camps were so often diseased. Enjoying their services was not worth the risk. He had seen enough disease to last him a lifetime, but it was difficult and unhealthy for a man of his capacities to abstain for long periods of time. He had learned that lesson well at Alder Gulch and thus far, his traveling companion had been well worth the trouble and expense of bringing her along. He had chosen well. He had known she was the one the moment he entered her shop and saw her posing before the mirror, a shop girl with the reflection of a courtesan.

Of course she could become a problem with all that talk about marriage and returning to his old family plantation. He had been a bit startled when she first mentioned the plantation one night when he was lying in bed smoking a cheroot. He had almost forgotten telling her the plantation story. He had so many stories. Still, it was satisfying to him that she had so thoroughly accepted him as a Southern gentleman, even a plantation owner. It went well with the name, he had to admit. Austin Avery, a fine old name, much better than the one he had used in Alder Gulch. And he needn't feel guilty about using it. It belonged to no one else. It was his. He had made it up himself.

He couldn't have fooled a real lady, of course. He knew enough about the Southern aristocracy to be sure of that. Nor would Emerald O'Brien ever be a real lady. But, decked out in the finery he had provided for her, she looked enough a lady to enhance his own appearance. She was, in fact, startlingly beautiful. Perhaps more beautiful than was necessary and perhaps more spirited, too. But he could handle her and he would never reveal his hand where she was concerned, not about the past nor the present. A man must be in control of his emotions. If he ever let a woman know how much he needed her, she would win something precious away from him: his independence, his spirit, perhaps his very manhood.

Emma had her faults, he told himself, almost wishing there were more to enumerate. He liked a woman who had enough faults so that he could leave her with neither loss nor guilt, because she laughed too loud or got drunk in public or did not accommodate his physical needs adequately. But Emerald was beautiful, didn't drink, and was charming and agreeable in bed. He had to do some thinking to decide on the ways Emerald annoyed him: She was preoccupied with her own appearance. She had the annoying habit of always reaching out to touch his face or sleeve in a way that sometimes flattered him but at other times seemed wifely and demanding. And she was certainly not the best audience he ever had!

She was far too concerned with her own performance

to be totally engrossed in his, though she did seem to instinctively say, "Poor Austin" or "Brave Austin" at the right moments when he told her his war stories. She thought he had fought gallantly to preserve and protect the bonnie blue flag. He enjoyed spinning the illusion for her as he enjoyed all the illusions he had built for himself. He did not dare play the hero when he was working. He too often found himself sitting across the gaming table from a real war hero.

Seeing himself reflected and glowing in her eyes, while he told her how he had fought Sherman's army in hand-to-hand combat made those war years seem glorious. Not that he thought the war had been a wasted effort. He had learned a great deal in the war. Neither entering the army nor becoming the general's orderly had been entirely his idea but once there, he had used his time well. For as he polished the general's boots, and served the general's meals, and held the general's horse; he had observed those affectations of speech, dress, and manners that marked the Southern gentleman. And he had learned one more thing, the most important thing. In the evenings, the general and the other officers amused themselves at cards. Gambling and gaming had never been allowed in his own home, squalid though it was, for his family had religion, but the reality of war soon got him over fears of eternal damnation. There was enough hell on earth. He was fascinated with cards, and he learned everything he could in the officers' tents. When he could slip away from his duties, he practiced his skills on the enlisted men. When the end of the war neared and conditions were difficult, he was able to provide himself with boots and rations and medicine when even some officers were doing without.

Some call gambling a sickness, but Avery knew that with him it was a talent. He had a natural genius for it. Perhaps he would have discovered it without the war, but more than likely he would have ended up as an overseer on some mediocre plantation. So the war had been fortunate indeed. Afterwards, of course, there had been a difficult period until he discovered those who had all the money, the Yankees and the carpet baggers, were anxious to increase their unholy gains at someone else's expense, particularly someone they thought to be a real Southern gentleman. He enjoyed taking their money. But, as he told Emerald, he would never be able to take another's money if that man had not first tried to get something without working for it. As a professional gambler, he told her, he was more honest and upright than the casual gambler. He worked for what he won.

He successfully made the transition from playing poker or shooting craps on the floor of a ragged army tent to dealing faro in the most splendid gambling parlors of New Orleans. From there, it was a natural step to work the Mississippi river boats. On one of his upriver journeys he had, purely on a whim, left the river and made the dangerous overland journey up the Bozeman trail to Montana and the notorious gold camp of Alder Gulch. The gold camp lacked certain of the Mississippi's conveniences, but having once been there, having once seen thousands of dollars worth of gold dust change hands over the gaming tables as casually as if it was the sawdust on the floors, having seen men made and men broken on the twist of a gold vein or the spin of a roulette wheel, he had to go back. He had to be where the stakes were the highest, where the play went on night and day and at any moment someone might pull a gun and the game would end in death.

There was no old family plantation to win back. There was no other way of life. He could only go on to the next game. And if Emerald didn't like it, well then, he had no doubt he could find some man, respectable or otherwise, in Deadwood to take her off his hands. He might miss her but he was certain he would never let his lust for her grow into a need he could not control.

When he stepped out of the hotel onto Cheyenne's main street, he felt a surge of anticipation. The streets were crowded with men on their way to the Black Hills. Stage coaches left almost daily for Fort Laramie where the passengers joined freight outfits to complete the journey. The route was dangerous, but as more left for the area, the danger was reduced. It was not danger that caused him to linger in Cheyenne. It was, as he told Emerald, that there were easier ways to get gold than to dig for it.

First come the miners to work in the mine, and then come the girls that work on the line.

Avery recited to himself the ditty sung in every gold camp since '49. He had made up another line to the verse:

And then comes Austin Avery to make it all mine

He did not let his pleasure show, although his little rhyme pleased him, as did the way the roughly dressed men in the street stepped around him. Not that he was a gun fighter. There were those to whom killing was an addiction and gambling just a way to pass the time until the next draw. But, although he wore saloon pistols in his belt and enjoyed commanding respect, to Austin Avery the guns were only tools of his trade, or his art, for to him gambling was a profession. Not exactly a gentleman's trade, but not a bad ending for a Cracker farm boy.

He stopped at the door to the Inter-Ocean. There was music and bright lights and excitement within. It was time to go to work. It made him happy. He was not a man to whistle or hum aloud. He made an art of keeping his expression impassive, but sometimes on the inside his thoughts ran wild, and he would tell himself little jokes or recite verses. Now he recalled the words of 'The Bonnie Blue flag':

> *We are a band of brothers, and native to the soil,*
> *Fighting for the property, ours by honest toil.*

Austin Avery had another thought as he pushed open the doors of the hotel and it almost made him smile: *It was time for a little honest toil.*

CHAPTER FIFTEEN

He had hesitated. For a long time afterwards whenever he would think about what had happened that morning in the camp beyond Custer City, and he would think about it often, Hugh would have to remember that he hesitated.

Later, he tried to tell himself it had been for only an instant and he had, after all, been half asleep when Luther shouted *Indians!* Hugh told himself he had to take time to be certain it wasn't an Indian, even though he knew Jake Lewis had been making trips back and forth to the bushes all night.

But when he got through all that, when he had made every excuse for himself he could, he had to face the fact he had hesitated because of his first, awful thought. *He's going to kill Jake. Luther is going to kill Jake and I can have Molly!*

And so, no matter how many times he told himself he had pushed the thought away the moment it came, that he had replaced it at once with the image of Jake his friend and the man Edwin called father; still he had known that instant of relief at the thought his brother was going to eliminate his rival.

He had hit Luther low, somewhere between his groin and knees, swinging his own body from a sitting position into a quick lunge with his shoulders that knocked his brother off his feet. The shot boomed out almost simultaneously with the moment his body collided with Luther's so that as they landed on the ground together, Hugh thought he had acted too late.

"What the hell?" Luther said from beneath him.

"Fool! You damn fool!"

Luther tried to break away from him and managed to grab his rifle again. "It's Indians, Hugh. Quick!"

"It was Jake." Hugh held him down and spoke into his ear. "You've shot Jake Lewis."

Luther turned and blinked at Hugh, suddenly sober. Shouts and footsteps surrounded them as men fell out of their wagons, half-dressed and waving their rifles.

"Who the hell's shooting?" A familiar voice boomed.

Not sure if it was his brother or himself he'd called *fool*, Hugh looked up. The moon had risen and he could see clearly. It was Jake standing there in his long underwear and boots, his beard and hair wild, his face showing a mixture of fear and anger.

"Who shot at me?"

Hugh let out his breath in relief and almost hugged Luther, now hanging limp in his arms.

"What's the shooting about?" Emmet Hobart demanded as he joined the group surrounding them. "Who fired that shot?"

Hugh waited for Luther to speak up but his brother just stared dumbly at Jake, one hand still clutching his rifle.

"I thought you was an Indian, Jake," Luther sobbed. "I heard something, and I woke up and I could see someone in the bushes and I thought it was an Indian."

"I was relieving myself."

"Oh my God," Luther moaned, rocking back and forth. "Oh my sweet Jesus, I thought I was saving us all and I almost killed you, and after all you've done for us!"

"Holy Mother of God!" another familiar voice boomed as Donnelly walked up laughing. "What a bunch!"

"Damn it, Jake," Luther moaned, hanging his head. "I would have killed you but Hugh ran into me and stopped me."

It was then Hugh first remembered that he had hesitated. He had almost let Luther kill Jake. He stood unmoving before his brother, knowing he should speak words of forgiveness, but his own guilt was too great. It was Jake who reached down to offer Luther his hand to help him up.

"It was a mistake. No harm done. I shouldn't have been in the bushes, but I been sick."

But Luther turned away from Jake's outstretched hand and remained on the ground, moaning "Oh my God" over and over. Hugh was embarrassed for Luther, lying there crying for everyone to see. By this time the whole camp had gathered around them. Molly broke through the crowd and hugged Jake. She had pulled a quilt around herself, but Hugh was aware of her nightdress beneath and her hair hanging loose around her face. He tried not to look at her.

The other men began to shift around uncomfortably. Donnelly was still laughing, "Man goes out to the bushes and almost gets shot. That would be a fine way to die, with your pants down!"

"Shut up."

"What?" Donnelly looked surprised. He was a big man, and mostly people took his jokes.

"I said shut up" Hugh made the words cold and hard. "Just let it drop."

Donnelly wiped his nose with the back of his hand, sheepishly, backing off a little from Hugh's anger. He looked around the group grinning, seeking approval.

"No need to get yourself in a tizzy. I was just making a bit of a joke to take the wife's mind off her troubles." Donnelly's eyes darted between Molly and Jake, still grinning. "It wouldn't be the first time some man got himself shot with his pants down. Am I right?"

Hugh's fist shot out. He saw Donnelly's shock as his face crumpled and he fell back into the crowd. Somebody caught him and he came up fighting, but Hugh was ready for him. Hugh's blood was up. He felt happy. He was going to kick the stuffing out of Donnelly, bloody his whole damn grinning face and knock his teeth down his throat.

Donnelly feinted and when Hugh swung, the Irishman got in a blow to the belly that almost knocked the breath out of Hugh. He realized, too late, Donnelly must have been a prize fighter, but Hugh wasn't afraid. He was conscious of Molly somewhere in the crowd and had to redeem himself in her eyes. He and the Irishman circled each other warily, fists in position until Hugh charged and began raining blows on Donnelly, oblivious to the beating he was himself taking. It felt as good to be hit as to hit. Then he was aware of other stronger arms around him. He was being pulled off Donnelly.

"Break It up!" It was Hobart's voice in his ear. "Break this up. Save it for the Sioux."

"Let me go!" Hugh tried to pull away from Hobart.

"What's with you, Hugh? Everything's okay. No harm done. Donnelly just made one of his jokes."

Hugh managed to jerk away from Hobart. He stood apart from the others a moment, still ready to fight. But Jake stepped between Hugh and Donnelly.

"It's all right, Hugh. He didn't mean anything by it. What's got into you?"

Hugh looked from Jake to where Donnelly stood, nursing his fist and looking as if he didn't understand what had happened. Hugh knew the Irishman had no grudge to pick with him, knew there was no reason for it but still had the urge to get in another punch.

"Please, Hugh," Molly spoke and he knew he had not won her respect with his anger. He had made things worse. He was worse than Luther. He had pledged his honor to her, but once again he'd been an animal, and now the whole camp was staring at him. The fight drained out of him. The only thing left to do was face up to it like a man. He apologized and shook hands with Donnelly; no one spoke of the incident again, but Hugh could not forget it. Worse than Molly's tears, the accusing looks of the other men, or Luther's sobbing apologies, was realizing the power for destruction that was within his own heart.

It took them nearly two weeks to make the journey to Deadwood, a distance of perhaps fifty miles. Donnelly had not been this far into the Hills, but they no longer needed a guide, for the trail followed the deep wagon ruts left by the Custer Expedition of'74, and even when it left the "Thieves Trail" the country had been forever scarred by the miners as they stampeded to the new diggings. The road was difficult and slow at best. At its worst, it seemed impossible. Trees had been cut down but the stumps remained. In some places the miners had used blasting powder to blow rocky outcroppings to bits, but in other places, the wagons had to be navigated around huge boulders. Always their desire for speed had to be tempered by the need to preserve the wagons. A broken axle would mean hours of delay. They crossed and re-crossed Spring Creek as it wound its way into the Hills. At one crossing, a wagon became mired and they lost hours pulling it out.

Despite their difficulties, the journey was not as tedious as the miles from Sidney to the Black Hills. Now each bend of the constantly winding road held the promise of the unknown. Hugh thought he knew how Adam must have felt in Eden, and he suspected some of the other men shared his sense of wonder because the grumbling and quarrelling ceased. The country was lush, fresh, and new, a wilderness unmarked by man except for the road they followed and widened.

The trail seemed to be always winding upwards. As they moved deeper into the craggy shelter of the inner hills, they were no longer so wary of Indian attack, but the trail seemed to be increasingly difficult, sometimes so steep Hugh and the other men on foot had to pull on ropes attached to the wagons to aid the weary mules. Then upon reaching the summit, they would lean back on the ropes to keep wagons from over-running the mules. Hugh marveled time and again at Jake's skill with mules. In descending, he reined them back until their chins touched the breastplates of their harnesses and they leaned back against the tongue, descending with short, sure steps.

Finally they crossed several miles of highland which formed the divide between Spring Creek and the next stream. They no longer knew the names of the streams they crossed or of any other landmarks. In every meadow they came upon deer so innocent of man they did not run away. Hobart rescinded the order against hunting and several men, including Hugh and Luther, took up the sport. Hugh thrilled at killing his first buck, but after days of killing and gorging on the fresh meat, throwing away less-choice cuts because there wasn't time to make jerky, he felt sick at the waste. He realized if the parties ahead and behind them slaughtered as many deer, even this last refuge of the Indians would soon have as little wildlife as the plains they had left behind. No one seemed to share his concern. He felt Molly would understand, but he was avoiding any serious conversation with her. He kept to himself.

There was a great deal of excitement early one morning when Morris came upon a bear and killed it. Jake judged it must have dressed out to as much meat as a cow; when the meat was passed around, the men said it tasted as good as beef. Morris rolled up the lushly furred bear hide and carried it in his wagon, declaring he would make a robe of it, but after several days it began to smell, so he dumped it over a bluff. Hugh looked down at the gleaming fur rotting there and was sorry for the slaughter of the bear.

When they crossed the second creek and camped on the north bank beside the blackened coals of previous campfires, Luther found a military collar button and a broken horseshoe from a cavalry pony. Donnelly said General Crook had likely camped there as he sought the Sioux. Everyone was glad the military had been through the area. They speculated as to where the army was and, as their wagons further invaded Sioux territory, wondered if they did encounter troops, would they be protected or turned back.

As they crossed more small creeks, the road grew so rough some wondered if they were still on the right path. Stumps crowded a trail hacked out just wide enough to let the wagons pass single file. Once again they began to climb. The road grew worse with each step. It was as if those before them, knowing they were close to their destination, had abandoned all effort to make a trail and clamored over the mountain top with no thought to those who would follow. *And why should they?* Hugh thought. The truth was they all came not to settle but to compete for the plunder.

At last, early one morning, they reached the summit and looked over the edge and knew somewhere in the gulch beneath them, clinging to the banks of Whitewood Creek and hidden in the pines, was Deadwood.

To descend the cliff-like slope by wagon seemed impossible; yet they knew it had been done, for at the bottom of the divide they could see both the skeletons of broken wagons and a trail heading on. The trees along the trail bore evidence of how the descent had been made. Wide bands of bark had been torn from their trunks as the ropes which had girded them were used to lower the wagons inch by painful inch. The men agreed it would be just about impossible to get the wagons down. And then, since there was nothing else to do, they unhitched the mules, and girding fresh trees with ropes, did what had to be done.

When they finished, sweaty and exhausted they looked back up the rocky slope, marveling at its size. Hobart spat and said now he knew why no one had come back from the new diggings. It was just barely possible to get down to Deadwood, but no one could get back out. They passed the joke around the group, savoring their accomplishment.

Hugh looked around at the whiskery faces of his traveling companions as they sucked at the new blisters on their hands and surveyed the mountain they had conquered. They all wore the same look of tired satisfaction, and Hugh felt that for the first, and the last time, on the journey they had all worked as a team. It was late afternoon and within an hour they would enter Deadwood, and their adventure together would end. In Deadwood each man would stand alone. Without anyone noticing that it was happening The Hobart Party to the Black Hills would disband.

Luther had been subdued since sounding the nearly fatal false alarm about the Indians. Hugh noticed he pulled more than his share in the back-breaking job of helping the wagons up and down the steep slopes. It was Hobart, however, who took the time to acknowledge Luther's efforts when they parted with a handshake and a word of praise. Luther blinked rapidly and for once, Hugh was proud of his brother.

They did not take long to rest from their ordeal; the trail to Deadwood beckoned. It was no problem to follow it as it moved along the gulch. It could not have been called a valley by any stretch of the imagination, for thickly timbered mountains rose on either side. The summits to the left were capped by towering white stones, while the outcroppings on the right were less rugged brown boulders. The creek the trail followed, which they assumed to be the Whitewood, had taken centuries to cut out even this narrow gully between the mountains. It seemed impossible a city could be growing in the cleft between the rugged slopes; yet they knew they were close to their goal.

Trees lined both sides of the trail. Hugh recognized white birch and quaking aspen as well as pine and spruce. The timber was thick, but as they progressed farther into the gulch, they came upon more fallen and rotting logs, the dead wood which gave the area its name. It was impossible to tell whether the trees had fallen to fire or disease.

Unlike the sparkling streams of their earlier journey, the creek they followed became increasingly muddy and disturbed. The reason was soon evident as they came across the first drainage ditches and crude sluice boxes; the creek was being diverted all along its course to wash the placer gold from the gravel.

Each set of drainage ditches and sluice boxes was guarded by a shack or cabin, and as the cabins grew thicker, Hugh wondered where everyone was. The cabins seemed unoccupied; no one was working the placer mines along the creek. Hugh calculated it was Sunday and wondered if the miners were in town, but it seemed unlikely they would be attending services. Surely they would not find that Deadwood, too, had been abandoned.

They heard the town before they saw it. First there was the sound of blasting or perhaps gunfire, distant and sporadic, then the recognizable whine of a saw mill and the rhythmic beat of hammers hitting wood. The crisp mountain air of the canyon gave way to pungent odors of chimney and campfires, road dust, manure and out-houses. They came around a bend in the road and suddenly the trail was crowded on either side with cabins. They saw one miner, then two, then a dozen,

As the wagons slowly progressed they were on a road which grew more crowded until there was only room enough for one line of traffic in either direction. The Hobart Party was quickly engulfed in the stream of horsemen and wagons. Men on foot darted between the wagons, and crowds lined the road on either side. Hugh realized Sunday must be the day the miners left their diggings to conduct their business in town. Seeing so much humanity was a shock after days in the silent wilderness. Now the road become a street lined so closely on both sides by brush shanties, dugouts, cabins, tents, and frame buildings in various stages of construction, that they seemed to touch, even lean on one another.

Hobart used his pistol to fire several shots into the air to mark their arrival. Luther copied their wagon master, and Hugh would have added his fire to the confusion, but a glance told him Molly was not enjoying the celebration, and even Jake was struggling with the frightened mules. Further shots would have been lost in the commotion anyway.

Everywhere men were sawing and hammering, surrounding the log cabins of the previous winter with siding of green pine, nailed in place as fast as the wood could be hauled from the sawmills. The cluster of cabins at the heart of town wore false fronts, suggesting two story buildings. Even as they passed, another front labeled 'Saloon" was raised. The road, now a street, consisted of a line of saloons. Other buildings, built too late to be fitted in along the street, were built clinging precariously to both hillsides of the narrow gulch, many of the log and frame buildings already sprouting second floors reached by narrow outside stairways.

An occasional pine tree still stood in the midst of the newly-hewn town, solitary reminders of man's making a forest into a mining camp. Evidence of mining was everywhere: piles of rubble, overturned sluice boxes, even buildings jacked up and set on stilts so the miners could tunnel beneath them to follow the vein.

Hugh marveled at the progress. Deadwood was a beehive of activity. Even the air, smoky and dusty as it was after the clear air of the trail, seemed charged with excitement. Banjo music and laughter escaped the saloons, and once Hugh thought he heard a piano, although it seemed impossible one had been freighted down that terrible hill. He estimated there were two or three thousand men in Deadwood that day. He tried to notice everything so he could record it later in his journal. He figured the city extended nearly a mile along the creek and contained at least two hundred buildings. The streets were littered with miners in various stages of drunkenness. They rubbed elbows with dandies in frock coats. There were Orientals too; men set apart from the crowd by their race and their willingness to do the washing and the cooking, work beneath the dignity of white men. There were few women. The respectable ones wore worried expressions; the others wore painted smiles.

Hugh took it all in. He breathed deeply of the fresh, raw smell of the place. He tried to sort out the voices and the banjo music from the pounding of the hammers and the squeaking of the rolling wheels and saddle leathers and the grunts of oxen and men. He wondered what was behind the false fronts of the buildings and he stared at the people, the miners, the gamblers, and the whores. He loved it.

He had actually done it. He was in Deadwood and it was both a hundred times better and worse than expected. The very air promised adventure. Hugh was charged with excitement. His breathing came fast. His manhood had risen and for once he was not ashamed. He lusted for his chance to conquer this raw, uncivilized city, to stake his claim and fight to win something from it. It was Poor Man's Gold, painted women and his terrible need for Molly all at once, but it went beyond any of the things he knew or understood. It was like the challenge of the stallion or the bull elk about to claim his territorial privileges. It was a feeling unlike any he had known before.

And Deadwood had brought it to him.

CHAPTER SIXTEEN

It was a terrible place. Never in her worst imaginings had Molly dreamed Deadwood would be so awful. For years she had looked out the tiny window of the sod house and seen vast, open fields meeting the sky low on the horizon. The openness of Iowa had seemed lonely to her then, but as Jake's wagon drove into Deadwood, the mountains on either side of the gulch and the buildings crowded together, like something Edwin would build with blocks, not to mention the swarming hoard of the worst kind of people one could imagine, all seemed to be closing in on her.

She could not believe this was their destination. She had pictured a city like Custer, or any other, set in a parkland. She had expected to come around a bend in the road, see the mountains drop away, and there before her a lovely valley with a city all laid out nice and proper. But it wasn't that way at all. Molly held Edwin close to her on the wagon seat. He was straining his neck to see, looking from one side of the road to the other, but everywhere they looked it was the same, cabins and shacks and buildings framed of green lumber, the purpose of at least half of them even more degenerate than their haphazard construction.

It was all so raw. It looked as if the whole city had been thrown up over night. Every other building was a saloon or worse. Wherever a narrow gap existed between buildings, a mountain of refuse filled the empty space. On the whole drive through town, she saw only one other woman who looked respectable, and her face was full of the anguish Molly was feeling. She tugged at Jake's sleeve to see if he shared her despair.

"Ain't it great?" he said, more to the mules than to her. "Ain't it exciting?"

He looked happier than she had ever seen him. She bit her lip. No use trying to talk to him. It was too noisy anyway. She could not imagine people discharging firearms right on the streets just for the fun of it. Fortunately the poor mules were getting too tired to react, but she held Edwin close, her poor little boy.

"Ain't it great, Ma?" Edwin sounded just like Jake. "Did you see that lady? Did you see her dress? Don't you wish you had a dress like that? And her face was all white and beautiful!"

"Edwin!" Such women had never walked the streets so brazenly in Pennsylvania or even in Iowa. But it didn't matter because Edwin was already looking in the other direction. "There's a man with a pigtail. Is he a Chinaman? Pa, why are all those men sleeping on that wagon?"

"They're drunk," Jake answered cheerfully and Molly realized he didn't care.

"How can they sleep with all that shooting going on? Can we shoot your rifle, Pa? How come there aren't any sidewalks and why are all the houses so close together and where are we going to live? I hope we don't have to live in one of those places."

Molly followed Edwin's gaze. The building was long and narrow, the front consisting of a line of doors. The rooms must be like stalls, Molly thought and then gasped as she realized what went on behind the doors. Half the town was whorehouses and saloons. And everyone seemed delighted about it. Everyone but her. Molly pulled her shawl closer around her. The sun was already low in the sky. They had better hurry and find a place to camp. She was sure they could not afford a hotel, even if there should be a decent one.

The men seemed blind to the squalor. One could have anticipated an old reprobate like Caleb Dexter would be in his element, but she had been shocked at the way the others had accepted his crudeness as they passed through

Chinatown. Almost every doorway in that area a bore the legend "Washee House," and Hugh had remarked at the number of laundries. The old man had laughed and pointed out that before each of the curtained doorways was a yellow-skinned woman.

"*Daughters of Joy*," he exclaimed.

"Daughters of Joy?" Luther asked, not getting it.

"Sure," the old man boomed. "The Chinamen got pretty names for 'em, Daughters of joy and Celestial Females, but let's face it, Luther, a miner goes to a Chinese laundry to get his wash done, and to a *Washee House* when he needs something else done!"

The men were all hooting with laughter before Molly got the joke. Her emotions went from embarrassment to concern. She knew many men had powerful needs, but in decent society such things were unspoken. Now a terrible thought struck her. She had aroused Hugh's passions. What if he visited such a place? The thought made her miserable. Even as Molly's uneasiness grew, the men seemed to become more jubilant. She wondered why the men did not notice the faces of the men she saw on the street, faces which were like Jake's when he talked about poor man's gold, but were also tinged with worry and discouragement.

Not everyone in Deadwood was lucky, but only Molly seemed to sense this; she did not transmit her fear to her husband. Jake was happy; she would do nothing to discourage him. She told herself that this time they would be among the lucky ones.

After they passed through the settlement, the road became a trail again, continuing up the gulch. On either side of it, the ground was pockmarked with exploration holes. They saw that some miners had begun to sink shafts, but most still worked the surface. It was like the scene of some terrible disaster; the trees struck down at random angles as in a tornado; the white splinters of their trunks gleaming in the last of the sunlight.

With the clamor of Deadwood behind them, the quiet of the trail seemed strange, as was their increasing aloneness. The Hobart party had dispersed along the way in two's and three's without saying goodbyes. Finally only the Lewis family, Caleb Dexter, Luther and Hugh remained. The men had agreed earlier to explore the Deadwood prospects together. Now, Molly wondered how much longer she would have the reassurance of Hugh's presence.

At last they found a bit of level ground and made a camp of sorts. Molly was starting to make dinner when the air turned cool and she turned and realized the afternoon sun had disappeared behind the mountain. There would be no purple twilights and orange sunsets in this canyon. The air was cold and sharp with the pungent scent of pine. She couldn't help shivering.

And then she heard the cry.

"Oh, Joe!"

At first it seemed hardly human. The mournful cry echoing up the canyon. Then it came again. It sounded like a cry for help. She grabbed Jake's arm. This time it was right behind her. She turned and saw Caleb Dexter, clutching a whiskey bottle, leaning back and wailing again, "Oh Joe!"

"What in heaven's name are you doing?"

The old man's grizzled face broke into a grin and he took a swig before answering her. "Why, just hollering, '*Oh, Joe!*' like the other prospectors. It's good to hear it again. Sure brings back memories. I figured they'd do it here too."

"Do what?"

"Holler 'Oh, Joe!' every night at sunset. They did it in Californy in '49 and in every gold camp since. It's an old gold diggers' custom. Shows who's an insider and who's a greenhorn."

"Can we do it too?" Edwin begged.

"Sure," Luther piped in. "We're insiders ain't we? We're in Deadwood in '76! That should count for something!"

"Well," the old man scratched his beard, "I guess you could figure it that way." He offered Luther the bottle. "Yep, I reckon you could figure since you're in Deadwood in '76, you could holler 'Oh, Joe!' just like the old timers."

Hugh got the bottle after Luther, took a quick drink and handed it back to Caleb Dexter asking, "Is there a reason?"

"Sure is. The story is some miner came home drunk one night and fell in a prospect hole. He spent the night hollering for his partner, a guy named Joe, to get him out!" Caleb reached for the bottle, but Luther took it again, put down another shot, leaned back and bellowed until the hills rang with it, "Ohhhhhhh, Joeeeeeee!"

"Oh, Joe! Oh, Joe! OH JOE!" It was Edwin.

Before Molly could stop him, he climbed up on the wagon seat to screech it out a dozen more times. At last even Jake and Hugh joined in. And every time one of them shouted, a dozen more cries echoing and re-echoing up the gulch.

Molly sat down on a rotten log and started to laugh. The men laughed with her. She hoped they didn't notice when her laughter changed to tears.

In the years of their marriage, Molly had learned to read Jake's mood and the next afternoon, she could tell the news was bad almost the moment she caught sight of him walking back from Deadwood. He didn't return her wave, but kept trudged along, his coat slung over his shoulder and his hat down against the afternoon sun.

"Daddy's coming!" Edwin squealed and ran to meet him. The mules on their picket lines looked up hopefully from their sparse grazing to watch him approach. Molly busied herself stirring her pot of ham and bean soup over the fire. *At least I have a good supper for him,* she thought. *I won't ask questions. I'll let him tell me.* He didn't come right out with it. He killed time hanging his coat on a wagon wheel, filling his pipe, sending Edwin off to pull some weeds for the mules to graze.

Finally she could stand it no longer. "Jake! Tell me! What did you find out?"

"Not much to tell." Tiredly he sat down on a log.

"What do you mean? Didn't you get a claim?"

"Didn't I *get* a claim? You think that's how it works. You think I just walk up to some office and ask for a claim, huh?"

It was obvious he'd had more than a little to drink. Molly stood before him and quieted herself, clenching her fists under her apron. Somewhere back in Deadwood someone was shooting again, she was almost used to it. Jake shook his head before he spoke.

"Every foot of land in this whole gulch belongs to someone. The good claims around the place they call 'Discovery' were taken up last winter; then when the big stampede came from Custer, everything else went overnight. Every damn foot. We're too late."

"Too late? With all this land? It can't all be claimed. How much land does it take for a gold mine, anyway?"

"The land's gone, Molly, All of it. We'd be lucky if we could buy a spot big enough to build a cabin. We're squatters on someone's land right now. They're throwing up some hotels, but we couldn't afford them."

"I thought everyone just went and panned gold at the creek. Can't we just pick up some nuggets?"

"You talk like Edwin!"

"I'm sorry," she said stiffly. "I don't know about gold. I thought you knew. I thought you knew what you were doing!" He looked like she'd hit him, but she couldn't stop. "What happened to this 'Poor Man's Gold' you're always talking about?"

He turned away, and once again, she held back tears. So Poor Man's Gold was just another dream. She would have to be brave. It was far from their first disappointment. She tried to think what to do next, though she knew that the decision was Jake's.

Jake said he might find work in Deadwood. Miners were being paid up to seven dollars a day, but prices were equally high. The mules were a problem. There was no grazing for them in the narrow gulch and feed was outrageously priced. Molly suggested it was best to sell the mules and wagon while they would still bring a fair price to those leaving Deadwod, but Jake pointed out they might need the outfit if they decided to go home themselves, and Molly could hold back her dispair no longer.

"Go home? We haven't any home."

As soon as she'd said it, she was sorry. Then she thought of something that hurt even more than realizing she was without a home. "What about Hugh and the others? What will they do?"

Jake allowed the boys might still have a chance. They could go out with Caleb Dexter to prospect in the hills. She asked why Jake could not do that also, knowing even as she asked that he could not leave her and Edwin alone in Deadwood. Jake also reminded her of the danger of prospecting. "You have to go in small parties and there's been a hell of a lot of miners scalped this spring."

"Then I don't want Hugh to go and . . ." her voice trailed off. She had said too much, but Jake didn't appear to notice. "And of course you can't take chances either."

"I guess the only thing to do is go on for wages," Jake concluded. He had accepted failure. He would be content to eke out a living, poorer than even homesteading, only now not even owning the land on which they slaved.

But Molly was not willing to settle for so little. If there was gold in Deadwood, she told herself, there must be a way to share in the wealth, and there must be a way to keep Hugh near her. The only alternative was to swallow her pride and write her parents, hoping they would send her tickets home to Pennsylvania. She dismissed the idea. She could not accept her family's charity, even if Jake would. He would be a defeated man. He would turn to drink..

She looked to her husband, hopeful he would think of a solution, but he was staring into the campfire, his eyes losing focus. She saw it would be up to her, and maybe to Hugh. She looked anxiously down the road where the others were still in Deadwood. Surely Hugh would think of something; together they could find a way.

Hugh was, in fact, trying desperately to think of a plan and wondering how all the promise of Deadwood had been snuffed out in just one day, but everywhere they turned, the answer was the same: *No*. People acted as if they were crazy even to ask about staking a claim. All the land was taken, unless you wanted to venture so far you had to prospect with a pick in one hand and a rifle in the other. Hugh was not afraid to do that, but it meant leaving Molly and Edwin. It would be difficult to leave them anywhere, anytime, but to leave them in such a precarious situation was untenable.

Jake was no help. They had gone their separate ways that morning, and when they met for a drink, Hugh could see immediately that Jake had given up. Jake and Caleb Dexter downed one whiskey after another until Hugh decided he had to get Jake home while he could still walk. Once he got him on the trail toward camp, Hugh returned to the saloon to make a plan. He would have no help. Luther and the old man sat staring into their glasses. Hugh finally said it seemed the best thing was to look for jobs.

"Hell, No!" Luther pounded the table. "The thing to do is head for the hills. Me and you and old Caleb Dexter will just go out prospecting with our trusty rifles; just us against the wilderness and the heathen Sioux!"

"I think it's better to stay here," Hugh said, intent both on staying near Molly and avoiding the old prospector. "Surely we can get some sort of work in one of the mines."

"Be a goddamn grubbing laborer?" Dexter roared. "No way! That's no life, grubbing away in the mud so the mine owner can get richer. Only life for a man is out staking your own claim." He drained his whiskey and stared into the empty glass philosophically. "Oh, it's not so bad buying into a claim, cause then you're still working for yourself, but the best way is out following the will-o'-the-wisp, striking out for your own bonanza, having the thrill of discovery."

"That's right," Luther burped. "That's real man stuff. Jus' the three of us against the whole Sioux Nation."

"Always moving on, never knowing what's over the next hill, Dexter rambled on until Hugh stopped him with a question, "What did you say about buying into a claim?" You mean you can *buy* a claim?"

"Sure you can if you got the money." Dexter looked at Hugh sagely. "But I don't suppose you do."

"How much would it take?" Hugh asked, fingering his belt where four twenty dollar gold pieces had been concealed since they left home.

"Oh, I reckon you could find a claim for a couple of hundred if you knew how to spot some outfit that was down on their luck and discouraged."

"But then it wouldn't be worth anything, would it?"

"Might or it might not. I reckon as there are lots of Greenhorns in this town don't know what they're sitting on. Folks as haven't been around like me, and figure if their gravel don't wash out much gold the first month or two, they don't have anything worth developing."

"But they might?" Hugh probed. "They might think their mine is no good and it might be worth something?"

"Could be," the old man yawned. He seemed to be feeling the effects of the day's drinking at last. "Could be a regular bonanza or could be worthless. That's the interesting thing about the gold mining business!"

Dexter put his head down on the table as if to go to sleep right there. Luther was watching with fascination at a large painting of a nude being hoisted above the makeshift bar. Hugh considered the matter. It was an important decision and he needed to use his head this time. Eighty dollars was all they had left in the world. It meant the risk of being really down and out in this godforsaken town or having to go back to Nebraska and listen to Phineas P. Crandall tell him what a fool he'd been to join the gold rush. He had Luther to think of. And eighty dollars wasn't nearly enough. He could probably talk Jake into selling his mules and wagon, but it still didn't add up.

He nudged the old man. "You got any money?"

"Sure, Drinks are on me," Dexter mumbled, without opening his eyes.

"No, I mean real money. Do you have any *capital*, like fifty or one hundred dollars?"

Dexter opened one eye and looked up at Hugh suspiciously. "Who wants to know?"

"I do. I was wondering if we happened to find a mine to invest in, if you would have enough for a share?"

"Could if I wanted to."

"You'd have enough cash? I mean you've collected enough dust since you've been in the Hills?"

The old prospector grinned toothlessly and made to

whisper in Hugh's ear. "I got my lucky nugget and a nice pouch of dust and I could buy me a share in any mine I wanted to." Here his voice became loud, "But I'd rather be out in the hills prospecting."

Having said his piece, the old man slipped back onto the table and began to snore. Hugh tried to sort it out. He didn't know how much of Caleb Dexter's company he could take. He didn't know if it was right to continue partnering with the husband of the woman he loved. In fact, he was pretty sure it was wrong. The whole scheme was crazy, but he couldn't see any other solution.

Hugh drained the last of his beer, sat back and groaned. It was either this or let Jake drag Molly and Edwin back to a life of poverty in a sod hut somewhere. Only now it would be worse for them because they had known hope. He couldn't let it happen to them; couldn't even rely on Jake to take care of them properly. He told himself his motives were pure: *to provide for Molly and his son.* He reached down and grabbed a hank of Caleb Dexter's hair and raised his head off the table.

"Wake up, partner," he said. "We're going out and find us a gold mine.

CHAPTER SEVENTEEN

"I'll be an old goat scroat if I didn't get us one hell of a fine gold mine!" Caleb Dexter declared, slapping the thigh of his filthy overalls, chawing a mouthful of tobacco and working up to a spit. *If he said that once, he said it a hundred times,* Hugh thought sourly, staring around the cramped little cabin in which they sat. *He's going to tell the whole damn story of how he got the mine again.* Why does he have to do this every single week? How long had it been going on? A month? Six weeks? Hugh had lost track of time, but it must be near the end of June.

"Yep, I'll be an old goat scroat if I didn't get us one hell of a fine gold mine!" The old man belched. He'd said it again. He'd actually said it again! Hugh stared at the point where Dexter's rooster-wattle neck wasn't covered by his grizzled gray beard or the top of the long-johns he wore for a shirt and had to stifle the urge to lunge across the table and choke the old man.

Molly looked strained but she kept smiling as she sat cups around the kitchen table and poured coffee into them. The smell of the coffee was almost enough to distract from the odor of Caleb Dexter, which confined in a small room was unbearable. It had not been a part of their partnership agreement for Molly to cook for the whole crew, and knowing she did not want the old prospector in her cabin, Hugh made it a point to discourage any invitations Jake extended for dinner, but it had somehow become a custom after their Saturday night clean up of the sluice boxes to share a plate of beans and bread together before dividing the week's dust.

And somehow it had also become a tradition of these Saturday nights that Caleb Dexter would tell again the story of how he had acquired the mine they optimistically named for their partnership, *The Lucky Six.*

Luther and Edwin gave Dexter their rapt attention from where they sat together on a crude log bench, the only furniture in the cabin in addition to the Lewis's double bed, Edwin's pallet, and the table and four chairs. The two never seemed to tire of the story.

"Well," the old man continued, finishing his coffee and spitting tobacco juice into his cup, "I hadn't moseyed around Deadwood for an hour before I knew exactly what was what. You can't fool an old goat like me. No sir, I been to Californy in '49 and I was at Cherry Creek in '58 and to the Comstock in '59, and Alder Gulch in '63, so I see pretty quick that the creek was cleaned out of nuggets and all the placer mines was taken up.

"Now a green hand," he continued, waving a piece of bread dipped in bean juice at Edwin, "A green hand like your papa and you boys here, you would have got discouraged and gone home or went out in the hills and got yourselves scalped trying to prospect. But me, Old Goat Caleb Dexter, why I wasn't in all those places for nothing. I know gold mining, partners. You remember that!"

The old man was looking at Hugh for approval, but he wasn't going to encourage the old reprobate who seemed to have forgotten that buying a mine had been Hugh's idea. Perhaps that was just as well, Hugh decided. It had been an uneasy partnership from the beginning; he'd as soon forget it had been his idea.

"So I says to myself, I says, Caleb Dexter, you old fart, there's more to mining gold than most folks know. Folks that wasn't there in '49 thinks you just go down to the creek and pan for nuggets and that's the only way. Don't know the finer points, like an old goat like me. Well, I knows, Edwin boy, I knows."

Edwin nodded. He never got tired of the story.

"So I just mosey around. I just go from one claim to another and I take off my hat and I carry it in front of me like a goddamn preacher, so they'll know I'm not out claim jumping, and I ask nice and polite how they're doin' and if they got any work for a laborer. Of course, I don't let on I was in Californy in '49, see? I don't let on I know all there is to know about mining gold, see? I just act dumb and if they're hiring, I ask a few questions but then I mosey on."

"Beats all." It was Jake's usual interjection.

"Cause I ain't lookin' for work, you get that?" Dexter leaned over and pinched Luther's shirt sleeve and winked conspiratorially. "I ain't really lookin' for work. I'm just reconnoitering."

He took a swig from his bottle, belched and went on. "So, if they looks like they're pretty happy, if it looks like they're cleaning up a lot of dust, and if they're hiring, I says I'll think it over, and I keeps moseying on cause I ain't lookin' for work and I ain't lookin' for happy miners. I'm lookin' for miners that are down and out and discouraged."

"And you found 'em!" Luther bellowed happily.

"And I found 'em! Sure enough. I found 'em!"

Again Dexter looked at Hugh for approval. This was supposed to be the best part of the story, but Hugh merely nodded. How could a man smell so bad, he wondered. And how could it be that only he and Molly seemed to notice? Maybe it had something to do with chewing tobacco. Jake and Luther had both taken up the habit and were lustily chewing away. Hugh had given it a try in self-defense, but he didn't care for the stuff and it was obvious all the spitting annoyed Molly.

"It takes me all day," Dexter continued, "but I finds 'em. One spindly lookin' kid standing there digging out a prospect hole up on the side of the hill. He looks like hell and I know right away this is it, but I just squats down and rolls myself a smoke and makes conversation kind of disinterested and pretty soon the kid's telling me all his troubles. Seems his partner is sick up in the cabin, got a hell of a fever and a bad cough and a case of poison ivy to boot, and the kid says his lungs don't feel too good neither. They been there half the winter and about froze and living for months on meat straight without even salt."

"Ain't that something!" Luther shook his head.

"But they found gold. Sure. They had a nice poke, he lets me know, tucked away in a safe place, he adds, just to let me know he's no fool. But it's been damn hard work and now it looks like their luck is petering out. They've worked out all the gravel on the creek, and they were only washing out six or seven dollars a day from the hillside, and they'll go broke fast that way with the cost of everything, and besides he finally got a letter from his sweetheart and she wants him to come home and his mother does too, and his partner's sick and, well, the adventure is over."

At this point in the story, Hugh leaned forward in spite of himself. Because it was always at this point that Dexter leaned forward conspiratorially, his eyes sparkling wickedly and his voice lowering to a whisper.

"And get this, folks. The whole time the kid's talking, he's shoveling out these big hunks of cement-looking stuff and wheel barrowing it over to the tailings pile cause he thinks it's just hunks of conglomerate rock. But me, I'm about to piss my pants, old goat scroat that I am, because I know. I know what he's got there."

"Conglomerate gold!" Edwin piped in.

"That's right!" Dexter slammed his fist down on the table, sending the plates dancing. "The kid knows. See Edwin already knows more than that greenhorn. He had conglomerate gold and he didn't know it."

He broke wind as if to emphasize the point.

Hugh groaned. Molly looked faint.

"Conglomerate gold!" Jake hit his side of the table.

"Yep." Dexter sat back smiling contentedly and lit up a pipe. "He's throwing conglomerate gold on his tailing pile and I'm about to piss my pants, I'm so afraid he's going to take a notion to hit one of those hunks of sand with his shovel, 'cause it could break open and he'd see the grains of gold because I know what's in there. He don't know, but I know, old goat scroat that I am."

"Old goat scroat!" Edwin piped in cheerfully.

"Edwin," Molly narrowed her eyes at him from across the table. "What did I tell you about that?"

"I'm sorry, Mamma. I forgot." Edwin lowered his eyes, but a grin played around his mouth.

"Let the boy go, Mother," Jake said. "You can't help but get excited when you get to this part of the story."

"This is the best part!" Luther agreed.

"Nope!" Dexter hit the table again. "Nope, the best part is the way I handled it. Some greenhorn would have bit right then, would have pissed right then and given the whole thing away. But not me. Not old Caleb Dexter."

"You old goat!" Jake said, then bothered to look at his wife and apologized with a shrug.

"He can't help it, Mrs," Dexter grinned at her. "'Cause this is the best part: the way I just sits there and tells the kid my troubles. How I guided this party all the way into Deadwood and how we had these two young bucks just dying to dig in the mines and how I had this responsible party with this fine wagon and the best set of mules you ever saw and how we were all anxious to have a try in the mines and now we couldn't find an inch of ground to work. How we didn't care so much for getting rich; we was just in it for the adventure since we already had a couple of hundred in gold between us, but we sure hated to go back to Nebraska without trying our hand at working a mine.

How we'd sure like to have just a little dust to show the folks back home to prove we was in the great Black Hills gold rush of '76, seeing as how none of us had been fortunate enough to have been in Californy in '49 and so on. And how this poor fellow with the team and wagon just didn't know what to do cause there wasn't any grazing for the mules and he just hated to buy hay at the price it was and they was such a fine team of mules all trail broke and how the poor man's wife and little boy —"

"That's me!" Edwin piped in.

"That's you, only he don't know that. Anyway —"

"To make a long story short," Hugh interrupted. Dexter frowned. "You got something to do, Hugh? You anxious to get to Deadwood? Maybe you got something to take to a Washee House?"

"Now see here!" Hugh stood up.

"Don't you two start in again," Jake broke in. "Finish the story, Caleb."

"Well" the old man frowned at Hugh. "To make a long story short, as Hugh says, pretty soon the kid's asking what I figure you'd need for the team and wagon, and I'm asking what they want for the mine, and the next thing you know we have ourselves a deal."

Yes, Hugh thought. They had themselves quite a deal. Only when he told his story Dexter never mentioned that digging conglomerate gold was like trying to pickax through cement. Nor that there was no way to get the grains of gold out of the conglomerate without sending it to a mill, and there was not yet a mill in Deadwood. Nor did he mention that the layer of conglomerate gave out within days, and they were now digging through layers of gravel which appeared to be practically worthless.

Nor did Caleb Dexter ever talk about what miserable, back-breaking work mining was. It was shoveling from morning to night. To the others, one shovelful of dirt looked like another; they never knew if they were in pay dirt or not. Therefore, Caleb Dexter, the expert, got to spend his time scampering about the diggings giving orders, while the rest dug until their hands were blistered raw and their backs so stiff they could hardly stand erect. Taking a turn at the sluice boxes, hauling water to run through it or shoveling the gravel in it, seemed like a break. Then at the end of the week, they cleaned out the boxes and picked out any tiny nuggets or grains of gold caught in the riffles at the bottom. And every week there was just enough gold there to make their expenses and keep them going. They kept their shares in spent cartridge cases and cached them away carefully.

But the endless, back-breaking, mind-dulling work was not the worst of it. The worst was when Hugh fell into bed at night, exhausted and yet unable to sleep. The cabin he shared with his brother and the old man was only yards from the Lewis's. And that was the worst of it, being in the cabin with the snoring men, or sleeping out under the stars when he had to be alone and always knowing Molly slept in the next cabin, just yards away.

Night after night he lay awake, exhausted, yearning for the oblivion of sleep. Yet his desire gave him no rest. He thought of visiting the cribs of Chinatown or the brothels in the area Deadwood called the Badlands. He suspected Luther would go if he ever had manhood, courage and cash at the same time. Hugh understood why men did such things, why they tried to buy love even at the risk of contracting a disease which crippled for life. But he knew that only one woman would satisfy his need, knew, too, if he gave in to his body's demands, he could face neither Molly nor himself. So he suffered and dreamed and tried to make the mine his mistress.

Sometimes when he saw Molly he would remember dreaming of her the night before in terrible and wonderful ways and feel shamed. He looked at her now, so calmly sipping her coffee as she watched Caleb Dexter divide the week's dust, and he felt his manhood rising.

He was a fool not to be in better control of his emotions. Molly looked up and, as if she read his thoughts, blushed. At such times, she would touch her collar button or caress her own arm nervously; he wondered if that meant she desired him. If she did, she had never spoken of it, and he knew women did not have the same strong needs as men. Yet he saw how given to touching she was; how much pleasure she found in holding and comforting Edwin when he was tired or afraid. Such a woman had to be warm and loving. It was of passion that she seemed innocent; yet he was sure he had awakened something in her in the past. Sometimes he took a morose satisfaction in thinking that if she had ever felt anything like desire, it was for him and not for Jake. That thought was followed by a sense of loss and guilt. If he had not squandered her innocence in that first love making, she would have had the freedom to marry a young man with whom she could have found joy instead of the dreary existence she shared with Jake.

As for himself, if he had never given his love to Molly, he could satisfy his lust with a woman of the Badlands, instead of driving himself crazy dreaming of his partner's wife, the partner who that moment stunned him with a casual question.

"What're you dreaming of there, Hugh? Poor man's gold?" Jake brought him back to reality with a start.

"Yes," Hugh didn't look at Jake. "Poor man's gold."

"Well, pay attention, we're ready to divvy up," Caleb Dexter declared, rolling more cartridges and caps onto the table. Hugh was relieved the weekly ordeal was about over. Their shares came to about thirty dollars each, before expenses. Jake pronounced it a fine week, and Luther and the old man nodded agreement.

"What do you mean?" Hugh demanded. "It's barely a week's wages!"

"Well, it's a hell of a lot more cash than I ever saw farming.'" Jake declared. "I'm ready to celebrate. Molly, hand me that jug."

"I say it's time for a real celebration," Caleb Dexter said, reaching for the jug himself. "Let's have a snort here and then go to town for a real gold miners' Saturday night. What do you say, men?"

"You can count me in!" Luther boomed.

"Okay with you, Mother?" Jake turned to his wife,

Molly disliked his calling her Mother almost as much as she disliked his drinking. She wanted to protest, though it was not a good wife's place to keep her husband from seeking release, especially when she could no longer offer him the comfort of her body. But as she was about to speak, her eyes met Hugh's and his look seemed to say, *Let us be alone.* Despite the closeness of their quarters at the mine, they had shared no more than a few private moments in weeks, moments always tense with the fear that if they dared to touch or to speak of what was in their hearts, someone would come along and discover their secret.

She found it hard to believe that anyone with eyes could see them in a room together, could see how they avoided looking at each other or sharing the same bench at the table and not know. But Jake and Caleb Dexter were so caught up with the mine that they seemed oblivious to everything else. Even when she said Jake should go, and Hugh said he'd stay and help her clear up, only Luther took notice. His eyes darted between them with the same look that Edwin sometimes wore when he sensed something was amiss between his parents, or he'd broken a rule.

"Come on, Hugh," Luther urged. "Doing dishes is

Molly's job. You been doing man's work all week; now it's time for fun."

"I had enough 'fun' breaking my back today. I'm going to turn in early," Hugh said firmly, picked up Edwin, who was too tired to protest, and took him to his pallet.

Molly sat silent until the men made their noisy exit and then loaded the dishes into an iron pan on the table, seeming to ignore Hugh. She fetched the kettle from the stove and poured hot water over the dishes while Hugh cradled the already dozing Edwin in his arms. Silently she busied herself at the stove, adding kindling to the embers and refilling the kettle with rinse water. She felt strangely reckless, as if something terrible yet wonderful was about to happen, and she was powerless to stop it. She felt as if she were sleepwalking.

When she dared look at Hugh again, his back was to her as he stood looking down at their son. Her vision of them seemed indistinct as if clouded by tears or illusion. She realized that Hugh had changed. He was no longer the boy she had fallen in love with in that faraway time and place. He was not even the lover of her dreams but a man hardened by the trail and the mine, a tall, bearded giant who wanted her and had been denied. She felt an uneasy premonition that Hugh's desire for her might be expressed in a way that could destroy them all, but even more disconcerting was the feeling growing within her, which she could not admit, even to herself, was also desire.

She only knew that since leaving civilization she'd been increasingly filled with yearnings as confused and primitive as the maze of shacks and mine shafts and lawless humanity which daily destroyed pristine wilderness in the name of the city of Deadwood.

Being alone with Hugh that night both frightened and thrilled her. She knew that as long as she stayed within the cabin she was safe. Edwin's presence kept them from being truly alone. She tried not to think of the temptation of Hugh's cabin only a door away or what it would be like to make love with him again. She wondered about his body, hard, lean and tanned in his workman's clothes. He had been little more than a boy that first time. She sensed this time it would be different. He would still be tender, but he would be a man and not old and weary as Jake had been almost since the beginning. This time she might know at last what it was to be a woman.

Hugh turned and looked at her. He seemed to be waiting for her to speak or move toward him. She could do neither. She sensed he wanted her to admit she had willed them to be alone, that she wanted something to happen. Did he not understand that she could not show willingness; that if he was to take her it must be his doing?

She turned back to her womanly chores, placing the kettle where it would heat faster. She tried to concentrate on her task, even as she began to tremble. Through her mind flashed the image of Hugh approaching her and putting his arms around her, caressing her shoulders, then touching his lips to her neck and sliding his hands to her breasts as his manhood pressed against her hips. Yes, that was how it must happen, with her caught in his powerful embrace, too weak and too aware of his terrible need to protest.

Even as the thought came to her, even as she thrilled to the certainty that it was about to happen, she pushed the image away. She grabbed the bar of soap and began to work it into her dish rag. She must not let being in this uncivilized place bring ruin on all she held dear. If she gave into temptation she would be no better than the women of the Badland bordellos. She must make polite conversation and not let Hugh think there had been an invitation in that look they had exchanged at the table.

"It's been strange, hasn't it, our being so close together here in Deadwood?" She kept her back to him. Her throat felt dry and her words seemed to echo in the small cabin. "I mean seeing each other every day, but not ever being alone."

She half turned to look at him.

"It's been hell."

She turned away as if she had been hit. He was not going to make polite conversation.

"It's been hell," he repeated. "It's driving me crazy." He was moving toward her. It was going to happen. He was going to come up behind her and embrace her just as she had pictured it. She tensed in fear and anticipation, her hand moving instinctively to her breast. She had unbuttoned her collar button while she worked over the stove; now she tried to fasten it again. Her heart was hammering.

"Look at me, Molly."

He was beside her now, but she could not take her eyes from the stove where the hot flames were licking against the kindling. Her skin felt on fire.

"Turn and look at me."

She obeyed, but crossed her arms over her breasts.

"I have to touch you, Molly," he whispered taking her by the shoulders, so that his strong, calloused hands covered hers. "I can't keep pretending you are nothing to me. It's been hell, seeing you every day but never daring to touch you, thinking about you every night, wondering what it would be like to hold you again."

She took a step backward, looking toward the corner where Edwin slept.

"I'll be quiet," he whispered. "We'll not frighten our son. I'll take you to my cabin; only let me hold you a moment first. I've waited so long."

She let him draw her to him, but could not embrace him even as she thrilled to his strength and warmth, the earthy smell of him and the roughness of his wool shirt as she allowed herself one moment in his arms. If only it could be like this forever. If only he would just hold her and ask no more. But she felt his hardness against her and knew it was impossible.

"Hold me too, Molly," he whispered. "Tell me you want me. Tell me you agree."

He held her away to see her face, "Say yes, and we'll go to my cabin."

She could not speak. Why was he such a fool? Why did he not just pick her up and carry her to his cabin? Couldn't he see that she could not agree but was powerless to resist?

She shook her head, her eyes downcast.

"God knows I want you, but you must want me too. Once I made you mine before you knew the consequences, and I brought ruin on you. Now I must somehow make it right. I want to make you my wife."

He was a fool. Couldn't he see that it could only be one way between them?

"I'm Jake's wife," she whispered, saying the only words her conscience would allow.

"We've got to change that. I can't go on any longer living this lie. We'll make a plan. We'll find some way to tell him, afterwards."

"*Afterwards*! How am I to know you'll still want me for your wife, *afterwards*?"

"Damn it woman!" He spoke through clenched teeth, holding her shoulders so tight her arms ached. "I told you I'd never leave you again. I want you so badly now I can't think straight. Feel my love, Molly. He took her hand and held it to his manhood, then held her whole body against his as he kissed her lips and neck. She was weak against the power of his desire. Surely he would take her now. Surely even God could not expect her to resist any longer.

"Tell me," he whispered. "Just tell me you love me. We don't have to make love tonight. I won't hurt you, but just say you'll leave Jake." He held her away from him like a rag doll and waited for her answer.

"I can't," she said. "I can't say it and I can't leave Jake. I can't hurt him that way."

"I don't want to hurt him either. He's my partner. But he can't need you like I do. I can't go on like this. I can't go on sleeping just yards from you, knowing he might be having his way with you and I can't even touch you."

"You make it sound as if I'm Jake's property. As if I'd be your property if I ran away with you. But it's not like that. Jake and I are not bound by desire. We are bound by what is right and holy. And," she spoke angrily now, "if it is any comfort to you, Jake does not *have his way* with me."

"What do you mean?"

"I mean Jake and I do not — do not — live as man and wife."

He let go of her and stood back, regarding her with what almost seemed suspicion. "You told me on the trail that you were a true wife to him."

"I was, or I tried to be, until the doctor said we could not have more children, at least for now. The doctor explained it to Jake, and so Jake does not do *that,* anymore, and so you and I, *we could not do that even if I would.*"

"The hell we couldn't!"

"What?"

"We could still love each other, Molly. We would find a way. I'd find a way. Don't tell me Jake hasn't."

"What are you saying?"

"There are ways, aren't there? When there can't be a baby? Those women in the Badlands have ways of protecting themselves. Maybe Jake wouldn't know about that, but he must find ways of loving you. He touches you, doesn't he? He has you touch him?"

"Jake has been considerate.'"

"So he pleasures you. He holds you and he kisses you and *finds ways*, doesn't he?"

"You misunderstand. I mean that Jake has treated me as a lady. He has not ... *touched me* ... in months. ''

She had begun righteously, thinking that if Hugh knew that Jake no longer treated her as a wife, it would make it easier for him to check his own passion. But now she realized that of all the wonderful and terrible things Hugh had said to her, this was the worst. For Jake had not touched her, he had not *found ways*. Saying it aloud to Hugh and to herself revealed the barrenness of her marriage in a way she'd never considered. She felt pain, but Hugh reacted with anger.

"Maybe you're lucky, Molly. Maybe he is right for you. Because if you were my wife, I couldn't leave you alone. I'd have to touch you. I'd find a way to love you."

He held her roughly as he spoke. When he raised a hand to touch her face, she flinched, and seeing her fear, he looked at his open hand, groaned and, filled with rage and frustration, turned and slammed it down against the hot stove. He spoke through teeth clenched in pain and anger.

"I'd burn in hell before I'd hurt you!"

Frantically Molly pulled his hand away from the stove. She kissed his palm and held his hand to her face, her tears soothing the pain. "Oh, Hugh, my dearest Hugh," she murmured, but he jerked his hand away.

"Don't do that, Molly. Don't be kind to me. I won't accept your kindness or your mothering. I want to be your lover. I want all of you. Jake can accept less, but I can't."

She wanted so badly to touch him, to hold and be held, but he was making it clear that it was all or nothing. They stood in the little cabin facing each other over what seemed a great distance.

"I'd not get you pregnant, but I want all the rest. I want you to be a true wife, to me. Clearly I can't have you now. Maybe I never will, but I'm giving you notice of how it would be between us. And that I can't go on much longer this way, staying in this crazy mining partnership just to protect you and Edwin and be close to you. "

"You'd leave? You said you'd never leave me again!"

"Not if staying with you means going crazy. And that's how I feel tonight. I'm going to my cabin now, and I'm taking this goddamn jug of Caleb Dexter's with me, because maybe if I drink enough I can get through another night without coming up here after you. But I can't promise you after that. You've got to resolve it with Jake and with yourself. I'll tell him if you can't, but you've got to come to me and be mine or you've got to let me go."

"Tell Jake? Tell my husband?"

"You've got no true marriage with him. I'll give you some time to admit that. When you're ready, Molly, when you can admit you belong to me, then you find some way to signal me, so we can make a plan. We'll find a way."

He took her by the shoulders once more and brought her to him and kissed her. It was a kiss full of resolution and power, one she would long remember, but it was his words as he left which haunted her.

"Remember, Molly. We can't go on like this!"

That night and the nights that followed, Molly lay awake, torturing herself with fantasies of giving herself to Hugh and with resolutions to tell Jake the truth.

In the daytime, remembering the night, she was ashamed of her thoughts. She almost hated Hugh for forcing her to realize her own desire. She tried to pray for answers, but did not dare to ask the true questions.

She asked how to be faithful to her vow to be one flesh with Jake. She could not yet ask whether their saying the words in a church had, indeed, made them one flesh.

She could only wonder if a man and woman are so bound, if it is words in a church that makes it so. And if it was words, she tried to remember if Jake had ever told her he loved her.

She resolved to try harder with Jake. Surely if she could again be a true wife to him, she would find the courage to let Hugh go. Hugh had said there were safe ways to give pleasure, and she thought she must find a way, not for herself, but for her husband.

And so one night when they had gone to bed, and she was sure Edwin was asleep, she tried to talk to her husband, knowing the time was not right but aware there might never be a better one. She knew the words would not come easily, for in all the years of her marriage, they had never discussed intimacy.

"Jake," she whispered. "I've been thinking." His response was mumbled and sleepy, but she persisted. "Try to wake up, Jake. This is important."

He struggled to one elbow, "You sick?"

"No, in fact I've felt very well since we've been in Deadwood. That's why I've been thinking that maybe we shouldn't worry anymore about what the doctor said."

"What doctor?"

"Dr. Morgan, back in Iowa. He said we shouldn't have any more babies, and so we shouldn't . . . you know."

"Why are you worrying about that? I been good, ain't I?"

"Yes, that's just it. You've been so good, and I've been thinking how difficult it must be for you. Men being made so needful and all, and I've been thinking that maybe the doctor was wrong, and that since I'm well now, maybe we could —"

"Not in Deadwood. I'd not have you risk yourself again, not in this place. I doubt there's a doctor in the whole Black Hills!"

"Then, maybe . . . maybe there's some way we could, just *please each other*, without making a baby."

Jake was silent. Surely he understood. She stumbled on, her heart pounding, knowing her cheeks must be burning in the dark.

"I was thinking about all those bad women in Deadwood. They must have some way of —"

"Molly! What a way to be talking! What those women do has got no place in the joining of man and wife. You got no business even thinking about such things."

Jake had shamed her, but she pressed on. "I was thinking about you. How you must suffer, doing without."

He patted her shoulder, "Why, that's sweet of you, Molly. You been a good wife, but you don't need to worry about me. I'm so busy with that mine, digging from daybreak to sundown, I don't have time or energy to think about what I'm doing without, much less suffering over it."

"But you must! You must want me. It's in a man's nature, isn't it?"

"A young man's, maybe. But I haven't got that problem anymore." He yawned. "Now you just go to sleep and quit your fretting. There's only one thing I'm needful of now and that's *Poor Man's Gold*. If the Lucky Six pays off for me, and I've a feeling it will, then it's all I'll ever need."

He reached over and patted her head in the same way he did Edwin's, planted a kiss on her forehead, turned over and went to sleep.

Molly lay awake, knowing she had received the answer to a question she had not dared to ask. It was over. Perhaps it had never been. Hugh was right; she had no true marriage to Jake. But what did she do now? How could she leave a good man who had believed all these years that she had not given herself willingly, but had been wronged? If only he wasn't such a decent man, if he beat her and gave her some reason to turn against him. Then, maybe such a decision would be possible.

She cried silent tears and touched her own body and knew the warmth and softness of her breasts and thighs. She was filled with yearnings she could not name. She touched herself more deeply and her longing surged, but she did not know how to still it. She thought of Hugh sleeping with his brother and the old man in the next cabin and knew she would find peace only in his arms, but the distance between them seemed impossible.

From Jake's side of the bed came a contented snore. Something had changed forever. She sensed that the next step would take them on a journey even more tangled and dangerous than the one which had brought them to the Black Hills. And that next step was hers.

It happened soon after that night. As June ended and the days grew longer and warmer, the men became increasingly discouraged with the Lucky Six. Each day less and less gold remained behind as they washed their surface diggings through their rocker on the creek. Finally when they divided the week's earnings, they had to admit they were making less than day's wages from their mine. Hugh brought them to a confrontation. His words were directed to Caleb Dexter, but she felt they were for her.

"We can't go on like this!"

"I can understand you being a mite discouraged," the old man said, undaunted. "Some weeks are like this. Now if you had been there in '49."

"I don't want to hear about '49!"

"Well, then, I guess it's time to tell you."

"Tell us what?" Jake broke in.

"The good news. We're almost to the bedrock!"

Caleb Dexter was beaming, but Luther answered for all of them, "So?"

"So, if you don't know what that means, it just goes to show you weren't there in —"

"Damn it, old man, *tell us!*"

"Well, as any experienced miner knows, gold is heavy. Even Edwin knows that. So since gold is the heaviest metal, as it sits in the gravel and hundreds of years keep passing, it drifts slowly downward. Then when it gets to bedrock, it stops," he paused dramatically, "So when you finally reach bedrock, there's a layer of solid gold!"

"Always?" Edwin asked, his eyes glowing.

"Well, not always. But sometimes. Sometimes there's a sheet of solid gold, and you just shovel it up by the bucketful!"

"Poor man's gold!"

"That's right, Jake! Poor man's gold!"

Only, in their case, it didn't turn out that way. When they finally dug out the gravel from their huge open pit, there was nothing on the bedrock but bedrock. It was called bedrock, Hugh discovered, because the ore was so solid you couldn't crack it with a shovel. Poor man's gold had eluded them again.

This time when they discussed it over Molly's dinner table, even Caleb Dexter was discouraged.

"So what do we do now?" Molly asked.

"Only two choices now," the old man answered. "And the best thing is to quit."

They were all stunned to silence, as for once the old man went on without prompting. "Quitting is the smart thing to do. Cash in here. Try to find some greenhorns to buy the mine, dissolve the partnership and head for the hills prospecting for a new strike somewhere else. That's the easiest thing to do in a situation like this. Safest, too."

"And what's the other thing?" Hugh demanded.

Dexter didn't answer right away. He rolled a cigarette and walked to the open door of the cabin to light it. He stood for a moment, puffing and looking at the hill which rose sharply behind their cabins and diggings. Under the old man's directions, they had dug a dozen prospect holes in it. Then he studied the creek a few yards below the cabin where they washed the gold. Finally he came back to the table and spoke.

"It's too dangerous. Too dangerous with me the only one to savvy mining. Too dangerous and too costly. It takes stuff. Timbers, a pump maybe, lots of blasting powder."

His voice trailed off and they all sat silent at the table, thinking. For even Edwin knew what he was talking about. *Going underground.*

They argued about it half the night. It was too expensive, Dexter said. They were talking about capital investment. It would take all the dust they had accumulated so far to finance it. And it was far too dangerous. He suggested they all cash in now while Molly and Jake had enough to get back to Iowa, or even home to Pennsylvania although they'd have to arrive with nothing to show for their years in the West. Dexter would, of course, help Hugh and Luther to head for the hills and prospect.

Luther was the first to state a different idea. He declared he wanted to join Emmet Hobart in the Spearfish Valley. The wagon master had stopped by the mine the day before and told them of the glories of the valley he had gone to after becoming discouraged with Deadwood. It was broad and lush, the perfect spot for a ranching venture. Their old wagon master would make his fortune supplying the mining towns with beef and produce, but he needed help in holding his land against the Sioux, who met the white settlers' invasion of the valley with constant raiding parties.

Luther was eager to go, and Molly knew that Hugh, too, would be happier ranching than grubbing away underground. But giving up the mine meant giving up Hugh. The Spearfish Valley was not safe for families and Jake was a farmer, not a rancher. If they separated now, she knew she would lose Hugh forever.

Jake declared they should stay. He loved the mine and had faith in it. They all had a sense that the Lucky Six might yet live up to its name. All around them fortunes were being made. If blasting into the side of the hill should lead them to a rich vein, they might attract capital from one of the investors who were rumored to be coming to the Black Hills on the first stagecoaches.

The mine and their partnership was a dream none of them was willing to give up easily, but instead of leading them on with more tales of poor man's gold, Caleb Dexter was brutally honest about the dangers.

Underground mining meant risking lives.

Somehow, the decision became Molly's. Hugh said that if they continued, they all must agree to the risk. And Molly knew that he was asking her to agree to more than the dangers of the mine. His eyes had been on her all evening, and she knew that he was telling her this was the time of decision. She must let him go, or she must risk all.

"We can't go on like this," she said finally, looking straight at Hugh and choosing her words carefully, "but I am not willing to give up. We'll find a way. I vote that we retain the partnership and go underground."

"You willingly accept the risk?" Hugh asked.

"I do," she said. And knew she had made a vow.

CHAPTER EIGHTEEN

Deadwood had immeasurably enhanced Emerald O'Brien's image of herself. She was easily the most beautiful woman in Deadwood. In fact, she decided, walking down Main Street putting her little French kid boots down carefully so as not to step in anything foul while at the same time keeping her chin tilted up proudly, she was the only woman in the entire Black Hills who wasn't downright ugly. She figured she had already seen every decent woman in Deadwood. There weren't many and they were all worried, used-up looking women, bone thin or gone to fat, clutching shawls around their shoulders, plodding after their miner husbands, some of them even dragging along a crying kid or two.

And as for the whores, she had not seen many of those either, as they kept to themselves in the daytime; but she knew whores were a cut below the dance-hall girls who sold their favors only to selected customers, and she had seen plenty of those doing their tired little kicks on improvised stages near the gambling tables, showing gaudy petticoats and plump white thighs. They were certainly not much to look at. Even as they danced and sang or draped themselves over the bar enticing the miners with breasts spilling out of their low-necked dresses, Emerald was certain it was she, Emerald O'Brien, the men of Deadwood were lusting for.

It excited Emerald to think how she looked as she graced the streets of Deadwood. Her black hair was swept up to reveal her delicate pink earlobes and flashing green earbobs before it curled down in ringlets along her neck. She wore the latest style, her tiny waist set off by the bustle-back of her daytime costume. She wore darling little gloves with the fingers cut out, and a fussy little beaded handbag dangled from her wrist, a tiny little bonnet perched on her head, and high-buttoned shoes on her feet. She felt as if she had just stepped from the pages of *Godey's Lady's Book*.

She paused in her stroll to look up to the second-story window of the hotel room she shared with Avery at the Grand Central Hotel. The name was imposing, but the hotel was merely a huge cabin of green logs topped with a tacked-on second story of rough green lumber. When Avery registered, none of the partitions between the rooms had reached the ceiling, and the cracks in the walls were wide enough to stick a finger through. Avery raised a terrible fuss about the lack of privacy and advanced a month's rent to properly furnish and complete their room. The next day, a huge brass bed and carved oak washstand were carried in and the walls reinforced and papered with white-washed newspapers. Although it was far beneath the accommodations to which Emerald had grown accustomed, she did have the finest room in Deadwood.

She couldn't tell from studying the hotel window if Avery was awake. He wasn't much good before he had breakfast, usually about four in the afternoon. It was not likely this was one of the days he would consent to be wakened early. He had gambled until dawn. Watching Avery gamble all night was only slightly less boring than going to bed alone, so Emerald usually went to bed by midnight and rose early to breakfast alone at the I.X.L. Restaurant.

She liked to eat before the crowd gathered. When she ate in a room full of men, all eyes upon her, it was difficult to maintain the lady-like posture of picking delicately at her food. When was alone, she could chew the meat off the bones and lick her fingers afterwards.

Maintaining her image was sometimes a chore, but more often part of the fun, Emerald decided as she stopped before a mud puddle and made a little mincing movement before lifting her skirts to reveal her ankles as she stepped around the edge of the puddle. Just as she expected, she looked up to see her dear little feet had been admired by several men sitting on empty whiskey barrels before the saloon. She gave them a look of offended modesty and tossed her head so her curls jiggled a little as she walked past them with her chin in the air and her bustle switching. She heard the men groan and could hardly keep from giggling. It was delicious. If only her mother and her hateful sisters could see her now.

The best part was the fact she knew the Deadwood men would not bother her. Women were so scarce, even the slightly- tarnished were valued, so even if some drunken miner lost his senses and approached her, a half-dozen others would instantly throttle him to prove their gallantry. Emerald thought it would be exciting to see men fighting over her, but such an event was unlikely, for it was evident she belonged to the gambler whose black frock coat did not quite conceal the pearl handled pistols tucked into the sash around his waist.

Despite her mother's warnings, the life of a rich man's mistress was quite satisfying. Avery bought her everything she wanted. Even among the barrels of flour and whiskey and nails that made up the stock of Deadwood's general stores, occasionally something suitable could be found: a bottle of lavender water, a gilt-edged mirror, a silver dressing-table set. It was as if in distant Cheyenne and Sidney, as the shipments were being loaded onto freight wagons for the Black Hills, someone knew there would be a woman like Emerald in Deadwood.

And Austin Avery was generous. Not that she didn't earn everything she got, although she shouldn't have put it that way. No, she *deserved* to be gifted. She gave herself freely to Austin out of love, and because he loved her, he bought her presents. That was the way it was.

She was certain Austin loved her. She hadn't made him say it yet, but if she were clever, he soon would. How could he not love her when any man in Deadwood would give his entire poke of gold dust for her? She was sure if she ever tired of Austin Avery, she would quickly find another man, this time one who would make her his wife. But for now she was almost content with Austin. For now, there were more pleasurable things than being a respectable wife, like becoming not just the mistress of Austin Avery but his master. He was a challenge to her for she had become a jealous woman. Sometimes it was as if gambling was his true mistress, and he turned to Emerald only when he had satisfied his deeper lust.

Just the night before, as she lay on the bed watching him dress for the evening, she had accused him of being possessed by the gambling fever. He had laughed at her, his gold tooth gleaming.

"It's my trade, my dear. Just as other men doctor or preach or practice law, it's *my profession*. It's what I do well. I understand gambling. There are odds and you play with them. And if you understand the game and are clever enough, you win more than you lose. You put in a certain amount of effort and risk and you get rewarded. It's only those who try to get something for nothing that lose. Work and honest toil is what is takes. Why, I don't even believe in luck. It's the amateurs who believe in luck, thinking they can get something for nothing. If everyone would be willing to work for a living as hard as I do —"

"Avery?" She interrupted. "Why don't you end the sermon and come to bed?"

He complied, but for once she failed to find her own satisfaction, and as soon as he finished, he got up, finished dressing and left for the tables. She did not believe for a minute that gambling was merely a line of work with him. It was as if he practiced magic.

He had an uncanny ability with cards. Tricks, he told her: tricks, practice, skill and a face that never betrayed emotion. But sometimes to Emerald, it seemed like magic.

It seemed like a sickness, too, because he could not leave it alone. He drank no more than a shot or two of whiskey in an evening, smoked his cheroots in moderation, and could go days without making love. He had not made love to her for the week it took them to get to the Hills, first on the stagecoach and then traveling with a wagon train of freighters, sleeping outside with a dozen men before the campfire. He had not touched her but kept just close enough to make sure the other men knew she was his property. But from gambling, he had not abstained. Even on the trail, he was always making a bet or dealing a hand. She noticed he refrained from playing for high stakes with his fellow passengers on the stagecoach. He explained to her it would not do to risk hard feelings with his traveling companions. Yet he managed to win a dollar or two off almost everyone he came in contact with. It irritated Emerald beyond reason.

She remembered the first night out from Fort Laramie with the freighters. After dinner they sat on their blankets before the fire and she, aware of the men's eyes upon her, brushed her hair by firelight, knowing she was beautiful in its reflection and knowing the men speculated about her relationship with Avery. She had turned to see if Avery was watching her, but he was spreading cards out on the blanket of a big, slow freighter who squatted across from him with hope in his eyes. It was a simple trick Avery performed for the freighter that night; yet Emerald watched him work it a dozen times before she figured it out.

He never repeated a trick on the same man and never took more than a dollar or two from each, so they could only grin foolishly, not out enough to get angry. Avery had over a thousand dollars in his money belt at the time, and her handbag was stuffed with jewels. There was no need to take the freighters' hard-earned dollars. That was when Emerald knew gambling was more than Avery's occupation; it was an obsession.

It was not that she had anything against gambling. Every man had his weakness. She learned that at her mother's knee and supposed if Avery's had not been gambling, he would have drunk too much or lusted after other women. It was the fact that Avery was not totally involved with her that she could not tolerate. She was the queen of Deadwood and yet, even though Austin made love to her almost every afternoon, he could turn his back on her afterwards. He did not worship at her shrine. He merely used her and then went on to his real mistress. Every time it happened, Emerald wished there was some way to get back at him.

That afternoon she had taken her time strolling up Main Street to think over her life with Avery. It was July and although Deadwood was infinitely cooler than Missouri, she felt a bit mussed. Now that she was before the hotel, she must make a decision. It was not quite noon. Austin might not wake for hours. She could slip into their room, undress in the afternoon light, hoping Austin would open one eye and peer at her white and naked body while she pretended not to notice. Then she could slip into bed beside him and if he were still not fully awake, she could grow a bit bold. Sometimes that worked and sometimes it didn't. It drove her crazy when he insisted on sleeping, and today might be one of those days. Besides, whatever time he woke up, he would make love to her.

She must not appear eager. He must never suspect

how much she enjoyed it. That would give him too much power over her. Besides, he seemed to like to believe he ravished her. She knew only fallen women enjoyed conjugal relations. Passion was not a desirable quality in a wife, and Emerald still planned to get Austin Avery to marry her.

She decided it would be better to make Avery come to her that day. She would return to the I. X. L. where Avery would find her when he came for his breakfast. Then he would need to find a way to persuade her to return to their hotel room. It was better this way, she thought as she returned to the restaurant and sipped tea.

She was bored. Watching men watch her drink tea was not an exciting way to spend an afternoon, so she looked up with interest when a man was bold enough to hesitate before her table. She knew instantly something exciting was about to happen. The man was small, nattily dressed and wearing a benign smile.

"Allow me to introduce myself," he swept off his hat with a grand gesture. "I am Jack Langrishe, proprietor of the only legitimate theatre in the Black Hills."

She knew him by reputation as did everyone in Deadwood. The whole city had turned out for his first show, for the showman's reputation preceded him. He and his wife had operated theatres in many of the mining camps of the West, bringing a brief illusion of beauty and magic to the drab lives of frontier towns. The performances at Langrishe's theatre had just begun, but were infinitely grander than the banjo music and off-color stories of the Melodeon or the vaudeville of the Gem Theatre, a place already more famous for what went on inside the curtained boxes upstairs than for any on-stage entertainment.

Avery had taken Emerald to Langrishe's opening night performance, and she had been enthralled, despite the fact the show was given in an unfinished theatre roofed with canvas, and when it rained she was almost drenched. She would have loved to go every night, but even in Deadwood, a lady did not attend the theatre unescorted, and Avery would not give up another night's gambling. Emerald decided to acknowledge him, even though it was highly irregular for a gentleman to approach a lady.

"Please sit down, Mr. Langrishe. I feel I know you from your performances."

"And I feel I know you, for you drew as much attention in my audience as I did on stage."

Emerald looked down at her tea, allowing herself to blush prettily. It was true, of course, and it had irritated Austin Avery in a most provocative way.

"Please do forgive my boldness, "Langrishe continued, "but I could not help but wonder, have you by any chance ever been on the stage yourself?"

Emerald knew what was coming. It was not a proposition; it was something much more exciting. She felt her blush rising beyond the point of attractiveness before she regained her composure.

"Why, Mr. Langrishe," she made her eyes wide, "why ever do you ask?"

"Because" the stocky little showman rolled his large eyes expressively, "if ever I've seen a woman who was meant to be on a stage, it is you!"

"Really, Mr. Langrishe, I hardly know how to respond!" She tried to look affronted.

"You must think I'm being terribly cheeky," Langrishe acknowledged. "I should have made my wife approach you. When we noticed you in the audience, she agreed you should be on the stage, and I had anticipated having her with me when we called on you, but when I saw you here today without your — escort, well, I could wait no longer to beg you to perform at our theatre."

"Why, Mr. Langrishe, I have no acting experience. Whatever makes you think I could do such a thing?"

She knew, of course, that she was going to accept, but first he must deal his hand. Besides, although she knew she acted her way through life, the thought of actually being on a stage was a bit frightening.

Langrishe made a flowery speech about her attributes and concluded by saying, "Frankly, my dear, whether you sing or dance or merely speak a few lines, you will always capture your audience."

Langrishe was Irish and he was full of blarney, but she knew he was speaking the truth. Still, she played coy, and let him continue trying to persuade her. The lilt of his brogue reminded her pleasantly of her father who had petted and praised her. Once he had gone off to the war, she was left with the jealousy of her sisters and her mother's constant reminders that her good looks endangered her chastity. Well, perhaps she had been right about that; still it was delightful to hear such an articulate man praise her.

"Just one song," he said finally. "Just come to the theatre and sing one song and see how it feels, see how well you go over. Then, if you like it and the audience likes you, as I know they will, my wife and I will coach you and you can perform in our regular plays and theatricals."

"I don't know about that, Mr. Langrishe. About joining your troupe, I mean. You see, I am engaged to marry, Mr. Austin Avery. He is acquiring some mining properties. And when he finishes his business, we expect to return to the South where we shall regain Mr. Avery's plantation lost in the war. We plan to wed there in the old plantation home. Generations of Avery brides have been married on the veranda of the old family mansion and my fiance would not hear of breaking the tradition."

"Fascinating," Langrishe said, ducking his bald head around to catch her speaking from various angles.

"The way you speak, I mean, it's utterly charming and fascinating."

"How you flatter me!" Emerald appreciated the interruption, as her impromptu explanation for her unmarried state, clever though it was, was getting onto delicate ground. "I'm afraid you *are* full of the blarney, Mr. Langrishe, but you have convinced me to give the theatre a try. Just one song, though. "

As they left the restaurant together Emerald tried to look demure, but her heart was beating wildly. She had the feeling something important was about to happen.

She was not quite so certain of herself later as she stood offstage while Langrishe introduced her. She knew few songs and no dances, but she was going to give it a try.

He played a little introduction to *Weeping Sad and Lonely*. It was a Civil War song, one that should bring tears to men from both sides. Besides, it was the only song they had been able to agree they both knew. The piano was the first in Deadwood and still a novelty. Emerald hoped no one would notice if her voice wavered.

She stepped very slowly to the center of the stage. It wasn't a real stage, just a large platform hastily made of green lumber, framed by a curtain and painted backdrop the Langrishes had brought from their last mining camp.

It wasn't a real theatre, either. The walls were of unpeeled logs, the floor was covered with sawdust. But it was a real audience, a hundred men and every eye on her!

Langrishe played the introduction, looking at her pointedly. It was now or never. She clasped her hands over her bosom as she had seen a real opera singer do on the river boat. She began to sing in a tremulous voice.

> *Dearest love, do you remember*
> *When we last did meet,*
> *How you told me that you loved me,*
> *Kneeling at my feet?*

There was not a sound in the whole theatre except the piano and Emerald's voice and her wildly beating heart. She saw she had them; her voice grew stronger as she began the next verse.

> *Oh! How proud you stood before me,*
> *In your suit of blue,*
> *When you vowed to me and country,*
> *Ever to be true.*

They were getting tears in their eyes! She had made all those crusty old miners weep! It was thrilling. As she sang the chorus she began to relax, to move her arms about, gesturing with her hands as she had seen real actresses do.

> *Weeping, sad and lonely*
> *Hopes and fears how vain!*
> *Yet praying*
> *When this cruel war is over,*
> *Praying that we meet again.*

It was over much too soon. She folded her hands as if in prayer and lowered her eyes; there was a tremendous burst of applause, but then it was over. And it had taken no time at all. Emerald felt bereft.

They were shouting, "More, more!"

Emerald couldn't think of another song. Her mother had approved of nothing but hymns. She knew a few, but they would hardly be appropriate. Langrishe was looking at her expectantly. She bit her lip, trying frantically to think of a jolly song. She had brought hardened miners to tears but that hardly seemed the mood in which to leave them. She could think of only one, another Civil War song. She ran over and whispered the title to Langrishe. He nodded and played an introduction. She ran back to center stage, struck a posture, took a deep breath and began, this time making her voice more lusty to match the mood of the song.

Sitting by the roadside on a summer day,
Chatting with my messmates, passing time away,
Lying in the shadow underneath the trees,
Goodness, how delicious, eating goober peas!

She saw the men breaking into smiles as they recognized the song, and it filled her with excitement and power. As she came to the chorus, she began to dance about the stage, shouting, "Everybody sing!"

Peas! Peas! Peas!
Eating goober peas!
Goodness, how delicious,
Eating goober peas!

She paused for just a moment, not quite able to believe she had done it. Not only had she sung a silly song to a whole theatre full of men, she had danced and kicked her legs and showed her petticoats. She felt wonderful and she wasn't about to stop. She repeated the chorus, gesturing for the men to join her in singing.

"Everybody: Peas! Peas! Peas!"

This time she put everything into her dancing, pulling her heavy skirts up and skipping around the stage. She was having fun. The men were applauding and stamping their feet to the music as she pranced and sang. She felt her carefully arranged hairdo coming down and her cheeks growing red, but she knew every man in the room was falling in love with her. And she loved herself! At last she truly loved herself.

Langrishe repeated the chorus again and again and she danced until she was breathless. She signaled to him *one more time* and he slowed the music to signal this was the finale. Emerald knew she should end with something sensational. As she made her last round kicking her legs up over the faces of the men in the front row, she thought of something she had seen dance hall girls do. She didn't know if it would work with her heavy bustled skirt. It was daring and terrible and not the kind of thing a lady would do. But then a lady wouldn't be doing what she was doing.

As the piano trilled its last chord of *Goober Peas,* Emerald turned around quickly, her hands on her hips, then grabbing her skirt on each side, she bent over and threw her skirts over her head. If she had done it right, her drawers would show. Thank heavens they were ruffled.

The audience yelled, stamped their feet and howled for more. She must have done it right!

Slowly, almost haughtily, she turned to survey her audience and saw something she had dreamed of. On the face of every man in the audience was a look of adoration.

They loved her.

Then, just as Langrishe pulled the curtain, Emerald saw a man who was not applauding. He stood in the back of the theatre, his face, ashen white.

It was Austin Avery.

Her first impulse was to tell Austin she was through with him and was going to stay right where she was, on the stage. The audience stamped their feet and yelled for an encore. Emerald was out of breath and couldn't for the life of her think of another song. She had worked Goober Peas for all it was worth. She was going to have to learn more songs and some real dances, and anyway, she couldn't let Langrishe open the curtain when she was so disheveled. Some instinct told her to quit while she was ahead. The same instinct told her it was not the time to leave Austin Avery. So when he appeared backstage and took her arm, she let herself be dragged away before the startled eyes of Mrs. Langrishe and the other actresses. She thought he might be going to spank her!

It was exciting to have broken Austin Avery's composure. He had lost his poker face, and looked furious, but he also looked vulnerable, and she knew in that moment that she had him. She didn't mind his hand almost crushing hers as he dragged her out of the theatre, down the street to the hotel and up the stairs to their room, where he would do to her exactly what needed doing. Avery thought he was dealing this hand; instead he was merely playing his part in the little drama she had created.

The next morning Austin was contrite. Emerald was tired, satisfied, and slightly bruised. She let Austin see the bruises and kept the satisfaction to herself.

Sometime during the night he had extracted from her the promise she would never again step on the stage of Langrishe's theatre or any other. It had been easy to promise. She could always change her mind. She let him think he had overpowered her, but his rage and his passion and need of her had been displayed for all to see. She thought at one point during the night, he had been close to saying he loved her.

Emerald had reached a new height of passion that night. It was no longer just Avery taking her or even Avery giving her pleasure, it was something she was doing for herself. It brought them both to a new ecstasy. It left Avery both delighted and confused. He kept his control by telling himself it was something he had done to Emerald.

But Emerald knew she was the one who had changed. She had discovered in herself something she had not known before — a sense of power, the knowledge she could control not only men but her own destiny. She didn't have to let things happen to her, but could go after whatever she wanted. And what she wanted now was to *own* Austin Avery.

CHAPTER NINETEEN

In the cabin in Deadwood, Hugh was close by now, just at the edge of her dream. Molly was alone, dozing in a cabin warm from afternoon sun. She wanted a bath, wanted to soak in a real tub filled with scented water, cool and clean and civilized, but in the dream, as in life, she had only a pitcher and bowl on a table. The pitcher, not the tin one in the cabin, but a pretty china one from her girlhood home, was filled with water now warm from the sun. She was naked, and began to sponge off her body, letting the water trickle down her skin, then lathering herself with soap. Her body had changed since the night she had promised herself to Hugh, as if she were ripening for that purpose. She felt almost feverish. The water would cool her. As she soaped her thighs and the place between them she knew Hugh had entered the dream and would soon touch all of her.

She had the curious sensation of being outside herself and so able to see the two of them together, like golden statues beautiful in sunlight which magically filled the cabin. Dust motes, more golden than any they had found in their mine, danced in the air. He knelt before her, and she pressed his face to herself and touched his golden hair, his smooth skin and rough beard. And then he kissed her breasts and belly.

Miraculously, they were alone in all the world and she was without shame or guilt. He was golden and warm from the sun, shirtless as she had seen him working a hundred times outdoors, the muscles of his chest and arms sculpted by light and shadow so now he was again a golden statue before her. Wonderingly, she reached to touch and found him warm and alive.

Then she dreamed his bare chest against her swelling breasts; his rough breeches against her nakedness.

They kissed. Molly willed him to take her. He carried her to a cloudlike quilt on the bed. He unbuttoned his pants and she saw his manhood and was not afraid. He brought his body close to hers, but he did not enter her, and although he held her tenderly, it was not enough. She wanted to possess and be possessed. She raised her hips, but she could not be joined with him.

And then she woke, alone, the empty cabin now shadowed, dark and empty. And she was bereft. She had given herself and almost been joined with him, but it was only a dream. She wept with the knowledge that she could not experience such joy with Hugh and remain Jake's wife and a civilized woman.

Then, even as she mourned for her lost innocence, a new thought struck her: Had the loss not made her free? She had left behind something of herself in Iowa with civilization and the miserable sod house and sad little graveyard. And whatever had impelled her on this journey, whether it was her destiny to be reunited with Hugh or her fear that she would lose her mind if she stayed in the sod house on the prairie, the threshold had been crossed.

On the trail to Custer, after she had insisted on a proper burial for the gold camp whore, Hugh told her what he had thought at the graves, that she, Molly Lewis, was destined to be remembered as a pioneer. She had laughed, saying she longed only for home and civilization; now she realized that pioneers do not always know the way; they simply meet the challenges of the journey. She had agreed to stay, knowing there were risks she could not even name, but to retreat now would mean going home defeated. And, in truth, she had no home to return to, and no true marriage with

Jake. Somehow she had been given a dream that showed the way, and a growing sense of certainty that she could and must seek her destiny.

Molly was not the only one in Deadwood that summer who thought of pioneer destiny. It was the year of the nation's Centennial, and the violators of the Treaty of 1868 now considered themselves no longer trespassers, but rightful citizens of Dakota Territory. They intended to celebrate not just the nation's one hundredth birthday on July Fourth but their own accomplishment in turning the narrow, rocky gulch into a thriving mining town and holding it against the Sioux.

They planned an elaborate Independence Day celebration, promoted not just by word of mouth, but by the printed word, for there was a newspaper, *The Black Hills Pioneer*, circulated in the city but also sent east with the stage. In its pages, which were written as much for the restless citizens of eastern cities as for the locals, the editor proclaimed that the rough and rowdy boom town was now a *CITY*, legitimate, respectable, patriotic, and, above all, prosperous! The reality that, according to the law of the land, the entire populace consisted of lawbreakers and trespassers did not enter into the editor's decision to declare the good news that *civilization had been carried into the wilderness!*

Molly looked forward to the celebration in hopes it would mark the beginning of a more orderly and civilized atmosphere in Deadwood. She bore little sense of guilt at being a trespasser, for certainly the Sioux did not till these lands, and she did not trouble herself with the notion of *sacred hunting grounds* for everyone knew settling to be a higher calling. She hoped only that the government would prevail and no more innocent women and children, white or red, would be killed or left fatherless. Molly did feel uneasy to know that their illegal status meant there was no form of law enforcement beyond the miners' courts, which were called only to protect property claims. The lack of sheriff and deputies did not concern her personally. She felt safe enough in Deadwood, for as one of the few wives and mothers in the camp, she was respected, although sometimes she wondered if respect was something she still deserved.

All the partners of the Lucky Six looked forward to the celebration, for they desperately needed a holiday. The men had not taken a day off work since they first drove the mine shaft into the side of the mountain. Molly, too, labored from sunup to sunset. She could not, of course, work underground, but they were so short handed that, in addition to the cooking and washing, she and Edwin helped with the surface work. She found the time spent outdoors, fetching and toting drinking water and relaying messages satisfying. She had become almost as obsessed with the mine as the men.

There was always the promise that with the next pickaxe of ore broken away from the mine tunnel, they would see the gleaming vein of the mother lode. The work was backbreaking and endless. For the men, it was sometimes dangerous. But all of them had caught what some called, *the gold fever*.

The Centennial Celebration would be a once-in-a-lifetime event, and Molly intended to enjoy it. The day began when she was awakened just after midnight with a series of terrible crashing sounds. Her first thought was that the world was ending or at least that the mine had caved in, but Jake proudly explained that it was the *one hundred-anvil salute*. He'd kept as a surprise his knowledge that the miners, not having real fireworks had something better, which was to set off powder charges packed between blacksmith's anvils, stacked and restacked one atop the other.

Edwin squealed with delight at the first of the

explosions; but by dawn when the one hundred blasts were finally completed, he and Molly both slept and so missed the first raising of the American flag over Deadwood.

Hugh and Luther later that morning reported it as a thrilling sight, accompanied by singing, shouting and shooting. Luther gleefully conceded that the red portion of Old Glory looked a bit strange, having been made from "an inner garment" donated by a patriotic lady from one of the Badland brothels.

Gunfire celebrations erupted in the smaller mining towns up and down the gulch all morning, so by the time the Lucky Six partners gathered to set off for Deadwood together, gun smoke wreathed the gulch like fog. Having initiated the midnight anvil serenade, Caleb Dexter was already somewhat the worse for wear, but still bursting with patriotic furor; so he brought his rifle and marked their joining the celebration with an explosion of gunfire. Then all the men had to fire a round; even Edwin, so that he would be certain to remember the Centennial. To Jake's surprise and Hugh's delight, Molly said she too would shoot. They had made her a full partner in the mine; now she wanted to be a full partner in the celebration.

"I'm a pioneer too!" she declared, hefting the rifle and firing a shot that, despite the pain the recoil brought her shoulder and the disconcerted expression on Jake's face, made her feel joyfully one with the celebrants.

When they reached Deadwood, they found Main Street packed with a happy, noisy, jostling crowd, drinking from bottles and sporadically bursting into patriotic song. When a dark-coated man mounted the crude stage of green lumber and began to speak, the crowd was slow to quiet, but when the word passed through the crowd that he was leading a prayer, the crowd hushed; men removed their hats, and the painted women who watched from the upper floors of the saloons bowed their heads. Molly was moved by the prayer and by seeing so many respectable women and families in the crowd. The city grew daily and for once it seemed that decent folk outnumbered the rowdy element.

The prayer was followed by a reading of the Declaration of Independence by the city's new tax collector, who was apparently so uncomfortable at having been sent to the Hills to tax a population the government called trespassers, that he then read and circulated a petition demanding that the U.S. Congress recognize the rights of its citizens in the Black Hills, numbered now at more than seven thousand "honest, loyal citizens."

Molly wished she could sign the petition. Being considered a partner in the mine had helped her realize how essential women's work was to the settling of the frontier; now she had the radical thought that when Dakota became a state its women should be granted the vote.

Isolated by its location and the lack of a telegraph, Deadwood hungered for news. Rumors circulated in the crowd that Generals Terry and Crook were somewhere in Montana seeking to chastise the Sioux, thus settling the question of the Black Hills. Among the military was the popular and dashing figure of General George Armstrong Custer. He had distinguished himself in the Civil War and was a popular figure. News of the military involvement made them all feel safer. The spirit of the crowd was jubilant, for they expected to receive at any moment word of a victory by Custer and the others. Soon they would be free from worry that they were building their hopes on land they did not own and from which they might yet be driven by the Indians or even their own government.

Edwin grew restless with the speechmaking, so Molly took him about the crowd to make the acquaintance of other families. They were both shy, having been so long isolated on the homestead and the mine. Edwin had been content to "work" with the men at the mine, but Molly wanted him to have playmates; he must not forget how to be a child. Although she enjoyed Deadwood's bustling crowds and the sounds of the tinny pianos and banjos reaching the streets from behind the swinging doors of the hurdy-gurdy houses and saloons that afternoon, to her Deadwood was still a place from which to escape.

The afternoon sun was hot, and when the men announced their intention to retire to a saloon called the I.X.L., Molly did not begrudge them. She had some gold dust of her own to spend, and Hugh made a point of telling her where he would be if she needed him. She thought there was an implication in his manner, some expectation that they might find a way to be alone in the confusion of the celebrating city, but what she wanted was a holiday.

She had not experienced happiness in so long, she was surprised to recognize the feeling and she wanted to share it with her son. Edwin had never known a real celebration. She wanted the day to be for him all he had missed: the fun of birthday parties, church suppers, sing-a-longs, and especially real July Fourth celebrations with fireworks and ice cream socials.

Sporadic gunfire, which she hated, continued all day, but the ice cream miraculously appeared, even as she tried to describe it to Edwin. They gorged on huge bowlfuls served in the dining room of the Progressive Hall, one of the city's more reputable establishments. Molly promised Edwin they would often have such treats when they returned to civilization.

"Civilization?" he asked.

"Yes, Edwin, that's places where there are real houses and other buildings made of brick. We'll see all sorts of fine things when we go back to Pennsylvania and meet your grandparents. That's what we'll do when we find enough gold."

"And leave the Lucky Six? Leave Deadwood?"

"Yes, Edwin. Won't that be wonderful? We can have a real house with real windows and live in a real city."

"But why would we leave Deadwood? Everything's here. The mine and Pa and Hugh and all of us!"

Molly was silent. She should not have mentioned the future. She had dreamed that everything would be solved when they could return to civilization; now she saw that her son was already part of the frontier. Her long-held dream of someday returning to her parents must likely be sacrificed if her dream of being with Hugh came true, but how could she even think of taking Edwin away from the only father he knew?

Her mood changed dramatically. She could no longer prattle to her son of places and things he neither knew nor cared about. Edwin was also quiet and Molly realized he was exhausted. They went to find Jake, but the crowd at the I.X.L. spilled into the street. She had no choice but to send Edwin inside. It rankled her that his maleness made it proper for him to enter a place she would have been mortally embarrassed to enter for any purpose, much less the task of fetching her husband away from his drink. She hoped Edwin would find him quickly and Jake would not leave her waiting long.

Edwin returned at last alone.

"Pa isn't ready to go home yet. He says can we wait in the restaurant or go on without him?"

Molly felt sick. It was almost dusk. Jake knew she would not want to walk home after dark with the whole town drunk. It was unlike him to be so inconsiderate. She wanted to know if he was drunk, but could not ask Edwin.

"Pa's drunk!" he volunteered cheerfully. "Him and

Caleb Dexter and Luther! They're drunker'n I ever seen anybody! But I think Hugh's sober. I don't know why."

"Than I ever saw *anyone*," Molly corrected before she realized the futility of reproaching the boy. He only told the truth. She felt helpless until she saw that Hugh was standing in the doorway of the saloon. She looked away, feeling shamed before him by Jake's indifference. She had seldom faulted Jake for needing his drink, for she knew how life had disappointed him, but he had never before failed in his duty to her or the boy.

"I'll take you home," Hugh said quietly, stepping out into the street with her. "I told Jake I would."

"And did he say that you should?"

"Pa's too drunk to say much of anything!" Edwin reported, happily taking hold of Hugh's hand.

"Jake thanked me for offering. He's not ready to leave. I expect Luther and I could get him home between us, though Luther's in no mood to end the celebration either, and Caleb Dexter's passed out underneath the table, but I'll get Jake home for you if that's what you want."

"No, I expect that would be even less dignified than letting them sleep it off in the saloon, but what about you? Do you mind leaving now?"

She saw the answer in his eyes. She realized fate had decided for her and let Hugh lead her away from town. Edwin skipped along and chatted amiably until exhaustion overcame him and he happily climbed onto Hugh's back. As they walked up the road to the cabin, Edwin fell asleep with his golden head on the shoulder of the man he so resembled, and Molly wondered who would be the better father for the boy.

They did not talk and Molly did not speculate on how it would happen. She knew it would happen and that was enough. When they reached her cabin, Hugh laid Edwin gently down and spoke at last.

"When you get him settled, will you join me on

the hillside? It's a beautiful night and there's enough moonlight to find our way."

She could not speak, but nodded.

"I'll be waiting for you."

She fumbled with Edwin's clothes, removing his belt and shoes so he would sleep more comfortably. When he half-woke, she helped him into his nightshirt and felt the need to reassure him if he should wake and find her gone.

"Edwin, it's still early. I thought I might sit outside where it's cool for a bit."

"With Hugh, so you'll be safe?"

Her heart was hammering as she laid him back down and covered him lightly. "Yes, with Hugh."

"Ma," he gave her what seemed a knowing look through sleepy lashes, "do you love Hugh?"

She could not help gasping, but she made her voice calm before she replied, "What makes you ask that?"

"'Cause I do. I love Hugh and Luther and Caleb Dexter, and I thought you might, too. Love Hugh, I mean. Not the others, I guess you just *like* them, but Hugh's special ain't he? I love him best, next to you and Pa."

"Well, I like all of the men. But you're right. Hugh is special. He's a very smart and well-spoken man!"

"I thought so," he seemed to be drifting back to sleep, but then his eyes fluttered open again. He had forgotten his prayers. Molly listened while he said his *God Blesses*, including all the men at the Lucky Six as he had since the beginning of the partnership, but Molly heard only Hugh's name, her heart full of confusion. She could not admit she loved this man, even to her son in the most innocent of declarations, but in a few minutes she was going to him. Now she could not ask God to bless her, but only hope for his understanding and forgiveness.

While she waited for Edwin to sleep, she freshened herself with cool water. She wished she had more than the scrap of mirror and a comb to make herself ready for him; then was surprised to see in the clouded mirror that she was already glowing and beautiful. She was ready at last, there was no time for hesitation.

He was waiting outside his cabin, holding a lantern and studying the side of the hill. She saw by the delight on his face when he turned to her that he had not been certain she would come.

"I found a place for us," he said, "There's a level space on the side of the hill. It's under a tree and cushioned with pine needles. I thought I'd leave the lantern here so we can find our way back to the cabin. We can make our way by moonlight now, but it might be dark when we return."

She saw he carried a blanket under his arm and was both touched and made shy by his planning. She followed him up the hill on a path that continued past the mine shaft to a high place she knew he sometimes used to get away from everything. From this place they could see the cabins and the road, but could not be seen themselves until they returned to the light of the lantern.

He spread the blanket over the pine needles and turned to her. "I hope this is all right. From this place sometimes I can almost forget the mine."

"Yes, it's lovely the way the trees make a shelter. And look how glorious the stars are. Away from the lights of town, the stars are incredibly bright and beautiful."

"I know. I've wanted to show you the sky for so long." He took his place behind her, with his arms gently around her so that she could lean against him while they studied the heavens.

"Take a deep breath. You can smell the pine and the mountain air so much better here. And you can still hear the creek and the night sounds of the crickets!"

"This must have been a beautiful land before everyone came here to spoil it. This reminds me of that time when we first found ourselves alone on the trail and saw the deer, and I said they were beautiful and you said —"

"I said it was you who was beautiful!" His breath was warm against her neck. "Do you want a compliment, Molly?" he teased. "Shall I say it again?"

"You don't need to. Tonight when I was getting ready to meet you, I looked in the mirror and I felt beautiful. Like a young girl whose beau is coming courting. I never felt quite that way before."

"You were never courted, were you? I spoiled that for you."

"Don't" she said, turning toward him. "Don't let's talk about sad times or the past."

"Or the future?" He took her hand. "Can we talk of the future, Molly? Can we make a plan?"

"No, Hugh. No, not that!"

"I thought you'd not say no to me again."

She closed her eyes as his arms enfolded her. They were warm and gentle around her, the rough weave of his shirt a blessing against her cheek; but she could feel his tension growing and was aware, too, of an answering yielding in herself.

"I can't say yes to anything. I can't speak my feelings, and I can't make plans or promises, *but I will not say no to you tonight.*"

"Oh, Molly, Molly, my love," his arms tightened around her and she raised her face to meet his kiss. Before their lips met, she thought only that she would at last give herself to him. But in the kiss, she not only yielded but took, as hungry for him as he for her. In that moment they were the whole world for each other. There was no mountain upon which they stood, no cabin below, and no Deadwood.

He lifted her then and laid her down on the blanket, smoothing it around her as best he could on the hillside.

"It makes me think of the first time," she said. "Remember us in the barn, arranging the straw and playing at making a home for ourselves in some magic place?"

"We were children then. Now we know that *home is us being together*. This is home, at last." He knelt beside her and touched her face tenderly, and she knew he was right. They had come home and everything was changed. She had come to him that night to fulfill a promise, to do what must be done to keep him at the mine, to hold him against her fear of darkness and loss. But from that first kiss freely given on the hillside, she became a different woman.

It was the first true lovemaking for both of them. With each other, in that time before, they had been teenagers exploring, pretending, caught up in something they neither willed nor understood. With Jake she had been a wife doing her duty, rewarding and comforting him for his protection and support. With others, Hugh had felt physical pleasure, but no more than that. Now, they truly *made love* as if it was eternity instead of a few moments stolen on the side of a Dakota hillside.

Sweet, almost shy kisses. Fingertips caressing her face and neck and then tantalizingly discovering the opening of the dress already made loose and ready for him. He touched with delicate strokes which warmed her skin and flooded her imagination with glorious color, so that as she sank into the blanket she felt herself a wildflower opening to blossom in this secret place. Blossoming to delight a lover. Only for him. Only for Hugh, at last.

Her dress was entirely open now and her skirts raised, petal-like around her hips. She felt wanton and willing, and his touch and her moans proved her readiness.

He stood and unbuttoned his shirt. He seemed to be moving slowly as if to tease. Then he was naked. She did not look away, but opened her arms to him.

He knelt at her side and then seemed to hesitate. "Molly, my love. I'm so foolish, and I don't know how to speak of it. I promised that I'd not get you with child, and I determined that when the time came, I'd have a sheath to catch my seed and keep you safe, but —"

"You're not afraid that I would be ashamed because they are what a man uses with a whore?"

"No, I'm the one who's ashamed. Ashamed and foolish. Even after you seemed to promise that we might at last be together, I could not think it would really happen, and I did not prepare myself. It seemed that if I planned for this, I would spoil it. I've wanted you so, my darling, and I made you promise you'd give yourself to me but I never believed it would happen."

"But you said if I did not give myself to you, you'd leave!"

"I lied. I could never leave you, even if I never did what I'm burning to do. Even now, you could deny me and I'd stay near you, always!"

How her heart leapt then to know that it was not only his desire that bound him to her, but that he would never deny his love for her. She felt infinitely tender and something new: *Impatience.*

"I'll not deny you."

He wanted her to say she wanted him, but he knew she could not speak such words aloud. As if sensing his thoughts, she reached out, and with an instinct as old as Eve, found the center of his desire and began to caress him.

"You said there were ways, Hugh. You said there were many ways to love me. You said you could never keep your hands off me."

"Oh God, yes. Many ways. A hundred ways that I can love you with my hands and with my mouth and with just the touch of this great need I have for you! I've thought of so many. And you! Oh, you have found how to pleasure me. Let me lie here against you, let us be close, and oh how we will pleasure each other!"

And so, because the ultimate joining could be theirs for only a moment, that which bound them together was not possession, but the joyous freedom of pleasuring and even squandering their love, one against the other. Their lovemaking was both tender and rough, greedy and giving; a riotous explosion of sensation, motion and mood, kiss and touch, of seed and soul spilled together.

At last they lay in each other's arms in quiet joy. Hugh touched her face and found it wet with tears. To his unspoken question, she said only, "I never knew before. I've lived so long and not known."

"And I thought I knew, and I was a fool."

And if their words made no sense, they both understood and said no more. The night grew cold, and Hugh pulled the blanket around them, so they seemed wrapped together in a warm cocoon. He slept, but Molly lay awake, her thoughts as radiant as the stars above her. Hugh's head was heavy on her breast and, though it was sweet to hold him so, his falling asleep made her think of Jake's snoring, and that all men were alike in some things. But even as she had that thought, Hugh woke to caress her and whisper, "Stay close, Molly. I love you."

She continued to hold him against her as tenderly as she had the newborn Edwin, but she could not answer him. She had thought of Jake. He would be needing porridge and strong coffee in the morning. And she must get it for him. Perhaps the men would not be home until dawn, but she did not dare stay longer with Hugh.

They had shared a gift. If she never knew a real home with a piano and glass windows, if she had nothing else in her life to treasure, she would always have the memory of this night, but now it must end.

She turned her head so she could see back down the

hillside to their cabins. The light of the lantern Hugh had left burning seemed far away and very weak. Even as she watched, it flickered and died.

She looked up at the myriad brilliant stars, heard again the explosion of gunfire echoing in Deadwood, and knew the mine and her cabin, her sleeping son and duty waited; and she wondered how she and Hugh would ever again find their way home.

CHAPTER TWENTY

Once again Emerald O'Brien stood outside the I.X.L. restaurant and tried to decide how to spend the afternoon. She had lingered over her brunch, taken her walk, and now was debating whether it was time to wake Avery. The only problem with being a bad woman, she decided, was that it took up so little of one's time. It was a shame Austin would not hear of her being on the stage. It would give her something to do. Still, her theatrical performance had produced results. Austin had been especially attentive since the afternoon he dragged her from the stage to their hotel room. He would have torn her clothes off, had she not decided to cooperate. She did not relish sewing on buttons.

In the days since then, their lovemaking had reached new heights as she realized her own ability to seek and receive pleasure. She kept her desires hidden from Avery, or so she thought, and instead encouraged him in subtle ways to replay the scene in which he ravished her. The pleasure was always worth the little bruises and the wear and tear on her chemises. Her only disappointment was in realizing there seemed to be definite limits to a man's energy for lovemaking, limits which left her so much empty time.

Her boredom made her lonely; sometimes she even experienced little nibbles of guilt. For even as she became her own woman, Emerald could not entirely forget her mother's lectures on sin and whoredom and the folly of loving handsome, dark-haired strangers. Sometimes she even missed the constant squabbling of her sisters. She could not associate with her "sisters in sin," in Deadwood's Badlands, for being the mistress of a man like Austin Avery was far above being a sporting woman or even a dance hall girl, but it was also far below the security of being a wife.

No married woman would speak to her; to respectable men she was *damaged goods*, no matter how much they might desire her for themselves. Knowing her whole life was built on one man made her uneasy, even as she told herself the romance was enough.

She did have the ability and means to distract herself: a new hairdo, a leisurely bath in the hotel's copper tub, or hatching a new plot to torment her man. That day, as she considered which amusement to chose, she noticed a commotion on the lower end of Main Street. A crowd was gathering at the disreputable end of the street. Glad for the diversion, she decided the location of the event would not deter her investigation. As she hurried toward the scene she was aware a decent woman would never go that far down the street, but there were some advantages to being tarnished.

When she joined the crowd, she quickly made her way to the front and found herself standing before one of the town's more notorious enterprises. A crudely painted sign labeled the street entry "Saloon" and the upper story "Boarding House," with "Rooms Rented by the Hour."

The crowd was enjoying a loud, three-way argument between a henna-haired woman in a dressing gown, standing on the outside staircase and obviously a tenant of the upstairs establishment, and in the doorway of the saloon, an oily-looking dark-haired man whose gartered rolled-up sleeves and apron marked him as a bartender, or perhaps the proprietor of the establishment. Between the two stood a frowning silk-vested gentleman carrying the black leather bag of a doctor.

"You can't just throw her out into the street" the henna-haired woman screamed, coming down the stairs and taking a stance before the saloon-keeper.

"Well, I can't keep her upstairs," he shouted, raising his clenched fist. "She's no use to me now!"

Emerald stood on her tiptoes straining to see who they were talking about. Someone shifted before her and when Emerald got a clear view, she gasped. Coming carefully down the outside staircase, two men balanced between them a door on which lay a woman. Her face and shoulders were draped with a fringed shawl, which could only mean one thing. She was dead.

"You're a cruel heartless man, Al Baines," The henna-haired woman screamed. "What would it hurt you to let her lie upstairs until we can make arrangements?"

The stretcher bearers reached the street and looked to Baines for orders.

"It's bad for business, Tiz, you ought to know that. Bad enough she had to do herself in on the premises. How do you think a man feels when he's out to have a good time and hears there's a dead woman upstairs?"

"He has a point," the man with the doctor's bag put in. "Even a vigorous man is apt to lose his libido when confronted with the harsher realities of cohabitating with the weaker sex."

"So what do we do with her, boss?" One of the stretcher bearers whined. "She ain't exactly light."

"Then you take her, Doctor," Tiz begged, clutching at his sleeve.

"Take your hands off me immediately." He pried her loose. "I told you, I have no facilities for laying anyone out. It doesn't look right for a doctor to run an undertaking establishment. Conflict of interests, you know."

"But, Doctor —"

"It's out of the question. You will have to make your own arrangements for your — friend. Now if someone will just take care of my fee, I will be on my way."

"Your fee!" Tiz screamed. "What did you do to earn a

fee? You didn't do a thing except say it was too late. You didn't even say what killed her!"

There was a rumble of sympathy from the crowd.

"Good heavens, men," the doctor addressed the crowd. "What difference does it make? She was dead when I got here. Probably an overdose of laudanum, as it often is in these cases. Or else she got herself in a predicament and took some drug to try to remedy her mistake. It hardly matters now." He drew himself up importantly, clutching his bag. "I have done my duty, offering medical assistance despite my natural reluctance to render my services in such an establishment."

"Hell, Doctor," a voice from the crowd yelled, "we seen you rendering your services at this place plenty times before!"

Another voice yelled, "and it wasn't in the afternoon!" and the crowd broke into laughter.

The doctor held his head high and spoke with anger. "I don't have to be subjected to this."

He started to march down the street, but before he had taken two steps, he turned back to Baines. "And you, Sir, will be receiving a bill for my services, and if you don't pay up, the next time one of your doxies makes herself sick, *the doctor will be out.*"

As he marched off down the street, a few of the hangers-on started to follow him, imitating his mincing gait. The crowd seemed about to dissipate when Tiz confronted the crowd. "What about Marabell? How is she to be repaid for *her services*? All you men were anxious to *know* her before, so now will you treat her like a dead animal?"

The crowd shifted uncomfortably; finally someone put some coins in a hat, and it was passed among the men.

"Can't we set her down, boss?" whined one of the stretcher bearers. "We can't stand here all day." They were moving toward the entrance to the saloon.

"Not in my place, you don't," Baines said, blocking the doorway with his hefty body.

"You let her in, Al Baines!" The voice came from an upstairs window, and Emerald looked up to see two women framed in the narrow window, ill-kept hair hanging around their shoulders and their eyes looking as if they had been crying. "You take her in, or we'll all go over to the Hidden Treasure to work!"

"The girls are right." Tiz put her hands on her hips as she confronted Baines."You lay Marabell out proper or we'll all go somewhere else to work." Here she cast a meaningful look at the crowd. "Or, we won't work at all."

At this, the hat which had been passed half heartedly began to fill more quickly as the miners dug deeper in their pockets and pouches. Finally someone handed the hat to Emerald. It was half-full of well-worn bills, coins and grains of gold. Emerald held the hat. She was struck by the incongruity of the picture she must make in such a crowd at such an event dressed like *Godey's Lady's Book*. The whole thing seemed unreal, as if it were happening on a stage.

"Excuse me, Ma'am," the man to her left took the hat, "this ain't no business for a lady."

Emerald gave up the hat and stood by as the men discussed coffins and burial sites and grave diggers. Baines, seeing which way public feeling was going, made a desperate attempt to save the day's business. "All right. We'll lay her out in her room. Drinks are on the house!"

It worked. Most of the crowd filtered into the saloon. Marabell was carried back upstairs and Tiz, taking the contents of the hat, followed the stretcher up the outside stairs.

Emerald, could not yet walk away. And then, as the

procession moved unsteadily up the staircase, a breeze caught the shawl and it blew away from Marabell's face.

Emerald gasped. Marabell was so young! She didn't look over sixteen, a round-faced farm girl, a girl like Emerald's little sister. A girl who thought she would find excitement and adventure in the gold camp and had died by her own hand. The doctor had declared that she had probably taken an overdose of laudanum, or else something to give her an abortion.

That's how whores end up, she could hear her mother say. They drink themselves to death or they get diseased or take too much laudanum or kill themselves trying to get rid of a mistake.

Emerald fled up the street, her heart pounding. *It could be me,* she thought. *Me, lying there dead for everyone to see. I have laudanum in my reticule. It helps me sleep when Austin has been aloof, or if I have a little pain. That's probably how Marabell started. Taking a little laudanum to dull the pain and the guilt and now she's dead. Or she got in a family way, which was as bad as suicide.* Surely that couldn't happen to her. Austin had assured her he knew the secrets of preventing pregnancy, but he wasn't always careful. And those girls must know all the secrets about not getting caught, but if something like that happened to Emerald, she would not even have sisters in sin to bury her.

Austin was arranging his silk cravat at his neck when Emerald burst into their room. He looked up, startled, one hand moving to the pearl-handled revolver in his belt. Emerald threw herself into his arms, weeping bitterly. He held her for a moment, then led her to the bed, made her sit down, and wiped her face with his handkerchief.

"Control yourself and tell me what happened!"

Hiccupping back her sobs, Emerald told him.

"Probably laudanum," he said. "Most of those girls are addicted to the stuff. Opium and alcohol; takes the edge off things. But why are you so upset? You didn't know her."

"But Austin, it could be me! Don't you see, it could happen to *me*. She was a bad girl and —"

"Don't be silly, Emerald," he stood up and moved away from her. "That girl was a common whore. Why you have too much pride to ever let yourself —"

"You don't *let* yourself get that way. *It just happens*. A girl gets . . . gets . . . in trouble and —"

"Gets pregnant, Emerald. Stop being coy. It doesn't, become you. Are you afraid of getting pregnant? Is that it? Didn't I tell you I've been taking care of that?"

"But sometimes you don't. Sometimes you get too excited!"

"I'll be more careful. I sincerely don't want to get you in any difficulty."

"But what if you did? What if it happened?"

"Well, then we would try to find a reputable medical man to take care of it, or else . . ." he shrugged.

"Or else *you'd marry me*? You'd marry me wouldn't you? Isn't that what you were going to say?"

"Don't put words in my mouth." His face was even more impassive than usual. "I was going to say I'd give you enough money to get you back East. You could pretend to be a widow and have the baby somewhere and we'd find a decent family to keep it and —"

"You'd make me give up my baby!"

"Look at me Emerald!" He demanded, taking her face in his hands. "Do you *want* a baby?"

"Of course not" she jerked his hands away angrily. "But you'd make me give it up? You wouldn't marry me so I could keep my very own baby?"

"I cannot stand it when you persist in being so

emotional." He picked up his frock coat and finished dressing while he talked. "You have witnessed an ugly scene and I understand your being upset. I suggest you lie down and compose yourself. I have business to attend to."

"Austin!" she screamed. "You answer my question! Do you mean you wouldn't marry me?"

He turned back to her. "I've told you before and I'll tell you once more. People like you and I are not made for marriage and respectability. You can't cage a wildcat. It would kill everything between us."

"But, Austin," she protested prettily, "I love you!"

"Don't start that, Emerald." He put a hand under her chin and forced her to look at him. "Now listen to me. If you decide you are meant to be married, or if you should find yourself with child and you want to play at being a mother, then I will set you up in some town where you can pretend to be a respectable widow until you tire of the game or else —"

"Or else, what?"

"Or you can find someone else to take a chance on."

"Take a chance on! You make it sound like one of your games. Like gambling!"

"Marriage is the biggest gamble of them all, my dear."

He picked up his hat and adjusted it on his head. "And all the cards are stacked against the man." He paused, studying himself in the mirror. "No, I'll take that back. Women lose too. Marriage makes them slaves and shrews. Marriage is the game no one wins. Oh, it might be worth it for those who are convinced they'll burn in hell without it. But as for me, I'd as soon take my chances on hell in the hereafter as deal myself in for a sure piece of hell on earth."

"I never heard anyone say anything so awful in my whole, entire life!"

"Then, it's obvious you've not been around many married people. They say awful things to each other all the time."

"I'd never say anything awful to you." She sniffed prettily and dabbed at her eyes with his handkerchief, but she knew she should have controlled herself. The subject of marriage should have been introduced in a way that made him think it has his idea. Now she had laid all her cards on the table and Austin was going to call her bluff. Somehow she must regain her advantage. Now, his handkerchief was full of black smudges, and worse, she had smeared the kohl around her eyes. She must look a sight. She tried to compose her face into a little-girl pout.

He moved closer to her. "Of course you'd say awful things to me. You'd say awful things to me if we're married, trust me. At least this way we can play it honest. This way when one of us wants out, we can just walk away."

"You'd walk away from me, Austin? You'd just leave me here alone without anything?"

"Of course not, dear little girl." He ran the tip of one finger along the side of her neck. "You've a whole bag full of plunder, don't you? If anything happened to me, you'd just cash in all those watches and jewels; you'd have more than enough to get you back East in style."

"You think that would be enough?" Emerald pouted. "You think it would make up for losing you?"

"I'm sure it would," Avery laughed. "I'm no prize. You'd soon find a man as good for you, or *as bad* for you."

He gave her a pinch on the cheek and left whistling, but his parting shot had given her an idea.

She *could* find another man. She could find one better than Austin Avery. One who would marry her. And she had seen that day the importance of marriage. It was the only way a woman could be secure.

If Austin Avery wouldn't marry her, then she would find someone who would.

And that would make Austin Avery sorry.

CHAPTER TWENTY-ONE

For days after their lovemaking on the hillside, Hugh and Molly hardly dared look at each other. It was not shame which kept them apart, but the thought that each had been so changed by what had happened that all could see. The physical expression of what had been in their hearts since their first meeting on the trail, indeed, since their first time together years before, had *changed everything.*

And yet it changed nothing. Destiny might promise that Molly belonged with Hugh, but she was still Jake's wife. It seemed impossible to Molly, but Jake did not notice the change in her. It was as if he had stopped seeing her. She wondered if it was his obsession with the Lucky Six that made him so unaware of her or if it was just Jake's way. She wanted to believe that he, too, had once loved just the sight of her, but she knew such emotion was simply not in Jake's nature.

Hugh didn't believe Jake's failings as a husband excused his own actions or feelings. Molly was still Jake's lawful wife; Jake was still a good man who did not deserve to be betrayed by his own partner. Hugh did not believe in predestination, that fatalistic theology which seemed to say man was doomed or saved only by the will of God. It was too much like the ancients' belief that man was but the plaything of the gods. It had always seemed to Hugh that man made his own fate, and the world operated on a principle of justice that would reward those who worked hard and did good. Now, finding a way to be joined with Molly and still respect himself seemed as impossible as finding riches in the dark and awful tomb they called a mine. Still, the hope of one more touch, one more kiss, even one more smile was, like Poor Man's Gold, enough to keep him imprisoned in that most torturous of traps: hope.

His inner turmoil grew as the atmosphere in Deadwood changed from hopeful expectancy and optimism to tension and fear. The city had celebrated its first Fourth of July and the nation's Centennial unaware that less than two hundred miles away Custer and his entire command were dead. It was a tragedy which those Deadwood "citizens" still capable of guilt would sense had been impelled by their own acts of trespassing. Even those who were beyond guilt realized the army's defeat put them in mortal danger.

Custer's massacre, the Battle of the Little Big Horn, occurred on June 25 and was regarded in the cities of America as almost as great a tragedy as Lincoln's assassination. Isolated as it was by the lack of a telegraph line, Deadwood did not learn of the event until July 20. Forever afterward, people remembered and related where they were and how they felt when they heard the news.

On the evening of that July day, Hugh had walked toward town, wanting to be alone to think. By the time he reached the upper limits of Deadwood, he knew something had happened. Men clustered in groups, talking excitedly. He hoped it was good news. Deadwood citizens had speculated for weeks on the location of the Terry and Custer commands, which one of the first issues of the city's newspaper, *The Black Hills Pioneer*, reported had been sent from Fort Abraham Lincoln in May to subdue the hostile Sioux. General Crook was also rumored to be campaigning, and hopes were high that a decisive military victory would be the first step in declaring the Black Hills officially open for settlement by whites.

Deadwood was tired of its common-law status. The Fourth of July celebration, glorified in the *Pioneer*, copies of which were sent to major cities in the East, was an attempt to portray Deadwood, not as a mining camp of squatters and trespassers, but a prosperous city of solid citizens, inviting more settlers and especially investors. So far, however, the only sign from the U.S. government of Deadwood's existence was a visit from the tax collector. The citizen/trespassers could have done without that, but they yearned for the other institutions of civilization: a telegraph line and official ways of dealing with the mountains of garbage that were filling the spaces between the crowded buildings, firefighting equipment, and, most especially, a legal system. Quasi-legal miners' courts were established to file mining claims, but the system was informal. Thieves and claim jumpers could not be tolerated, but without a sheriff or jail, they had only two ways to deal with lawbreakers: *banishment or hanging.*

Although the value of property and mining claims was growing rapidly, so was the number of those who had no regard for law and order. The pioneers who braved hardships to come to the Hills in the winter of '75 or the spring of '76 were men willing to break their backs to get their gold. In the summer of '76 came those who knew there were easier ways to get rich. So when Hugh saw the crowds that evening, he hoped it meant a peace treaty had been made, and they could truly establish the rule of law.

Even before Hugh joined the noisy crowd that day, the men's faces told him the news was bad. He heard of the massacre in bits and pieces and could not comprehend the magnitude of the disaster. Even when he managed to buy a copy of the *Pioneer's* special edition and read the story for himself, it seemed impossible that nearly a month before Custer, his brother, and his entire command of over two hundred men were lost, without a single survivor. According to the newspaper, Custer's men had met what seemed an impossibly large number of Indians — *five thousand Sioux and Cheyenne.* Now all could understand why there had been only a few raids against isolated settlers that summer. It was not that the Sioux did not intend to retaliate against Custer who had led the first invasion of their beloved Pahasapa in '74, but they had chosen to make their stand where they could mass in numbers and fight in open fields. So what would happen now? With the soldiers' scalps, waving triumphantly from their lances, surely the Sioux would turn their wrath toward Deadwood and those who had followed Custer on his *Thieves' Trail.*

Throughout July, the situation seemed to grow more precarious. Travel into and out of the Hills was reduced to parties of well-armed men, and even these were subject to attack. No one knew where the five thousand victorious warriors were, and every issue of the Pioneer rumored new battles; yet some said that since more copies of the paper were distributed in the East to encourage capital investment and immigration to the gold fields than were sold locally, the *Pioneer* was downplaying the danger in their determination to "Ballyhoo the Black Hills."

Then on August 2, two events occurred which, had they happened on different days would have been disturbing enough but, occurring as they did, within hours of each other, made Hugh feel the whole town had gone mad. The first incident, the murder of Wild Bill Hickok, would quickly become local folklore to be recounted in years to come as part of the legend of "The Summer of '76." The second happening was one most pioneers would choose to forget.

It was a Tuesday evening and toward sunset Hugh, Luther, Molly and Edwin strolled into town. As they reached the city, once again Hugh noticed clusters of men talking and arguing in the street. They soon learned that James Butler Hickok, commonly known as Wild

Bill, had been sitting in Saloon No. 10 (there were so many saloons, some were known only by numbers) when Jack McCall entered and shot him dead. Hickok was habitually cautious, having killed many men in his career as a law officer and in other pursuits. But that day he had violated his custom of watching the door and was sitting with his back to it when he was slain. McCall was chased through the streets by an angry mob and soon captured. He was tried almost immediately by a miners' court convened in the Bella Union theatre. McCall testified Hickok had killed his brother, and for that or other reasons, the jury promptly acquitted McCall with the provision he leave the Hills. McCall had left immediately.

Hugh thought it a terrible miscarriage of justice and others in the crowd agreed. One man speculated McCall had been hired as an assassin by those who feared Hickok might bring law and order to Deadwood. Even as he spoke, the man realized the significance of his words and his voice trailed off as he glanced around the crowd.

Hugh was still pondering the remark when he became aware of another disturbance at the upper end of Main Street.

As the crowd watched, a horseman charged down the street at a gallop. The rider brandished something in one hand. Hugh assumed it was a dead animal of some sort. Then as the rider reined in, setting his lathered horse back on its heels almost directly before him, Hugh saw with horror that the object held aloft was a human head.

The head had been severed at the neck and spattered drops of congealing blood. Instinctively Hugh stepped before Molly and Edwin to protect them from the sight. But it was too late. Molly looked as if she were going to faint, then steadied herself and grabbed Edwin who was standing on his tip-toes trying to get a better look.

Hugh picked Edwin up. "Let's get out of here."

"Wow," Luther sputtered. "Would you look at that!"

Hugh, holding Edwin's head against his own shoulder, couldn't resist taking another look himself. The horseman was now the center of a large crowd. The head was that of an Indian and the rider held it aloft proudly, swinging it to and fro. Edwin was struggling in his arms, wanting to see.

"Please, Hugh." Molly cried, and Hugh held on to her arm and the protesting Edwin and broke a path through the crowd. He knew without looking back that Luther would not follow.

And indeed, Luther stayed and reported later that the head was auctioned off to the highest bidder. The Deadwood Board of Health paid the bounty on the grounds that killing Indians contributed to the health of the city. It was not the first time Hugh had heard there were those who would pay a bounty for an Indian scalp; yet if he had not seen such a thing with his own eyes, he would not have believed a white man could behave so savagely. Hugh knew that if he been alone that day, he would have protested. He doubted that the crowd would have supported him. He felt no particular horror at Wild Bill's death. He believed that men like Hickok who lived by the gun could expect to die by the gun.

But that people could hold life so cheaply they behaved as did Deadwood over the Indian head made Hugh question again what kind of men they had all become. He no longer felt even a vestige of pride in being one of the pioneers *spreading civilization*.

He tried to explain to Edwin that there was no excuse for men to be so barbaric, even in war, but he doubted that his words could counter what the boy had seen, not just the face of the dead Indian, but the faces of the crowd — fascinated, excited, approving.

As for talking to his brother, Hugh knew it would

be effort wasted. He had given up trying to set Luther straight about anything.

He would wonder later if he should not have tried harder to be a brother to Luther. He would think often about his brother's last trip to Deadwood and wish that he, Hugh, had done something — anything — different.

It happened on a Sunday afternoon. It was their day of rest, but the cabin was hot and flies buzzed incessantly. They were all irritable and discouraged. Hugh was sitting at their plank table trying to write in his journal while Luther and Caleb Dexter dozed in their bunks. Unable to find the words to express his feelings about the mood in Deadwood, Hugh drummed his fingers on the table nervously.

"Please stop that noise!" Luther suddenly barked. He sat up with a groan and put his head in his hands. "I can't stand it anymore. Working in that mine all day all week and laying around here all day Sunday. I was having more fun back in Nebraska."

"Yep, it gets to you after a while," Dexter said.

"I know how you feel," Hugh closed his journal.

"Just remember partnering in this damn mine was your idea, Hugh! I wanted to be free, out somewhere prospecting or working for Hobart. Someplace where I'd have a chance for action."

"For shooting Indians, you mean."

"So? It needs to be done, doesn't it? I thought we came to the Black Hills to have an adventure, not to muck around in the ground like a bunch of moles. Look at my hands. I've got calluses on my calluses!"

"We have man's hands now, Luther." Hugh looked at his own hands, so different from the hands that had set type for the Nebraska newspaper only months before. "There's nothing wrong with the marks of honest labor."

"I didn't didn't leave home to be a laborer. Look at my boots. Ruined! And I can't buy new ones. Every speck of gold we get out has to go back into the mine for supplies. When are we going to get anything out of it?"

"We just got to hit the right vein," Caleb Dexter interjected, "One of these days —"

"One of these days! I've heard it all before. I'm sick of hearing about it. Poor Man's Gold, and conglomerate gold, and bonanzas on the bedrock. I'm sick of you acting like you know everything and I'm sick of Hugh bossing me around and I'm especially sick of this cabin."

"Well, I reckon it's time then." Dexter rolled off his bunk and picked up his boots.

"Time for what?" Luther demanded.

"Time for you and me to make a trip to town. When a man's got cabin fever; there's only one cure."

"What's that?" Hugh asked suspiciously. "Luther doesn't need to get drunk again. He's only sixteen."

"And ain't sixteen almost a man?" Dexter grinned. "Ain't sixteen old enough to know what's what? Especially for a lad that's working twelve hours a day in the mines. That grows you up fast, but it makes you tense too, and there are certain natural urges that got to be met!"

"Hey!" Luther grinned wickedly.

"I hope you're not talking about taking him to a bawdyhouse!"

"I *hope* that's what you're talking about," Luther grinned happily at the old man.

"Well, it all depends," Dexter spoke casually as he drew on his boots. "I figure well start with a venison steak and a little drink at the new General Custer House, just to start the evening with a touch of class. Then we'll work our way down to the hurdy-gurdy houses, see the show, dance with the girls, maybe stop and do a little gambling."

"Then?" Luther urged from the top bunk.

"Then," Caleb Dexter straightened his suspenders over the red-flannel underwear that served him as a shirt, "then, we'll see how we feel. We might take a little walk down to Chinatown and look over the —"

"You're not going to take Luther to one of those *whores!*"

"*Whores?* Why, Hugh, I'm surprised *a refined gentleman like yourself* would use such a word! Now the Chinamen, they got the right idea. They know their trade is an essential service in a mining camp. They use respectful names, like *Daughters of Joy* and *Celestial Females!*"

"How can you say they treat those women with respect? The girls in those Chinese cribs are practically prisoners. They're sold as children and brought here for —"

"Don't get so excited, Hugh. You may be right," He actually looked thoughtful. "Luther should start with a woman of his own race. No sense getting him off on the exotic stuff at such an impressionable age. I myself started with a Chilean and after that I never could get enough of Spanish whores with dark, flashing eyes and lots of spirit. Why if you'd ever known Lola Montez, wouldn't no other woman —"

"You knew Lola Montez?" Luther was impressed.

"Why sure I knew Lola Montez," Caleb Dexter said, washing his hands at the basin and slicking back his ragged sideburns with his wet hands. "I was in Californy in '49 wasn't I?" He smiled philosophically, "I reckon I knew 'em all. All the famous sportin' gals of the mining camps, Ragged Ass Annie, French Emma and Dutch Erma and Big Nose Bertha; except for that nose, she was a beauty!"

"I can't wait," Luther clamored down from his bunk. "I been thinking on it and hoping you'd take me. Is it hard to know what to do? The first time, I mean."

"Luther! Don't tell me you're really going to —"

"Quit being such a prig, Hugh, and come with us," Dexter prodded. "Don't you have an itch too? Don't tell me you haven't been sneaking off to the Badlands yourself."

"Not Hugh," Luther grimaced. "He's too good!"

Anger surged through Hugh. "Listen, Dexter, I know you don't care about yourself. You're probably syphilitic already, but Luther here is just a kid and I don't want him going down there and getting some old diseased —"

"Don't need to worry about that, son. They got the *means to prevent that. Course it costs a bit more to wear an overcoat* and ain't quite as much fun, but you're right, a boy like Luther shouldn't take any chances."

"What are you talking about?" Luther asked. "Taking chances on what? And what's an overcoat?"

"Don't you see, Dexter? He's just a kid. You can't take him to a place like that!"

"He's got to grow up sometime." Dexter said, picking up his hat and starting toward the door. "But I don't want to interfere in family business. You two decide. I'll wait outside. If you're coming with me, you better hurry up."

He left the cabin, shutting the door behind him with a meaningful look at Luther.

Luther faced Hugh defiantly and started to push past him toward the door, but Hugh grabbed his shirt collar. "Listen to me!" he began angrily, then, seeing the look of frightened determination on his brother's face, tried to speak more calmly. "Luther, I'm supposed to watch out for you, and I must tell you this is wrong. I know it's tempting. I know how you feel, but it's wrong to —"

"Wrong?" Luther blinked. "You're a fine one to talk about wrong. The way you've been mooning around Mrs. Lewis! You think I'm too stupid to see you want her?"

Instantly Hugh brought up his other hand and hit

Luther full in the face.

Luther reeled back, jerking free from Hugh's grip.

"Luther, I'm sorry. I shouldn't have —"

"No, you shouldn't have." Luther said, sniffing back tears, "but don't think I'm going to forget it. You think I'm so dumb, but I'm a lot smarter than you think, and I know there's something funny between you and Molly. Jake just mentioned the other day where they came from in Pennsylvania and it's a funny coincidence that we used to live there and —"

"Did you tell him?" Hugh whispered.

"No. I got that much sense."

"Luther, you've misunderstood. There's nothing —"

"Then how come you didn't want Jake to know you used to know her?"

"I never said I knew —"

"I know you didn't *say* that; just like you *never said* we lived there. That's what made me start to thinking. Why, if you did know Molly before, you wouldn't have said so right away. And why you always look at her so funny and why she's always blushing and holding onto her collar buttons when she's around you."

Hugh reached toward his brother, his hand trembling a little. "Come sit down. We better talk this over."

"I'm sick of you and your talk. I'm sick of you acting so holy when you're no better than me. I'm going with Caleb Dexter to have some fun and you're not going to stop me!"

"Luther, damn it, listen to me," Hugh began, but Luther was already out the door. Hugh started to follow as Luther ran down the hill to where Caleb Dexter waited, but he knew it was no use. He went back to the cabin and hit the wall with his fist, trying to dispel his anger. He considered following them, but Luther might make a scene and Jake was just next door.

The cabin was too small to contain his anger, so he

grabbed a pickax and climbed the hill to the mine shaft. Letting himself down by windlass in the iron bucket which raised the ore, he lit a torch and strode down the tunnel to the stope, the room hollowed out by mining. He fixed the torch in a metal spike and drove it into the wall of the stope with the blunt end of his ax, hefted the pickax and attacked the wall with a fury. He knew it was a strange place for a man who hated the mine to be on his day of rest but hitting with the pickax helped to drive away pictures coming unbidden to his mind.

Women in red silk with full breasts spilling out of transparent garments, rustling skirts lifted above black hose and garters and white thighs. *Such women could be had for the asking, for a price which did not involve right or wrong, love or the betrayal of a friend.*

CHAPTER TWENTY-TWO

Hugh stayed in the mine until long after dark, but when he returned to the cabin, Luther and Dexter were still gone. He did not wait up for them, but was surprised the next morning to see their beds had not been slept in. So, they had spent the night in a bawdy house. It must have cost a fortune.

He was on his way to the mine, still feeling out of sorts, when he spied Luther and the old man trudging up the hill from Deadwood. They looked exhausted and downcast and guilty. Hugh's first impulse was anger, but he decided he'd be tolerant, for who was he to judge? Luther was sixteen, the same age he'd been when he'd sinned with Molly. The two approached slowly, exchanging sheepish glances. Hugh was glad to see they were contrite. Perhaps Luther would settle down now. Maybe the experience had even been good for him.

"Well," he asked when they stood before him, "how was it? Did you get lucky?"

Luther didn't speak but stood with his head down. He looked as if he had been crying.

"What's the matter, Luther? Did it cost too much?"

When Luther still did not speak, Hugh began to feel uneasy. He turned to Dexter. "What happened?"

"Well, it's like this," the old prospector began sheepishly. "We had our dinner and a few drinks and were sitting in this hurdy-gurdy house trying to decide if we could find a pretty girl to go upstairs with, or if we should just go across the street and take pot luck at a bawdy house, and then we notice there's some gambling going on, and Luther never had done any real gambling, so—"

"So? Get on with the story, please!"

"So we started watching the gambling and amongst

the pot on the table, they had these brass tokens from the Hidden Treasure."

"What brass tokens? The Hidden Treasure's a mine isn't it? You don't mean they were playing for a *mine*?"

Dexter and Luther exchanged guilty looks. "There's a Hidden Treasure mine," Dexter said, "but there's also a Hidden Treasure that's *a house*. I don't suppose you'd know, being so pure and all, but when you go into *a house,* you start with a drink at the bar, and you make your arrangements with the bartender or with the madam, if they have one, for whatever girl you want or can afford."

"I don't need to hear all this."

"I think you do." Dexter said, glancing again at Luther who was now studying his boots. "Anyway, you can't set your own price with the girls, cause they might hold out on the house or you might not pay them beforehand like you're supposed to, so at most places they sell you a token downstairs good for one —" he hesitated and looked around as if Molly was nearby. "Good for *one trip upstairs.*"

"Get to the point!"

"So me and Luther sees they've got some tokens on the table. Some guys like to buy a fist-full of tokens when they got extra cash. It feels good to have a few jingling in your pockets so you won't have to do without in case you run short of funds. So anyway, along with the dust and the greenbacks in the pot there was a bunch of tokens for the Hidden Treasure, and Luther suggests —"

"It wasn't my idea," Luther spoke up, "It was yours!"

Hugh was getting the picture. They had spent the night gambling. He supposed not too much harm could have been done. Between them, they couldn't have had over ten dollars in dust.

"Well, maybe it *was* my idea," Dexter admitted.

"Anyway, we decided to sit in on a game or two and see if we could win some tokens to the Hidden Treasure. It would be a real *sporting way* for Luther to get his *first!*"

"Get to the point. How much did you lose?"

"Twelve dollars in dust," Dexter said sadly. "And my gold pocket watch."

Another long silence. Hugh reassured himself his father's watch was still in his own pocket.

"And Ma's locket." Luther said quietly.

"Ma's locket!" Hugh gripped his brother's shoulder, "It had Ma and Pa's pictures in it!" Luther looked so guilty, Hugh let him go. The locket was Luther's part of their inheritance, but still only a trinket.

"And the mine." Dexter put in quickly. Hugh turned from his brother's ashen face to the old man, not sure he'd heard right.

"What?"

"I said we lost the mine."

"The Mine? *Not Our Mine?* How could you lose the mine? Surely you didn't gamble with our mine?"

"Just our shares." Dexter said.

"What?"

"Only our shares. Mine and Luther's. We figured our luck was about to change, so we put up our shares and then this slick gambler, well, he won both shares."

"Your shares of the mine! You lost the mine at cards."

"Only our shares! Dexter repeated as if he had a right to be indignant. You and Molly and Jake's shares are just the same. You'll have a new partner, that's all."

"A new partner?"

"Austin Avery. That's his name. The gambler. He'll be your new partner in the mine."

"Oh my God."

"Now don't carry on so. There's no real harm done. We'll get it back. Mr. Avery seems real fair. He said since he can't work the mine himself cause of his other interests, he's going to let me and Luther stay on to work for wages!"

"You're going to stay on?"

"Just like it's always been. Since I'm the one with the mining expertise, I'll be advising and overseeing the development of the mine. And Luther will be working, same as always, only instead of being a partner, he'll be like me, working for Mr. Avery. Working for wages."

"A *gambler*. You lost our mine to a gambler."

"Just our shares. And you'll like Austin Avery. He's real smart. You'll meet him tomorrow. So don't worry. Everything will go on like always."

"I'll work real hard!" Luther said. "I'll work real hard like always and I'll give my wages to you, Hugh, and you can buy back my share. And . . . and keep it for yourself."

"No!" Hugh bellowed.

"I'll make it up to you! I promise!"

"Get away from me!" Hugh shouted, pointing down the hill. "Both of you, get away from our mine."

"I'm sorry," Luther blinked back tears, and Dexter added, "Don't be so hard on the boy."

"Luther, I'm sick of hearing you're sorry. You've been trouble ever since I brought you along! I should have left you in Nebraska. You never do anything right!"

"Okay," Luther swallowed hard. "I'll get my gear and I'll go. Hobart said I could have a job ranching with him in the valley anytime I wanted." He went into the cabin and began to gather up his things slowly, like he was expecting Hugh to stop him. Caleb Dexter had judiciously disappeared.

Hugh stormed away from the cabin and started for the mine, passing the startled-looking Jake just leaving his own cabin. He didn't explain why he looked so angry, and Jake didn't ask. There was time enough for that later. Jake went underground for his shift, and Hugh marched to the tailings pile to take out his anger on the rock, breaking and shoveling it with a fury.

After he'd filled a wheelbarrow of ore to take to the sluice box, he calmed down a little. Luther was still his brother, his responsibility. He figured he should go back to the cabin and tell Luther he didn't have to leave. Not that the kid would actually have the nerve to take off by himself. Then again, he thought, maybe it would be better if he did go off to ranch with Hobart. The older man had always been a good influence on him, and it might be healthier for Luther to be free of Hugh's constant scrutiny. And perhaps better for Hugh to be away from Luther's gaze. The truth was, it would easier all around if Luther went away for a while. He had just made up his mind when he saw Molly walking toward him.

"Hugh?" she approached wearing a worried look. "What's happened with Luther?"

"Didn't he tell you? Didn't he tell you he lost his share of the mine to a gambler? And so did the old man!"

"My God, is that what happened? Luther wouldn't talk to me. He just said you'd fought and he was leaving."

"He didn't actually go, did he?"

"That's what I came to tell you. He took his bedroll and pack and he's gone. Caleb Dexter too. I tried to talk to Luther, but he just brushed on past me. You better go after him. You can't let him go."

"It might be better. He suspects."

"Suspects?"

"About us."

"Oh." She was shocked but not surprised.

"So you see, it's better if we let him go, unless —"

"Unless?"

"Unless you're ready to tell Jake!"

She looked agonized. As if she had not expected him to say it. As if their lovemaking had not happened and he had not told her she must make a decision about leaving Jake. He knew she was not good at facing up to things and sometimes that made him angry, even as he loved her for her decency and her loyalty to Jake. He didn't want to hurt Jake either, but one of them must do it.

"Will you tell him, Molly? Or do you want me to?"

"No, we can't tell him."

He winced from her words, though they had been softly spoken, then looked down the hill, away from her, thinking he should throw down his shovel and follow Luther. *Walk away from her*, he thought and was on the verge of doing it. Then, as if she sensed his thought, she reached out and touched just the tips of her fingers to his shoulder and added one word.

"Yet."

He knew she was trapping him. Holding him to her with that one word of promise. He would insist on more.

"You'll do it then? You'll leave him?"

She would not, or could not answer

"You know if we let Luther go," he said, it's not just my decision. Sending him away will be your doing too."

She nodded and voiced his own thought, "It will be better for him to leave Deadwood. It's a terrible, uncivilized place. He'll be happier working outdoors. Hobart will watch out for him."

"That's true. He won't listen to me, but Hobart might make a man of him."

"He said something about that. He said to tell you something. I almost forgot."

"What did he say?"

"He said that he would make you proud of him yet."

Before they parted, they stood for a moment and

looked at each other as if aware they had just added another twist to the invisible cord that seemed to bind them together.

She came to him that night, just as he had dreamed it a hundred times, but before she appeared he was not thinking of her but of his brother. He was lying on the crude bunk in his cabin, staring up at the log rafters barely visible in the narrow shafts of moonlight admitted by the cabin's single small window, but familiar from the many hours he had counted them to try to sleep without thinking of Molly.

The cabin door was open to clear it of the day's heat, and he was naked, a thin blanket at his feet for later when the night turned cold. To Hugh, the cabin seemed strangely silent without the sound of his brother's breathing. They had shared a room for most of their lives. Caleb Dexter was gone too; whether escorting Luther to the Spearfish Valley or scheming with the gambler in town, Hugh neither knew nor cared. He knew the old man would be back, to entice them with more plots for easy riches.

Luther was a different story. The boy was proud and stubborn, and Hugh knew he would not see his brother again until he went after him or sent him word to return. Luther's losing their mother's locket made him remember he'd promised her he'd take care of his brother, and he felt more guilty than angry. For he knew the real reason he had sent his brother away was that he could not bear to face his brother with the truth about his own weakness.

Hugh had taken pride in playing the part of the big brother, older, wiser, stronger. He'd always told himself that he was simply setting a good example; now he had to admit that sometimes his feelings had bordered on righteousness. He loved his brother and he wanted his brother's love but, most of all, he wanted his respect. How could he look Luther in the eye and admit his own wrong? It seemed impossible that his loving Molly should have the power to bring ruin on those he cared for most, but he believed it had.

Yet when he saw her there in the doorway, his resolution to be civilized and decent abandoned him.

She wore only a nightgown with a shawl around her shoulders, and her silver-blond hair was loose and haloed by the moonlight in the doorway. She was silent and he was aware of his nakedness.

"Are you awake, Hugh?" she asked softly.

"I'm not sure. I've dreamed of you so many times. Come here and touch me to prove you're not a vision."

He touched the blanket, but did not cover himself. She did not move from the doorway.

"Step inside, Molly, and bar the door behind you."

She obeyed but still did not approach him. He pulled the blanket up although it did not conceal his excitement. "Is something wrong? Where's Jake?"

"He's asleep. Passed out, really. He was very upset about Luther and Caleb Dexter leaving. He drank a good deal."

"He hasn't hurt you, has he? "

"No, of course not," she took a step toward the bed and sighed, "It might be easier if he had, but Jake has never raised a hand to me. Even if I were to tell him about us, I wouldn't fear him. It's just that I saw how soundly he and Edwin slept, and I could not, because I kept thinking that with Luther and the old man gone, you were alone and —"

"And you wanted me? You wanted to come to me?"

She was standing at the side of the bed now, looking down at him, and he saw she was trembling.

"I thought we should talk. We were both so upset about Luther's leaving and the gambler coming and —"

"And what happened between us last time? You're ready to talk about telling Jake now? About leaving him?"

"Oh, Hugh, be silent. The truth is I don't want to talk about anything. I don't want to talk at all."

And then it was she who acted, she who let her shawl fall away and she who pulled aside the blanket and who knelt beside him and sought his mouth and body.

He barely had time to find the protective sheath he had bought in Deadwood and explain its use to her. It was she who helped him to contain himself within it, and it was she who raised her gown and mounted him. For a moment he wondered if she had gone mad or if it was he who had lost his senses and confused a dream with reality. But then whether a dream or a madwoman, she was exquisitely demanding above him, taking as well as giving. Then he thought of nothing else until they were released by sweet shuddering explosions of pleasure and could at last lie tenderly together to begin their reluctant return to reality.

"I had to come to you," she said at last. "I ached so."

"I know the aching. I've dreamed of you every night, but nothing as wonderful as seeing you above me."

"I never knew it could be done that way until I touched your manhood and wanted to capture you inside me. Am I different from other women? Is there something unnatural about me, about how I mounted you, and the way I move and feel when we join? It starts a trembling I can't stop and then a terrible explosion as if I'm going to die, and then a wonderful feeling of peace."

"Sweet Molly, it's a natural thing. It's just your release coming over you."

"But I never had that happen before. I didn't know that women had such pleasure."

"I don't know about other women, but I'm very glad it happens to you. That I make it happen to you."

"But you've known other women?"

"Molly, what questions you ask!"

"It's all right. I know I can't have been the only one for you, and I've had Jake, but I have so many questions now. So many wonderings I never had before. It's like I thought I knew what a mountain was before we reached the Black Hills, and then when I actually saw one, it was so much greater, so much more beautiful than anything I'd imagined. And now I feel confused as if I've been a child before, and I'm finding the whole world is somehow different than I knew it to be. It's more terrible and more wonderful."

"You are more wonderful, and you are my whole world. You are not just the first, but the last woman in my life. My only love, forever."

They talked of other things then, tried to sort and reason it out, to agree on what must be done about Jake. But all they agreed upon was to hope that somehow the mine would pay out and that would resolve their fates.

"Jake is sure his luck has finally changed, and I pray it's true." Molly said, raising her eyes to the ceiling.

Hugh could not believe as easily as Molly, but he kept silent. He feared they had all been seduced and made believers by Caleb Dexter's tales of Poor Man's Gold. There had to be great veins of gold somewhere; perhaps the "Mother Lode" as the miners' called it was just a pickax blow away. It was true they had put in too much work to give up now, and if they did strike it rich, Jake would be rewarded for his hard work and his faithfulness, and maybe then it would be easier to tell him. They could use their own share of the riches to buy their freedom. These thoughts he did speak and Molly nodded her agreement.

The next day and in the days to come, she denied to herself that she had promised that when the time was right, she would leave her husband.

In the daylight as she saw Jake going about his work so faithfully or saw how Edwin followed after Jake and walked and talked like him, she could not face the reality of what she had said and done.

She remembered only that Hugh had told her she was his first and last love. She was the only woman in the world for him. That seemed promise enough.

CHAPTER TWENTY-THREE

Hugh was stunned by his first sight of Emerald O'Brien, so beautiful did he find her and so unexpected was the sight of a woman standing at the entrance to the mine when he winched himself up from the shaft. He'd finished his shift knotted with worry over Luther's leaving and his dread of meeting the gambler who was now a partner in the mine. He hoped he could contain his anger.

And there she stood and he found himself looking into the most unusual green eyes he'd ever seen. Eyes set in a face that would have been heart-shaped enough without the little curving bonnet that framed it so perfectly. She was a small woman. Smaller than Molly and much more fragile looking, though her body was full and round, revealed as it was by the bustle-back green suit she wore. After his months of frustration and loneliness, the white skin, the black hair and the green eyes stunned him. He could not imagine why she had appeared before him, and he felt his mouth dropping open foolishly as he stared at her.

Then he heard Jake say his name and realized there were others present. He turned and saw Austin Avery, the gambler. The slick, crooked bastard who had tricked Luther and the old man out of their shares of the mine, He looked just like one would expect a professional gambler to look: handsome, sly, shrewd, dressed in a pin-striped cutaway coat and a ridiculous ruffled shirt and wearing an ascot tie with a diamond stick pin. He made Hugh want to laugh, until with a deliberate gesture the gambler moved so his coat opened just enough for Hugh to see his gold watch and chain, the sash at his waist, and the pearl-handled revolver tucked inside. Hugh got control of himself. He was still full of anger, but he knew he'd have to extend a certain degree of politeness. Avery held the deed to two shares of the Lucky Six.

Caleb Dexter was standing with the gambler and the woman, and Hugh had just time enough to realize that the woman belonged to Austin Avery before the old man stepped forward and began making introductions cheerfully. It was obvious he was going to nuzzle up to the gambler for whatever it was worth to him.

"This here's your new partners, Mr. Avery. Jake Lewis and Hugh Everett."

"I don't believe you can consider me *your partner*, Mr. Avery," Hugh said quietly, noticing the gambler was regarding him coolly, not extending his hand. "I think I can speak for Jake also."

Jake gave an affirmative grunt.

Avery was nonplused. "Therefore, I suggest, Mr. Everett, we simply regard ourselves as temporary business associates. I understand how disconcerting this change of affairs must be to you, but let me assure you, there may come a day when you will look back on this association as the beginning of your good fortune, for I do bring a certain expertise in mining affairs to this venture!"

"I told you he talks good," Caleb Dexter broke in. "He's a real gentleman."

"I hardly consider a man who makes his living taking advantage of boys and foolish old men —"

"Who you calling foolish?" Dexter bristled.

"No one forced your brother or Mr. Dexter to sit at my table. They might as easily have been the winners. I trust you are not seeking to impugn my honesty?"

"He means do you think he cheated," Dexter said with a meaningful glance to the gambler's pistol. "But he didn't. We lost the mine fair and square."

"If there is any doubt in your mind about that, Mr. Everett," Avery said, "then let's call your brother out here and settle this question!"

"My brother is gone. He went to the Spearfish Valley."

"But I assured him he could stay on."

"I didn't think it was your place to assure him of that," Hugh said, noticing that his remark seemed to cause the woman to glance at the gambler uneasily, as if she expected trouble. He wasn't afraid of this man, and he wanted the woman to know that. He certainly wasn't going to have this so-called partner questioning his judgment.

"It was a family matter and it has been settled. Luther will no longer be associated with the mine."

"I see. Well then, Mr. Everett, Mr. Lewis," Avery, removed his hat and held it before him. "I have no wish to enter into any business venture where there cannot be good will between the members. I can see you harbor some natural feelings of resentment. Perhaps it would be best for me to buy out your shares of the partnership. Unless, of course, you would prefer to buy mine?"

Hugh and Jake exchanged uneasy looks. It made Hugh feel angry and impotent, but there was no way he and Jake could afford to buy two shares of the mine. Hugh had only a few dollars in gold dust cached in a buried tobacco can. Jake probably had even less.

As if to save them embarrassment, Avery stepped smoothly into the awkward silence, "I would, however, prefer to buy your shares."

Hugh didn't speak, but he could see Jake was interested. Throughout the conversation the woman had been pouting prettily, as if annoyed that no one had paid attention to her. Hugh had never lost awareness of her standing there, but he'd kept his attention on his business.

Now she broke in with a question. "Austin, aren't you going to look at the mine first?"

The gambler ignored the question, but Hugh sensed

he was annoyed; yet she seemed pleased. The trace of a mischievous smile played between her mouth and her eyes. Avery was being forced to acknowledge her in the midst of his business deal.

"Allow me to introduce Miss O'Brien." He made a courtly gesture with his hat. "Miss Emerald O'Brien, meet Mr. Lewis and Mr. Everett. You met Mr. Dexter on the drive out, of course."

Emerald O'Brien. Such a name. It fit her. Her dress, hat, and even her eyes were green. She smiled graciously to Jake and then offered her hand to Hugh. She was wearing tiny little gloves with the fingers cut out. Hugh had never seen such gloves or such a woman. He took her hand and held it for longer than was necessary, hating Avery for having her, for she was obviously his mistress.

There was another awkward silence and, once again, Caleb Dexter tried to smooth things over.

"Are you sure you don't want to inspect the mine, Mr. Avery? We could lower you in the bucket there."

Avery took a few steps forward and peered past the windlass with its chains and pulleys into the darkness of the mine shaft. There was hardly room to stand near the shaft, littered as the area was with piles of rubble and mine tailings. The pump they had rigged spewed spurts of brackish water out its hose and down the hillside. A dank smell rose from the shaft. Hugh could not imagine a man like Avery going down there. Emerald seemed amused by the prospect.

"It won't be necessary," Avery said. "I see you have a water problem. You didn't mention that," he frowned at Caleb Dexter.

"Well, it didn't come up, now did it? It isn't exactly like you *bought* the mine, is it? Anyway, since you aren't planning on working the mine yourself, a little water ain't going to hurt you."

"But it certainly isn't going to look good to a prospective buyer, is it? One would hardly miss a pump system like that would one? I've never seen one rigged quite that far." Avery's gaze followed the system of aspen poles rigged all the way to the creek and raised and lowered rhythmically by a flume of water flowing upon the water wheel in the stream.

"Well, you got to get your water power where it runs, don't you?" Dexter said. "I'm right proud of it. Designed it myself and had the blacksmith forge the axle-tree and the pivots, and then I showed the boys how to rig it. Besides, don't worry about your buyer. Capitalists as would be buying up mines can afford the equipment to work them proper."

"Of course," Avery smiled, revealing a gold tooth.

"You don't intend to work the mine?" Hugh asked.

"Of course not, but why don't we sit down somewhere and talk about it?" He was entirely gracious. Hugh could hardly refuse to discuss the matter with him, although he wanted to throw him off the property.

"We can step down to my cabin," Jake offered. "My wife will make us coffee."

Hugh had to nod agreement, so Avery took Emerald's arm and followed Jake and Caleb Dexter to the Lewis cabin. Hugh watched Emerald walking away from him, noticing the way her bustle back swung as she walked, and the way her raven hair was fixed in fat little curls that jiggled beneath her bonnet.

He wondered what Molly was going to think of the woman and wished they were not about to meet. Then, as if knowing he was thinking about her, the woman turned slightly, and gave him a knowing little smile.

It made him angry. He would be damned if he would let some fancy piece of baggage take his mind off his business. She was probably in league with Austin Avery to cheat him further.

Besides, she wasn't half the woman Molly was.

Emerald had been as much affected by her first sight of Hugh Everett as he had been by his first glimpse of her, the difference being that Emerald was willing to admit it to herself. Hugh Everett was tall and ruggedly handsome. He looked raw and unfinished, but somehow clean as if he belonged outside on a horse instead of down in a filthy mine. His hair was bleached golden by the sun and it seemed to Emerald there was an almost halo-like glow about his head. His short beard was golden and his skin tanned. His hands were terribly big and when he'd held hers, she'd felt ever so delicate. She had almost expected him to kiss her hand. She liked his courage in confronting Austin, and when she had glanced back over her shoulder and seen him staring at her, she had been thrilled. Meeting him had made the boring trip to inspect Avery's first mining interest worthwhile.

Jake Lewis was old but not as bad as the disgusting Caleb Dexter. The cabin was dreadful, tiny and shabby. The little boy was cute enough, but the wife she disliked at first sight. She was stirring something on the stove while her son watched as if fascinated. That is, he watched his mother until he saw Emerald. Then he, too, stared at her. When the wife saw Emerald, she turned away and wiped her hands on her apron and tidied her hair in a gesture that spoke of respectability and annoyed Emerald. The wife was surprisingly young and pretty, although for someone so fair, she had spent too much time in the sun. Too bad she'd probably never get the time and money to make the most of her looks.

Hugh began the introductions. He hesitated as he turned from the wife to Emerald, and Emerald knew he realized she was Avery's mistress and wondered how to introduce her. Avery stepped forward to fill the awkward gap. "Mrs. Lewis, allow me to present *my intended*, Miss Emerald O'Brien."

My intended! That was a new one. Avery had never before felt the need to sanctify their relationship. What made Mrs. Lewis so special? Why did a man assume a woman was decent just because she was dressed shabbily and had a brat hanging onto her skirts? And did he think calling her *his intended* would make them any more respectable to Mrs. Lewis? For an instant Emerald wished she had stayed in the carriage, but when she noticed the wife's hesitation in acknowledging her, she bristled. Why did everyone assume that just because she looked so good, she was bad? She did not intend to let his woman snub her.

"Pleased to make your acquaintance, Mrs. Lewis," she used her stage voice, thrusting out her gloved hand, pleasantly aware that her elegant appearance made Mrs. Lewis seem even shabbier.

"Please, call me Molly," she took Emerald's hand and smiled in a way that Emerald had to admit seemed gracious. It could have been that her earlier hesitation had been from shyness. She looked to be the kind of woman who blushed easily — her skin was all flushed and rosy.

And then, almost in that same moment that Molly was shaking her hand, Emerald noticed something. Noticed that Molly turned from her and looked at Hugh and the expression on her face was almost like fear.

Emerald thought about it while they found places to sit and declined Mrs. Lewis's hesitant offer of coffee, it being obvious there weren't enough cups to go around. Emerald realized the look of fear meant the wife felt threatened by Emerald. But why had Molly turned her concern to Hugh and not to her husband? Emerald studied Jake Lewis. He was a weather-beaten man, decidedly middle-aged, especially standing by his blushing wife. It seemed unlikely that Molly feared her husband would stray. He'd hardly noticed Emerald when they met at the mine, and now he gave his full attention to talking business with the others. Hugh, too, was ignoring her; yet Emerald felt he was all too aware of her where she sat on the edge of the double bed.

Being stared at was an everyday event for Emerald, but she noticed that while Molly pretended to be giving all her attention to her son and whatever was cooking, she revealed her uneasiness with glances that seemed always to travel between Emerald on the bed and Hugh Everett sitting across from Austin Avery at the table.

So, Emerald decided, there was something going on between Jake Lewis's wife and Hugh Everett.

It was understandable; them being thrown together in such a place and Lewis being so much older than his pretty wife, and Hugh so handsome. *Were they lovers?* She studied them as Avery expounded on his offer to buy the mine. She decided it was not likely. There could not be much privacy about the place with a little boy like big-eyed Arnold or Edwin, or whatever his name was hanging on his mother; besides, Hugh seemed too upright a man to cuckold his partner.

And, Mrs. Lewis was a respectable woman. That was obvious from the neatness of the cramped little cabin, the worn but clean quilt on the bed, the flour-sack curtains at the window and the Bible proudly displayed on a top shelf. There was an attraction between Hugh and his partner's wife, but Molly Lewis had not given Hugh what he wanted. What a man needed. She was not a woman who knew how to please a man, nor how to please herself.

Emerald smiled. The situation seemed full of possibilities. She was making Mrs. Lewis uncomfortable sitting here on what was probably her bridal quilt. She liked knowing the woman was really no more respectable than she, Emerald O'Brien. She was just not as brave. Emerald knew how to get what she wanted.

And at that moment, she began to think that what she wanted was Hugh Everett. He was more handsome even than Austin Avery, and Hugh was a decent man, one who would feel obliged to marry a woman he'd seduced. That made him even more attractive to her. But with the thought of being married to Hugh came the realization that he was poor. Being married would certainly not be worth being poor. Still, it would be thrilling to make him want her. It would be satisfying to see if she could take him away from Molly Lewis. Besides, making Austin Avery jealous always led to sparks between them.

She turned her full attention to Hugh, lowering her chin slightly and making her eyes look wide and luminous. She let her lips part and curve in a smile both mysterious and promising.

But Hugh's attention was on Avery. "I don't care how much you offer," he said, slamming his fist on the table. "I'm not interested in selling out."

Jake Lewis cocked his head at Hugh. "Are you sure? That's a generous offer."

"You take my advice, you'll sell out," Caleb Dexter declared. "Underground mining's a risky business. We already took too many chances."

Hugh seemed to be considering it. Then, to Emerald's annoyance he turned to Molly. "We've risked so much already. If we stop now, it's been for almost nothing. "

Lewis also turned toward his wife and Emerald wondered if he suspected, but his face was guileless.

"What do you think, Molly? We need to decide right now. We'd have enough to get back home."

"But that's all you'd have," Hugh retorted. "If we stick it out, we still might make sense out of this crazy journey. We shouldn't make a rash decision. I hate to give up if there's still any promise."

Emerald again sensed something going on between the two. When Molly spoke at last, she seemed to measure her words.

"I think there is promise. I'm not willing to give up."

"You vote to stay then?" Hugh asked.

Molly nodded as her husband broke in. "I vote to stay. This mine's the first thing I ever had, except Edwin, that there was any hope to. I'll risk it."

"Then it's settled." Hugh declared. "We won't sell."

Avery was furious. Emerald admired the way he did not betray his anger almost as much as the way Hugh stood his ground.

The old man, however, was not ready to give up. "What if Mr. Avery doubles his price?"

"Give it up, Dexter!" This time there was no mistaking the cutting edge to Avery's voice. "I've already made a generous offer. I'm sure it's more than the mine is worth in its present stage of development."

"But you said you could unload it on some eastern capitalist for a tidy profit," the old man declared, and Emerald had to stifle a giggle at seeing the way he had revealed Avery's hand.

"You were planning on reselling the mine then?" Hugh asked. Avery delayed answering a moment by taking out his silver cigar case and lighting a cheroot.

"You can hardly expect a gentleman to grub about in a mine. My purpose is to have the Lucky Six developed a bit more and then, when the time came, sell it to someone with the capital to profitably operate a lode mine."

"You know folks like that? Capitalists, I mean?" Jake asked.

"I wasn't aware of any outside money coming into Deadwood," Hugh said.

"There will be, Mr. Everett, you can be sure of that! I've had considerable experience in mining affairs, and with things continuing as promising in Deadwood as they have these past months, it will be only a matter of weeks before any number of entrepreneurs will be on the scene. Men with money for machinery who will buy up whole sections of claims, forming large companies. That's what it takes for quartz mining — Capitalists. These placer operations will be played out in a matter of months."

"I don't think I like that." Hugh said. "I don't see why Easterners have to come in here and take over what we've been building up. If there's gold to be mined in Deadwood, the men who came in here first ought to get it!"

"Well then, Mr. Everett, I suggest you continue to develop your mine and we'll just bide our time. I'll come by every week to go over the books with you, but I'll be keeping my eye out for a prospective buyer. Then when the time comes, we can re-evaluate the situation. Does that seem fair to you?"

Hugh nodded slowly. "I guess that's the best we can do under the circumstances. We'll put your shares of dust aside. Jake and I will continue to work the mine."

"With Caleb Dexter's help, of course."

Hugh looked at the old man with disgust. "No, I draw the line there. You've caused nothing but trouble, Dexter. I think it's time we parted company."

"I know I done wrong with Luther, but he was *your* brother and you should have spent more time with him 'stead of leaving it up to me to educate the boy."

"Now, listen here!"

"I *said* I was sorry about Luther and for losing our shares of the mine, but you wouldn't even *have* this mine if it wasn't for me. You got to admit that. And you didn't know squat about developing a mine. You'd have had all your prospect holes in the wrong places, and the mine would have caved in on you the first day if I hadn't been there to show you how to shore up the stopes."

"He's right," Avery interjected. "I'm afraid his mining

expertise is essential to the operation. I do know a great deal about the business side of mining, but I cannot match Mr. Dexter's knowledge of mining methods. It would be absolutely foolhardy for you to attempt to continue working underground without him."

'He's got a point there," Jake declared. "We already got a lot of water seeping in the mine; that little vein we been following is about to peter out, and I ain't got the faintest notion of where to open another stope."

"So, it's settled then?'" Hugh stood up so abruptly he nearly knocked the table over. "It seems like every damn thing is settled before I have a chance to do anything. So we're partners then, Mr. Avery, and you can pay Dexter for his expertise until we figure out a way to get out of our so-called partnership. Now, if you'll excuse me, I have to get back to work."

He had to walk past Emerald to get to the door. He stopped and stared at her for just a moment. There was something in his eyes that made her feel he might just pick her up and carry her out the door with him. There was something in her that made her wish he would do just that.

And then he was gone.

That evening as Emerald lay on the bed admiring herself in the red silk wrapper she had purchased in Deadwood's Chinatown and watching Avery dress for the evening, she was still thinking of Hugh Everett. She knew she should put him out of her mind. It would be foolish to become involved with him, though it would be a pleasure to take him away from Molly Lewis. True, he was the kind of man who would marry a woman and she did want to be married, but she was hardly the type to be happy in a miserable little shack built next to a mine shaft.

Avery had been in a jubilant mood since the visit to the

mine. Now, studying himself in the mirror, he declared, "I've done it. I'm a mining entrepreneur at last!"

Emerald decided to ignore him. He was wearing his ruffled shirt and his white under drawers, and she was amused to note how knobby his knees were. Why, she wondered, had God made women's bodies so beautiful and men's so downright funny?

"You don't seem very excited, my dear. I said I'm a mining entrepreneur at last. This is my chance to make a real fortune."

"All you care about is money," Emerald said annoyingly.

"And I suppose you don't? You only care about spiritual values like truth and beauty and —"

"And love. Yes, that's right. That's the kind of thing I care about."

"And you don't care about money. That's strange. It seemed to me you care a great deal about the things money can buy. Like that kimono thing you just bought."

Emerald was tempted to take it off and throw it at him. It would be a grand gesture and it would surely lead to some exciting action, but that night a tumble with Avery did not hold its usual appeal. She wanted to turn the talk to the subject of Hugh.

"I don't see why you're so excited about the Lucky Six. It doesn't look to me as if the mine can be worth much. Jake Lewis said their vein was about played out. And they certainly all looked poor enough. What if they don't find another vein?"

"It hardly matters if you know how to play your cards right."

"What do you mean?"

"Just that if one knows what one is doing, if one is clever, and we both know someone who is, then, one can get quite wealthy on a gold mine — even if it doesn't happen to have any gold."

"I don't get it."

"I don't expect you to, my dear. You shouldn't clutter your head with business schemes. It isn't womanly. Just trust me. When the capitalists start coming into this town burning to buy mines, I'll have a grand mine to sell!"

"But, Avery, you haven't even been down in that mine. How do you know anyone is going to buy it? Don't they have to see some gold or something?"

"Certainly, they do, my dear. No one is going to buy a mine without seeing a favorable assay."

"So if there's no gold —"

"Then it's a little more difficult to get a favorable assay. But not impossible!"

"Oh," Emerald smiled. So that was how it was. She lay on the bed and traced with one finger the embroidered design of the Chinese wrapper, enjoying the look and the feel of the red silk against the curve of her hip. She thought it over for a while and then she turned back to Avery.

"Tell me more about the mine. If you sell your share, will Molly and Jake and Hugh get rich too?"

"There may be no helping it. They don't seem inclined to sell out. I'll keep trying to get them to bail out, of course, but if they don't, I guess they'll just ride in on my coattails"

"I see."

Emerald sat up on the bed, removed her hair pins and lovingly brushed her glossy black hair until the air was full of electricity. While she brushed, she thought. For once she hardly noticed when Avery left for the gaming tables.

If Hugh was going to be rich, then it changed everything. Of course, Avery would be rich too, but there was no real security for her with Avery. Avery might never make her respectable. But Hugh was different.

Such a man could be led into marriage. She could get out of Deadwood and go East or even South as the wife of a successful and decent man. She and her handsome and rich husband might even stop in at her mother's dress shop. Wouldn't that be a surprise! Yes, she could be a real lady if she played her cards right and she could make Austin Avery real sorry. It would be a pleasure to see Avery squirm.

And besides, she thought, her heart beating faster. There was something so strong and noble about Hugh. He would appreciate her beauty, call her his beloved, and carry her to bed in his strong arms. There would be nothing of the tawdriness she sometimes felt with Avery, but surely their lovemaking would be as exciting. She saw she'd have to hold back at first. It might not be easy to win him, but if she could, it would justify everything.

There was just one problem. Hugh Everett was a man with ideals. That was obvious from the way he acted toward Avery and the fact he had not consummated his lust for his partner's wife. Hugh Everett was a man with ideals, and Emerald O'Brien was no virgin. Hugh had to have realized she was Avery's mistress and while that might make her desirable to him as a man, he certainly would never consider marrying a soiled woman.

So, she thought, *forget about marriage.* She'd take Hugh without condition, but then when she was ready for sleep that didn't come she started obsessing about the attitude of men toward soiled woman, and then the dead woman at the saloon. Marriage was the only solution, There was no other way to be safe. Her mother had been right about that much. Somehow she had to convince Hugh Everett she was a good woman. She had to trick him into believing she had changed, had given up Austin Avery and was worthy of marriage.

It seemed an insolvable problem. But there had to be a

way. She climbed out of bed and got down on her knees. Her mother had always told her prayer was the answer to everything. It might be worth giving it a try.

Winning Hugh Everett was such a noble cause, surely God would show her the way.

Molly, too, was praying that night. She had known the moment she saw Emerald that Hugh would want her. How could any man not want a woman like Emerald O'Brien? She had such a knowing look about her; there was something in those mysterious, dark-lashed green eyes and in her smile that made Molly remember a picture she'd seen once of a famous painting called the Mona Lisa. The book said the Mona Lisa's eyes seemed to follow you everywhere, and her smile made men think she knew some secret. It was not just the secret of loving and pleasing a man or of knowing that woman, too, could find exquisite release in lovemaking: it was the secret of daring to do whatever you and your man wished. Emerald had defied society by openly living in sin with a man.

If she could do such a thing, Molly reasoned, there must be nothing she was afraid to do, nothing that would make her deny either her love or herself. Emerald would not be afraid to leave one man for another. And Emerald wanted Hugh. Molly knew that, and knew that her every pretty gesture, even her pretended friendship with Molly herself, were only ways to get to Hugh.

She told herself that Hugh was an honorable and civilized man; that he loved her and would not want another woman, even one as beautiful and desirable as Emerald. She told herself a person could not love two people at one time; then heard a voice within remind her of her own divided loyalties.

She prayed against temptation, thinking at first it was Hugh's temptation that must be guarded against. But if she received any answer to her prayer it was only the reminder that the worse temptation was hers.

And so at last it seemed to be clear that there was only one way she could ensure the safety of them both, and that was to honor her promise to leave Jake. Hugh could wait no longer. She would persuade Hugh to secretly sell their shares of the mine to the gambler so that they could get away for a start somewhere else. It would not be enough to get them back to civilization, but they could join Luther and Hobart in the Spearfish Valley. Holding the valley against the Sioux could be no worse danger than they now faced.

She would tell Hugh in the morning as soon as she could find a moment with him alone. It would not be hard to convince him. Then they would face Jake together.

Tomorrow night, when Jake came out of the mine, they would tell him.

CHAPTER TWENTY-FOUR

Jake walked through the mine tunnel carrying his pick and shovel over his shoulder, holding before him a smoking torch which trailed acrid smoke and cast eerie shadows on the tunnel walls. His footsteps echoed before him. The only other sound was the pump working ahead in the stope. The floor was wet beneath his feet and here and there water trickled down the tunnel walls. The smell, dank and stagnant, was sharpened by the smoke from the torch and a lingering odor of blasting powder.

Reaching the stope, Jake threw down his tools and drove his torch into a crevice. The light was feeble but all a man needed for pick and shovel work. Jake checked to be sure he had candles and matches should his torch burn out. Satisfied, he took up his pick ax and began to work at the face of the ore. Jake was happy. He was always happy these days, but when he took his turn working the stope, he was especially happy.

The work was divided into shifts. One man worked in the room they called a stope, breaking out with his pick the ore loosened by the previous day's blasting and shoveling it into a wheelbarrow. Another man worked the tunnel, wheel barrowing the ore from the stope to the shaft where he would dump it into the huge "bucket" to be hauled to the surface by the man on top who also wheel barrowed the ore to the sluice box on the creek.

Jake knew Hugh did not like the underground shifts. He'd never said so, but Jake knew, because Hugh only went to work whistling when he had the outside shift. Jake offered to work all the underground shifts, but Hugh said the work must be divided fairly, though they both knew Caleb Dexter used his expertise in mining to shirk the physical work of the operation. He guarded his knowledge, too, refusing to drill the precisely set blasting holes or measure powder into them unless he was alone. And when it came time for washing the broken ore through the sluice boxes, he acted like he was the only one who could spot the flicker of gold dust or know the difference between fool's gold and an actual flake of gold.

They were terribly short handed. Austin Avery had offered to advance the wages if they'd hire some laborers, but Hugh stubbornly refused, either from his reluctance to be indebted to the gambler, or, Jake speculated, because replacing Luther would acknowledge the fact his brother was not coming back. Jake had urged Hugh to go after him, but Hugh was unwilling in a way that seemed to Jake to be uncharacteristically unforgiving.

And so with Caleb Dexter so lazy and Hugh just a bit spooky underground, Jake figured he was the best miner. He liked knowing there was something he did best, and he loved the mine. The temperature was always the same, so they could work no matter what the weather. Many an Iowa blizzard had kept him in the sod hut for days, with nothing to do but whittle, teach Edwin his numbers, and listen to Molly read from the Bible. And with farming there was always the unexpected. You'd want to plow, but it would be too wet. When the crops needed rain, it was dry. When you needed it dry so as to hay, it would rain. If you once got a good crop, then came the grasshoppers. With farming a man had to always keep one eye on the sky.

But in the mine it was always the same. A man had his day's work laid out for him. Today he had to break down this wall of ore and get it into a pile, and beyond that he didn't have to think. Hugh would haul the ore to the entrance; Dexter would hoist it out. Nothing to think about. You were almost sure of washing out enough dust to feed your family. And it wasn't boring! With each pick of the ax, you strained forward to see that gleam that meant you had cut into that great golden vein that Caleb Dexter promised led to the mother lode. Mining was exciting business. He supposed it was something like gambling. Made you understand a man like Austin Avery. Jake had always been unlucky with cards but with mining he knew he had only to keep plugging away and he had as good a chance as anyone of winning.

Jake was happier than he'd been in his whole life. He could forget about failure and people looking down their noses at him, saying how some folks just had worse luck than others. This time he would among the lucky ones. He could feel it in his bones. He was glad he'd let Hugh talk him into going underground. Hugh had been a real friend, urging him to stick it out, making them partners. Jake valued the partnership and had told Hugh that more than once.

He only wished Hugh could be as happy as he was. Hugh was a worrier; that was his problem. He thought too much, worrying about Luther working in the valley, worrying about the Sioux getting closer to town, trying to decide if they should sell out to Avery. There was no sense in it. A man couldn't change things by thinking. Custer was dead and all the weeping and wailing and talk of revenge wasn't going to bring him back. Jake wasn't going to let anything get him down. He kept chipping away with his pick with the narrow sideways arch he had developed to adjust to the low ceiling of the stope only inches above his head. It was a graceful movement. He hardly ever broke the rhythm. Until he heard the sound.

He paused for a moment then. It had been a cracking sound, like something breaking. Jake cocked his head and listened. There was nothing but the steady wheezing suck of the pump and the sputter of the torch. The sound did not come again. If he had been a jumpy fellow like Hugh or Luther or some greenhorn, he would have stopped work to run ask Dexter what the noise was. But Jake wasn't that kind of a man. He wasn't going to let anything interfere with his work. He hoisted his pickax and drove it into the ore with a mighty blow.

When Hugh heard the noise he had been midway through the tunnel on his way to the stope with an empty wheelbarrow. He stood still for a moment listening. It had been a curious sound, like something breaking somewhere underground. Hugh looked around the tunnel as far as the torch resting in his wheelbarrow would allow. It was not far. He could see only the nearest of the massive timbers which at intervals supported the roof of the mine. He tried to decide if he should go forward and warn Jake or turn back to the entrance and ask Dexter what the sound had been. It was probably nothing, and Dexter would laugh at him. It wouldn't be the first time. Jake and Dexter probably sensed he always felt uneasy underground. His idea of hell was working underground for eternity. He was more than a little afraid, even having listened to Caleb Dexter's lectures that gold mines were not that dangerous. Gold mines bored into solid ore. It was coal mines with their soft structure that shifted and sent black death down on miners. Still, Hugh's notion of following the gold rush had been to find *Poor Man's Gold*, the glittering nuggets one found in the creek, needing only a gold pan and maybe a sluice box. Reality was working underground. Long days, so that you might go underground before dawn and only on summer's longest days get out in time to see the sun set. The whole gulch was now pockmarked with crude mine shafts and as fall approached miners would be going underground. According to Dexter everyone would want to be in deep diggings when cold weather came. Gold mines were fine places. There was no reason to feel you were working in your own tomb.

Still, when Hugh heard the noise, he was afraid. He was still standing there, holding on to his wheel-barrow and trying to decide what to do, when the mine caved in.

When Jake came to, he was lying belly down in the darkness — the complete and utter darkness of the underground. His torch was gone. It took him a while to think where he was and then to decide what must have happened. There had been a cave-in and he had been knocked unconscious. Now he was awake and lying on his face in the mine, and a terrible weight on his legs kept him there. He reached around behind him as best he could and discovered he was buried from the waist down in loose ore. That nearly brought him to panic, but when he brought his arms over his head, he found that as far as he could reach before and above him, he was clear. Part of the roof must have held, he reasoned. He tried shouting, but his yells seemed so soon lost he decided to save his energy. There was plenty of air to breathe even if it was full of dust. He hurt all over but not as bad as if his legs were smashed. He could wiggle his toes so it couldn't be too bad. His shirt front was wet, but it was a cold kind of wetness, so Jake reasoned it was just water on the floor of the mine and not blood. He could hear the pump still working away, its steady sucking at the water reassured him.

A feeling of calm settled over him. He was all right. His luck had not changed. It was a set-back, but he was alive and it was just a matter of time until they dug him out. If he rested his head on his arm, he was fairly comfortable. He worried about Hugh back in the tunnel. There was no way of knowing how much of the mine had caved in. He hoped Hugh was safe. He should have taken warning when he heard the first crack. Hugh was more cautious, so maybe he'd gotten out in time. If he hadn't, Jake hoped he, too, was in an air pocket and not badly hurt.

The thing to do, Jake told himself, was to relax, take it easy and not get into a panic. He would just rest his head on his arms and lie there on his belly and try to keep his mind on other things. He would try to visualize what was going on at the surface. He figured he knew pretty much the steps they would take to rescue him, and if he thought each step out slowly, then he could figure when they were close to him and he should start to yell.

Jake reasoned that when the cave-in happened Dexter would have run for help. Maybe sent Molly and Edwin to do that while he started digging. It wouldn't take long for word to spread, and Jake knew within minutes a hundred men with shovels would be coming to the rescue. Caleb Dexter had told them often that one of the first rules of a mining camp was in case of a cave-in, everyone dropped everything and kept digging until everyone was out. Every miner knew he might someday be trapped underground; so in case of a cave-in, every man was a brother.

With all those men digging in shifts, they could move a lot of rock fast, Jake reasoned. He wondered if the shaft was still open. If the cave-in was only in the stope or in even the stope and the tunnel, then the men could get down into the mine, and might be only a matter of minutes before he was rescued. If they had to re-open the shaft or dig a new one, it would take much longer.

Jake tried to calculate how long it had taken the four partners to sink their shaft so he could divide that by a hundred men digging in shifts round the clock, but he found he could not remember even how many days they had worked on the shaft. He wasn't good with calculations at his best; now he suspected he was not thinking clearly. There was no sense worrying about it. He couldn't make them dig any faster. The dust had settled now and the air he breathed seemed good. He was pretty sure there would be enough to last even if it took a day or two to get him out. He'd have quite a story to tell Molly and Edwin. He hoped they were not too worried. He wished there was some way he could tell Molly he was safe. That he had left his curse of bad luck behind in Iowa and everything was going to be all right.

Then the pump stopped.

It had been churning away steadily for minutes or hours; however long he had been trapped. But now, quite suddenly, it stopped. Jake held his breath and strained to listen, but there was no sound except that of his own heart pounding away in his chest.

Something had happened to the pump.

Jake felt cold sweat breaking out on his forehead. The pump had held all through the cave-in. That was one reason he had figured most of the mine was still intact. But something had happened. It was a long way from the mine to the water wheel on the creek which powered the pump. The connecting rod between the water wheel and the pump was a line of aspen poles nearly two hundred feet long, supported every dozen feet or so upon standards fastened on pivots to firm blocks on the ground. The standards moved backward and forward with the lifting and sinking of the pump. It was a simple system and worked well enough, but with two hundred feet of aspen poles a lot could and did go wrong. It was not unusual to go to work in the morning and discover some animal had knocked down one of the poles during the night and the water had risen to a depth of a foot or more within the mine.

Jake tried to calculate how long it would take the water to rise above his head. He reared up as high as he could and figured he had his nose at least a foot off the ground. But he could not stay that way for long. Fear was making him weak. He lay back on his arm and willed himself to be calm. Surely someone on the surface would notice the pump was broken. It would take only minutes to set it up again. He had nothing to worry about.

But even as he lay there, telling himself his luck was going to hold, he could feel the water rising.

Hugh had stood still clutching the handles of his wheelbarrow and watching in amazement as great chunks of the tunnel caved in around him with a roar, raining blows on his head and shoulders. It seemed to take a long time to happen; yet it was only an instant before the torch was snuffed out and he was left in absolute blackness and silence, still hanging on to his wheelbarrow. There was so much dust in the air, he felt himself strangling.

He took deep, frantic breaths until the fact he could still breathe reassured him, and he began cautiously to grope through the darkness, not daring to move his feet as if a great pit might have opened up before him.

He felt in the wheelbarrow for his torch, but his fingers met only rock. He dared a step or two and found debris packed around him as if he were in a giant pocket in the earth. Fighting panic, he leaned on the wheelbarrow to steady himself and reached into his pockets with trembling fingers until he located a candle and the matches he kept in a waterproof container. He held a candle and the match safe in one hand and with the other carefully removed a match from the block and struck it, concentrating on getting the candle lit despite the trembling of his hand. The wick did not catch until the match burned his fingers. He held his breath until the flame grew and then he dared to raise the candle and look around.

He saw he had been standing under one of the heavy support timbers; that had saved his life. He reached up to touch the great pine log thankfully. He wondered what would have happened if he had heeded that first warning crack, would he have gotten out in time or been caught in that pile of rubble in the tunnel behind him? What if he had gone forward to warn Jake? Had the roof of the stope held? Was Jake dead or was he, like Hugh, buried alive? Hugh stood, holding the candle in both hands, trembling so the hot wax dripped on his hands. He willed himself to be calm, to be strong.

Caleb Dexter always said that every miner in camp came running if there was a cave-in. With enough men digging, they might be saved. Miners never assumed a man was dead, Dexter said. Men had been brought out of mines alive after being trapped for days. No one gave up until everyone was out. It was just a matter of time, Hugh told himself. The key was not to panic. Not to go crazy at the idea of being buried alive. If only he could do something to help. He noticed the handle of his shovel half-buried in the wheelbarrow. Carefully balancing the candle in a pile of soft dirt, Hugh pried the shovel out. It felt good to hold it. God must have meant to give him a chance. He studied his situation. Although there was debris all around him, he could move quite a lot of the loose ore himself, and in the tunnel, there must be other pockets of air where the timbers had held.

Propping the candle between two rocks, he prepared to dig. Then he realized he might have lost his orientation and be digging in the wrong direction. He studied the situation. The wheelbarrow had been in front of him when the roof fell in. Therefore if he dug behind the wheelbarrow, he would be going back through the tunnel toward the shaft and freedom. Possibly the cave-in didn't go all the way. He might meet the rescuers in an hour or two. The shaft might be clear. He tried to think how far into the tunnel he was. Not so far; he could surely get himself out before he used up his air.

And then he thought of Jake. Jake was back in the stope. It might take the rescuers hours to reach Hugh, and then more hours to get to Jake. Maybe too long. If he dug in the other direction, he might be able to find Jake in time. Jake could be dead already. It was possible, likely even. But there were strong support timbers in the stope. A hard section of ore formed the roof. It might have held, but Jake would have only enough air to last a few hours.

Hugh slumped back against the prison of rock and groaned. He had coveted Jake's wife, maybe even wished Jake conveniently dead; now God had given him a choice. He could get himself out or turn back and try to save the husband of the woman he loved.

He began digging toward Jake. He was crying in rage and frustration and fear, but it didn't matter, no one would ever know. The candle flickered in the narrow passageway, and Hugh realized it was burning up precious oxygen. He would have to snuff it out and work in the dark. He could light a match from time to time to be sure he was moving in the right direction. Without the hopeful flame, he was stunned by the darkness. There is no place on earth darker than the inside of a mine. He made himself keep digging.He succeeded in making a shallow passageway back toward where Jake must be. A passageway so small he had to lie on his side and use his shovel like a pick to hack the dirt before him and pull it back over his shoulder. There was no way to shore up his tunnel as he worked, and he realized much of it was falling in behind him as he went. But it didn't seem to matter. He was getting closer to his partner.

Then instinct told him something else had gone wrong, but he ignored his new fear and kept working. Finally, lying there on his side in the place he had hollowed out, a place no bigger than a coffin, he realized he was lying in water. He had forgotten the pump. It was broken and now the mine was filling with water. For a moment he was too shocked to move. Finally he got his father's pocket watch and checked the time by the light of a match, trying to calculate how much longer he had to live. As he put the watch away, he pictured someone giving it to Luther. Poor Luther; he wished he had done better by him.

His heart beat faster at the thought he was going to die. He tried to picture what it would be like. He supposed he should ready himself to meet his maker, but he could pray only for Molly and Edwin, for who would take care of them if neither he nor Jake got out alive? He could not just lie there and wait for death. If there was to be salvation, it was up to him. There was no longer room to use the shovel. He began digging at the rocks before him with his bare hands.

CHAPTER TWENTY-FIVE

Emerald was weeping in great choking sobs and Avery was annoyed. He had expected her to cry prettily at the funeral. In fact, he had suspected her insistence on attending the burying had something to do with the fact that she had a new handkerchief of Brussels lace and she fancied the picture she would make dressed in her favorite green velvet traveling costume and drawing attention to her eyes by dabbing at them with the new handkerchief.

Now, with the preacher still droning on, she had thoroughly soaked the handkerchief, and he must give her his. She actually blew her nose into it, hardly a pretty gesture. The hot August wind had kicked up dust on the hillside graveyard and soiled her dress and rumpled her hair. The black stuff she used to accentuate her eyes had run down her cheeks and she looked thoroughly disheveled. She was sniffing like a child. It was hardly the performance he had expected of Emerald, and because he couldn't account for her behavior, Austin Avery was getting angry. He liked women to be predictable.

He had gone along with her when she insisted on attending the funeral. After all, it was proper for a man to attend the burying of a partner. It would build good will and make it easier for him to buy the other partners out when the time was right. He had admired the way Emerald had fluttered into the arms of Mrs. Lewis, hugging and kissing her as if they were true friends. And he had to admire the way she stopped to plant a kiss on the little boy's forehead so gracefully only Avery was aware of the care she took to keep her skirt out of the earth turned up around the open grave. She had managed to come out of the kiss with her hands clasped to her breast and her face tilted toward the child in a perfect picture of tragedy, and yet somehow raise her eyes to meet those of Preacher Smith at exactly the right moment to give him the full effect of her beauty. Avery had to admire a woman who could look like an angel at the very moment she was enticing a minister of the gospel to let out an involuntary gasp of desire.

But this sniffing and sobbing and hiccupping was not in character! He was about to whisper that she was overdoing it, when she took his arm and teetered as if she were going to faint. Despite the fact the minister was still sermonizing, the crowd behind them surged forward as if each man wanted to be the one to catch her. Avery put his arm around her protectively and let her lean on him. The feel and scent of her excited him as did the knowledge he alone possessed her. In some ways, he had to admit, it was her unpredictability that made her desirable.

Emerald felt terrible. She had ruined her new handkerchief with tears and mascara; her face must be a sight, but she didn't care. All her schemes and plots had come to a bitter end. It had been going so well. She had accompanied Avery on his visits to inspect the mine and fetch his share of the profits. Although she had carefully avoided flirting with Hugh, she had made conversation with Molly and Edwin and established a friendship, if not with Molly, at least with the little boy. She had brought Edwin small gifts, things Molly could hardly make him refuse without appearing harsh. True, she had not figured out any way to see Hugh away from the watchful eyes of Molly and Avery, but she knew it was just a matter of time before she could contrive some excuse to get Hugh to visit her hotel room while Avery was out gambling.

How she wished now that she had not delayed, but she had been waiting for inspiration, for a way to make Hugh think she was respectable without simply throwing herself on his mercy, telling him Avery had tricked her into eloping, promising her the ship's captain would marry them, then taken her against her will. She would then weep that she could not leave the gambler now because she had no money, and no decent man would have her. She'd been sure that would work, especially as Hugh was overcome with desire, nature took its course, and further sobs inspired Hugh to do the gentlemanly thing and marry her.

It might well have worked, but Avery had taught her to hedge her bets, and she'd had to delay action until Avery completed whatever devious scheme he had in mind to sell the mine and make Hugh, as well as himself, rich. She certainly didn't want to be married to Hugh badly enough to risk being poor, nor did she wish to give up the attentions of Austin Avery any sooner than was necessary.

Thinking about how close she had been to landing Hugh sent Emerald into a fresh paroxysm of weeping, just as the coffin was lowered awkwardly into the grave. When it hit bottom with a thump, Molly Lewis stifled a scream. It was time for the widow of the dead man to cast the first earth upon his coffin. Instead she had to be held back from throwing herself into the grave. *What acting!* Emerald thought almost admiringly; then how convincingly she sobbed as she threw the first handful of dirt into the grave. But Molly didn't fool Emerald for a moment. Molly's husband was conveniently in his grave and Hugh was alive. She had lucked out!

Molly must have had some bad hours when she learned the mine caved in, as had Emerald, especially when the word came that only one of the men was alive. But no matter how sad Molly looked now, Emerald remembered the looks Molly and Hugh had exchanged in the cabin, the something that always seemed to run between them telling her, if not the stupid husband, that they were determined to be lovers. And now with Jake Lewis dead, they would wait to be wed only for whatever would pass as a decent interval in a place like Deadwood.

And it was so unfair! Just when Emerald had realized her true destiny was to be married to a respectable man like Hugh, a man who was sufficiently handsome and brave and noble to make her forget Austin Avery and his lovemaking. And just when that man was about to become rich, the whole scheme had come crashing down in a stupid mining accident. Why should Molly get another husband so soon, when Emerald hadn't had even one!

Emerald dared a glance at Hugh from behind her hanky. She had not dared have him see her eyes since she had ruined them with weeping; now she saw any efforts to attract his attention would be wasted. He looked terrible, and not just from the bruises suffered in the accident, but genuinely anguished, as if he had lost his best friend. Hugh's hands were bandaged, so he must have been digging with them, but surely not back toward his partner as was the talk of the camp. That was just a story. Avery said the story of a man going after his partner instead of saving himself was the kind of heroic tale miners liked to believe in. No one would do such a thing, Emerald agreed, then realized he might have if he felt guilty about wanting his partner's wife.

Guilt could do funny things to you. Like sometimes she would remember that her mother would call her a sinner or worse, and she would feel strange inside. Sometimes she almost liked the feeling. It made her episodes on the bed with Avery more delicious, made her twist and moan and call out his name.

But in the clear light of day in a cemetery, new dug into the side of a mountain with only crude wooden crosses marking the graves, knowing she was living in sin made Emerald uneasy. Avery had made it clear he was never going to marry her, and as long as she was his mistress, he would have power over her. Even when it was she that enticed him, it was as if he owned her passion. She sensed that with Hugh love would have been different, tender and beautiful, like in a love poem.

If only Hugh had gotten Jake out of the mine alive! Then she would have had time to make Hugh forget whatever it was he saw in Molly. She studied them, trying to see the situation clearly. They looked terrible. No doubt they felt both grief and guilt. They might not get married right away, and they couldn't leave town, married or just together, until they sold their shares of the mine. Emerald might somehow get Avery to delay that. Perhaps if she was very clever Emerald still had a chance.

The service ended at last and the crowd began to disperse from the graveyard. Emerald wanted to give Molly another sisterly hug of condolence to show Hugh what a loving, ladylike sort of person she was. But Avery was tugging at her arm, anxious to leave and Emerald didn't want to annoy Avery just then. She intended to hang onto him and to enjoy him as long as possible.

She watched Molly and Edwin, uncertain of what to do, and then saw Hugh step forward and pick up Edwin and hold him close, even though with his bandaged hands it must have cost him considerable pain.

She could not see the look Molly and Hugh exchanged, but she could imagine it. And she knew that Molly had one important advantage. In her faded gingham and tattered old shawl she wasn't half as beautiful as Emerald, but Hugh's mother had probably worn homespun, and some instinct told Emerald that when it came to taking a wife, men looked for their mothers.

Emerald sighed and let Avery lead her down the hill from the cemetery. She wasn't defeated, but she knew if she was going to get Hugh away from Molly Lewis, she would have to be very clever indeed.

CHAPTER TWENTY-SIX

Fourteen miles northwest of Deadwood lay the broad, fertile, and lovely grassland known as the Spearfish Valley. Surrounded on every side by mountains, it was a land perfect for men who found the rugged interior of the Black Hills confining and were more comfortable in the open air riding a horse than digging in a mine. White men tried in that summer of 1876 to establish farms and ranches on the fertile grasslands. The price they paid for their homesteads was constant warfare with the Sioux. The Indians sought revenge for the violation of their sacred lands, not against the first trespassers, the miners who crowded into the narrow gulches of the interior, but against the ranchers of the valley, seeking as their war booty the cattle and horses sheltered in the valley and the scalps of the men who defended them.

On a hot August day Luther Everett tied his horse to a bit of brush halfway up the steep slope of what the ranchers called Lookout Mountain. He climbed to a spot on the rocky face of the slope where he could best stand guard over the haying operation in the valley.

Luther was unaware of the disaster in the Lucky Six, and he felt confident he had made the right decision in joining Emmet Hobart's ranching operation. Ranching was the life for a man, he knew, not grubbing away underground, never seeing the light of day, chasing some bonanza which maybe didn't even exist. He would choose to stay on with Hobart even if Hugh begged him to return to Deadwood. Not only was ranching healthier work than mining, it was easier, too. Of course, cutting hay with a hand scythe was no picnic. His shirt seemed always soaked through with sweat, but with the need to post guards over the valley, even in haying season a man was bound to get in a few hours a day on a horse.

It turned out that ranching was mostly riding around on horseback keeping an eye on the livestock and watching out for Indians. Luther liked that. It gave him plenty of time to dream. At first he'd been so nervous he'd thought he saw an Indian behind every rock or bush. Now that his imagination no longer plagued him, he feared he might never have a chance to shoot an Indian.

He didn't understand his rotten luck. Everyone in the valley constantly complained about the Indians. How the Sioux had run off half the parties that had been trying since early May to settle the valley and how they might need to build a stockade if the new town site of Spearfish was to survive. But despite the fact Indian raids, or at least rumors of such, had been almost daily occurrences since the Custer massacre, Luther always seemed to miss the action. Still, ranching was a great business, he decided sitting cross legged on the hillside, his rifle balanced across his lap, a sprig of grass between his teeth, watching the men working in the valley. From where he sat, he couldn't see Hobart's cabin, but he had a good view of the livestock grazing just south of where the men were haying.

Luther was looking forward to fall when Hobart would cull stock from the herd he had built that summer, and they would drive those not worth wintering to Deadwood for sale. Then Hobart would give him his pay and he'd buy himself a real outfit — one that Hugh would envy. He'd have a broad-brimmed Stetson hat and boots with high heels for riding and maybe he'd even get his own saddle. Cowboys always had their own saddles, and he reckoned that was what he was going to be, a cowboy and an Indian fighter, if he ever got the chance. He'd borrow one of Hobart's best horses for the trip, and he'd ride up to the Lucky Six at a gallop. Would Hugh be surprised to see him! He was sure he'd grown stronger and taller, and if he stayed on the horse, he'd be able to look down on his brother for once. He'd stay on the horse, holding it in and spurring at the same time, so it would prance a little. He'd be riding like he was glued in the saddle and wearing his new boots and a hat. Maybe he'd have enough money to buy a revolver. To have a six-shooter in his belt would be great; he'd let Edwin shoot it. That would get to Hugh.

He bet Hugh never would have a revolver, even if he did get rich off his old gold mine, which Luther was pretty sure he wouldn't. Yes, it would be really fine when he rode into Deadwood side by side with Hobart.

He'd learned a lot from Hobart about riding and handling horses and livestock; by fall he reckoned he'd know all there was to know about ranching. Emmet Hobart was a real man and ranching was a real business. He should have listened to Hobart and gone with him in the first place. He could have saved all that trouble over his getting hoodwinked by the damn gambler. In the fall he'd make it up to himself. After he saw Hugh and the others at the Lucky Six, he'd head for the Hidden Treasure and take care of his business like the man he was. He wouldn't take chances on winning his tokens in a card game this time. He'd pay and he'd get his business over with quickly, and let Hugh know about it. That's how a man would do it.

Luther was concentrating so hard on watching the men cut hay, he didn't notice the rider at first. It was the cattle moving away from a rider in the tall grass that made him notice someone was coming. He'd finally stopped hoping every rider was his brother coming to get him. He could tell by the way the man sat in his saddle, it was Emmet Hobart coming to relieve him. Luther squinted at the sky and tried to judge how long he had been on guard duty. It didn't seem like long, but he supposed an older man like Hobart couldn't stand the haying for too long. Well, he was glad to pull a little extra weight if it would help. Hobart had been like a father to him. Luther was watching Hobart leaving the valley floor for the gentle slope leading up the side of the mountain when he caught some other movement in the periphery of his vision. He turned and squinted, then felt his eyes grow wide and his jaw slacken.

Off to the left, moving through a ravine that skirted the edge of the valley was a group of horsemen.

For a moment, Luther couldn't move or think. He had acted the fool so many times, thinking he was seeing Indians when it had been only a coyote moving through tall grass or a cow and her calf wandered away from the herd.

But this was it. A war party! Hobart rode slowly up the side of Lookout Mountain toward him, unaware of the Indians approaching through the ravine getting closer to him. It wouldn't be long before they would meet. Hobart had to be warned. The men in the valley had to be warned. Luther stood up and began waving frantically. Hobart rode on up the hill. It seemed a long time before he looked up at Luther, and then he merely answered his frantic signals with a cheerful wave.

He must get mounted! Luther looked down the hill to where his horse was grazing peacefully. He'd have to ride down and warn Hobart; then together they would meet the Sioux in combat. He started down the steep hillside, sending the loose gravel clattering down before him and almost falling in his haste. He gripped his rifle awkwardly in his left hand, using his right to keep his balance.

When Luther reached the spot where his horse grazed, he saw Hobart rein in, wondering why he was in such a hurry. Then Luther realized what he should have done first. *Shoot his rifle.* That was how you were supposed to warn everyone! He could no longer see the Indians, and there was no time to aim anyway. He cocked the hammer, pointed his rifle at the sky and pulled the trigger. The shot boomed out, and the horse whinnied and bolted sideways, tearing the branch she was tethered to from the bush.

Oh my God, Luther thought. Don't let her get away. Without stopping to see if Hobart and the others had reacted to his warning, he grabbed for the horse. She rolled wild eyes at him and pulled away frantically, but the branch dragging from the reins caught in something, and Luther was able to grab the cheek strap of her bridle. He flung the reins still dangling the branch over her head and tried to mount. The horse danced away from him, but he hung on and managed to scramble into the saddle. He turned the horse and started downhill, almost going over her head in the momentum of their motion. He leaned back in the saddle as Hobart had showed him, keeping his legs stiff before him. Hobart had finally seen the Indians. They saw him at the same time and kicked their ponies into a charge, yelling and brandishing their rifles. Hobart wheeled his horse and started to make a run for the valley, but a shot rang out and he fell from the saddle.

They got Hobart, Luther thought, stunned, but then Hobart was on his feet clutching his side with one hand and pulling a pistol out of his belt with the other. He looked around, dazed, then went after his horse, but it was galloping away with Hobart's rifle still in its scabbard. Hobart spotted an outcropping of rock and ran to it.

We'll have to make a stand, Luther thought. *I've got to join Hobart and stand them off.*

The Sioux wheeled their ponies and re-grouped, shouting and waving their lances and rifles at Hobart and at him. It was like they wanted to be all lined up to charge, so each would have an equal chance to make a kill. It gave Luther time to get to the shelter of the rocks.

"Don't worry," he shouted as he reached Hobart's side. "Well make a stand of it!"

Hobart was slumped against a rock. He looked like he couldn't decide if he should fall down or try to stand up and do some good against the Sioux with his pistol. Blood was seeping between his fingers where he held his other hand against his side.

"Glad you're here, kid," he said. Then he clenched his teeth as if it had hurt him to talk. Luther got off his horse and made as if to touch the sticky wound. Hobart shook his head. "Leave it alone. Nothing vital. Just hurts like hell." He strained to raise the pistol while slumping himself over a boulder so it could both prop him up and give him shelter. "See if they're coming."

They were. Eight, maybe ten warriors. There was no time to count. They were riding at Luther, whooping and hollering. There wasn't even time to be afraid.

"Just sight in on one," Hobart gasped, leaning over the rock and using both hands to aim his pistol. Luther tried to keep one of the braves in his gun sight, but they were coming too fast. The sight started to waver wildly before him. His eyes were watering so he could hardly see.

"Wait till they're closer," Hobart commanded, but Luther had to do something. He cocked the hammer and pulled the trigger. To his amazement nothing happened. The rifle was a single shot and he had forgotten to reload. Cursing, he fumbled in his cartridge belt for a fresh cartridge. He nearly dropped it as he slammed the rifle's hammer to full cock and cammed the breech-lock open. The empty shell ejected just as he heard Hobart take a shot. It seemed to take forever to get the new cartridge ready to fire. The Indians were almost upon them when he raised the rifle and without taking time to sight, pulled the trigger.

At the same moment a burst of fire came toward them, but Luther saw a red stain open in the belly of one of the warriors as he fell from his pony. The boulders protected him and Hobart, though rocks broke all around them. The Sioux were upon them, almost up to the boulders and then they seemed to wheel their horses as one and veer off sharply to Luther's right.

"What the hell?" Luther said, blinking.

Hobart slumped back weakly against the rock, allowing himself to drop to his knees. "They're going for the livestock. It's our luck they'd rather steal horses than risk lives charging us. Your shot warned the herders, so the braves are going to have to make their raid fast if they're going to get any booty today." Hobart sat down and, pulling a handkerchief out of his back pocket, pressed it into his wound. "I think I'll be okay if I sit quiet until help comes."

Luther wasn't listening. He was looking at the Indian he'd seen fall from his horse. Wonderingly he said, "I got one. I killed me a Sioux!"

"Plug him again to make sure," Hobart advised, not looking up from his own wound. "They'll play possum."

Luther considered it. It didn't seem sportsmanlike, but maybe Hobart was right. Better to make sure. He'd played the fool enough. He reloaded and aimed the needle gun and pulled the trigger. The body of the Indian ripped open again.

"I'm going to scalp him," Luther declared.

"What?"

"Sure, what the hell? I'm going to scalp him and wear it on my belt. That'll be something to show Hugh!"

Luther started out of the shelter of the rocks, reaching for his knife.

"Be careful!" Hobart yelled. "They'll be coming back for the body."

But Luther had already left the boulders, clutching his rifle and his knife out. He'd have to be quick, and wasn't sure how to go about it, but he wasn't going to lose his nerve. It was his trophy and he deserved it. He had held off a Sioux attack almost singlehandedly! What a story it would make!

He heard the shot at the same moment he felt something bite into his back. It knocked him to the ground. He came up on his knees, still holding his rifle. He looked around incredulously, thinking for a moment that Hobart had tried to stop him.

Then he saw the other Indian.

The Indians had posted a lookout too! On the mountain not a hundred yards from where he had been standing guard. He'd been shot in the back by a damn redskin and now the sneaky bastard was getting ready to plug him again.

Frantically, Luther raised his own gun, knowing it was too late. The damn Indians weren't playing fair!

CHAPTER TWENTY-SEVEN

In her cabin near the shaft of the ill-named Lucky Six Mine, Molly sat, rocking endlessly, her arms folded tightly. She had spent most of the three days since Jake's funeral in her rocking chair, feeling numb, often with Edwin in her arms. She stared straight ahead, grieving, tormenting herself with her loss and her guilt. She had no other purpose in life but to mourn. The people of Deadwood had rallied around her, bringing food, helping to lay Jake out, and minding Edwin. Just that morning a subdued Caleb Dexter had come with his hat in his hand and offered to take Edwin for a walk to town. She had let the boy go, knowing it was not good for Edwin to see her as she was. She had hardly been able to say the necessary things about Jake going to heaven.

She wished she could cry. She hadn't really cried, though she had felt her face crumpled with anxiety since she had heard Caleb at the cabin door shouting those terrible words, *cave-in at the mine!* Something had knotted up inside her, hearing those words, and moments later when he'd told her Hugh and Jake were both trapped in the mine it had grown tighter until sometimes she could hardly catch her breath. And then she thought of how it must have felt for Jake suffocating in the mine. Poor Jake, she thought, over and over, poor Jake dying alone down there in the dark. She could not rid herself of the picture of Jake dying alone in the darkness.

He had been happy in the mine. That was some consolation. But he had been happy with her too and, just like the mine, she had betrayed him. At least he had never suspected his wife was unfaithful, but it was something she would never forget. Jake was a good man, he'd worked hard all his life and should have earned more than the glittering hope of hitting a vein of gold.

Tormented with her thoughts, she was at first oblivious to the knocking at the cabin door. "Come in," she finally said, not caring who it was. When Hugh stepped quietly into the room, she was not surprised to see him. Despite his own narrow escape and his injuries, he'd taken charge as best he could, arranging for Jake's burial, and holding Edwin as he cried, and supporting her at the graveside. She saw he had taken the bandages off his hands, and his cuts and bruises were healing. She was relieved, but she couldn't look at him for long. She folded her arms tighter and kept rocking, not even speaking. He pulled a stool over and sat before her.

"Have you eaten, Molly?" he asked quietly.

She nodded but he looked around as if he didn't believe her. Two plates on the table still held most of the meal someone had brought her and Edwin last night. The stove was cold. Hugh got up and took the plates to her wash pan on the stove and poured water from the kettle over them.

"That's my job," she said, but Hugh poured a little soft soap into the pan before wiping his hands on his pants uncertainly. He looked awkward standing there; a big, rugged man trying to do women's work. He must have realized he had forgotten to heat the water and the stove was cold. He got kindling and started the fire. She kept thinking she should tend to things, but felt unable to move. She should not have let the stove go out.

While the water heated, he returned to the stool and sat facing her. His didn't seem to know what to do with his hands or how to make her look him in the eyes. "I have to talk to you, Molly. I need you to know I tried to save him."

"I know that. Everyone said so. Even if they hadn't told me, I knew you'd try to save each other."

"He was my partner and my friend. If it hadn't been for him, we wouldn't have gotten a place on the wagon train. He was a good man, always so steady. He never saw bad in anyone."

"It isn't your fault he's dead."

"But it is. I'm the one that made us go underground. Dexter said it wasn't safe, but I insisted. I didn't want to give up the partnership because — well, you know."

"*I know,*" she shut her eyes. "It was my doing too. We knew dissolving the partnership, would mean the end for our time together."

"And that might have been the right thing, but I just couldn't leave you once I'd found you again. It was hard to sort out right from wrong, not just my being Edwin's father, but my still loving you." He paused, looking at the stove as the fire caught and crackled. "Besides Jake didn't want to give up the mine; he loved the damn place."

"I know," she almost smiled. "I tell myself that too."

"But I take responsibility for everything."

"It's not your fault the mine caved in."

"I keep wondering what I should have done differently."

She saw him looking at her as if she had answers, but she could only keep on rocking.

"Molly, look at me. It was right for us to meet again, wasn't it? It was our destiny."

"I don't understand destiny, Hugh. Nor God's will, nor even if there is a heaven, no matter what I told Edwin. You know, it was my idea to join the gold rush! I thought it would make Jake happy."

"And it did. He died with hope in his heart."

"And he was spared knowing about me *and* —"

"And the man who always loved you." He took her by her shoulders and made her look at him. "We *did not* will Jake to die. And somehow I think that if we had explained it all to him and found some way to keep him close to Edwin, he would have understood we should be together. I've been thinking all along what it meant, us meeting again. Edwin is my son and now you can be my wife. We didn't want to hurt Jake and we didn't. He never knew, but now it's all different. Don't you see we must be together to make sense out of what's happened!"

Still she rocked, but she could feel her tears falling at last. She wanted desperately to believe him. He took her hands.

"Molly, stop that rocking and look at me. You're hands are cold as ice. Let me warm them."

She was surprised his touch still thrilled her, surprised that she could feel anything but numb. Something was breaking loose within her, so she could look up and into his eyes. It need not be her decision, she saw. Fate had settled it for her. Once she had followed Jake, now she could follow Hugh, if she could just take that first step, if she could even speak.

"Tell me what you're thinking, Molly. I know it's too soon, that we shouldn't be making plans when you're in mourning for Jake, but if you agree, then in the fall —"

His voice trailed off. The question unasked but understood. She was on the verge, not of answering, but of letting the fact she did not withdraw her hands speak for her. They were as close in that moment as they had ever been, but then there was a knock at the door.

It must be a stranger, she thought. Caleb and Edwin would have just entered, but even for them it would be too soon to reveal their intimacy. She snatched her hands back from Hugh's. She felt herself blushing. Jake was hardly cold in his grave. What kind of woman was she?

The knock persisted.

"Shall I get it?" Hugh asked.

Molly shook her head and went to the door, wiping her hands on her apron and making the habitual check to be sure her collar was buttoned. She opened the door to a stranger. No one she'd seen in Deadwood. He was tan and bearded and smelled of sweat and something else, horses.

"Is this the Lewis cabin?" he asked and she nodded.

"I was looking for Hugh Everett. I understand he lives in the other cabin on the Lucky Six, but nobody's home down there and I got to find him."

"Mr. Everett is here." She stepped aside. "He was my late husband's partner and . . ." her voice trailed off as Hugh came to the door and stood beside her.

"Hugh Everett? I'm Pete Simpson. Emmet Hobart sent me."

"Come in," Hugh said eagerly. "How is Emmet?"

"Maybe you better come outside," Simpson took his hat off and held it in front of him. Molly thought he did it awkwardly. If the man hadn't taken his hat off to meet a lady, why was he taking it off now? She followed the men outside, feeling uneasy.

"I see you have Hobart's wagon," Hugh said.

"Yes, Hobart's wagon. Hobart asked me to bring ... this to you. He would have come himself, he said to tell you that, but —"

They moved closer to the wagon as they talked. Molly noticed there was something in the back covered with a tarp. Simpson was fingering his hat nervously, looking uncomfortable.

"I don't know how to go about this —"

"My brother's working for Hobart," Hugh made conversation. "I guess they've got quite a livestock business started up in the valley. Do you know Luther?"

"Well, we never exactly met. You see I was just passing through on my way to Deadwood and —"

"I hope Luther thought to send us some beef. We could sure use some fresh meat," Hugh said, reaching over to lift the corner of the tarp.

Molly suddenly understood. "No!" she gasped, but it was too late.

Hugh lifted the tarp and cried out, "Oh, my God!"

Molly tried to stifle her own sob.

"Oh, my God," Hugh said again, still holding the tarp and looking down. It was Luther, in the wagon. Dead.

"Hobart said to tell you he'd have come himself, only he's got a pretty bad side wound. Same outfit as did in your brother."

"Indians?" Hugh asked after a long silence.

"Bloody Sioux. Probably the same bunch that got Custer. Tried to steal Hobart's horses."

Hugh climbed into the wagon, and putting an arm under his brother, raised him up so he could hold him. Luther was cold. Luther was as cold as ice. His head hung back awkwardly. Hugh looked at the body, denying, unbelieving, remembering Luther as a little boy. A little boy tagging after him. A little boy always wanting to impress his older brother. A little boy wanting to be a man.

"You can be proud of him," Simpson kept talking. "Hobart said to tell you he saved Hobart's life for sure. He warned the herders and the haying crews in the valley, and he saved Hobart, and he killed one of the goddamn Indians too. Got a shot right near the heart Hobart said."

I'll make you proud of me. How many times had Luther said that? *I'll make you proud of me yet.* That's what he had said that last day. The day Hugh sent him away. Now, when it was too late, he tried to hold Luther close, not caring about the blood.

"He done real fine. Mr. Hobart said to be sure to tell you that. To tell you he was really growing up there in the valley and he died like a man."

My fault, Hugh thought. My fault. *Take care of your brother*, his mother had said, and Hugh had sent him to his death. There was a buzzing in his ears like he was going to pass out, and for a time Hugh was conscious of nothing but the terrible pain and guilt that descended on him.

Finally he heard Simpson saying, "So you see, I got to get back, Mr. Everett. I got to pick up supplies tonight so I can get started back first thing in the morning. I don't want to be alone in that valley after dark. So I got to get unloaded now." Hugh realized what the man was saying. He needed to unload his wagon. Unload the body.

With a great effort, Hugh laid his brother down.

"So if you'll just tell me where you want him, I'll help you to get him laid out, but then I've got to go. It don't seem quite decent and I'm sorry, but I was just passing through when Hobart gave me the job; him being short handed and wounded and him figuring you rather have your brother buried near you."

Still sitting in the wagon Hugh reached to replace the tarp and noticed Luther's feet. The beautiful boots Luther had spent his savings on were worn completely through. Luther had been so proud of them. They were the only fine thing he had ever owned and now they were trash. Hugh wondered how he could have walked in such ragged boots. Luther fighting Indians and dying with ragged boots. It looked as if he had tried to mend the boots with bits of leather. Luther had never been very skillful at things. There was a great crack in the right boot and Luther's big toe was showing. It was more than Hugh could bear. The naked toe was harder to look at than the wounds. A man could be proud to die fighting but not of dying too poor to cover his nakedness.

Simpson drove Hugh and his brother to the other cabin. Molly walked. They had to put Luther in his old bunk. Hugh's table wasn't long enough. Hugh covered him with a blanket. There was an undertaker in Deadwood now, but he would lay his brother out himself. He'd promised his mother to take care of him.

"Caleb Dexter will be back soon," Molly said after Simpson left. "I have a clean shirt of Jake's. I'll fetch it."

Hugh nodded. Of course, Luther couldn't be buried in his own shirt. His best shirt, blood soaked. Hugh wondered how to keep the blood from staining the clean shirt. Maybe Caleb Dexter would know. Caleb Dexter knew everything. Hugh knew nothing.

Molly came back with the shirt and set a kettle of water on the stove. "You better fetch more water. We'll need hot water."

"We don't have to lay him out right away, do we?" Hugh asked. "Can't we just ... mourn for a while?"

"It's better to keep busy. Keep doing what has to be done, and if you're lucky, you won't run out of chores. Then you don't have to think."

Hugh was like a man sleepwalking. Molly was afraid for his sanity. She ached for Hugh. She felt his grief more sharply than her own. She knew the guilt he would feel. Knew he would remember the way he had sent Luther away to keep him from hinting to Jake that he and Molly were lovers. And, of course, now she too had Luther's death on her soul. She had somehow known the moment she'd seen the tarp covered form in the wagon; she should have held Hugh back. Now, faced with the need to act, to care for Luther's body and to comfort Hugh, she found some hidden strength within. Hugh needed her. A moment before she had been unable to bring herself to bridge the space between them and accept his love, but now that his own pain was so terrible, her whole being demanded she try to bear some of it for him. She took off her apron and opened her arms to him.

"Let's hold each other."

He came to her and she felt she supported him, as if she were the strong one, the pioneer, and only she had the power to give comfort. And in comforting him, her own pain at Jake's death receded for an instant, and she knew Hugh had been right to ask her to marry him. Only together would they find peace. She wanted to love and nurture him, to take him away from the horror in this cabin and take him inside her and ease his pain.

"Hugh," she whispered, "let's go to my cabin. Let me comfort you. Let me help you forget, just for a moment." She felt the anger tense within him even before he pushed her away.

"Make me forget? Make me forget what I've done to Luther? *What we've done?*"

"Just for a time," she was stunned by his reaction. "I just wanted to ease you from this shock."

"With your body? You wanted to trap me again like the night you left Jake's bed to beg me to let Luther go!"

She was stunned. Of course, she remembered.

"You did that. Don't deny it. I wanted to bring him home, but I couldn't because of you; because of what we were doing to Jake."

His truth crumpled her, but she tried to deny it.

"Luther wanted to go. He knew he had to be away from you to grow up. And Jake wanted the mine. They made their own destiny. Not us."

"No, it was our doing. It was my lust that brought all this down upon us. Pearson, Jake, and now my brother are all dead because of me. Because of you."

She saw she could not reason with him. Whether the fault was theirs or fate they would never know, but she must not let him go. She reached out for him one more time. "Please, Hugh, please let's just hold on to each other. Just for a while more."

His eyes betrayed an instant of longing and uncertainty, but when he spoke his voice was harsh with determination. "Go away, Molly Lewis. Leave me alone to bury my brother in peace."

The pain was sharper than anything she'd yet born. She breathed deeply against it and although she wanted to scream back at him, made herself speak calmly, "I'll leave you alone now and come back later. Later we can —"

"No. *No later*. You held me with promises too long. Now it must be ended. I'm sorry I ever laid eyes on you. You are like a curse on me. Go back to your cabin. Go home now. Go back to your father if he'll have you."

He did not know when she left. So great was his own guilt and loss that he was unaware of the pain he had caused her. For a time, he did nothing but sit and stare at his brother's corpse. The blanket did not quite cover Luther's feet, and the broken soles of his brother's boots seemed an accusation. He remembered Luther as a little boy. And all the times he'd been impatient with his brother, the boy who had followed him everywhere, even into Sioux lands, and who had left with the promise that he would make them all proud.

Hugh knew he had to do something or he would go mad. He would tend to the burying. That was the thing that had to be done now. Now was not the time to think of Molly nor of the terrible things he had said to her.

He took the tobacco can with his share of the gold dust from its hiding place in the dirt of the cabin floor. He would use it all on a proper burial. He'd buy a real coffin and he would buy his brother a new pair of boots to be buried in. Hugh would give his brother the finest boots Deadwood could offer and he would order a real gravestone. His brother would lie beside Jake on Mt. Moriah, and Hugh could visit them both in peace, for he had rid himself of the woman and the promise that had become a curse.

CHAPTER TWENTY-EIGHT

Luther Everett was not the only man to lose his life that day. By sunset of August 20, 1876, five men including Luther and Preacher Smith, the gentle itinerate minister who had set out to walk to Crook City to preach the gospel, saying his Bible would protect him, were all victims of a raiding party, or parties, of Sioux.

As if this were not enough for one day, that evening once again a man rode into Deadwood with the head of an Indian dangling from his saddle. And once again, the trophy was auctioned to the highest bidder. This incident, the second in as many months, inspired the editor of the *Pioneer* to write against the practice of decapitating dead Indians, for "we should always keep in mind that the eye of the world is upon us," and "the practice makes Deadwood appear uncivilized." Citizens were reminded that to encourage immigration and investment in the Black Hills more copies of the paper were distributed in the railway depots of the east than in the town itself. The editorial concluded, "Kill all the Indians that can be killed. Complete extermination is our motto. But when once killed, leave the body intact where it falls."

The editorial stirred controversy in Deadwood, but Hugh did not take his usual interest in local issues. August ended in a blur for him. Only two things were real: his brother was dead, and his relationship with Molly seemed irreparably broken. He knew he'd said something terrible to her after Luther's death, though what he could not remember. And he could not ask. He had tried to apologize, but, her manner was distant. There seemed an icy wall between them. She had declared her intention to leave Deadwood as soon as stage service was available. Travel was at a stand-still and, although there had been efforts to organize a local militia, they had failed, for the city preferred to escape its fears in a frantic search for gold and sin. Millions of dollars in gold were found in the gulch that summer. Sin was even easier to come by.

The fact that leaving Deadwood was virtually impossible for an unescorted woman and child saved Hugh from making any decision in Molly's regard. He suffered from the same shock that had paralyzed her after Jake's death. He thought he had said something to her about their love being like a curse; sometimes he believed that. Because he had loved Molly Lewis, three men were dead, one of them his brother.

He continued to work the mine with Caleb Dexter. His heart was not in it, but he knew Molly and Edwin had needs, and work gave him an outlet. His days were full of grief and his nights with tortured dreams. Dreams in which Molly offered herself, Luther and Jake and even Custer called for his help, and although he struggled mightily, he could never complete the ordeals needed to save them. Emerald O'Brien also appeared in his dreams, but he refused to recognize her and never put a name to the dark-haired, green-eyed woman he sometimes remembered when he woke. When she accompanied Austin Avery on his trips to the mine, Hugh would avoid looking at her, but when he did allow himself a glance, she would smile as if she knew what troubled him.

August drifted into September, the weather turned unseasonably cold, and still nothing was resolved.

And then General Crook and the two thousand men he commanded marched into Deadwood. It was the event the city had waited and prayed for. Crook announced they had avenged the massacre of Custer by attacking a village at Slim Buttes, capturing two hundred ponies, the winter food supply and blankets, and a Seventh Cavalry guidon flag as proof the Sioux bore the guilt of Custer's blood. The troops and Deadwood were triumphant, although history would reveal the battle was a victory over a village occupied by women and children.

It had been a discouraging campaign. Sitting Bull and his warriors had fled to Canada. Crook had run so short of supplies the men were resigned to eating the flesh of the horses and mules that dropped from exhaustion. Still, they claimed to have broken the backbone of the Sioux nation. Indeed, the tribes had scattered to the winds and a massed attack on the Black Hills was no longer a threat. Crook was given a hero's welcome.

Hugh stood in the crowd to hear Crook speak from the balcony of the Grand Central Hotel, but he did not share the crowd's jubilation. To Hugh, the news meant Molly's path of departure was now safe. Not an hour after the news of Crook's victory reached Deadwood, Austin Avery called on Molly to offer to buy her shares of the mine. She told him she must consult with Hugh about the price. Hugh had to admit the gambler's offer was generous, so she had just that morning sent Avery a message saying she would sell and Hugh might also. As much as he hated to accommodate the gambler, Hugh saw little point in retaining his own share of the mine.

It was, therefore, not from a desire to celebrate that Hugh joined the throngs welcoming Crook to Deadwood. Whether history would regard them as pioneers or trespassers he was not certain, but he had been among those who had defied both the U.S. Cavalry and the Sioux Nation to invade the Black Hills; so now he would be present for the event which marked a turning point in the city's brief history. The summer of '76 was almost over. The military presence amounted to official government recognition of the white occupation of the Black Hills. Deadwood would become civilized. Saloon interiors would no longer be just boards placed across whiskey barrels. Carved back bars, brass foot rails, pianos, and gilt-framed portraits of nudes were being hauled in by ox train. Deadwood was no longer a glorified mining camp, but something like a real city complete with an assortment of lawyers, doctors, and a dentist, and although Preacher Smith had been killed, others had come to take his place.

Hugh wondered if all the so-called *progress* had been worth the price. He listened to the sounds of celebration, the cheers and the music of the hurdy-gurdies, the gun powder blasts from anvils and the random shooting and the whistle shrieks from the saw mills. He turned his eyes from the bustling, jostling crowd and the painted women who leaned from the upper windows of the brothels waving their handkerchiefs to the troops and looked away, to the steep slopes which would always surround them, now glowing with bonfires lit in honor of Crook. He thought how barren the hills had become as they were stripped of their timber for the cabins and mines and bonfires of the city, and he remembered the promise of the Black Hills and how he'd once called them *beautiful*. Now all seemed changed, most especially himself.

Hugh Everett did not welcome civilization that night though he followed the crowd from the Grand Central to Langrishe's theatre, which instead of a canvas roof now flaunted a two-story facade. The theatre was jammed and he did not try to get in although he caught a glimpse of Avery and Emerald entering. Emerald saw him and waved with her fan, but he could not get through the crowd. He supposed Avery had reserved a place. It was like him. Hugh lingered in the street, not ready to leave, but telling himself it had nothing to do with wanting to see Emerald. He realized if he sold his share of the mine to Avery, he would have no reason to see her again. There would, in fact, be nothing to hold him in Deadwood. He felt at a loss. His adventure was almost over and what had he proven? He had lost Molly and Edwin and had found neither poor man's gold nor himself.

Those who had managed to squeeze into the theatre passed word to those waiting outside of handshaking and speech making inside. When the vaudeville performance finally began, people started drifting out of the theatre. Hugh imagined it was stuffy inside and wondered if Avery would leave. Gold must be crossing gaming tables elsewhere. Sure enough, Avery and Emerald appeared in the doorway. She scanned the crowd and when she saw him, flashed a smile which he acknowledged with a tip of his hat. When they approached, Hugh tried to keep his eyes off her, but she seemed to be seeking his attention. Her eyes were wide and sparkly, her color high.

Hugh and Avery exchanged a few words about Crook's victory and when there was a lull in the conversation, Emerald reached over and slipped a paper into Hugh's pocket.

"I saved this playbill for dear little Edwin to reminder Crook's coming to Deadwood by. Soon everything will be changed."

Hugh touched his pocket wondering, but kept his attention on Avery, agreeing to meet him at the hotel the next day to talk business. As he turned to leave, Emerald reminded him again to give Edwin the playbill. Hugh stepped into the nearest saloon and in the dim light opened the folded paper. Across the bottom Emerald had scrawled a message, with parts underlined for emphasis:

> Hugh! <u>Do not</u> sell your share of the mine to Austin! He has a plan to make himself rich reselling the mine <u>and he will make you a lot of money too if you only hold out!</u> Mrs. Lewis <u>better sell</u> so she can leave town. It's safer for her and the boy to get back to their people, <u>but don't you sell out</u>. I beg you!
>
> Your friend,
> Emerald O'Brien

So he was right. Avery did have a scheme. But why was Emerald telling him about it? He couldn't answer that question, but if there was any possibility of a fortune to be made on the Lucky Six, Molly must have her share.

Only Molly didn't feel that way. She wanted nothing to do with the mine, Austin Avery, or, he suspected, himself, she told him when he went to her early the next morning. Without showing her Emerald's note, he said he thought she should not be so quick to sell her share to the gambler.

Molly didn't understand why Hugh was acting as if her leaving was only about the mine. Did he think money was what she cared about? Had he forgotten his brutal rejection of her after Luther's death, the way he'd all but accused her of killing Luther and told her to get out of town? True, he had been kind and gentle to her since then, stopping by each day to see if she needed anything, but she could not forget how he'd acted that day.

"Don't ask me to stay, Hugh. As soon as the route's safe and the stage starts operating, Edwin and I will leave."

"Please, Molly, I know turning down Avery's offer will mean a delay, but if you stay until he locates a buyer, you might still make a fortune on the mine!"

"Just yesterday you said his offer was generous. What makes you think the mine is worth more today?"

She was angry. It was painful for her to be near him; getting angry at him, was safer than admitting her true feelings. She would not risk more rejection nor more accusations. "We've never washed out more than day's wages!"

"You don't understand mining. Someone with capital to invest in a proper underground operation could make a go of it!"

"You're right. I don't understand mining, and I don't understand why you want me to stay now when before you all but ordered me to get out of town, and I don't understand how we find this entrepreneur who's going to make us all rich!"

He was surprised by her anger, and not willing to discuss his confused feelings, he tried to focus on business. "That's why we need Austin Avery. Apparently he's got connections with eastern capitalists and he'll be able to make the kind of deal I can't."

"And are you sure you want the kind of deal Austin Avery would make?"

"What do you mean by that?"

"You know what sort of man he is, a gambler, no doubt a charlatan and a crook, a man who openly consorts with a woman like Emerald O'Brien!"

"Don't drag Emerald into this! This has nothing to do with Emerald. She's been nothing but kind to you and Edwin, and she's warned us about Avery and —"

"I don't trust her. She thinks she can win me over by making up to Edwin, but she doesn't fool me." She was about to go on, but she suddenly realized she could not say aloud what she suspected Emerald of scheming for. Hugh's revelation of a private contact with her and his passionate defense of the woman was sign enough the green-eyed beauty was winning him over.

"Now, Molly. You're upsetting yourself. Please let me take care of this for you."

"Don't you 'Now Molly' me! You sound like Jake!"

He was treating her like a child, when he was the one showing poor judgment. She'd already sounded like a shrew, but, she could not resist a parting shot, "Austin Avery is a crook!"

"I can handle him. Besides, he's got something I don't have — luck! I've heard about him. He almost never holds a losing hand."

"And why do you suppose that is?"

"Maybe he cheats. Maybe he doesn't. But he can't pull the wool over my eyes about the mine."

"So, you'll attach yourself to his coattails?"

"Damn it, I'm sick of losing. Everything I've touched this summer has turned to dust. The man's no Preacher Smith, but Preacher Smith is dead. It's all luck, Molly, and this man has it. If he could get us a thousand dollars a share for the mine, think what a difference it could make to Edwin's future —to *our* future!"

"*Our* future?"

It was not the time to admit that he had once again thought of that, so he went back to talking business. "There's fortunes to be made here and I don't see why we shouldn't have our share."

"Our share? What of Jake and Luther's shares? Shall we take theirs too?"

She immediately wished she hadn't said it, but she'd wanted to hurt him as he'd hurt her by hinting again that their futures were one and then talking only of fortunes to be made.

"Must you remind me, Molly? I've taken it upon myself to protect your interests and get you the best price for the mine, so that Jake's dying will not be for nothing."

He had again reminded her of her guilt.

"Be quiet, Hugh," she spoke sharply in her anger. "I don't want to discuss it any more now."

"Well, we can't resolve it now anyway. We need time and that's why selling the mine is still an issue. Why we must talk business."

"Then talk business. Talk business with Austin Avery. I want to be finished with this mine. I want to be finished with everything. Tell him I accept his offer. Two shares are mine and only one is yours, and I wish to sell, and I want you to know: *I am not your responsibility.*"

They faced each other as if across a great distance. There seemed nothing he could do but agree to bring the papers.

"It's settled then," he said as he stepped to the door to leave, but she detained him with a touch.

"Just one thing, Hugh."

'Yes?" he asked willing her to somehow come into his arms again, to forgive him.

"If you take my advice, if you still care about anything decent, you'll have nothing to do with that man *or that woman.*"

He pulled away from her and left without an answer and she knew that her words had been wasted.

Avery had three hundred dollars in gold dust in a plump leather pouch ready for Hugh when he came to the hotel dining room that afternoon. Hugh wondered how many turns of the cards it had taken Avery to win that much dust, more than Hugh had earned in a summer of back-breaking labor. Emerald smiled at Hugh and let her eyes dart between him and at the pouch on the table.

"It's all here." Avery patted the little bundle, "Three hundred in dust. We'll weigh it at the bar after we finish our drinks and talk. Then you can take it to Mrs. Lewis and tell her I'll be out this evening with the papers for her to sign."

Hugh supposed Avery must be happy that Molly was selling, but the gambler had not betrayed his emotions by so much as the flicker of an eyelid. He offered Hugh a cheroot from a silver case. Hugh declined but could not help but admire the smooth way Avery picked out his own cigar and snapped the case shut with a flourish. He had never seen a man with such graceful hands. Avery held the cheroot until Emerald removed a tiny match safe from her beaded handbag and leaned over to light it for him.

Hugh was fascinated with the idea of a woman doing that for a man. It meant she would do anything for him. He'd tried to avoid looking at her, but now as she held the flame so it seemed to dance within her eyes, he wondered for a flashing moment what it would be like to have her.

There would be no hesitation in her, he knew, no obligation and no reminders of guilt. He felt his manhood responding to her and was glad the table hid the fact. Then a little smile played around her mouth as if she knew.

Hugh forced his attention to the gold pouch. If Avery said there was three hundred dollars in dust in it, he was sure there was, but for Molly's protection he'd have it poured and weighed.

"I suggest you open an account for Mrs. Lewis in the new bank," Avery puffed on his cigar. "They'll exchange the dust for bills or a bank note if she's going East."

"She is going, isn't she?" Emerald suddenly entered the conversation.

"She says so. Just as soon as stage service commences."

"How wonderful," then catching herself, "I mean, I hate to see her go, but it will be better for her and Edwin to be with their people." Emerald smiled knowingly.

"Now, as to you, Mr. Everett," Avery leaned back to draw on the cigar. "I assume that after the loss of your brother, for which I offer my condolences, you, too, might be ready to return home, so I am prepared to offer you a bit of a bonus, say two hundred for your single, remaining share in the mine."

"I'm not interested in selling."

"Oh?" Avery said with just the slightest raise of an eyebrow. "Is my offer not generous enough?"

"The price is fair. But I've no interest in going back. I've put a lot into that mine. I'll stick with it."

"You're aware you can't hope to develop it properly without capital?"

"I know that all too well," Hugh said quietly. "Jake lost his life and I nearly died myself because we didn't have enough timbers to shore it up properly."

"Then why do you think you can continue to mine it yourself?"

"I don't. I'm willing to sell to the right party, but I figure if it's going to some eastern capitalist, I'd like to sell directly to him."

"Understandable," Avery smiled, although Hugh had as much as called him a crook. "And you have contact with such men?"

"No. But I figure you do, or you will. Otherwise you wouldn't be so interested in the mine yourself."

"So," Avery drew on the cigar and sent out a screen of smoke, "So, you'd ride in on my coattails?"

Hugh winced inside at his words and the reminder of Molly's warning, but he kept his voice even. "You can put it that way if you wish. I prefer to think of it as an exercise in patience. And a certain trust in your field of expertise."

"Well, I admire your honesty. No one appreciates honesty more than I do. You flatter me, of course, but I do have a certain skill in such matters. One would suppose, if one had been to Alder Gulch and had some experience, that one of the first stagecoaches to hit Deadwood will disgorge a real live eastern capitalist."

Hugh suddenly was reminded of Caleb Dexter and wondered if the old man fit into this deal somewhere.

"Winter is coming on," Avery continued," and the miners will have to decide if they're going underground or getting out. And, as your unfortunate example has proved, underground operations are not for amateurs."

He doesn't mind hurting a man, Hugh thought. *He's not the gentleman he pretends to be.*

"You are aware," the gambler pressed his advantage, "that your mine could be worthless? That there's no way of knowing until an accurate assay is made?"

Hugh nodded. All summer miners had conducted their own primitive tests; now rumor said an assay office would open, staffed by a metallurgist from a foreign university. "I'm willing to take a chance on the assay."

"So you're a gambler too! Well, there's some of that in most men. That's what enables me to make my living. That's what I always say, don't I, Emerald dear?"

"Hugh must have heard of your reputation for holding winning hands," Emerald patted the diamond ring Avery wore. Her hands were small, Hugh noticed, and delicate, compared to the work-worn hands of Molly.

"Some might think it luck," Avery put his hand over Emerald's, "but I work hard for what I get. Emerald and I know it's like we sang of our lands in the Confederate anthem, *Ours by Honest Toil*."

Hugh didn't like Avery's using words men had died for to glorify what he did for a living, nor did he like the gambler's hand on Emerald. There was something indecent about a man wearing a diamond ring and having hands that white, a man who flaunted his mistress and called gambling honest toil. Impulsively Hugh thrust out his own hands.

"See my hands! Here's how you tell a man who does honest toil! By his hands. See these calluses? These are where I froze my hands panning for gold in the creeks. And these here, these are where I blistered my hands raw opening up that mine. And these fresh scars here, these I earned digging Jake and me out with my bare hands when the mine caved in!"

Avery remained impassive. Hugh knew he was losing his own control, but he could not stop. "It was my idea to buy that mine and my idea to go underground. It was because of me and that mine that Jake is dead. Jake gave his life for that mine. It's all I've got left. All I've gotten out of this crazy, damn trip to the Black Hills, and I'll stick with it to the end!"

The gambler stared at him for a moment and then pushed away from the table. "I understand, Mr. Everett. You're emotionally involved. Not a good idea in business, but understandable. You have an attachment to the Lucky Six, so I won't try to change your mind. Just take this dust to Mrs. Lewis and tell her I'll bring the papers tonight. Then you and Caleb Dexter hire some laborers and keep working that mine. Clean up all signs of the cave-in and get a new stope opened somewhere, anywhere, and keep that damn pump working, so when I bring some capitalist to look it over, it looks like a going operation."

"Okay," Hugh choked down his resentment. "I'll do all that."

"Well, then that settles it for now. Agreed?"

"What about the assay? Should I arrange for one?"

"Leave that to me," Avery said sharply. "Tend to the diggings and leave the business end to me." He stood up to signal the meeting was over and offered his hand to Hugh.

Hugh hesitated. He didn't like the way Avery was giving orders, implying Hugh was fit only for grubbing in the earth. He felt like he was making a pact with the devil, but when he looked at Emerald, she was smiling and nodding encouragement.

He shook Austin Avery's hand.

The three hundred dollars in gold dust seemed heavy as he walked back to the mine that evening. At eighteen dollars an ounce, it had weighed out at over a pound, but it wasn't just the weight of the gold, it was the knowledge it would enable Molly to leave town and start a new life without him. It spoiled any pleasure he might, have felt at withholding his own share from

Avery. He did not want her to go, but their relationship seemed doomed.

Molly met him at the cabin door. Her face was white and her eyes were wide and frightened.

"Thank God you're here. I was about to send Edwin to look for you."

"What's wrong?"

"It's Caleb Dexter. I think he's dying."

CHAPTER TWENTY-NINE

The doctor's face was solemn as he examined the old prospector. It was not the forced solemnity doctors, like preachers, sometimes assume to conceal being faced with something beyond their understanding, Molly decided, but an expression very close to fear, and that frightened her as much as did the way Caleb Dexter had slipped between delirium and unconsciousness ever since he'd stumbled into her cabin late that afternoon burning with fever and complaining of a headache and collapsed as suddenly as if he'd been struck dead.

She'd been afraid to leave him alone and been about to send Edwin to town for help when Hugh had arrived; he'd been helping her ever since. The old man had retched so violently she was afraid he would choke. Even as the doctor examined him, he was overcome by dry, strangling heaves. Then he passed out again, his eyes rolling back in his head, a phenomenon that fascinated Edwin who persisted in watching the goings on, despite Molly and Hugh's efforts to busy him outside.

The doctor took his time with the examination, then stood up and grasped his stethoscope with both hands before announcing importantly, "He has all the classic symptoms. His skin is burning with heat, but you will notice it is quite dry. His pulse is hard and frequent. He's complained of headache and pain in the epigastrium. He's vomiting and delirious, verging on the point of convulsions. They are all classic symptoms."

"Of what?"

The doctor took off his stethoscope and dropped it into his bag, closing it with an ominous click. He stood for a moment, his bag in his hand, regarding Caleb Dexter with an air of sorrow. He rolled his sleeves down.

"Smallpox."

"Oh, my God," Molly snatched Edwin away from the inert form of Caleb Dexter and held him close to her.

"How could you let the boy stand so near if you suspected smallpox?" Hugh demanded.

"He was exposed long before I arrived. Smallpox is so virulent just being in the same room with a victim is sufficient. If the boy has not been vaccinated, it is already too late; he will contract the disease, and if he has —"

"Too late?"

"If he has not been vaccinated. Has he?"

Molly finally sorted out what the doctor had said and pulled Edwin's shirt roughly off over his head and jerked up his arm for the doctor to see.

The doctor knelt down and examined Edwin's arm. "Very good," he said. "The cicatrix is well-defined. It obviously took."

"He was quite sick at the time."

"Excellent, then he's in no danger at all." The doctor beamed, but then put on a more solemn expression as he turned to Molly and Hugh. "What about you two? Have you both been vaccinated?"

Molly looked at Hugh anxiously, but he was nodding, touching his own arm. She touched hers also. "I have a good scar."

"When were you vaccinated? As children?"

They nodded.

"Then I assume you have never been revaccinated?" When they shook their heads, he continued. "Vaccination is completely effective for only six to ten years. That's why the boy is completely safe. But for adults, there is a chance of becoming infected."

"You mean we could get it?" Molly touched her face. Smallpox marked you for life.

"Unlikely, but possible. Seldom fatal in such cases, though you'd likely be scarred. Actually half the town is vulnerable."

"Let's get the old man out of here," Hugh said to the doctor. "I don't want him near Molly."

"It's too late now. You're both exposed. It's better not to move him."

"Is Caleb going to die?" Edwin wailed, returning Molly's attention to the old man.

"That depends."

"On what?" They spoke as one.

"First of all, on which form of the disease he has, the confluent form or the discrete variety."

"What's the difference?" Hugh frowned.

The doctor hooked one thumb in his vest so his gold watch fob showed as he recited: "Variola discreta pustulis paucia, discretis —"

"In English, damn it!" Hugh interrupted.

"If he was variloa discrete he may live; if he has variola confluens, he will most likely die."

"How can you tell which he has?" Molly asked.

"I can't at this point. Although the severity of the pain, vomiting and delirium in the early stages is some indication, we won't know until the pustules form. The eruptions will begin on the third day and must be examined to determine which form he has. If it is confluent, when the secondary fever begins on the eighth day, it will be very severe, most deaths occurring then. So you see," he concluded brightly, "we won't know until the second week "

"You'll be gone by then, Molly," Hugh said. Molly had almost forgotten. She had plans. She could not be expected to nurse the old man.

"You're leaving town?" the doctor frowned.

"I'm taking my son and going to my people in the East. Unless I can't go? Because of the exposure?"

"No reason you can't. As I said, it's unlikely you'll get it, but if you did, you'd be home where you'd have better care. Better yet, you could stop in Cheyenne and get revaccinated and be completely safe. Yes, my advice would be to leave town as soon as possible. This is the fourth case I've seen today. I expect an epidemic."

"That's terrible" Molly said.

"It is," he said calmly. "Especially as most of them will die!"

"But you said smallpox isn't always fatal!"

"It is when there's no nursing care or hospital. I can prescribe treatment, but with no one to administer constant care, there just isn't hope. The other three men all live together. There's no one to care for them. And I certainly can't act as a nurse, especially if I'm as busy as I'll be once news of this gets out."

"But surely," Hugh interrupted, "someone will volunteer."

"One can hardly expect volunteers to care for a disease as filthy, disgusting and contagious as smallpox. It's a woman's job, but all the women in Deadwood are otherwise occupied."

"But if that's the case," Hugh said. "The whole town could be infected!"

"The situation is not entirely hopeless. After I diagnosed the initial cases this morning I informed the sheriff who has already dispatched a rider to the nearest telegraph line. They will have vaccine at Fort Laramie, so we should soon be able to inoculate anyone who is not protected. The situation is only serious for those who already have it. I had hopes for Mr. Dexter here, thinking Mrs. Lewis would be caring for him, but since she's to be leaving, we'd best move him now. We may as well dump him off with the others; at least they'll be together when I make my rounds."

"We can take him to my cabin," Hugh said. "He's my partner. I'll take care of him."

"That's the spirit!"

Molly turned away from the men as they began to

make a blanket stretcher to move Dexter. She had heard about smallpox. It was the most dreaded of all diseases. It made one sick just to look at someone who had it. She had already had enough of the vomiting and delirium. Besides she was going home. She needed someone to take care of her for a change and her parents would do that. She was a widow; surely she deserved some comforting. She had spent her whole life doing for others. What's more she had disliked Caleb Dexter from the moment he'd stumbled into their lives.

If it were Hugh, she would lay down her life for him. If it had been Luther, dear foolish Luther, she would have nursed him night and day, but Luther was dead. Hugh had sent him away to protect her secret and now he was dead. And Jake was dead and she was guilty there too. If only it were someone else. Even those three unnamed miners alone in their cabin must have wives or mothers or sweethearts somewhere who would bless her if she saved their lives, but Caleb Dexter meant nothing to anyone. He had done nothing but cause trouble. Except for the day the mine caved in and he had worked so frantically to get Jake and Hugh out. He had shoveled continually, never letting anyone take a turn for him. Caleb Dexter, who liked to lie in the sun and drink and belch while others were working, had shoveled until he dropped.

"Put him down." She was surprised to hear herself speak.

"What?" Hugh asked. They had just rolled the old man over onto the blanket and started to lift him.

"I said, leave him. He's not to be moved. I'll nurse him."

"But you're leaving town!

"I can wait. I don't have to go right away."

"Mrs. Lewis," the doctor said. "Smallpox is a very ugly disease. Are you sure you can stand to —"

"I can stand what I have to stand. I can do whatever needs to be done." She held herself proudly and tried not to think of how good it would be to go home and be her father's little girl again.

"I don't want you to do it, Molly," Hugh said. "If you should get it, you could be scarred."

"I've already been exposed. It can't matter now."

"I'll have to admit," the doctor interjected, "it would give the old man a chance if he had a nurse. There's nothing like a woman's touch. Even if he should have the severe form, he'd have a good chance. He looks like a sturdy enough old geezer."

"It's settled then," Molly spoke with determination. "Hugh, could you drag the bunks and some bedding from your cabin over here for the others? We'll set up a hospital and I'll nurse them all."

"It's too much for you, Molly. You're still suffering from your loss. You can't do this."

"I've made up my mind. Someone must care for those men or they'll die."

"Then I'll help you. It will be me and you."

Molly hesitated, but the doctor repeated that she'd need help. "There will be a lot of lifting and carrying if the men are to be bathed properly, not to mention the laundry and the cooking. You'll need a fire going and water boiling continually." Molly knew he was right. Hugh would be near her day and night, but with the sick men to care for she'd not have the will to make a fool of herself with him again. She accepted his offer.

Later that afternoon Hugh remembered the gold dust and set it on her table where she was preparing compresses for the sick men. "Here's the money for the mine. Avery's supposed to come out this evening with the papers for you to sign, but now that you're going to be staying for a while, shall I tell him to forget it?"

"For heaven's sake, Hugh! I've made up my mind about that! I told you I'd sell and I will. I never want to hear about that mine again!"

It was on the tip of her tongue to add, *and don't think because I'm staying here it means I'm still hoping things can work out between us.* She decided she'd already made that clear, both to Hugh and to herself.

Emerald looked forward to going with Avery to sign the papers buying Molly's share of the Lucky Six. Not only would it give her the opportunity to see Hugh again, but it would be a great satisfaction to know her rival would be on the first stagecoach out of town. She arranged her face and hair with great care for the occasion, but when the knock on the door of their hotel room came, she was wearing only her chemise and the Chinese silk wrapper.

"Who is it?" Avery asked, and when she recognized Hugh's voice, Emerald was delighted that he would see her in the red silk wrapper, but Avery frowned warningly and stepped outside to talk to him. Emerald listened at the door but could not make out their words. What was Hugh doing there? She hurried to the mirror and frantically adjusted her hair and powdered her cheeks against the rising blush, planning to slip on her dress and join the men in the hall, but in a few minutes Avery came back into the room.

"We won't be going out to the mine."

"Is something wrong?"

"Just a smallpox epidemic. What luck they have at that mine! It looks like Caleb Dexter has come down with the smallpox."

"So why can't we go to the Lewis cabin?"

"That's where he is. Molly and Hugh are setting up a smallpox hospital there. Three other men have it and they are afraid of an epidemic."

"Molly and Hugh are setting up a hospital?"

"Well, that's an exaggeration. A pest house would be more like it."

"Molly and Hugh together?" She sat down on the edge of the bed feeling she might faint.

"Don't take it so hard. Hugh says there's little danger to anyone who's been vaccinated. You have been vaccinated haven't you?" He looked genuinely concerned.

It was simpler to nod yes than to explain.

"Then there's no skin off our hides. I gave Hugh the papers to have the Lewis woman sign so the sale won't be affected. It should be two or three weeks before any capitalists show up anyway, so the quarantine won't hurt."

"Quarantine?"

"Yes, they'll be stuck with those disgustingly sick men for a couple of weeks at least."

"They're going to be in that cabin *for two weeks together*? How can they do that?"

"It beats me! That Everett has a noble streak a mile wide. It'll get the best of him one of these days, mark my word. Show me a man with a touch of nobility and I'll show you a fool. But then some people like to be miserable. They'd be unhappy if they ever won anything in life."

Emerald didn't hear the rest of Avery's speech. She sat clutching her stomach, actually feeling pain. Avery bustled about getting ready for his evening of gambling and just before he left, he stopped by the bed and patted her shoulder solicitously.

"Now don't worry your pretty little head my dear. Hugh says it's unlikely anyone who has been vaccinated will come down with the disease." He touched her cheek with a tenderness rare for Austin Avery. "Your skin will always be perfection."

Emerald did not acknowledge the compliment and

was glad when he left. She had to think about what this sudden change of events was going to mean. Avery was right about one thing, you'd have to be a fool to take on smallpox. She'd seen it and she knew. But Avery was too cynical to see the nobility of the gesture. Molly and Hugh together nursing the sick men! It made her sick.

She could just picture Molly Lewis, eyes downcast, offering to delay her trip east and stay with Hugh and nurse his poor sick partner. What a gesture! Whatever it was that had kept Molly and Hugh apart in the past, two weeks of togetherness while Molly played angel of mercy, and Hugh would be trapped. By the time the disgusting old man was on his feet again, Hugh would be over his guilt about coveting his partner's wife, and he and Molly would be calling for a preacher! And just when her own schemes were working out so that she had Hugh set up to make a fortune on the mine and Molly on the first stage out of town! It was so unfair! That Molly Lewis with her gingham dress and her great cow eyes could have come up with such a scheme to snare Hugh, when Emerald had been working so hard on a plan! If only there was some way she could take advantage of the situation.

Emerald caught a glimpse of herself in the mirror across from the bed. Her wrapper had slipped open and her bare white shoulders were showing. She did have lovely arms, she thought, caressing them. She had always been proud of their perfection. The idea came to her slowly, almost reluctantly as she stared at herself in the mirror. She pulled the wrapper down to her elbows to examine herself. She touched the smoothness of her own unblemished skin, then shuddered and jerked the wrapper back around her shoulders. Smallpox was a filthy disease. She couldn't do it. Even if she were sure it would work but even as she denied the idea, she knew if it would work for Molly Lewis, it would work for her. And she was in no real danger.

But it was no use. She couldn't do it, *wouldn't* do it. Just then the door burst open and Avery came in without knocking.

"Emma dear, I'm afraid I've run short of gold. Would you give me a couple of baubles from your bag?"

Emerald got her beaded bag and handed it to Avery, pretending meekness. She was used to acting as his bank. He'd gambled with her jewels before, and she got them or better jewels back, but she resented handing her trinkets over to him. Avery poked through the bag and extracted a heavy gold watch and chain and a few stickpins and something else. Her new ear bobs.

"Not the garnet ear bobs! You just bought them for me. You didn't win them. I thought they were for me."

"But it doesn't do to lose more than one watch a night. They like to think they're getting your personal property. But since you favor the ear bobs, let me have the ring then."

"The ring?"

"Yes, that plain gold one. It's not much, but it will do to sweeten the pot."

She hesitated, looking down at the ring. She liked this one because it reminded her of a wedding band. But if it was between the ring and the garnet ear bobs, she'd give him the ring.

When he was gone, she sat studying her left hand and thinking. There was a white mark where she had worn the ring on her third finger.

If Hugh put a wedding band on her finger, you could bet he'd never ask for it back. Hugh would cherish her and take care of her. Hugh was a decent man and Austin Avery was a cheat and a crook. That was all there was to it. It didn't matter how a man thrilled a woman. Surely decent, married men could do the same. But, if a woman wanted to win a respectable man, she had to find some way to win his respect.

She turned back to the mirror, slipped off the wrapper and smiled bravely at her naked reflection.

She would do it.

CHAPTER THIRTY

Of all the plagues God had rained down upon man, Molly decided, smallpox was the worst. The pain was so severe the sick men raved with delirium. Caleb Dexter's convulsions were so violent, Molly and Hugh tied him to his bed in fear he would harm himself. On the third day, the eruptions appeared. Despite their efforts to lessen the outbreak with saline purgatives and tepid sponge baths, the pox spread like wildfire from face to neck, to wrists, spreading and growing until the men's entire bodies and even their tongues were covered with the angry sores.

When the eruptions began, the fever, pain and vomiting stopped, but the agony from the itching began. Molly and Hugh would hardly finish bathing one man with the soothing lotion of olive oil and lime water when the next would begin screaming and clawing at himself. By the eighth day it was necessary to tie all the men's hands to their beds to keep them from scratching. Molly shuddered to think of the scars they would bear for life.

The glands of salivation were somehow affected by the illness so the men sometimes choked and gagged for breath. Their faces swelled until their eyelids were all but shut. It was impossible to find their pulses in their swollen wrists. The men were so hideous, Molly could hardly bear to look at them. Sometimes the thought she might contract the disease made her tremble.

Molly was relieved when the doctor made his call on the fourth day and confirmed his opinion the disease was the milder, or discrete form. Even so, he cautioned, the men were in danger of death until after the secondary fever appeared on the eighth day of the eruption.

It was the smell of the disease Molly hated most. She thought at first it was just the smell of sick men unused to bathing, but no amount of washing seemed to relieve it, and finally the doctor confirmed her suspicion that it was the odor of the disease itself. He said if he were taken into a sick chamber blindfolded, he could diagnose smallpox by the smell. Molly could only describe it as a greasy odor, but she knew she would not forget it, nor the sweetness of the mountain air when she could steal a moment outside for greedy gulps of air fresh with pine.

Edwin helped by fetching and toting, but she saw he spent most of his days outside or with a neighboring family. For Molly it was a nightmare of washing bursting sores and carrying reeking bedpans and basins. Yet it was also a time of peace. She knew God could not send such an awful plague upon them if some good were not to come of it. The illness was so terrible, even the sins of so determined a sinner as Caleb Dexter must be expiated. And so, for hours at a time she was so busy with her work she forgot herself and her own guilt. The numbness she had experienced since Jake's death began to melt and she started to feel again. She allowed herself to admire the gentle strength and bravery of Hugh as he helped care for the men. It was not easy for him, she knew, to be confined to the cabin and woman's work, but he did what had to be done, and it was good to be working beside him.

It seemed natural and right for them to be a team. They worked well together; they were often able to communicate with just a look or gesture, and thus could share their concern over the course of the illness without troubling the men with worried talk.

Yet there was tension between them. Though each longed for the comfort of the other's arms against the ugliness that surrounded them, they avoided touching. And there was no privacy. One of them always needed to be on duty, so they had to take turns slipping down to the other cabin for a few hours' sleep. It seemed that if they so much as stepped outside together for a breath of fresh air while the men were sleeping, Caleb or one of the other miners would sense their absence and cry out for help.

It was more than lack of privacy that kept them from touching, however. They were held apart by the terrible things Hugh had said on the evening of Luther's death. Hugh did not remember that he had accused Molly of causing his brother's death or of saying that their love was like a curse. Now, watching her as she nursed the sick men so patiently, he thought of her only as the most noble and holy of women and that made her seem as forbidden to him as when she had been Jake's wife. He never doubted that he loved her, but there was a barrier between them. There seemed no easy way to reach her or to find his own salvation; he concentrated on what had to be done against the smallpox. It had become an enemy he could fight. He put his energy into hating the illness.

Molly knew it was Hugh's own guilt over his brother's death that had made him strike out against her. She understood guilt, and if it would lighten Hugh's burden for her to carry some of his, she was willing, for her own heart was already heavy with remorse, not just for her sin with Hugh, but for secret thoughts she hardly dared admit even to herself. But Molly understood something else, and that was forgiveness. She had already forgiven Hugh for his terrible words, and as she began to have hope that the men would live, she thought that their act of love in saving the lives of men who were strangers to them must surely count for something against whatever wrong they had done in loving each other.

And that she loved Hugh she was at last able to say aloud, if only to herself. The words came to her a hundred times a day as their eyes met and they seemed to be standing, not in the horror of the sick room, but somewhere on a mountain top, alone with all the fresh and promising world before them. Even if he rejected her again, she knew she must someday tell him the words that her loyalty to Jake had so long imprisoned within her. He deserved to hear from her lips the expressions of love he had so freely given her from the beginning, and she determined she would tell him someday when the time seemed right.

The eighth day of the outbreak was the worst, although the doctor assured them the crisis had passed. Molly and Hugh were exhausted and, as the secondary fever struck, the men became restless to the point of tremors and violent outbursts of temper. The doctor prescribed more purgatives and an opiate solution to keep them under control. By late afternoon the men had finally all descended into a drugged sleep, and Molly found time to start a fresh pot of soup. Hugh was dozing, leaning back in his chair, his feet propped up on the end of a bunk. She turned and studied him, thinking he looked younger since he'd stopped wearing a beard. She noticed that he needed a shave and thought she would heat some water for him. Perhaps she could also find time to wash her hair or slip down to the creek for a bath.

It was nice to have things peaceful again; the worst, she decided, was surely over. She hummed as she heated the water and got Hugh's razor and basin. It felt good to be doing a wifely chore again. Perhaps when her hair was clean and pretty again, they might find time to sit outside the cabin together. She felt light and hopeful inside. And then came a knock at the door.

Hugh woke with a start and got to the door before Molly could maneuver her way around the bunks. "My God, what are you doing here?" She heard him say as she hurried forward to see who he barred from entering the cabin.

It was Emerald O'Brien.

Molly noticed how different she looked. She was wearing a plain blue dress, her hair was demurely tucked behind her ears, and her face looked freshly scrubbed. She could have played the role of Purity in a tableau.

"Stay back," Hugh warned Emerald. "Don't you know we've got smallpox in here?"

"I know. I came to help."

Molly gasped.

"That's good of you but I can't let you come in." Hugh said. "Even if you've been vaccinated, you could get it! I can't let you take the chance."

"Send her away," Molly said sharply. "She should not be here."

Emerald looked to one and then the other beseechingly. "Please, Hugh, Mrs. Lewis, let me help. I've got nowhere else to go and I want to be of use."

"What do you mean? What happened to Avery?"

"I've left him," Emerald said with a proud lift of her head and a determined narrowing of her green eyes. Then she lowered her lids demurely. "I've been living a life of sin with him, and I just can't go on. You're the only decent people I know, and I hoped you'd take me in."

Molly stepped closer to the door. Some instinct warned her she must keep this woman outside. Hugh seemed just as determined not to let her enter the pest house. "I'll give you money for a hotel room. You can't stay here and expose yourself to this terrible disease."

"But I have to. Don't you see? It's the only way I can make up for what I've done. I thought he'd marry me. I know it's no excuse, but when he begged me to leave my mother he promised we'd be married by the captain of the ship. But once the ship was underway, he came into my cabin and —"

"You've told us enough." Hugh said, "Of course I'll

help you get away from him. I'll get my pouch." As soon as he stepped away from the door, Emerald stepped inside.

"Don't!" Molly shouted, but it was too late. Once inside, Emerald breathed deeply of the contaminated air.

"There, I've done it," she announced. "Now it's too late to send me away. I've exposed myself and you'll have to let me stay and help nurse these poor men."

The men had been awakened by the commotion, and by the way they were looking at Emerald, Molly knew they too were thinking of how smallpox might ravage her face. A face with skin as white and perfect as alabaster against her jet black hair.

"You'll ruin your face!" Molly declared. "A woman like you can't afford to take chances." She knew she was saying too much, but she felt threatened by Emerald's invasion of her cabin. "If you take the pox, no man will ever look at you again."

"That would be what I deserve. I have prayed that someday I will be forgiven for my sin with Austin Avery and might still be a wife and mother, but if God chooses to mark my face so no man will have me, then I will bow to his will."

Molly was appalled by the way the men, even Hugh, seemed to be taken in by the woman. Molly was about to insist Emerald leave, when the green eyes were turned on her.

"It's you who have inspired me, Mrs. Lewis. You have set such a wonderful example staying here in Deadwood to nurse these poor homeless men, endangered your own health and your own prettiness. You look exhausted. Surely you will let me help you."

Molly wilted. What more could she say without the men and Hugh thinking she was a jealous shrew? Besides, it was true that she was exhausted. She must look awful. Too confused to argue, she hesitated, and the next thing she knew Emerald was standing at her stove, wearing her apron, and stirring her soup.

As she watched Emerald fluttering around the sick men that afternoon, Molly could not help thinking it was terribly convenient that Emerald O'Brien's conscience hadn't troubled her until the worst of the disease was over. She tried to force such ideas from her head. She knew she was too tired to think sensibly. She told herself she was being unreasonably suspicious of a woman who had never done her any harm. Besides, what motive could Emerald have for exposing herself to such a terrible disease if she were not truly repentant? Surely Molly could understand repentance.

Later that day there was another knock at the door. This time it was bold and insistent. Molly opened the door. There in his topcoat and ruffled shirt, his face more darkly handsome and solemn than she had ever seen it, was Austin Avery.

"Is Emerald here?"

"She is," Molly said, "but you can't come in. We have smallpox within."

"I know that! And what in God's name is Emerald doing here? She left me a crazy note saying she was going to the mine and telling me not to follow her!"

"Don't let him in," Emerald shouted.

"Emma O'Brien, come the hell out of there," Avery shouted, trying to get around Molly who still blocked the doorway. "What do you think you're doing?"

"I told you," Emerald shouted. "I've left you and I've turned over a new leaf!"

"The devil you have!" Molly felt Avery was about to walk right over her as he continued to shout at Emerald. "Get the hell out of there and come to me right now!"

"Really, Mr. Avery," Molly said, "obscenity is not necessary."

"Slam the door shut or he'll get in!"

Even as Emerald shouted the warning, Hugh sprang up behind Molly, pulled her inside, and slammed the door in the gambler's face. "Hugh!" Molly began, "I don't think this is our —"

"Bolt the door, quickly," Emerald beseeched Hugh. "He's crazy when he gets like this."

Molly watched as Hugh slammed down the bolt. "Stay out, Avery," he shouted through the door. "She's already exposed herself. It's too late."

In reply the gambler pounded on the door, shouting, "Emerald you little fool, do you know what smallpox could do to your face? Come out of there! Come back to me."

"Never!" Emerald turned so her back was against the door and stood with her arms outstretched so that, despite herself, Molly thought of Joan of Arc. Emerald's cheeks were flushed and her eyes were sparkling, tendrils of dark curling hair had come loose from her severe hairdo and ringed her face. "Never," she repeated. "I've given up our life of sin!"

"What are you talking about? You didn't mind it last night!"

Emerald blushed but held her head high. "I pretended, just as you deceived me. You promised to marry me and I believed you, but you are nothing but a profligate and a scoundrel."

"Come back to me, Emerald."

"You don't get something for nothing, Austin Avery. That's what you always say!"

"All right then, Damn it. I'll marry you."

When those words came through the door, Molly noticed Emerald hesitate in her pose. So that was what she was after, Molly decided. Then, Emerald noticed how Hugh was watching her and, as if she were too caught up in the drama to quit before the final curtain, she repositioned herself with her back to the door and shouted her reply.

"It's too late now. You had your chance. Now I'm going to be a decent woman and repent for my sins!"

Again, Molly had the sensation she was watching a play. She looked at Hugh. He seemed totally absorbed in the drama. How could he be taken in so easily?

Austin Avery continued to plead, his tone more intense. "You don't know what you're doing, Em. You don't know what it can do to your face. I saw my sister after the war. The army got to her, gave her the clap. It was awful, just awful. She had sores all over her pretty little face. Come out, Em. Don't let them ruin your face. Don't do it, Em."

Avery pounded on the door again, before he realized he had lost control. He stopped, his hand in mid-air. He had not bargained for this. He was not a man to be made a fool of by a woman.

"Have it your own way, then," he said quietly and turned and walked down the hill to where his hired rig waited.

He hoped the driver wouldn't tell anyone what he had seen and heard. Austin Avery in such a state! He had let his emotions betray him for the first time since the war. It made him feel almost afraid. He should have known better. What did this woman mean to him after all? What made her so special? Perhaps there was not another like her in Deadwood, but it did not mean she could not be replaced. He didn't know why she had left him, but he didn't think it had anything to do with decency. He knew her that well. He would sort it out later when he was calm. And when he had figured out why she had moved into the quarantined cabin with the sick men, then he would figure out how to get her back. That is, if he still wanted her.

When Austin Avery finally left, Molly somehow felt

it was she who had been defeated. Emerald had ignored Avery's proposal of marriage; therefore she had to have some other motive for nursing the sick men. Molly could think of only two. Either Emerald O'Brien was truly repentant or she was after Hugh.

Molly was suddenly aware of how awful she must look. She had hardly combed her hair in days and it hung in limp tendrils around her face. Her eyes must be circled with dark shadows and her dress was dirty. Emerald, although she wore only powder and was without rouge, looked as if she were ready to step out on a stage. How could Hugh not notice the difference between them? Not only was Emerald more beautiful, but she was *worldly*. She was all the things the Bible preached against. A soiled dove, a tainted woman, true, but wouldn't a man like Hugh, a man with such strong passions, be attracted to such a woman?

In the days that followed, Molly often found herself watching Emerald and watching Hugh watch Emerald. Emerald ministered to the sick men with no more care than Molly had used, yet the men regarded Molly as a mother, while it was obvious, they all fell in love with the raven haired vixen. Emerald obviously knew how to use her body in just the way Hugh had accused Molly of doing, to entice and trap a man, but she would never be trapped by her body. To a woman like Emerald, desire would be a way of getting what she wanted from a man and for pleasuring herself. It would never be the aching need that made Molly want to cast aside all sense of integrity to beg Hugh's touch.

Molly was tempted to try to be like Emerald, to beat the vixen at her own game and win back Hugh's love. But guilt and the memory of Hugh's accusations held her back as did her image of herself as a mother. Remembering that she came from decent folk had sustained her during her years on the homestead; it had kept her from Hugh's arms during the weeks they were on the trail, and prevented her leaving her husband. Now her image of herself kept her from a confrontation with Emerald and from telling Hugh how she still longed for him.

She had been taught all her life that a good woman did not take action but only hoped and prayed for what she wanted. Even in her prayers, she asked that God's will and not just her own be done. Destiny still seemed to promise that she and Hugh belonged together; that they had not come this far for him to be won away by a green-eyed Jezebel, but Molly still believed that being good brought its own rewards. And in a curious way the back-breaking and often loathsome labor did reward her for she grew stronger. Her sense of guilt and sin was worn away by the good she knew she accomplished. If there was truth in Hugh's accusation that three men were dead because of her, there was greater truth in the fact that because of her, four men would live.

The smallpox ran its course. Although Caleb Dexter's delirium had been severe, once it passed, his natural vigor asserted itself and he made a speedy recovery. Days before the other men were able to venture out of their beds to again breathe fresh mountain air or bathe their weakened bodies in the creek, Caleb Dexter was able to make brief visits to the mine to ensure that the day laborers Austin Avery supplied were keeping the mine ready for the anticipated arrival of the Eastern capitalists. Occasionally Avery drove a buggy out to the mine on his own inspection tour. Molly suspected he and the old man were plotting something in their meetings held within the confines of the shuttered buggy, but when she expressed her suspicions to Hugh, he all but said that since she had sold out to Avery and was determined to leave Deadwood she should forget the mine.

Living and working together with nothing settled between them and each waiting for the other to somehow bridge the gulf of hurt and misunderstanding made them increasingly tense with each other. Caleb Dexter was more irritating than ever. He was intensely grateful to Molly for saving his life and followed her with his eyes like some mangy old dog that had outlived its usefulness and which, except for its devotion, one would have taken outside and shot. He seemed to take morose pleasure in lying about Molly's cabin, picking at his scabs and greeting each sick man's return to consciousness with a thorough recounting of any gory aspects of the disease the poor man might have managed to forget in his delirium. Finally Hugh persuaded the old man to move back to their old cabin so he could more closely supervise the mine.

Edwin, however, was delighted that their saving of the old man's life seemed to have bonded them to him forever. He took to "camping out" at the smaller cabin when he was not playing Indians with the neighbor's family. Since discovering the companionship of Deadwood's growing gang of children, he had run wild, but Molly was too exhausted to care.

To everyone's great relief the vaccine arrived and most of the city lined up for vaccination. Deadwood also ecstatically greeted the arrival of the first stage-coach September 25. Then, at the end of the month the *Pioneer* announced the news they had waited for all summer: The Sioux, under protest, had signed a treaty at the Red Cloud Agency to cede the Black Hills for all time. The city erupted into a joyous celebration, but the news was barely mentioned at the Lucky Six. The smallpox sufferers were too weak for celebration, and Hugh was only too aware that with the crisis passed and safe transportation available, Molly and Edwin were free to leave. He was aware, too, that their Black Hills adventure was ending in a way that seemed to offer no sense of victory but only more questions as to what it all had meant, if, indeed, it meant anything.

The nights turned suddenly cold, reminding them that Deadwood was a city built in the cleft of a mountain and not a place for anyone not already securely established to attempt to winter. Hugh knew decisions must be made, but he felt unable to act. The loss of his brother and his alienation from Molly had robbed him of the certainties that had driven him all summer, and he asked himself if the Black Hills were not to bring them good fortune and if he and Molly did not belong together, what was there left to believe in and to act upon?

Molly's work load lifted as the men grew stronger, but her spirits grew heavier as the time of decision neared. When the doctor vaccinated them, he assured her that the men were nearly well, and that the newly vaccinated Deadwood residents were in no further danger of contracting the disease, though they might anticipate severe reactions to the shot. Molly's arm was soon so tender she could not stand to touch it, and the convalescing men, persuaded Hugh to let them go back to their own cabin so that the women could rest from their nursing ordeal. Caleb Dexter borrowed a wagon and he and Hugh helped the men aboard; they departed with great rounds of thanks and promises of undying devotion.

Emerald accepted their accolades as if she alone had saved them, and Molly could hardly enjoy her own satisfaction at seeing the men well, so annoyed was she by the pretty pose Emerald assumed as she waved the men out of sight with a lace handkerchief vigorously wielded by the same arm she'd complained all morning she could hardly lift.

When they were finally alone except for Edwin, it occurred to Molly that she might soon be rid of the temptress, but no sooner were the men out of sight than Emerald fluttered about exclaiming that she would just stay another day or two to help Molly return her cabin to order and recover from their reactions to the vaccination. She even offered to help Molly pack. That suggestion nearly impelled Molly to throw Emerald off the property, but Edwin was as entranced as the other males with Emerald's portrayal of charity, and Molly did not want him to see his own mother as a shrew. Nor did she want Emerald running to Hugh with tales of Molly's ingratitude. Surely the woman would soon depart, and surely once she was gone, Hugh would not find an excuse to follow her to town.

Or would he? The realization, that if she and Edwin left Deadwood, it would be like giving Hugh to the other woman stunned Molly. She did not trust herself to look at Emerald who, since the departure of the men, had prettily arranged herself for a nap in Molly's own bed. Instead she stood at the window and watched for Hugh to return. She needed to think of a way to let him know Hugh had no need of a woman like Emerald, and that it was time for forgiveness on both their parts, but she must accomplish this in a way that would show that she was a virtuous woman herself, despite the fact that she, too, had sinned.

She caught sight of movement down at the mine. It was the gambler's usual hired carriage; this time followed by a buckboard. She announced, "Austin Avery's here again."

Emerald lay still, but her fluttering eyelids revealed she'd been listening. She always feigned annoyance at the gambler's visits to the mine, but Molly noticed that she also made sure that "the villain" would be certain to catch a glimpse of her in a pose calculated to be both demure and seductive.

"He's got a man following him in a wagon, but he's

not a Black Hiller. He's a fat man in a frock coat and top hat."

"*A capitalist!*" Emerald shrieked as she shot out of the bed and joined Molly at the window. "Avery's found a genuine capitalist and Hugh's going to be rich at last!"

Molly looked at her curiously and Emerald, sensing that she had said too much, backed away from the window.

"I'll need to change into something more presentable; perhaps you had better run see what they want. I'm sure Hugh will want to know."

"Yes, it's curious that they've chosen to arrive when Hugh and Caleb Dexter are gone."

"Well, if it's mining business, Austin can handle it." She stripped off the simple cotton gown she had been wearing and began rummaging in her trunk which was crowded under the kitchen table of the little cabin. "I'm sure Austin will beg to see me, hoping that I will come back to him and of course I won't but —"

"But you'll want to look desirable when you tell him that." Molly's voice was sharp.

Emerald looked up at Molly, her arms full of silk and lacy things and her plump breasts spilling over the top of her chemise.

"Well, I can hardly meet him in my nightgown, now can I? And I do think it might be time to talk to him. He still has my other trunk and things at the hotel. Besides, I'm dying to know what he's cooked up with the capitalist!"

"And you think he'll tell you more than me or Hugh?"

"He did beg me to marry him." Emerald sat back and gave Molly her most innocent look, but the Mona Lisa smile betrayed her. "Besides, Hugh isn't here and you've already sold out your shares and will be leaving town in a day or two. Therefore, since I'll be in Deadwood, and understand Austin Avery, it seems only right that I try to protect Hugh's interests."

Molly was furious. She wanted to lunge at the woman, tear up all her lovely clothes, pull the adorable, fat curls away from her perfect face and scratch out those bewitching green eyes. She allowed herself the fantasy, but she knew she must not lower herself to Emerald's level, especially if she might be seen by Hugh or Edwin. She clenched her fists until her fingernails dug into her palms and strode to the cabin door. Before opened the door, she turned back to Emerald and said primly. "It's not decided that I'm to leave Deadwood. I belong here more than you."

Molly did not so much as get the satisfaction of knowing the other woman had heard the determination in her voice, for Emerald had donned a dress and slipped out of the door before Molly had it half opened.

Instead of walking toward the mine where the carriages had stopped, she ran away from the cabin, calling after herself, "When Austin asks for me, tell him I'll be sunning myself on the big rock by the watering hole."

Whatever game Emerald was playing, Molly felt she had become a pawn.

Austin Avery did not use the word *capitalist* when he introduced Molly to the portly man standing outside the mine, but it was evident by the cut of Carson D. McPherson's city clothing and the size of his girth that that was what he was. He did not name for Molly the eastern firm he represented, but she knew that if he was pleased with what he found at the Lucky Six Avery would be selling to a company with the capital to bring in the machinery and manpower needed for profitable and safe hard rock mining.

Despite the fact that even before Jake's death Molly

had hated and feared the mine, she resented the man for the reality that he might so easily acquire that which they had earned with their hopes, their labors and their very lives. His manner was presumptive.

"I'll be gathering the samples myself, of course." He addressed his remarks to Avery as if her presence, and the absence, of Hugh and Caleb Dexter did not matter. "One wagon load will be sufficient for the mill, so just have your men lower me into the mine and load the samples as I direct!"

The gambler was all ingratiatory smiles as he helped the portly capitalist into the set of white workman's coveralls McPherson had brought along to protect his fine clothes and watched the two hired workmen lower him into the shaft, but Molly knew he must be irritated at McPherson's insistence at gathering the samples himself. She knew there were all sorts of ways of salting ore samples with gold to make it appear that a mine bore high grade ore, and she was convinced that Austin Avery would not be beyond perpetrating some scheme to ensure that the Lucky Six would be one of the mines bought up by McPherson. But once McPherson was out of sight, the gambler appeared strangely indifferent to the mine.

"And where might I find Miss O'Brien?" he asked, almost as if he knew she'd be waiting somewhere for him, posed somewhere prettily. Molly directed him to the secret place on the creek where the men had bathed since Hugh had diverted the creek into one of their old prospect holes. She watched him retreat in the buggy, hoping that when he returned he would have Emerald with him. She was sure the unscrupulous pair deserved each other and that Emerald would try mightily to manipulate the gambler to serve her own ends and not Hugh's. She was certain that Emerald cared for no one but herself.

Molly would stay at the mine, watching and waiting and doing what she could to be certain that Hugh would not be cheated.

In truth, Emerald was very much concerned about Hugh's interests. It was crucial that Austin Avery's scheme to make a fortune on the Lucky Six include Hugh, for Hugh must become rich. Emerald had removed herself from much of the suffering and ugliness of the smallpox epidemic by arriving late and often reminding herself that she was only playing a part. Nevertheless, the horrors of the illness had been much worse than she had expected; the prize for her efforts must be worthy of such a fine performance. She had convinced Hugh that she was not only repentant but a veritable angel of mercy worthy of any man's love, and she had convinced herself that not only would marriage to Hugh bring her respectability, it would be a delightful prospect in itself. She was, however, thoroughly disgusted with the squalor and discomfort of her brief return to respectability. She wanted Hugh, but she wanted him rich. And she did not intend to wait much longer. She'd had enough of poverty and dirt-floored cabins.

That Hugh wanted her and was ripe for the picking she was sure. The trick was to reel him in while at the same time eliminating the competition. She had been delighted when Molly announced that Avery was back with a capitalist. She had avoided any discussion with the gambler during his previous visits to the mine, though she'd always let him catch a glimpse of her just to tease him. Now it was essential that she discover just what it was he plotted. Still, she was surprised that seeing him again brought a strange sort of rushing pleasure. Being around Hugh warmed her hands and heart, but the sight of Austin Avery made her blush inside.

It would never do to let Austin know that his

presence excited her, so she concentrated on her pose and pretended not to see him. She was wearing a dressing gown of delicate layers of pale green batiste and her hair was down. She sat on the large rock which overlooked the swimming hole, brushing her hair, her gown slightly asunder so the sun could momentarily play upon her delicate skin.

"You look lovely posed like that, my dear," he said while she pretended surprise at the sound of his voice. "You're a regular Psyche, goddess of nature and love."

"Why, Avery, how gentlemanly a compliment," she purred. What an apt description, she thought. She'd have to find some opportunity for Hugh to see her posed against nature this way.

"And now that the preliminaries are over, come and get into my buggy. I must talk to you."

"How dare you order me about! You forget I no longer belong to you. And if you think I would step into that buggy with you so that you might close the curtains about us and do what you would with me —"

"Emerald, I don't have time for your pretty fantasies today, nor for doing what you would have me do with you. I've got to talk to you about selling the mine, and I want to do it before Hugh gets back and sees us together."

Emerald glanced about uneasily. It would not do for Hugh to see them together. "Why do you want to tell me about selling the mine? What do you have in mind?"

"Come with me and I'll tell you. If you want your precious Hugh to be a rich man, then I'll need your help."

It was amazing how the man understood her. Soon she was sitting beside him as he drove the buggy farther up the trail and then off into the woods. He stopped the horse and pulled the curtains around them so that it was deliciously private inside.

"I don't think we need to be this private," she put on a haughty expression. "Are you sure you don't mean to ravish me once again?"

"Dear Emerald, I'm sure you hope so," he took her into his arms and kissed her neck at the open front of her dressing gown. "And I shall if there is time, I promise you I shall, but first to business! It is essential that you help me tomorrow!"

She pushed him just far enough away that she could look into his eyes, yet still enjoy his hands on her body. His promise to ravish her had sent such delightful shivers through her body! He'd not have her without a fight, though she must be careful not to protest so loudly that someone would hear and stop him.

"How could I help you, and why should I?"

"You can help me by keeping Hugh away from town tomorrow morning. And why you should help me is so that Hugh doesn't blunder in and foul up the assay I've arranged for the mine."

"Hugh will never stand for you salting the samples. I've heard him telling Caleb Dexter that when the samples are taken from the mine he's not to attempt to high-grade the ore. Hugh wants everything to be done right."

"Hugh's a fool and you know it. Something as important as selling a mine can't be left to chance."

"But when Hugh comes back and discovers you've already taken the samples, he'll know something's fishy."

"No, he won't. I carefully instructed the laborers to let McPherson select his own ore from anywhere in the mine. Hugh will know there's no way I could have salted the whole damn place. He'll believe that I did not salt the mine."

"But of course you did."

"I most certainly did not. McPherson is much too smart to fall for something as obvious as high-grading the samples or shooting gold dust with a shotgun into the stope. I've something much more clever in mind, but I need your help."

"To keep Hugh away from the assay office tomorrow morning."

"Precisely, My Dear. I've told the laborers to instruct him that the assay is set for noon if he cares to be present. But by noon the assay will be completed, a very favorable assay, I might add, and I'll be on my way back to the mine with McPherson's generous offer to buy the Lucky Six."

"But why should I help you to deceive Hugh?"

"For his own good, my dear. You know he's much too noble to allow me to help him get rich, and you know you want him to marry you despite the fact he's so obviously destined for Molly Lewis, and you know you'd never be happy with a poor man, so —"

"So you're resigned?" Emerald had never felt so hurt. "You'll let Hugh have me?"

"Of course not, my dear. I intend to have you back myself. We both know where you're destined to end, but if you intend to take your chances on playing respectable in the meantime, you may as well do me some good. I'd cut Hugh out of the deal in a minute if I could get him to sell out to me, but he won't, so I've no choice but to bring him on my coat tails. And if he gets a taste of you in the meantime, well, I'm sure it will do you no great damage and perhaps only serve to convince you that you're not made for a great lumbering fool like Hugh Everett."

"And I suppose you think I'm made for you?"

"Yes, Emerald. You are made for my hands which even now you let touch your breasts, and for my mouth which will soon be kissing you again, and for the rest of me which has been ready for you since you first stepped inside this carriage, and don't pretend you haven't noticed."

"Oh, Avery, you're a beast," she began to struggle prettily against his hands which were hot and insistent through the foamy green layers of her gown. Her own squirming against the smooth leather seat of the buggy excited her almost as much as his hands until he touched the places only Austin Avery seemed to understand. And then she stopped being afraid that Hugh would discover them together and was only afraid that Austin Avery would not take the time to satisfy them both.

From her vantage point at the mine, Molly was surprised when the gambler's buggy returned to the cabin. She thought he must have gone on to town by now. She was even more surprised to see Emerald's figure slipping out of the buggy and into the cabin. She hoped the gambler had persuaded her to return to him, but he didn't linger at the cabin or go in to fetch her trunk; instead he drove back to where Molly stood.

"You've missed McPherson," she told him. "He just left with a wagon load of ore."

"That's quite all right," he said, leaning out of the buggy and removing his hat to her in a sweeping gesture. "I needed the opportunity to try to persuade Miss O'Brien to return to me."

"And did you?" She knew she sounded anxious.

"Not yet. She still has her pretentions of achieving some notion of respectability I can't give her. But I've got faith she'll yet be mine. For I have faith in you, Mrs. Lewis."

"You have faith in me? What do you mean?"

"Just that my gambler's intuition tells me that it's you Hugh Everett truly wants and needs. And I think that if you're pressed hard enough, you'll see that you must do something to win him."

"I don't know what you're talking about!" Molly was

astonished by his boldness and made herself answer with ladylike evasiveness, but she was thrilled to know he was on her side and thought she still had a chance to win Hugh.

"I think you do, but I must advise you that you must take a risk if you intend to play to win, and you must do it soon or you'll lose him to Emerald and that would be disaster for all of us."

"But how? I don't understand. How do I play to win?"

"Like a woman. You use the cards and the tricks that fate has dealt you. Haven't you learned anything from watching that little baggage in there?"

"I could never do that. I could never win Hugh through some trick!"

"In that case, don't use a trick. Simply be honest. I've always said honesty pays." He picked up the reins and prepared to drive away. "Just remember, Mrs. Lewis, that if by some stroke of luck Hugh Everett should come into a stack of greenbacks, say enough to set up housekeeping in style, that it's you and your son who deserve him. Oh, and when the time is right, don't be afraid to get rid of that little baggage in your cabin."

He started to turn the horse to leave, but Molly was moved to reach out and stop him. "You love her, don't you? You'd take her back despite the awful things between you, wouldn't you? You wouldn't let the past stop you from having the woman you love?"

"That's a romantic view, Mrs. Lewis," he said looking up at the cabin with a speculative smile on his face.

"Let's just say two of a kind belong together."

Molly stepped back and he walked away, but then turned back to her with another of his secret little smiles. "Do me a favor would you? Ask Miss O'Brien to truly think over what happened this afternoon. Tell her I cherished the time we spent together."

Molly stood in the clearing before the mine and watched him drive away. She turned back and looked at her cabin, knowing Emerald probably watched her from the window. Down the road somewhere Hugh would soon be coming home. She sensed they were nearing a turning point. Fate was about to deal the final hand in their summer of '76. And that whether she and Hugh fulfilled any portion of the promise that had brought them to the Black Hills was somehow up to her.

CHAPTER THIRTY-ONE

Emerald was up and dressed before Molly awoke the next morning, if one could call wearing the delicate wrappings of silk and lace being dressed. Molly opened her eyes just as Emerald slipped into her frothy green batiste dressing gown, and so caught a glimpse of what she wore underneath, an embroidered silk chemise with matching ruffled pantaloons.

Molly closed her eyes against the realization that her jealousy of Emerald extended to envy of the woman's undergarments. Molly's hasty marriage had not merited a bridal trousseau, and the years at the homestead had starved her for the touch of anything pretty. When she had first seen Emerald in the green velvet costume, she had felt a terrible temptation to make a fool of herself by asking to touch the fabric. Seeing Emerald's wardrobe had made her yearn for the feel of garments made not for sturdy duty but for pleasure in themselves. She could not blame Hugh for wanting Emerald when Molly herself ached to see such beauty. Nor could she be comforted in knowing that Emerald had earned her pretty things with sin, for Molly, too, had fallen and had nothing to show for it but the memory of glorious moments that seemed destined never to be repeated.

And now, seeing the confident way Emerald dressed, as if certain of winning what she wanted, Molly wondered if there was any use in fighting. Perhaps she should just give up Hugh and her place in Deadwood and go home to her parents. Emerald seemed to be counting on that. But leaving would negate all she had struggled for that summer. Even if she could never overcome the terrible rift between them, abandoning Hugh to this woman and the gambler's plots would make a travesty of all their sacrifices and even of the graves on Mt. Moriah.

Edwin stirred beside her in the big double bed they'd shared since Emerald had taken over his pallet on the floor. Molly touched his face and golden curls as he woke and remembered she had been given something far more beautiful and precious than anything Emerald possessed, and that was her child. Hugh's son. And he was reason enough to continue the struggle.

She sat up and faced Emerald. "You're very elegant for morning. Are you planning something?"

"Just to help you get this ugly little cabin back to order and pack for your journey," Emerald smiled sweetly as if she had not heard the sharpness in Molly's tone. "But doesn't it cheer you to put on something pretty after such an ordeal as saving the lives of all those poor, dear men? It's just good to be myself again after all that sickness. I was so exhausted last night I didn't get to talk to Hugh about the sale of the mine."

"Yes, I'm sure your visit with Mr. Avery must have been quite an ordeal."

Emerald blushed and Molly knew she had hit a nerve. Emerald had taken to bed complaining of a headache immediately after the gambler's visit, but to Molly her expression had been strangely serene. When Hugh returned she wanted to voice her suspicions, but he expressed concern for Emerald and implied that Molly should have protected her from Avery's advances. Hugh was also suspicious that Avery had shown up with the long-awaited capitalist and taken ore samples in his absence, but the laborers assured Hugh that the sampling procedure had been honest, and that Hugh was invited to the test at the assay office at noon.

Remembering that it was the day of the test gave Molly the notion she might accompany Hugh to the assay office. It seemed her place as one of the original owners to be present for the test which would determine the mine's worth. Edwin could be sent to the neighbors once more, and surely Emerald could find no excuse to intrude on mine business; so that afterwards, when they were alone and at last knew the value of their labors, she could find the courage to ask Hugh if they might still have a future together.

If Hugh were rid of the mine, then she might persuade him to return East with her. There in a civilized place, the calamities of Deadwood and their terrible journey could be forgotten and they could regain the love begun in innocence so long ago.

Feeling hopeful, Molly arose quickly, despite the throbbing pain in her arm and the feverish, unsettled feeling that had plagued her since the vaccination. She dressed in her everyday dress, thinking she would heat an iron and make her better dress more presentable. She realized she might even take a little of her gold dust and buy decent traveling clothes for herself and Edwin. She had more than enough for their stagecoach and rail tickets home, so why not honor Jake's memory by arriving there, wearing a smart traveling suit and her mother's cameo necklace, thus presenting herself as the widow of a man who had at last succeeded? Hugh would be presented as Jake's former partner and her gallant escort to safety, and when, after a decent period of mourning for Jake, she married Hugh, her family would surely sense the rightness of the union and Edwin could be taught to call Hugh father. Then all her past wounds would be healed.

"Edwin, please dress and run fetch Hugh. Breakfast will be ready in a few minutes."

It was Emerald who had given the order, usurping Molly's position, and Edwin's hurrying to please her hurt his mother almost as much as the fact he had once confided in her he thought Emerald "the prettiest woman in the whole world." *Steady,* Molly told herself. Continue to behave as a lady and surely it would soon be resolved, with both Emerald and herself in their rightful places.

Hugh arrived for breakfast fresh from a bath at the creek, drops of water glimmering from his sun-bleached hair and his skin ruddy. It was all she could do not to throw herself into his arms. Emerald played the part of hostess as she seated them for breakfast, somehow superseding Molly's spot across from Hugh, so Molly was made to feel out of place at her own table. They ate their oatmeal in silence and then when a lunch had been packed for Edwin and he'd been sent off to the neighbor's and the adults lingered over more coffee, Emerald made her move.

"I'll bet the creek was just lovely this morning," she trilled. "As I was sitting beside it yesterday I could not help thinking how lovely it would be to bathe there in the warmth of the sunlight instead of having to sneak down at night and shiver and stumble about as poor Molly and I have been doing."

"The creek is in full view of the road," Molly spoke too loudly. "You know why only the men can bathe there in daylight!" She too had longed to enjoy the cold clear water of the creek when the sun warmed and dappled the rocks.

"Goodness, I know it wouldn't be quite proper. But I thought if I kept my chemise on and went in mid-morning when there's hardly ever anyone on the road —"

"I hardly think that would be a good idea." Molly responded. "You'd get your pretty things all wet and muddy; besides, now that your nursing services are no longer needed, you can move back to the hotel and take your baths in the style to which you are accustomed."

"Molly, you don't sound very hospitable," Hugh said. "Emerald came to us for help in leaving Avery; we can hardly expect her to move to the hotel where she'd be at the man's mercy, or at any man's mercy for that matter."

"Oh, Hugh, you are so considerate, but Molly is quite

right. I've overstayed my usefulness. I've no real place here, nor anywhere for that matter. I'm sure my mother will never forgive me for running away with Avery, even if I did believe he would marry me. But I've a few jewels I can sell, and I'm sure I'll be quite safe in a hotel, especially if you'd escort me to one, Hugh. I think if the proprietor knew that you were my protector, he'd be sure the men would respect me. Perhaps you could escort me to town when you go in for the assay this afternoon."

"I thought I would go with you, Hugh," Molly implored.

"There's no reason we can't all go," Hugh said brightly. "Then, if there's something to celebrate, we can make a day of it."

"Yes," Emerald smiled, "and we can stop at the stage depot and make Molly's travel arrangements."

"Travel arrangements?" Hugh looked at Molly. "I'd almost let myself forget. You swore before Caleb Dexter got sick that you'd go home. Are you still determined?"

They both looked at her and Molly felt herself blushing and confused. How could she announce before Emerald that her plans, her whole future, in fact, depended on Hugh? And how could she now suggest Emerald continue living with her just because she realized the little vixen would be a greater threat in a hotel room in Deadwood than sharing her cabin?

"I'm not sure what I'll do," she said quietly. "I was too busy with the sick men to make any plans. And what of your plans, Hugh? If Edwin and I go home to the East will you come also?"

"Go East? I have no home there. I have no home anywhere. If Luther were here, I'd probably have taken him back to Nebraska, but I can't go there now," Hugh's voice was full of emotion, but he kept his eyes on his tin mug as he spoke thoughtfully. "It's strange; all our hopes have been based on making our fortunes in that mine, and now when I think it might happen today, that I might be rid of the mine and have the cash in hand to get out of Deadwood, why I can't think of anywhere I want to go or anything I want, except —"

His voice trailed off but his eyes met Molly's. He had wanted her from the beginning and he had not forgotten how love had bound them together on that glorious night in July. In her joy at seeing the love still in his eyes, she brushed aside his saying he'd not return to her home. Surely she could persuade him that only in a civilized place could they be the couple their childhood love had destined them to be.

"Oh, Hugh," Emerald intruded, forcing his eyes from Molly. "I'm sure that once you're rich, you'll think of many things you want. You've never had the freedom before to discover what it is you really desire."

She isn't going to give up, Molly realized. She can see that Hugh loves me, but that won't stop her for a minute. Molly realized she must take a stronger stance. She remembered the gambler and what he had said about playing to win.

"By the way, Emerald," Molly said sweetly, "Before he left, Mr. Avery asked me to give you a message. I'm sure it's not important, but he did say to remind you to think about your time together yesterday. He said it meant a great deal to him."

"Oh, the beast!" Emerald blushed furiously.

"What happened?" Hugh demanded, "Did he try to win you back?"

Emerald nodded prettily, as if relieved Hugh had supplied his own explanation.

"That man's as unscrupulous as they come." Hugh banged his cup down on the table, "I hate having my name associated with his as partners in the mine. I've a good mind to go to town early and warn McPherson about him."

"Oh don't do that," Emerald protested. "You could spoil everything!" Seeing Hugh's startled expression, she changed her tone. "I mean, it wouldn't do for you to question your partner's honesty before the capitalist. You could make McPherson refuse to even give the mine a fair test. Besides, Austin assured me that he'll not try to cheat you out of your share of the mine sale."

"That's because he doesn't dare try anything with me. He knows I'd call his bluff. Still, I might as well go into town early. Neither Caleb Dexter nor the laborers have shown up for work, so I can't get anything done here. I'll make sure of the time and place for the test, and then I can rent a buggy to fetch you ladies into town later."

"No, Hugh, please don't leave," Emerald interjected, her eyes flashing around the cabin for an excuse to delay him. "There's so much to be done here. All the sick beds must be carried out. Poor Molly has a ton of washing to boil, and I'd like a bath."

"Let me think for a moment. Of course, I'll haul water for you. Molly, do you want a fire in the yard for your wash? That would keep the cabin cooler and it wouldn't be much extra to heat some water for Emerald to bathe."

"Oh, no, I can't make extra work for Molly. I'll just bathe in the creek. It would be so lovely and cool and I felt so feverish since the vaccination, and my poor arm is so sore, and I'm sure I'll be safe there if you'll stay close by, Hugh, watching over me, I mean watching the road while you fetch Molly's wash water."

"Why, of course, Emerald, there's no reason why being a woman should deprive you of a cool bath. I'll take my rifle, and if someone should come along the road, I'll be sure they don't tarry."

While Poor Molly does the wash! Molly burned in shame and anger. Hugh was taking her as much for granted as had Jake! He'd believed the vixen again. Of course, he would behave as a gentleman, keeping his back turned while Emerald went to the creek, but if she should pretend to slip on a rock or see a snake and make a little shriek, why then of course Hugh would have to investigate, and once he saw her as good as naked with the wet silk clinging to her body. Well, Hugh was no saint. Molly knew that.

But there seemed to be nothing she could do to stop it. Hugh got the water buckets and carried her wash tub out to the yard without even asking her if she meant to do a wash on a day that was supposed to be special and while she herself was aching and feverish from the vaccination.

Emerald was like a cat into the cream as she gathered her scented soap and Molly's last clean towel. They were gone before she could think what to say or do to stop them and Molly could only sit at her kitchen table and worry.

Here I am again waiting, she thought *waiting*. Like I waited to see if I could really be pregnant, and I waited for Hugh to come back, and I waited to see if I could be a good wife to Jake if I but tried harder, and I waited in the wagon while the men fought the Indians and Pearson came to rape me, and I waited and I waited when Hugh and Jake were lost in the mine and they said only one of them was alive.

And then she knew she would wait no more. And she remembered what Avery had said about beating the little baggage at her own tricks. And she stood and took off her plain cotton dress and examined herself in her simple muslin chemise. It was not inset with lace and tucks like Emerald's to show the outlines of her body, but when it was wet, she, too, would be as good as naked. And hers was the body Hugh had loved and would love again.

Hugh was startled to see her. He was sitting on a stump near the road, not even taking a place on the big rock overlooking the waterhole, just cleaning his rifle and watching the road.

"Molly, what are you doing out here in your shift?"

"I'm going to take a bath. I'm hot and feverish too, and I've as much right as any man and certainly as much right as that woman to enjoy a bath in broad daylight."

She strode past him and made her way down the steep path to the creek. Her slippers sent little bits of gravel skittering down the bank before her, and Emerald, wading in the creek with the water just reaching the ruffled hems of her pantaloons heard the noise and looked up smiling. When she saw it was Molly, her expression changed.

"Don't mind me," Molly said sweetly, removing her shoes and stepping into the cold water. Having come this far, she realized she wasn't sure of her next step, but, oh, it felt right to be taking action at last. She sat on the warm surface of a rock in the middle of the creek and began to bathe her arms and legs in the deep water which swirled around it. Getting into the deeper water of the icy mountain stream was always a challenge best begun by cooling one's limbs. Her arm was swollen, hot and sore, from the vaccination; the center already forming the ugly sore that would eventually match the scar from her previous inoculation.

She told herself that her body, even with the marks of child-bearing, was as desirable as Emerald's, but she was not certain. Feeling again the foolish jealousy of the morning, Molly studied Emerald. Emerald's body was round and firm, her skin flawless, her hands unmarked from work, her arms and neck as perfect and graceful as a swan's.

Molly stared. Something was wrong, something out of place. Emerald was flawless, unmarked. Emerald was unmarked.

"Emerald," she said quietly. "Let me see your arm. Where is your scar and where is the awful sore from your new vaccination? You've been complaining all week how sick the shot made you; you almost fainted when it was your turn to be inoculated; now, tell me — why isn't your arm swollen and throbbing like mine?"

Emerald backed away from Molly, stepping deeper into the creek, her pantaloons now wet to the thigh. She tried to turn away, to conceal her arm with the other hand, but it was no use, Molly followed her into the creek, oblivious to the soaking of her own underclothes.

"So it didn't take! So my vaccination didn't take. That's no crime, is it?" Emerald stood proudly at the edge of the deeper pool of water, thrusting forward her breasts and flaunting the perfection of her white arms and shoulders. Molly came closer.

"But you don't have *any* marks on your arms. If you were vaccinated before, where is that scar? And you must have been vaccinated or you'd never have dared nurse those men. The doctor said you were in terrible danger anyway, that you could be scarred for life. All the men feared for you. Hugh feared for you. Even I feared for you!"

"I was vaccinated on my hip. Yes, on my hip where no one can see. My mother made the doctor do it that way because she was so proud of my beauty."

"Show me,"

"Molly!" Emerald backed away, slipped on the rocky creek bottom and fell into the water. She came up soaked and shrieking, her hair falling about her face and her nipples showing hard and pink through the wet silk. As she tried to wipe the streaming curtain of wet hair away from her face, she slipped and went under again, screaming.

Molly waded deeper, wetting her own chemise to

the shoulders and grabbed Emerald by the hair, pulling her out of the water. "Show me!" she demanded of the sputtering woman, still holding her by the hair. "I'm a woman; there can be no sin in showing me. You've shown yourself to Austin Avery and half the men in Deadwood at the theatre, and you'd show yourself to Hugh, so show me!"

"What's going on here?"

It was Hugh, standing on the bank, clutching his rifle, his face full of alarm.

"Save me!" Emerald screamed. "She's trying to drown me!"

For just an instant, the lady in Molly reacted in horror, realizing the picture they made standing now in hip-high water, Emerald's hair soaked and tangled about her face, Molly's streaming wet around her shoulders; both of them covered only by wet and clinging cloth, their breasts high and nipples hard from the icy water. For an instant she was tempted to hide herself with her arms or retreat into the deep water. Instead she held herself proud and faced Hugh squarely as she spoke.

"Nonsense! She slipped in the water and I pulled her out."

"Don't listen to her. She tried to kill me! She's wanted me dead from the first!"

"Emerald, stop being hysterical!" Hugh set the rifle down on the bank and stood with his hands on his hips. "Will one of you please tell me what's happened?"

"I confronted her. I asked to see the evidence she's been vaccinated. I've discovered she's lied to us and let us think she was in danger nursing the sick men, but look, her arm isn't sore and she's got no old scar either. She claims she was vaccinated on her hip, so I merely asked her to show me!"

"Why she's right, Emerald. You haven't a mark on

you. I saw the doctor vaccinate you. Why aren't you sick like the rest of us?"

Molly had the answer.

"Because she's a witch, that's why!"

"Now who's hysterical?" Emerald shouted. "I told you I was vaccinated on my hip so that I'd not have an ugly scar like you do. You're jealous because I'm so perfect and all the men want me!"

"I want to see that scar," Molly demanded. "I want to know if you really were in danger of being scarred or if you just used us to make everyone think you were good."

Emerald was backing up again, this time toward Hugh on the shore, but she had regained much of her composure. "I won't let myself be questioned by you," she taunted Molly. "Jealousy has driven you crazy!"

"Then let me question you," Hugh demanded. "I don't believe there's such a thing as a witch, but even if you were vaccinated somewhere we can't see, your arm would still be swollen like ours. How did you escape that? I want to know."

"All right," she posed defiantly, one hand on her hip, the other pulling back her hair, which was already springing back into perfect curls. "If you must know, it happens I'm a natural immune. My mother had the pox when she was carrying me. I've been vaccinated before and I've been through epidemics before. They don't affect me. Nothing will ever mark my perfect skin. It's like a gift from God."

"Gift from God! Why you little tramp!" Molly shouted. "It's the mark of a Jezebel! You used us. You made us think you were risking everything to nurse those men!"

"Why?" Hugh interjected. "Why did you do that?"

Emerald was silent for a moment, thinking, and then she took the part of the contrite sinner. "I had to make you think well of me. I knew you'd never accept me as a decent woman after what Avery had done to me, and I wanted your respect, Hugh. I wanted you to think well of me."

"You wanted him period!" Molly shouted. "You wanted to take him away from me."

"You never had him! He was free for the taking. I had as much right to go after him as you. More right! At least I wasn't married. You wanted him when you were married to Jake. You wanted to commit adultery with him. Would have too, if you weren't such a goody-two-shoes!"

Molly started to speak, then bit her lip, but Emerald had seen something in her face.

"Oh, so *you* did commit adultery! And *you* condemn *me*! You treat me like a sinner when you fornicated with your husband's partner!"

"Leave Molly out of this!" Hugh shouted. "I want to know about you. I want to know what you wanted from me!"

"I wanted you to marry me," Emerald spoke with quiet sincerity. "I wanted you to make me a respectable woman. And to love me." Then she almost shouted, "Yes, I wanted you to love me!" Then her voice fell to a whisper, "I still do."

"But that's crazy. I love Molly."

He had said it! He had not only said it but shouted it to the other woman! Joy soared in Molly's heart. Half naked and dripping wet, and as crazy as she was behaving, he loved her. Emerald was surprised that Molly had fought for her man and might even be winning, but she was not backing down herself.

"Well, loving Molly doesn't stop you from wanting me," Emerald accused, holding her head high like a queen and flashing her wonderful green eyes so that they touched first her own silken splendor and then Hugh's strong body. "You did want me and you do want me. You want me now! Look at you!"

Molly was still reeling from Hugh's admission of love when she followed Emerald's gesture and blushed to see outlined in his trousers, the evidence of his desire.

Hugh was embarrassed and furious. "Molly's right! You are a witch! Coming here and using those sick men to make us think you'd repented and all the while you were flaunting yourself, flaunting your beauty. Of course, I've wanted you. Any man half alive would want you, but that doesn't make it right. It doesn't give you the right to manipulate people!"

"You're such a hypocrite!" Emerald shrieked. "And you're a fool. Austin Avery is right. You're a fool and you don't deserve to have him make you rich. And to think I was going along with it! Keeping you here so you wouldn't be a fool and ruin Avery's scheme —"

"What scheme? What do you mean keep me here so I won't ruin Avery's scheme?"

"To salt the mine. To fix the assay. To make you rich enough to be worthy of me, you fool! He's doing it right this minute. Austin Avery is making you a rich man while you're ashamed to have your precious name associated with his. Well, it's too late now. He's going to pull the mining fraud of the century with your mine, and Deadwood will remember you both as crooks!"

"Damn it! I knew he'd pull something. Where is he? What's he going to do? Get out of that creek, woman, and tell me!"

Emerald climbed out of the creek and stood on the bank, dripping, her proud and almost naked body just inches from Hugh's as she confronted him defiantly. "He's got a plan to rig the assay. This morning before you get to town. That's all I know. Except that Austin Avery is twice the man you are and I was a fool to leave him. Austin Avery knows how to enjoy life, and how to pleasure a woman!"

"Then go to him!" Hugh demanded, striding up the hill as Molly joined Emerald on the bank. "But I'm going to find him first and I'm going to do my best to stop him and see he gets what he deserves!"

"He will!" Emerald shouted. "Austin Avery will get what he deserves because he knows how to make things happen. And he knows how to enjoy what he's earned. You and Molly deserve each other. You deserve to be miserable together forever. You two ought to build a damn church!"

Hugh turned and looked down the bank at the two women. He was the picture of frustrated rage.

Molly took over. She leaned down and picked up the gun.

"You go on into town, Hugh, and do what you can to stop him. I'll put away your gun for you, and I'll take care of Miss O'Brien. Just stop at the livery stable and have a rig sent to collect her things. I think she'll be leaving soon."

Hugh shook his head, but gave Molly a trusting wave and was off for Deadwood at a run. Emerald started to call after Hugh, but realized it was no use. She turned and looked at Molly, her eyes wide with disbelief.

"Now then," Molly said, hefting the heavy rifle and slowly swinging it so that it was pointed toward Emerald. "I suggest you get back to the cabin and get into your clothes rather quickly. And then I suggest you get packed and be sitting on your trunk when the rig comes for you."

"You can't tell me—"

"And then you get out of town. You've been reminding me all week that stage service has commenced. So when the next stage leaves Deadwood, you be on it!"

She stepped toward Emerald, not aiming the rifle, but holding it squarely before her. Emerald backed up the hill, then turned and ran toward the cabin.

Molly climbed up the creek bank and stood in her dripping chemise watching the woman retreating and looking proudly over the scene before her, the cabins and the mineshaft and the rubble of the Lucky Six Mine. What she had said to Emerald sounded melodramatic, she knew, like a line from one of those cheap novels they had begun to write about the west, but it also sounded right.

She felt like a true pioneer.

CHAPTER THIRTY-TWO

The proprietor of the hotel, delighted at Emerald's return, gave her the key to Avery's room without question. The first thing she did upon entering the room was to throw herself across the bed and cry out her rage at the humiliation she had received at the hands of Molly Lewis. Not only had the scene at the creek become a travesty of the way she had scripted it in her mind, but all her suffering and sacrifice to save the lives of the filthy, disgusting miners was a waste. Of course, the story of how Emerald O'Brien had risked her perfect beauty to nurse the pox-covered sick men was already becoming a Deadwood legend that would not be tarnished by any spiteful detractions from Molly Lewis, but she had failed to trap the noble Hugh Everett; worse, she had given up Austin Avery for nothing.

But was he truly lost to her? Although lying on the bed she had once shared with him and smelling his bay rum on the sheets had sent Emerald into new rounds of sobbing, she soon realized she'd not yet forfeited her winning hand with the gambler. He had been most attentive to her in the buggy, ravishing her not just with his body but with words, even promises. Obviously she could get him back.

It would not be necessary to let him know she had failed with Hugh. Austin had, after all, been her first choice. In fact, he was the better man for her, she realized, sitting up on the bed and staring at her reflection in the mirror across the room. Austin was right, Hugh Everett was too noble for his own good. He would never know how to enjoy life. He would always be struggling for something. The woman he married might be respectable but she'd soon be worn out with hard work and child bearing. He'd probably run for mayor of Deadwood and expect her to stand by his side. Respectability did not come cheap, and her ordeal with the sick men and Edwin always whining for attention should have made it obvious to her she was not destined to give up all for marriage; however, if marriage did present a gain for her, she need only trick Austin to think he was the winner.

As she considered and shuffled through new plots for her life, Emerald left the bed and went to the larger of her trunks, the one she had left behind. She took out a bolt of cloth, one of the purchases she had made in the afternoon of self-gratification with which she had fortified herself before beginning her self-imposed exile in the pest house. The cloth was of deep red embroidered silk and when she bought it, she had pictured herself wearing it on her honeymoon with Hugh, but by the time she brought it back to the hotel she had become aware of an uneasy feeling and known that her pleasure in her purchase had been spoiled.

She had felt wonderfully excited when she found the silk in the shop of Wing Tsue, Deadwood's leading Chinese merchant. The color was perfect to be worn with her latest gift from Avery, a pair of garnet earrings, and it had excited her to think that the silk had come all the way from China to adorn her, once a simple shop girl. But her feeling toward the silk had changed by the time she left the shop, and she realized now, it had something to do with meeting the merchant's wife. For Wing Tsue, believing she was a respectable woman, had invited her to step through the damask wall hangings to the room behind the shop and be presented to his wife, Hal Shek Wong. At the first sight of the tiny little woman dressed in layers of rich embroidered silks and perched on a pile of silk pillows, Emerald had been enchanted, for she was just like the china dolls displayed in glass cases on the other side of the curtains. Her face was chalk white; her expression was painted on, just like the doll's. Her hair was even blacker than Emerald's and was arranged in an elaborate pyramid laced with carved ivory pins and combs. The merchant's wife spoke no English, but she offered Emerald tea by gesturing with her delicate hands, and Emerald took it from her in a tiny cup as delicate as an egg shell.

She would have gone away still enchanted had she not seen Hal Shek Wong's feet. She knew that Chinese women bound their feet to make them tiny and pleasing to men, and she, having small and pretty feet herself, had thought it a clever idea. But then she saw that Hal Shek Wong's feet were not pretty at all despite the doll-like slippers she wore. They were grotesquely deformed. A woman could barely walk on such feet, and she certainly could never run away. And that was how it was meant to be, Emerald realized. Wing Tsue kept his wife in a silken prison, just like the dolls in their glass cases.

She had put away her insight about the merchant's marriage with the garnet-colored silk and not let her doubts distract her from her plot to win Hugh, but now, sitting on the floor and fingering the silk, she realized that her insight about Wing Tsue's wife was true of all marriages. Had she won Hugh as a husband, he would have become not just her husband, but her master. Marriage might offer a woman security and respectability, but whether the walls were made of silk or logs, the price was still imprisonment.

Emerald laid the bolt of silk on the bed and bathed her face with water from the pitcher, then examined herself in the mirror of the mahogany dresser. She was not only more beautiful than most women, she was smarter, and she was destined to be a winner.

The window of the hotel room was open, and as she arranged her face and hair she heard music drifting up from the hurdy gurdy across the street. She hummed along and remembered her moment of glory on the stage of Langrishe's theater, and then it came to her at last where her destiny lay. She laughed out loud, looked at her sparkling eyes and pretty white teeth in the mirror and wondered why it had taken her so long to see who she must be. An actress! Of course, that was destiny's promise for her. If the men at Langrishe's had gone wild for the unknown woman who had dared to show her bloomers on stage, what would they do to see Emerald O'Brien, Deadwood's Angel of Mercy! It was a title that would play in Cheyenne or even San Francisco. Such a woman need not depend on Hugh or Austin or any man to save her. She was destined to be a star!

Emerald again picked up the bolt of cloth. The silk shimmered in the sunlight, and as she turned back to the mirror and draped the full length of the fabric around her, she was amazed to see how the deep rich red enhanced her skin and eyes. She was suddenly sparklingly alive and different, a new and exotic woman. Putting aside the role of Deadwood's angel almost as soon as she had created it, she saw what she needed. Not just a new dress and a new career but a whole new personality and a new name.

Garnet, she thought. I've been Emerald O'Brien long enough. I've been Irish long enough. Garnet and something Spanish and exotic. She would learn to dance and be the new Lola Montez.

Gabriel! That was it. Gabriel, the angel. How perfect for the legend who had saved Deadwood. She might still use that story, but she would be Garnet Gabriel. And although she would always be remembered in Deadwood, she would move on to new places and new adventures. Molly had ordered her to be out of town on the next stage. Well, she would leave town, all right, but not because Molly had ordered it, but because her disappearance would serve her legend. How the men would yearn for her return when they read of her appearances elsewhere! How those she had saved would struggle to do justice to her beauty and her goodness as they described her!

She stuffed the silk and her toilet articles back into the trunk and got out her green velvet traveling costume, but as she dressed, she caught a glimpse in the mirror of the unmade bed behind her and she remembered Austin Avery. It was a long way to Cheyenne and a long time before she'd find another man like him. She remembered their last encounter in the buggy. They had both known he was not ravishing her but servicing her, and he had serviced her well. He was the one who had awakened such needs in her; how could she be certain another man could satisfy them as completely? Besides, he might soon be rich from the sale of the mine, that is if Hugh didn't spoil the assay for everyone. Austin would surely be furious at her for tipping Hugh off. If he caught up with her, he would probably spank her.

She remembered the night he had dragged her off the stage and back to their hotel room. There would certainly need to be some concessions made if Austin Avery were not to be an encumbrance to her stage career, but she had no doubt she could win concessions if she let him win her first. But she certainly couldn't let him return and find her in the hotel room waiting for him. Getting on the stagecoach was still the best plan, but how to be sure Austin knew about it in time to stop her?

She could leave a note, but he might not find it in time. A messenger would be better. She leaned out of the window to find a likely candidate for the honor of serving as her messenger. To her delight, she saw the familiar figure of Caleb Dexter hurrying along across the street. She hailed him with an unladylike call, and he interrupted his progress to stand underneath the window with his hat in his hand. He clutched a bottle of whiskey to his chest.

A dozen men, alerted by her yell, joined the old man standing underneath her window and gazed up at her adoringly as she gave Caleb Dexter his instructions. She didn't mind the audience.

That morning after Hugh stopped at the livery stable at the edge of town to send a rig back for Emerald, he decided to rent a horse for himself. The assay office wasn't far from the stable, but he had a feeling he might not find the gambler and his unsuspecting capitalist there. He was right, he discovered when he rode up to the office. The man in charge suggested that if a whole wagonload of ore had been taken from the mine, the first step would be to have it crushed at the new quartz mill which had only recently been built. The quartz mill was located in another of the small mining camps some distance from Deadwood, so Hugh was glad of the horse, even though it was a typical livery hack and needed constant reminders from his heels to make the trip at a gallop.

When he reached the mill, Hugh had to admire Austin Avery. He must have been furious to see Hugh galloping up, but he kept his face expressionless as he stepped down from the wagonload of ore he and McPherson appeared to be guarding and acknowledged Hugh.

"Ah, Mr. Everett, you're just in time to witness the first part of the test. I didn't think it was necessary for you to be here for the ore crushing, routine as it is, but you may as well watch, and then go along with us as we take the crushed ore to the assay office."

Hugh swung off the horse, feeling unsure as to how to express his defiance in the face of the gambler's exaggerated politeness and the curious look McPherson gave him and his lathered horse. The gambler turned his attention to McPherson.

"I don't believe you've had the opportunity to meet

my partner, Hugh Everett. Hugh, this is John McPherson. He represents a company which is buying mining properties in the area."

"Excuse me for not getting off the wagon," McPherson said, "but my orders are not to let this ore out of my sight until I have the results of the assay. I slept with it last night!" He was wearing some sort of white overalls open at the front to reveal an embroidered vest and cravat.

"Glad you could make it for the test, Everett. I understand you've been something of a silent partner in the Lucky Six."

Hugh was startled by the remark. So that was how Avery had presented him. Yes, he thought. I've been a *silent partner*, all right. Just sweating underground, tearing my hands open on the rocks, struggling and fighting for my life and killing my partner and my brother. He hesitated before he shook the soft, white hand McPherson offered him.

He realized McPherson was from another world, a world of security and comfort and high finance. If cheating and fighting went on in McPherson's world, it went on over a board table. Fortunes were made or lives were broken with the stroke of a pen. McPherson was like Phineas P. Crandall, the crusty little newspaper editor who had called him a fool to believe the promises he wrote; they were men who made their fortunes on the struggles of others. Hugh wanted nothing to do with such men. What he wanted was to beat the dickens out of Austin Avery; yet Hugh knew it wasn't just the gambler that made him mad; it was the way men like Crandall and McPherson could make nothing of other men's sweat and tears.

McPherson noticed that Hugh had hesitated before shaking his hand, and his eyebrow raised in question. Hugh made his handshake firm, knowing he'd have to meet these men on their own ground. He spoke with false bravado, "So, we're ready to see what the old Lucky Six is worth, eh?"

"That's right," McPherson said cheerfully. "And from what Mr. Avery has been telling me, you have some promising ore here. If it assays out as high grade as he thinks, I'll be able to offer you a price that will send you home in style."

"I don't have a home."

"Well, then you can buy yourself one, somewhere far away from this miserable place."

"How much of Deadwood do you expect to buy?"

"I personally won't buy anything. The offer will come from my company, the name of which I'm not yet authorized to reveal. You must understand, Mr. Everett, that mining gold is big business, scientific business. Capital is essential, if not everything. If these Deadwood diggings are as rich as your newspaper has been making the world believe, thousands of dollars of capital will be accrued this winter. It takes a good deal of money to properly develop a quartz mine, you must realize. Geologists and mining engineers, like myself, trained at foreign universities and hydraulic mining equipment, that's what it takes."

"So 'Poor Man's Gold' was just the bait for fools like me who took all the risks so that —"

"Not all the risks, son. Why, the entrepreneurs will be taking risks too. Capital investment involves considerable risk, even for men like George Hearst and J.P. Morgan; men who have already made fortunes in banking, shipping and railroads—"

"While we've been dying in the mines!"

"What's that?" McPherson asked. He paused to light a cigar.

"Nothing."

"I was merely trying to explain to you that I am not speaking as an individual, and that is why I'm not authorized to make you an offer until I have an accurate assessment of the potential worth of your holdings. And, of course, you must realize the vast difference between what the mine would be worth to you as an individual who could hope to grub out only a few more months' wages with your primitive placer methods, while we can provide the capital to—"

Avery interrupted politely to inform them the mill operator was ready, and the three turned their attention to the mill as the heavy doors were hauled open, revealing the huge machines which would pulverize the ore to a fine powder so the gold could be freed.

"Ah," McPherson said almost reverently. "The Blake Crusher and Balthoff Ball Pulverizer."

"The first quartz mill in the Black Hills!" the operator declared proudly.

Hugh stared at it. In a few minutes the ore from the Lucky Six would be dumped into the yawning mouth of the huge cylinder where it would be rolled and tumbled with iron balls until the rock was broken into bits small enough to allow the gold to be freed through one of several mechanical and chemical processes. The gold would normally be extracted from the ore at the quartz mill, but in the case of a mine test, the crushed samples would be taken to the assay office.

The mill operator and a couple of his flunkies produced wheelbarrows and stood ready to transfer the ore from the wagon to the mill. Avery was leaning back against the wagon, seeming to take no interest in the process. It made Hugh wonder. Maybe Molly and even Emerald were wrong about Avery. Hugh had made it clear he wanted the test to be conducted honestly and it looked like Avery was going along with him, or perhaps it was simply that since McPherson had been experienced enough to select the ore samples himself, there was no way to high grade it.

Hugh relaxed a little and entertained the thought the Lucky Six might actually be worth something. It would make a difference, he realized. McPherson was right. With enough money he could buy a house somewhere, maybe even a business. If he gained enough to make it possible for him to take care of Molly and Edwin, then perhaps he could still find some meaning in whatever had brought him to the Black Hills. Hugh started to feel almost cheerful. Then, just as McPherson climbed off the wagon and was preparing to supervise the transfer of the ore, they heard a shout.

"Hey, wait for me!"

Hugh turned around. Someone had just come around the corner of the mill. He was staggering and lurching and waving a whiskey bottle as he approached. It was Caleb Dexter.

"Well, I see Mr. Dexter has decided to show up for the test after all," Avery told McPherson. "He was one of the original partners in the mine and after he stopped being associated in the partnership, he still has worked in the mine itself."

"Looks like an old drunk to me," McPherson said.

"Frankly, he is somewhat intemperate," Avery whispered to McPherson. "That's how he lost his partnership, but when it comes to practical prospecting experience he's an expert! Without him, we might have missed all that conglomerate ore I told you about. We humor him along."

Hugh, old buddy," Dexter stumbled up to the group and threw his arms around Hugh. "Thanks for waiting for me, old buddy. Sorry for being late, I got detained in town. But I wouldn't miss the test of the Lucky Six for the world." His speech was slurred and he seemed hardly able to stand up. He straightened up a little and addressed himself to McPherson. "I'm proud to meet you!"

"Can we get on with the test?" The mill operator asked Avery, and then, turning to McPherson, spoke more deferentially, "That is if you are ready, Sir?"

It's amazing how people can smell capital, Hugh thought. Maybe money couldn't buy happiness, but it sure got you a lot of deferential treatment.

"We sure as hell ought to get on with the test!" Caleb Dexter roared waving the whiskey bottle. "This is what we been waiting for ain't it? To see what the old Lucky Six is worth? I'll be damned if it ain't a hell of a good gold mine. I always said it was, didn't I, Hugh? Right from the start, and now here we are getting ready to test our first ore right here at the good old Balthoff Ball Pulverizer."

Funny, Hugh thought. He can hardly stand up but he can say Balthoff Ball Pulverizer.

Caleb Dexter climbed up on the wagon and looked down at the ore lovingly. He seemed to sway a little and he kept swinging the bottle to and fro like any minute he might pitch over backward off the wagon. It made Hugh nervous. He wondered if he should make the effort to catch the old reprobate if he fell off the wagon. The mill workers had put their wheelbarrows in place behind the tail gate of the wagon and were leaning on their shovels waiting for the old man to move away so they could unload the ore.

There was something funny going on, Hugh thought. Something didn't feel right, but he couldn't put his finger on it. He stared at Caleb Dexter and then realized what was bothering him. As often as Hugh had seen the old man drunk, he had never seen him quite so loose. And it was strange he would choose this morning to get stumbling drunk. Caleb Dexter had put his whole heart into the Lucky Six. Why hadn't he been around when McPherson selected the samples? He had obviously known the test was this morning, so why had he just now shown up and why so drunk? The old man stood on the wagon, brandishing the whiskey bottle, waving it about recklessly. It looked like any minute he might pass out or drop his bottle.

The bottle, Hugh thought. There is something funny about the bottle. He realized Caleb Dexter was not drinking from it, nor had he offered a slug off it to everyone in sight as was his custom. And the bottle had a funny, gleaming look about it as if the contents were heavy and slippery, like amalgam. *Amalgam! That was it.* Caleb Dexter had amalgam in the bottle! How many times had Hugh watched the old man use his little bottle of quicksilver to attract the gold particles from the residue caught in the riffles of their sluice box? The mixture of quicksilver, or mercury, and gold was called amalgam. He would put it into a bag and squeeze the quicksilver out to use again, leaving behind the pure gold. While the amalgam was in a bottle, it would be a sort of liquid gold. And if that liquid gold could be dropped into a load of ore awaiting assay, it would make that sample look like it came from a mine full of high-grade ore. If one could risk dropping $100 worth of amalgam into an assay sample, it could add thousands of dollars to the mine's value!

Even as Hugh figured it out, the old man staggered forward, just as McPherson signaled the mill workers to unlatch the tailgate of the wagon and prepare to dump the ore into the pulverizer. The old man was going to play his scene for all it was worth, waiting until the last possible moment to drop the bottle. He leaned over the ore as if to give it a final inspection, then raised the bottle as if he were about to drink, but Hugh knew he was keeping his thumb over the neck. He knew, too, what would happen next. When the old man brought the bottle back down, he would stagger back a little as if he were going to pass out and as he caught himself, the bottle would come crashing down in the ore, shattering and spilling its load of pure liquid gold into the ore, just as the tail gate dropped and the ore tumbled into the wheelbarrows.

It would all be over in a second. McPherson would never suspect a thing and would pay a highly inflated price for the mine. Hugh looked at Avery. The gambler met his eyes and he was smiling. *He's glad I figured it out,* Hugh thought. He could have found an easier way to salt the mine, bribed the assayer or the mill operator, but he wanted to take a chance on it. Make a game of it. And he's glad I know. He wants me to play along.

And why not? Hugh thought. *I've done everything else. I've got murder and lust and the whole Sioux nation on my conscience, why not this too?*

And then, even though there was no time to articulate the answer in words, Hugh knew. He stepped forward and, with one sweeping motion of his big hands he caught Caleb Dexter by the seat of his pants and hauled him off the wagon.

"Hey, old partner, you were about to fall!"

"What the hell?" Dexter shouted as he spun around to face Hugh, just as the tailgate was released and the ore began tumbling into the wheelbarrows.

"How about you share a drink of your whiskey there?" Hugh said, reaching for the bottle.

Dexter hugged the bottle to his chest. For once he was speechless. Hugh looked at the bottle. Through the amber glass, he could see the glimmering slippery gliding of amalgam. He had the satisfaction of knowing he was right and the satisfaction of seeing Austin Avery's jaw drop open before the gambler regained control of his expression and regarded Hugh with narrow eyes.

Hugh clenched his fists. He'd have to move fast if Avery went for one of the saloon pistols tucked in his belt.

"That's right, shovel it in, boys!" McPherson directed the mill workers. Avery went white around the lips, but he could say nothing to Hugh without showing his hand to McPherson. The men were already shoveling the last of the ore into the mill.

"I'll be a son of a bitch," Caleb Dexter said to no one in particular. He made as if to take a slug off the bottle, and then at the last minute he remembered and lowered the bottle and stared at it in bewilderment.

Hugh decided there was no point in hanging around any longer. He knew Avery was maintaining his control and in the hope the mine might by some chance still prove worthy of capital investment. Hugh had stopped believing in miracles.

He untied the horse and swung into the saddle. He was turning to go, thinking of how to explain his sudden departure to McPherson, when Avery stepped before his horse, blocking his way.

"Not staying for the test?"

"I have business in town," Hugh said more to McPherson than to Avery. The capitalist nodded absently, intent on watching his ore samples being loaded into the grinding mill.

"You're a fool, Everett," the gambler whispered; Hugh said nothing but met the gambler's steely eyes with feigned innocence until Avery's eyes darted back to McPherson and then, with a threat in his eyes that only Hugh could see, let him pass.

He's right, I am a fool, Hugh thought as he rode away, realizing that he now felt but little satisfaction at having thwarted the gambler's plan, but, he told himself, had he gone along with the fraud, he would have felt guilty forever.

So, I've got my integrity, he thought, *is that enough to show for my struggles in the Black Hills?* As he galloped the horse toward town, he decided that maybe it was enough. For he felt a lightening in the heavy load of guilt he'd born since he first knew he wanted his partner's wife. Perhaps it was saving the lives of the miners during the smallpox epidemic that had lifted the burden from him; perhaps it was seeing Molly so confident and free in her anger against Emerald that morning. He only knew that for the first time in months he did not feel guilty and anguished over what he wanted. And what he wanted was to find Molly and settle matters between them.

He forced the horse to gallop past the livery stable and on to the mine. It seemed imperative that he find Molly as soon as possible, but when he reached her cabin she was gone. There was a note on the table telling him that Edwin was still at the neighbor's and that she had gone to Mt. Moriah "to say goodbye."

He crumpled the note into his pocket and climbed back on the horse, concerned. If she had gone to the cemetery to say her goodbyes, that must mean she still intended to leave Deadwood. He did not want to let her go, but he would not follow her to Pennsylvania. Either she knew by now that they were destined to be together, or she would never know. Whichever her answer, it was time for resolution. He forced the tired nag toward the steep trail leading up to the graves on the hill which overlooked Deadwood. It seemed an appropriate place for he and Molly to end the journey that had begun in innocence so many years and miles distant.

When he saw her at last, she was only a blue speck high on the mountain near the graves. He tied the horse to a small tree and, on foot, climbed to meet her.

Caleb Dexter had a hard time keeping up with Austin Avery as he strode purposefully down Deadwood's Main Street. He figured the gambler was in a black mood after what had happened at the quartz mill, and it seemed important that Caleb try to make up to him somehow. Dexter felt rotten. Hugh had blown not only his own last chance for a bonanza, but Caleb's too. Oh, eventually there would be another stampede and he'd strike out for the new diggings, but he knew in his heart it was never going to be as it had been in Deadwood the summer of 1876. He wanted to prolong what he had found in this last gold rush, an excitement that was as close to lust as the old man could remember. He felt he could hang on to hope a little longer if he could just stick close to Austin Avery.

"It wouldn't have hurt us to stay with McPherson till the assayer finished his job," the old man said, trying to walk fast enough to keep an wary eye on Avery's "That smart-assed young fool thinks just cause he's got a university degree, he knows everything. We might have been able to give him a wink that we'd made it worth his while if he upgraded the results!"

Avery was silent. And Caleb rattled on, "McPherson might have thought it was funny, us not sticking around for the assay."

There was still no response from Avery, so he tried another angle. "Of course, on the other hand, it looks sort of casual. Like we was so confident about the Lucky Six we didn't even have to stick around to see how it panned out. ''

There was still no sign from Avery that he'd even heard. He wished the gambler would slow down. Caleb was getting short of breath walking fast and trying to keep up both sides of the conversation.

"He still might buy the mine, you know." Caleb wasn't sure Avery had even heard him. The gambler hadn't broken stride since they left McPherson clutching his bags of crushed ore at the Assay Office. Caleb figured Avery was headed for a saloon and he had to admit there was not much else to do at this point but get drunk. He was all for that, but he'd like to know the boss wasn't mad at him. After all, it wasn't his fault. He'd played his part according to the plan. Their scheme would have worked perfectly if Hugh hadn't shown up.

"Yep," he said louder, trying to sound cheerful. "He might just up and surprise us and buy that mine anyway, even if the assay ain't too good. Of course, the assay could be better than we expect. I mean there was all that conglomerate ore, and we have been pulling enough gold for wages out of there all summer, and then again, even if the Lucky Six don't pan out too hot, it depends a lot on the properties surrounding us. An outfit like McPherson works for, capitalists like them, they like to buy up a whole series of claims. That way you can follow the vein without any worries about water rights and claim jumping and such. Yep, chances are you and Hugh will get a pretty fair price on that mine anyway!"

"Caleb Dexter, old man," the gambler finally spoke.

"Yes sir?"

"Shut up."

"Why, Mr. Avery, that's no way to talk to a partner. It ain't my fault Hugh got all righteous and —"

Suddenly Avery stopped in mid-stride, turned and grabbed Caleb by the throat of his red-flannel shirt.

"One more word out of you, old man, and I'm going to shoot you dead right here on the street."

Caleb looked into Avery's cold steel eyes and thought of the pistols the gambler wore in his belt. He'd do it, all right. The old man let himself go limp and Avery released him as abruptly as he'd grabbed him. They continued to walk up the street in silence.

Caleb Dexter was hurt and he wanted Austin to know it. He sniffed a little, trying to think of the best way to get back into the gambler's good graces. Then as they passed the hotel, Caleb finally remembered.

"Well, I guess I can't tell you then!"

Avery didn't take the bait.

"Miss Emerald said to be sure and tell you, but if I'm not supposed to say anything —"

Suddenly Avery had him by the shirtfront again. "What are you supposed to tell me about Miss Emerald?"

Caleb would have liked to draw it out, make himself more important, but something in the gambler's eyes told him to spill it.

"She said to tell you she was leaving town!"

"When? When did she tell you that?"

"This afternoon when I was on my way to the ore crusher."

"Why didn't you tell me?"

Caleb hesitated. Why hadn't he? He'd forgotten, that was why, but he couldn't say that. "I was supposed to be drunk. I was supposed to stumble around the corner of the mill just as they were getting ready to dump out the ore. I had to do it just right, act dead drunk, so when I spilled the amalgam in the ore, McPherson wouldn't get suspicious. I couldn't run up to you first and say I had an important message from Miss Emerald, now could I?"

"What did she tell you exactly? Did she tell you to tell me?"

"Well, I don't remember her exact words, but she was leaning out the window of her hotel room right up there," he pointed to the window. "She was attracting quite a crowd, and she says she'd had it with Deadwood and she was going off to become an actress!"

"An actress?"

"Yep, and she could do it too. You should have seen all the men gawking at her."

"That damn little baggage!" Avery looked up at the hotel window, his eyes narrowing dangerously.

"That's the way I figured you'd take it, boss. I reckon' you don't care at all that she took off."

"Took off? You mean she's already gone?"

"Well, she said she'd take the first stage out of town and since I don't see no stage parked in front of the freight office over there, I figure it's gone."

"She was bluffing. She was just trying to attract attention. If I know Emerald, she's up in her room right now, pouting and plotting something else."

Avery was staring at the hotel window. He seemed uncertain. Caleb figured he ought to help out. "One way to find out," he said.

Avery looked at him, but didn't speak.

"We could mosey on over to the office there and just ask."

"Just ask?"

"That would be one way. Just slide in there and ask if there was a Miss Emerald O'Brien on the passenger list."

"No," the clerk said, holding the passenger list at arm's length to peer at it through squinted eyes, "No, no one named Emerald O'Brien bought a ticket."

"I told you!" Avery said to the old man. "She was just putting on a show to get my attention again."

"Course there was a lady," the clerk volunteered.

"A lady?" Caleb Dexter said. There weren't many ladies in Deadwood.

"*Quite a lady.* And if you don't mind my noticing, Mr. Avery," he offered Avery a diffident smile. "She did appear to be the same *lady* you have been escorting this summer."

"Emerald?"

"That's what I thought her name was. But that's not how she bought her ticket. She registered under the name of — let me see here," he peered at the passenger list again. "There's only one woman's name here. Garnet something."

"Yes, that's it," the clerk brightened. "I remember she

had to say it for me. Garnet Gab-ri-el. Real Spanish, it sounded."

Avery snatched the list from the clerk and studied it himself before asking, "Did she actually get on the stage?"

"Helped her on myself," the clerk beamed, then feeling Avery's gaze on him, he whitened a little. "Of course, I had no idea, that you, I mean —"

"That I what?"

"That you cared if the lady left town. I would have stopped her, if I'd known!"

"What makes you think I care?" Avery stood taller and regarded the clerk coolly.

The situation tickled Caleb Dexter. "The boss don't care." he volunteered. "He could have any one of them saloon girls, just like this." He snapped his fingers.

"Anyone can have one of the saloon girls just like that," the clerk grinned," provided they got the fare."

"Well, there's nothing we can do about it anyway." Dexter said. "She's gone and it's too late to stop her."

"Oh, I reckon a body could catch the stage, all right," the clerk said. "If you wanted to rent a horse, I mean. The stage took out of here on a gallop, showing off those matching white horses and making a production of it, but just between you and me, they stop at the first camp out of town and switch to a regular team. The whites are just for show. Can't keep up at a gallop all the way to Cheyenne, now can they?"

"You could catch her then," Dexter said, grinning. "I'll just run over to the livery stable and rent you the fastest horse and —"

"And why would I want to do that?" Avery's voice was infinitely cool.

"Why, to get her back. To get Miss Emerald back."

"What makes you think I want her back? That I'd even take her back?"

"Well, uh," Dexter hesitated, "uh, because she's such a looker, and women are scarce and well, uh —"

He hated to say anything about love, and he figured a word like that wouldn't apply to what was between Mr. Avery and Miss Emerald anyway.

"Well," he finished up lamely, "because she wants you to come after her?"

"She wants me to?"

"Sure, why else would she have made such a point of telling me to tell you she was leaving on the afternoon stage? If she wanted to get away from you, she'd just have snuck out of town."

"He's got a point there!" The clerk put in cheerfully. "I noticed how she kept lookin' around like she was watching for someone. She acted sort of funny at the last minute like she wasn't going to get on the stage, only by then there was a bunch of miners hanging around waiting for her to climb in the coach, probably so as they could get a gander at her ankles when she stepped up."

"Sure sounds like she was expecting you to stop her," Dexter interrupted, realizing the clerk was on dangerous ground. "We would have too, if the test had gone like we expected and I'd remembered — I mean if I'd had time to tell you she was leaving."

"Yep, you might say she left a trail a mile wide," the clerk mused. "Garnet Gabriel. It wouldn't be hard to trace a woman with a name like that, especially one with a face and body —"

"You could catch her," Dexter interjected.

"I could catch her if I cared to."

"Sure could."

"I could get her back if I cared to."

"Yep, you could catch right up to that coach and —"

"Only I don't care to."

Not hearing him, the old man rattled on, "You could gallop up to the coach and stop it and drag her off and sling her across the saddle. Boy, I'd sure like to see that!"

"He said he didn't care to," the clerk pointed out.

"What?" Caleb blinked, pulling his hat back off his head and scratching his bald spot. "You don't *care* about getting Miss Emerald back?"

"That's what I said. She hardly meant anything to me."

"But boss, women are scarce and she's so tasty looking and so high-spirited and all. You won't find another one like her, and it ain't like you couldn't get her back. You could drag her off the coach and make her come back."

"Of course, I could get her back. I'd drag her off that coach and sling her across my horse and gallop back to town with her kicking and squirming and yelling. That is, If I wanted her back. If she mattered to me."

"But she don't?"

"She's just a woman. The fellow here is right. A woman like that is ... well, shall I show you how much I care about her? Here, look. I'll show you."

While Caleb and the clerk watched fascinated, Austin Avery took a $5 gold piece out of his pocket. "I'll show you how much I care about her. I'll toss a coin, to see if I go after her. Should I?"

Caleb Dexter shook his head. "She's quite a woman, Mr. Avery, if I could have her, I'd — Hell, I'd go after her even if I didn't care, just for the fun of it."

"That's what I'll do then!" Avery said, paying no attention to the old man. "I'll show you how little she means. I'll toss a coin. Heads I go after her and tails—"

"Tails?" the clerk and Caleb Dexter asked as one.

"Tails I walk down to the Hidden Treasure and pick out another woman."

By this time a crowd had gathered, and sensing something was going on, moved in closer. Avery came close to grinning. He held the gold piece aloft, twisting it so both the Liberty head and the eagle flashed in the late afternoon sun. Then he lowered his hand, the crowd stepped back to give him room as he repeated the words.

"Heads I go after her. Tails, I forget her."

He threw the coin, and Caleb held his breath as it spun higher and higher, then seemed to hang in midair for a moment before it tumbled down and Avery snatched it with a theatrical gesture. He slammed it on the sleeve of his frock coat, then held his hand over the coin and paused a moment, eyeing the crowd. When he saw every eye was upon him, he slowly raised his hand and looked at the coin.

His expression did not change.

CHAPTER THIRTY-THREE

Like most frontier towns, Deadwood called its cemetery Boot Hill because most of those buried on Mt. Moriah that first summer died, not in sickbeds, but in skirmishes with the Indians or in brawls with their fellow miners. Mt. Moriah was a lonely spot, as visiting the graves of Wild Bill and the other pioneers had not yet become a popular pastime. The path to the cemetery was steep, as was the cemetery itself, for with level ground at a premium in Deadwood, none could be yielded to those who had ceased to contribute to the economy.

Molly watched Hugh climbing the hill toward her and waited for him, thinking that this must be the last time for waiting.

Seeing Molly standing before the graves with her hair down and haloed in the sunlight, Hugh thought she was like a heavenly apparition, but whether of hope or loss, he did not know. The cemetery itself looked as stark and raw as when they'd buried Jake and Luther. Dug into the side of the mountain, the graves sloped downward, their rough-sawed wood headstones tilting at precarious angles over the barren mounds of fresh earth. The timber grew thinner as the trail climbed, but compared to the barren gulch in which the city crowded, Mt. Moriah seemed lush, and Hugh was reminded of his first vision of the Black Hills and their beauty before he and the other "pioneers" spoiled their pristine beauty. The grass was high around his boots as he walked, and he noticed it was yellowing, reminding him that summer was over.

Hugh sensed even before his eyes met Molly's that whatever happened on Mt. Moriah would either unite them forever or mark their final parting. When he saw the determination in her stance and the tears shining in her eyes, he knew she was also aware of the significance of their meeting. He remembered their joining in love and desire on that other hillside, and that it was he who had broken their bond with his angry words, and realized they could no longer avoid a confrontation.

They stood for a moment, not speaking, but holding each other with their eyes. A breeze played with the strands of hair falling around her shoulders, and his throat ached with the pain of all that had kept them apart. He was jealous that the breeze could caress her while he dared not. The new spirit he recognized in her excited him, but also made him shy. She had, after all, never even said she loved him.

"I don't know where to begin," he said. "There's so much to be settled between us."

"Then start with what's not between us. What happened with the test? Are you rid of the mine at last?"

"No, I blew it. Avery and the old man had figured out a way to rig the test so McPherson would pay us a fortune for our shares, but I blew it."

"So Avery was out to cheat you?"

"Not me but McPherson, or his company to be exact. It was a beautiful scheme. Caleb Dexter played drunk, a part he does well, and was going to break a whiskey bottle full of amalgam into the ore just as they were dropping it into the quartz mill. Our ore would have tested out like the mother lode, and it wouldn't have hurt me, except for the truth of what Emerald said. Sooner or later all of Deadwood would know that I was part of the fraud!"

"Then you did the right thing to stop it. So why are you sorry?"

"Because I'm such a fool, Molly. Suddenly I saw it all. What a fool I'd been to think joining the trespass to the Black Hills would be an adventure so I selfishly dragged poor Luther along when he should have stayed in school; then not being man enough to tell Jake about you and me, but thinking it would all work out in some honorable way, even after I'd made love to you again. It's like I've been driven by some obsession to win the easy way, to think that fate owed me something. That I was destined to win, or even to be happy."

"You mean you just found out there's no *poor man's gold*?" There was a trace of mockery in her voice.

He had to laugh at her irony. "I guess I really believed there was such a thing, that glittering bonanza on the surface, and we'd just find it and pick it up, and all our problems would be solved."

"I didn't believe in it," she said softly. "I tried to believe, for Jake's sake and later for yours, but I think I knew all along that it was only an illusion. I think women always know."

"So we're all fools. All of us. Look at this graveyard! Jake and Luther and crazy old Preacher Smith and all the rest, all of them coming here dreaming they'd find something wonderful. All of us chasing rainbows. Even Wild Bill thought he'd get himself one last stake so he could give up gun fighting, and instead he gets shot in the back."

"Hugh, don't —"

"Let me finish. It's got to be said. They fooled us! They've been using us! We gave up what little we had at home to rush in here by the thousands, and we scraped our hands bloody panning for gold in the streams, and we got scalped by the Indians and crushed in the mines, and it was all for nothing. There's no poor man's gold. Never was a poor man that got rich off a gold rush. You know who's going to get rich off Deadwood?"

She didn't answer and he kept talking, the words tumbling out, so fast he was really thinking aloud. "It will be men like George Hearst, Capitalists, Entrepreneurs, as Crandall called them. Men who already have money. Men that don't sweat or need, Molly. That's who will make fortunes here. Not those who risked. It's those who have who get. That's the way of the world."

"But, Hugh—"

"Sure there's gold in this gulch — millions of dollars worth —but it's low grade and it's underground and it's going to take machinery and real mining engineers to get it out. "

"What can I say, Hugh? You're right."

"I don't expect you to say anything. I just had to tell you. Maybe I'm just finally admitting it to myself. I didn't want to believe that the world operates that way but it does, and I had to say it to you. This all started with you, and now, today, it's got to —"

"End? Are you saying it's got to end today?"

"It's got to be resolved. And yes, today. I've got to have answers about this summer and about you. "

"It didn't start with me, Hugh, and I'm not responsible for your disappointment. You didn't know I'd be on that wagon train. You were looking for something when you started, and I don't think it was just gold. Was it adventure or were you out to prove something?"

"Adventure's as good a name for it as any, except maybe destiny. Something vital was happening in the West and I felt driven to be part of it. But if my destiny didn't start with you, it soon became you, and now it seems we'll never get it all untangled."

Still thinking of destiny, he took her hand and started to pull her close to him. She put her hand over his, but stepped back, indicating he should follow her. "There's something I want to show you. I don't know if it will help, but I discovered something today that seems important."

She turned and began to climb up a narrow path which wound between the graves and then above them.

Wondering, Hugh followed her as the path trailed away into the high grass above the cemetery. Above them the white rocks of the summit looked down. Hugh wanted to question her but she did not look back, and he knew she needed her breath for climbing the steep hillside. He saw she was not going to the summit, but toward a point perhaps halfway up the mountain where a rocky outcropping, smaller and less imposing than the summit, but of the same granite, formed a natural overlook. When she was almost there, she turned to him.

"You've never climbed this high before, have you?"

He shook his head.

"Neither had I until today. I'd visited the graves before, but I never took the time to climb higher. We might even be the first, since there's no path. I don't think most folks in Deadwood have much interest in exploring, but today when I came to the cemetery, I was full of emotion and I too wanted answers. I knelt back there and said my prayers and my goodbyes to Jake and Luther. I thought that might free me to return to Pennsylvania, but I only felt more uncertain. And then I looked up and saw these rocks just ahead there at the point all shining in the sun and something seemed to call me. So I climbed up here and discovered that from those rocks you can see the whole valley. I stood there looking down at Deadwood with the wind whipping about me and suddenly I felt calm and certain and almost happy."

By the time she finished speaking she had reached the summit and he joined her, wondering what she had discovered there. She turned back to look at him and he saw that there was indeed something new in her eyes. It looked like happiness.

When she turned away to look out over the valley, he followed her gaze. He gasped at the view. The scene was as perfect as a painting of a Swiss village nestled against the Alps. The steep hillsides, which in town were awkward obstacles to orderly building, from a distance, provided a magnificent setting for a city that suddenly seemed not a sprawling mass of shacks struggling to climb the hillsides, but a jewel in the folds of velvet-blue hills.

Hugh looked out at the city, marveling at the way it nestled into the gulch and then spread its way up the steep sides of the mountain. It was like a toy village, the men swarming through its streets visible, but as tiny as toy soldiers. The mountains, too, were no longer the brooding slopes that sometimes made him feel claustrophobic, but beautifully serene guardians of the valley. The city grew in the largest gulch where Deadwood Creek flowed into the Whitewood, but there were also dozens of side gulches cut by melting snow in the spring; each bearing the potential of gold laced gravel. The side gulches deepened in the late afternoon light as shadows grew. The afternoon sun was hot on his face as it sank behind the mountain he faced, causing the shadows, ever present in the narrowest of the gulches, to lengthen and make one aware of the sometimes fleeting nature of the gift of light.

Hugh was surprised to see the city was so large. He had lived so long within the narrow confines of the gulch that for days at a time he had seen but not been aware of the beauty of the mountains which surrounded them, but had focused only on the confusion of the city which seemed to daily grow more crowded and ugly. Cabin crowded upon cabin so that the smoke of one cook fire swirled around its higher neighbor's window, while the seepage from outhouses higher up leaked into the down-slope neighbor's yards. In the heart of the city, space was so scarce buildings were almost stacked upon each other. Some were even raised on stilts so that the miners could follow the veins underneath. Rickety outside steps lead to tacked-on second stories, and the narrow spaces between the buildings were filled with rubble from the diggings, trash, discarded whiskey bottles, and worse.

Since that day in June when he first left the serene beauty of the pine-scented mountains to follow the road that became Deadwood's Main Street, an ugly river of humanity fed by muddy tributary streets which traversed the steep gulches or tumbled downward at impossibly steep angles, Hugh had never again been completely free of the sights and sounds and smells of the mining camp.

Now it was quiet. He could hear birds and insects and the wind blowing. The blasting and shooting and the hurdy-gurdy music of Deadwood became, like the sound of the creek, only a distant murmur.

The colors surprised him. Deadwood was almost all the same color, that of uncured logs and timber weathered by the sun. But the hills were varied tones of green and yellow, gold and brown. The somber stands of timber killed by whatever had laid it waste, giving Deadwood its name, were broken by an occasional pine still standing, and patches of green new grass renewed the burned-out areas. In some spots, aspen and birch had already become established and their leaves formed patches of yellow in the distance, while those nearer to them trembled in the breeze and looked like the golden coins of men's dreams.

The lengthening shadows and the occasional pine tree standing alone in a patch of dead wood or clinging precariously to the summit, sentinel-fashion, made Hugh understand why those in the gulch had lost awareness of the beauty of the mountains surrounding them. Shadows reminded one of the cold darkness of the mines and the perpetual darkness of death. A man looking up some morning at a view he hadn't committed to memory might mistake one of those sentinel pines for a Sioux scout seeking vengeance on the trespassers in the gulch.

But the Sioux were gone forever; a treaty forced upon them in retaliation for their victory over Custer. Whatever the right or wrong of it, it was decided — the white man had won. And the gulch was in peace. Smoke from evening cook fires trailed upward. One could make out the figures of men going home from their diggings or making their way down Main Street and disappearing into saloons.

Hugh marveled at how far he could see. The two creeks formed a Y at the heart of the city, the trail following Whitewood creek to his right leading to Crook City and the other mining camps in hidden gulches. If he had known of the view, he would have climbed the mountain before. He could not have imagined Deadwood would look so different from above.

"It's beautiful," he said at last.

"Then you see it too."

He nodded.

"That's what struck me. After all these months of thinking it was the ugliest place in the world, of being so closed in by the mountains and the shacks and the mines and the people, I climbed up here to plan my escape and to think how to persuade you to come with me, and then I looked out and saw that it was beautiful!"

"Everything looks better when you are away from it. Every place is beautiful when the sun's about to set. Everything is more precious when you think you've lost it." He said the last with special significance.

"It's not just that. Not just that it looked beautiful to me. It was the feeling I had. It was almost the feeling of being home. I thought I could see our cabin way over there to the left, and suddenly it looked like home. Not just the cabin, but the whole place, the city and the hills all around and the people. I just had this feeling I haven't had since I had to turn my back on Pennsylvania. I never felt I was home in Iowa. We'd get in sight of the sod house after a long trip to town and I'd be glad to be back, to have the trip over and get supper started, but I'd never look down the road and see our place and think, 'there's home!' I'd forgotten that there was such a feeling, and then today I looked down at Deadwood and I knew it was home. I knew that it is here I belong."

"It's with me that you belong."

"I knew that too. I knew that this morning when I chased Emerald away. I've always thought I belonged to you, but after all that happened there was so much that made me feel it was wrong for me to even think we could be together. But today when I stood here looking out on it all, I knew that it was right. Right that I be in Deadwood and right that I be with you."

He started to reach for her, but she stopped him. "Let me finish. It's important that I tell you what I've discovered."

"That we've built something here? I see that. Maybe that's why I couldn't go along with the mining fraud. Jake hallowed that ground with his death and I couldn't let it be part of something cheap and dirty. But does it really matter? Are you saying we can't leave this place because we've left Jake and Luther on this hill? Forget the view, Molly, and think about what Deadwood really is. It's just another boom town."

"But it's ours, Hugh. It's not much, but it's the city we helped build. And it's up to people like us to make it better. That's pioneering, Hugh. Not pillaging the land and killing the Indians, but building a decent place to live."

He remembered the words Emerald had taunted him with that morning. *You and Molly ought to go build a damn church.* He wanted to laugh, but then it didn't seem so funny. Maybe this is how it was meant to be. They had been tricked into coming, into thinking they would go away rich, but instead they would stay to build a civilization. To build a city, a life. To make their own destiny. He started to share that idea with her, but he no more than got out the name *Emerald* than her expression told him Molly wanted no reminders of that woman. "Can you forgive me for her?"

"There was nothing to forgive was there?"

"There was nothing except my being a man and she being a woman who wasn't afraid to go after what she wanted."

"But that's part of what I've got to tell you. I learned something from Emerald, or maybe she just made me realize what I'd learned from becoming a pioneer.

Hugh, I'm different. I'm not the girl you fell in love with so many years ago, and I'm not the woman who only waited and didn't dare do anything but try harder to be patient and good. I knew today that I could never go back to Pennsylvania and be my father's daughter and the genteel widow. I don't belong back East anymore. I belong here. I suffered here. I saved those men from dying and I earned my place in this town. And my son is the son of pioneers and this is his place, too."

She took a deep breath before finishing, "and if you don't want to stay here, if you don't want the kind of woman I've become, then Edwin and I will stay on alone. And I can do that too because I'm strong!"

"I know you're strong and I know you can survive without me. You've always been strong, Molly, but now you're wondrous and I love you more because of it."

She let him take her hands now, her eyes glowing. "Then it's settled? We will stay here and be married and someday even tell Edwin the truth."

"No, it's not settled. There's something left unsaid. There's still something wrong between us and I won't pretend it doesn't matter. I can't marry you just to make what's happened between us right and to give Edwin a father!"

He dropped her hands and turned away from her, his eyes searching the mountains as he tried to articulate what it was he still wanted from her.

There was a sudden movement beside him and he felt her hit him as if she had stumbled or thrown herself at him. He turned and she caught hold of his shirt and held on.

"Don't turn away from me, Hugh! Don't ever turn away from me again! You want *to hear me say it*? That's it, isn't it?"

He was shocked by her response. Why was her face so anguished?

"You want to hear me say it! That I wanted you. That I wanted you to make love to me. That I want you now. All right I'll say it. I wanted you from the first moment I saw you again. No, even before that. I wanted you on my wedding night with Jake. I cried for you then. I lay awake after giving myself to my husband and wanted you! Even as I birthed Jake's babies, I wanted to cry out your name. And, then, just when I finally began to forget — just when I thought it hadn't even been real that time with you but only a dream, then you finally came back, and how I suffered for wanting you and for letting you make love to me again! And how I suffered for wanting you so much that I left my husband's bed to go to you in the night, and then when you accused me of using my body to trap you and —"

"Molly, don't —"

"No, let me finish. I'm going to say it all. I'll keep no more secrets! You shall hear the worst of it. I wanted you when you were down in the mine. Yes! When you and Jake were buried in the mine, it was you I feared for, more than for my lawful husband, and when they said that only one of you was alive, I prayed that it would be you! I felt so guilty."

She began to cry. "I felt so damn guilty. It was like I'd killed Jake. Do you know that the night before he was killed, I'd resolved to leave him? You'd met Emerald and I knew you'd want her and so I was going to leave Jake, and then later at the cabin that awful day when you accused me of killing Luther—"

"Hush, Molly, I never meant that."

He was holding her now, comforting her, but she pulled away once more.

"There I've said it all. All the awful things about wanting you and loving you, all except what I've waited so long to say —"

"Say it now, Molly."

"I love you, Hugh. I've always loved you."

"Say it again, Molly."

"I love you. I love you. I love you!"

She was laughing now, her eyes sparkling and her whole being transfused with light so that she looked as young as she had been the first time, and yet this time she was infinitely more in every way. He knew there was nothing else to be said. He reached for her and she came to him, in his arms and in his heart and so within him that he did not know where one left off and the other began. He did not need to know anything except that they were together at last, *forever*. Kissing, laughing, and even crying together. He held her away from him so he could look at her again and then they kissed more deeply, this time with passion as well as joy, their mouths almost awkward in their urgency. He desired her and knew he would have her soon and forever. He felt infinitely happy and complete. He lifted her into his arms as if to carry her away.

She grabbed hold of his neck and buried her face in his shirt, feeling in his strong arms both child and woman.

Then, feeling his hardness against her, she whispered, "There is no place here for what you have in mind."

"What do you mean? We've got a whole mountain top! And why are you whispering when at last we can shout our love to the heavens?"

"But we've a cabin and a bed waiting below."

"And a son who'll be wanting explanations and a preacher who will say tomorrow is time enough. But I want to marry you now. Here on this mountain top. I want this to be the sacred place where we at last are one."

And there was a place. A little patch of clover which formed a nest between the white rocks that looked over Deadwood. As he lay her down and busied himself with her buttons, she laughed again. "And someday, husband, when we bring our grand-children to Mt. Moriah to see where they buried Wild Bill Hickok and Preacher Smith, you'll tell them the pioneers made this into a holy mountain, and I'll have to hold back not to look up to this place and make them wonder why I'm smiling so!"

And then her eyes met his and she saw he was right. This would be their true marriage ceremony; the preacher would be for their son and the town, but it was the act of love which had bound them together from the beginning, and it was this new act of love that would end the long journey which had kept them apart.

They would be trespassers no longer.

He took her hands and for a long time they simply looked at each other, each to the other's soul. The words were unspoken, but each touch, each tender breathing and sharing of the other's essence became their sacred promise: *To have and to hold.*

From this day forth. For time and eternity.

It was the setting sun which finally brought them back to this world. They took a moment to walk back to the look-out point, and stood storing up their memories of what had happened and how beautiful the city was and could be.

At last they remembered their son and the cabin that was home waiting below. As one they turned and began to pick their way across the summit to the path leading back to Deadwood. He took the lead on the narrow path, holding his hand out to her so they moved almost sideways down the mountainside.

They were perhaps halfway down, in sight of the cemetery, when the thought occurred to him.

A complete love — a man and woman destined to be together forever, body and soul. Perhaps this too was like poor man's gold — an illusion, a trick of the gods to taunt men and drive them on. Maybe once again he was being a fool.

He turned and looked back at Molly. She smiled. And he knew that if he was a fool, he no longer cared.

Far below Mt. Moriah, down on Deadwood's Main Street, the street where a man could live for months and never really see the beauty of the mountains around him, Austin Avery swung into the saddle of the big bay gelding Caleb Dexter had rented for him.

The old man stepped back and studied his boss. He made a fine picture, sitting there on the horse. It was the best mount to be had in Deadwood and it was dancing and champing at the bit. Caleb thought his boss looked like a real Southern planter gentleman, sitting there firm in the saddle in his frock coat and striped pants, his watch fob gleaming across the front of his ruffled shirt and the motion of the horse dancing beneath him causing his jet black hair to blow down a little over his forehead. What a sight he was!

Avery wheeled the horse around so as to face Caleb. He leaned down in the saddle to speak to him. "You tell McPherson to write up his best offer on the mine, assuming he makes us an offer, and you leave it for me at the hotel."

"Sure thing, boss. You can count on me!"

Avery straightened up and suddenly the old man realized he was about to spur the horse and gallop off. Dexter grabbed the horse by the bridle. Avery looked down at him, surprised.

"Boss, wait up. There's just one thing."

"What's that?"

"The coin. You didn't show the coin."

"What are you getting at?" Avery frowned, pulling at the reins so Caleb could hardly hold the horse.

"Boss, you said heads you'd go after her and tails you'd forget her."

"So?"

"So you just said it was heads. You didn't show us the coin."

Avery relaxed his grip on the reins. He looked down at the old man with one eyebrow raised.

"Are you implying that I'd cheat? You insist on believing that I care about that woman enough to cheat on the toss of a coin?"

"Well, no . . . I mean . . . I don't know, boss. It's just that you didn't show the coin and —"

"And you're wondering if it really was heads?"

"Yep," the old man grinned."That's it, Boss. Was it heads or was it tails?"

Avery jerked the reins up and kicked the horse so it danced away from Caleb's grip. Then he wheeled it and turned back to look down at the old prospector. For the first time since he'd known Austin Avery, Caleb Dexter saw the gambler laugh. His gold tooth gleamed as he leaned down to whisper his answer.

"That will just have to be something for you to wonder about."

About the Author

Both the reality and the romance of the old west are as real to this author as the towns she's called home: Casper, Laramie, Riverton, and Cheyenne, Wyoming; Lead, Deadwood and Spearfish, South Dakota.

She especially loves the Black Hills region. When circumstances took her and her family to Oklahoma she earned a master's degree in professional writing and for a history of journalism class, read every issue of Deadwood's first newspaper *The Black Hills Pioneer* from June 1876 to June 1877, and wrote an article for *South Dakota History Quarterly*. Further research resulted in an illustrated booklet, "Annie Tallent, the Mystery of the First White Woman in the Black Hills."

In addition to accuracy in historical themes and details, this novel expresses her skills as a writer of fiction. She began this aspect of her writing career by writing short stories for such magazines as TRUE CONFESSIONS and MODERN ROMANCES.

Today Nancy Kovats Lea makes her home in Fort Collins, Colorado.